"[This book] has a great plot, but it's the characters who kept me reading most of the night."
—*Toronto Globe and Mail*

"Compelling . . . densely textured, character-rich . . . Both a realistic police procedural and a forceful portrait of a world where a passion to do the right thing can sometimes lead to doing a grievous wrong."
—*St. Louis Post-Dispatch*

"This dark and brooding tale is an outstanding candidate for best of the year awards."
—*Lansing State Journal*

"Certain to be on Top 10 lists by the end of the year."
—*Halifax Chronicle Herald* (Nova Scotia)

"A rich and pleasing page-turner . . . a gripping and smart read."
—*Columbus This Week*

"Sure to appear on a lot of year-end 'Best of' lists."
—*Crimespree Magazine*

"An excellent mystery novel."
—*Booklist*

PETER BLAUNER

SLIPPING INTO DARKNESS

WARNER BOOKS

NEW YORK   BOSTON

Copyright © 2006 by Peter Blauner
Excerpt from *Slow Motion Riot* copyright © 1991 by Peter Blauner
All rights reserved. Except as permitted under the U.S. Copyright Act of 1976, no part of this publication may be reproduced, distributed, or transmitted in any form or by any means, or stored in a database or retrieval system, without the prior written permission of the publisher.

Warner Books and the "W" logo are trademarks of Time Warner Inc. or an affiliated company. Used under license by Hachette Book Group USA, which is not affiliated with Time Warner Inc.

Cover design by Jesse Sanchez
Cover photo by Mike Yamashita/Getty Images

Warner Books
Hachette Book Group USA
1271 Avenue of the Americas
New York, NY 10020
Visit our Web site at www.HachetteBookGroupUSA.com.

Printed in the United States of America

Originally published in hardcover by Little, Brown and Company
First Warner Books Paperback Printing: February 2007

10 9 8 7 6 5 4 3 2 1

To Peg, Mac, and Mose

With special thanks and respect to
Rob Mooney and Michael C. Donnelly,
two of the best.

PROLOGUE

HUNGRY GHOSTS
2003

As soon as he walked through the wrought-iron gates and out into the pastoral green expanse of Cricklewood Cemetery, Francis X. Loughlin heard the tranquillity of a mid-October afternoon being torn open by the *crunk* and whine of a hardworking backhoe.

He looked around, trying to figure out where they were making the hole. Nothing was where it was supposed to be anymore. Another rude metallic thud sent a flock of geese flying high over a mausoleum down by Cypress Pond. He watched the birds disappear from his line of vision a second before he expected them to, another sign of the natural order being disturbed.

Twenty years.

He took a left at the first granite angel and followed the sound of the machinery up Hemlock Avenue, passing the tree-shaded urn gardens, catafalques, and overground sarcophaguses, the society matrons not far from the stevedores, the nuns near the baseball stars, the Indian

Princesses beside the Hat Check Kings, the Natural Causes next to the Sudden Demises.

Would it make his job any easier if they could all talk about their last moments? Or would the sheer cacophony and confusion just be overwhelming? *What happened? Is that all there is? Nine-one-one is a joke. But I wanted so much more!* He shielded his eyes from a gust of flying specks. Would you even be able to hear one soft high girlish voice saying, *"Excuse me, but I don't think I'm supposed to be here"?*

He lumbered on past a Civil War memorial, a bruiser-weight white guy in a three-quarter-length leather coat, with boxing-glove shoulders, an Etruscan chest, and more or less the gut he deserved at forty-nine. His hairline had retreated up to the grassy hinterlands, revealing a pair of dark rapscallion's eyebrows over a debauched cherub's face. Women still liked him, though, because he could listen without interrupting to talk about the Giants and because he seemed like a man who could take broken things and give them back fixed without a lot of pissing and moaning about how hard it had been.

Maybe not quite twenty years, he decided. The ground had no give to it then. There was frost on the headstones, icicles on the crypts, and the trees' branches were broken blood vessels against a bleak white sky. Maybe after Thanksgiving.

A sharp breeze shivered the red maples and sent a wash of dead leaves past his ankles. He felt something catch in his pant cuff and reached down to find a fifty-dollar bill stuck there. He picked it up and examined it, seeing it was not just fake but half burnt. Another gust carried the odd mingled scents of roast duck and smoldering incense. His eyes searched for explanation, over the stone crosses and up the hill, before finding a Chinese family gathered on a rise, traditional candles and flowers arrayed around a casket covered in netting.

"Hey, Francis X. *qué pasa?*" a voice called out from behind him. "Wake up. Didn't you see us waving to you?"

He turned and saw about a half-dozen people standing by an open grave, staring at him like a groom who'd shown up drunk to his own wedding. One by one, he recognized most of them as either being from the DA's office or the medical examiner's office. Behind them, the backhoe kept working, digging a hole near the headstone: ALLISON WALLIS, 1955–1983. A steel claw reached into a shallow hole and emerged with a mouthful of dirt. It pivoted and disgorged its load out onto the plywood boards laid out to protect the grass, the smell of topsoil hitting wood setting off a writhing of worms in his gut.

"Hey, hey, Scottie, word up." Francis put on a game face as he went over to greet the video tech setting up a tripod over the trench.

"Not the same old same old, eh, Francis?" said Scott Ferguson, a big bluff ponytailed guy from the Visual Evidence Unit who was always handing out business cards, trying to get weekend work filming weddings, bar mitzvahs, and christenings. "Usually when you put 'em down, they stay down."

"Absa-fucking-lutely."

Normally he ran into Scottie only at crime scenes, when there was literally still blood on the walls. "So whassup?" said Scottie. "I tried to ask Paul, but he said this is your clambake."

"Did he now?"

Francis looked across the grave where Paul Raedo, his erstwhile friend, the prosecutor, was having an animated discussion with a lady from the ME's office, pointing his way every few seconds, trying to reassign the blame, no doubt. Four members of the gravediggers' union stood by in their green uniforms, leaning on picks and shovels, waiting to do the more exacting work of digging around the coffin.

"Well, he told me one thing," Scottie admitted. "He said it's the fucking weirdest case he ever heard of."

"Don't believe the hype."

"Well, I don't know what the hell else you'd call it. Girl's dead twenty years and her blood shows up on another body last week."

"Sounds like fucking Paul told you plenty." Francis glared into the mid-distance.

The backhoe grunted and rocked on its stabilizers as little brown plumes wafted from the gouge, drizzling dust on the people nearby. Francis took some small measure of satisfaction in seeing Paul cough and try to brush the grit off his lapels.

"So, what's up with that?" asked Scottie. "You got the wrong girl buried?"

"That's what her mother thinks," said Francis, remembering how he'd stood on this very spot with Eileen Wallis, a hand on her arm to keep her from jumping in back in '83. "I'm trying to keep an open mind."

"And what about the guy you locked up for it? Paul said he was in the can twenty years."

"He's not the happiest horse in the race, but what are you gonna do? I still got one eye on him. Everybody did something."

The machine kept digging. Each *chooff* of metal into soil another dig to his solar plexus, another reminder that something had gone wrong on his watch. The doctor brings you into the world, the undertaker signs you out, and if something goes wrong in between, you call a cop. He might have had his lapses, but if you needed someone to get you from crime scene to the grave, he always figured he was the man for the job. Not necessarily to comfort the bereaved the way a priest or a funeral director would — just to keep the game honest. But now he felt like he'd let down his people. He was supposed to be their representative, their public servant, their envoy: a Politician for the Dead. Who else was going to make sure their needs got met? Who else was going to twist arms, make phone calls, knock on doors, and filibuster on their behalf? Who else was supposed to speak up and fight for these constituents?

"So do I smell a lawsuit in the wind or is somebody burning incense?" Scottie sniffed.

"Chinese funeral up the hill."

Francis pointed with his half-singed bill to where a bell was softly chiming, joss sticks were fuming, and a monk in saffron robes was leading the family in chanting.

"They pay people to come or something?"

"Nah." He stuck the bill in his pocket. "It's hell money."

"Say what?"

"Hell money. Spending cash for the afterlife. You let the dead go hungry, they might come back and haunt you."

"Maybe you ought to toss it in there instead." The tech nodded as one of the gravediggers looked down into the pit and gave a thumbs-up. "*Somebody's* getting an attitude."

"Might be a little late for that already," said Francis.

Slowly the steel claw retracted and the men climbed into the hole with their picks and shovels, ready to start separating the casket from the dirt.

PART I

IN A LITTLE ROOM

1983

1

Time was in a cage, a yellowing Bulova clock with a hatchwork of thin silver bars across its face.

The boy sat in the cinder-block room, as fragile as an egg in a carton, staring out into space, the needle of the second hand jerking in tiny increments above him. A red-and-white tie was knotted at his throat and a green book bag sat by his feet. His long eyelashes fluttered and a wispy virginal mustache, no thicker really than the hair on his arms, twitched on his upper lip.

He looked more like twelve than seventeen. Too chicken-chested to have done the kind of damage they were talking about. Nine of the fourteen bones in the girl's face had been shattered, leaving just a pulpy maw between her hairline and lower jaw. They couldn't even use dental records to identify her: her brother did the ID based on a mole on her thigh. The mother couldn't bear to look. There was minor vaginal bruising, but what disturbed Francis X. more for some reason was the injury to her right eye. Something had pierced the lid, spilling the aqueous humor that had made the iris blue.

"He lawyer up yet?" Francis watched the boy through the one-way glass.

"No, but he's thinking about it," said his sergeant, Jerry Cronin. "He's no dope, this kid."

The boy's fingernails drummed on the wooden tabletop, a little lopsided rumba beat. Hearing the echo in the empty room, though, he stopped and stared into space again, vaguely aware of being observed. His slender shoulders rose and fell in his maroon parochial-school blazer, sagging with the weight of accumulating time, two small red scabs on his chin plainly visible.

"Sully get anything out of him?"

"You know Sully." The sergeant made a hissing sound. He was a small tight man, rapidly becoming smaller and tighter. "He's got a touch as soft as John Henry. He came on hard and tried to put the fear of God in the kid. It was mutually decided another approach was needed."

"So you giving me the keys or putting me in the rumble seat?"

"You're getting the keys. With conditions."

"Yeah?"

"Grown-ups are watching."

Francis saw the Bosses gathering in the office down the hall like crows on a phone wire. Al Barber, his father's friend from the First Dep's office, talking to Robert "the Turk" McKernan himself, the chief of the department. No longer creatures of the street, but products of administration. Reflexes dulled, bodies thickened, eyes shrinking as they became more adept at spotting threatening memos than concealed weapons.

Francis locked eyes with McKernan for a half-second before the chief closed the door. "He don't like me. The Turk."

"Of course he don't like you," the sergeant said, shrugging. "Two years out of Narcotics, eighteen months off the Farm? Get the fuck out of here. You wouldn't even be standing here if it wasn't for your old man. But I told him, honestly, 'The kid's a fuckin' great detective.' I reminded him you got the Harlem Meer shooter and the one threw that little girl off the roof. I said, 'You put Francis in a room with a guy, *he's gonna give it up.* Best interrogator I've ever seen. Great natural talent, like Mantle hitting a baseball or Pavarotti singing opera. We got people talking over each other to tell him what they did.'"

"So he said all right?"

"Fuck no," said the sergeant. "He still wants you out of there. But Barber and me ganged up on him, and the old man put in a good word. You get one shot."

"Thanks, Sarge."

"Don't thank me. You make me look bad, you will rue the fucking day, my friend." The sergeant tugged his sleeve. "Francis, one other thing."

"Wha?"

"Sully never got around to reading him his rights. Bosses are a little concerned, Julian being seventeen and all."

"I'll dance around Miranda like Fred Astaire."

Francis brushed past him, picking up a black canvas bag and putting his game face on. Not letting on the fact he was bothered. *Wha?* Just because the story had led the news for two days running? Just because the mayor and the police commissioner had already both given press conferences? Just because everyone was acting as if he, Francis X. Loughlin of Blackrock Avenue in the Bronx, would be personally responsible for a third of the city's tax base relocating to the suburbs if the killer wasn't caught by this weekend? Just because this was his best shot at turning things around after his little stint in rehab? Just because he'd met with the girl's family and personally promised he'd do right by them? Just because the old man had interceded on his behalf and would probably be up here any minute, looking over his shoulder?

He stepped into the interrogation room and the door closed behind him with a cool unnerving *clunk*.

"Whaddaya reading?"

Julian Vega looked up from the book he'd pulled out of his bag, like a fawn peering out from behind a thicket, and then shyly raised the futuristic-looking silver-and-black cover of a book called *Childhood's End*.

"Arthur C. Clarke. What is that, like, sci-fi?"

"It's the third time I've read it." Julian looked sheepish. "It's not the greatest writing, but every time I understand it a little better."

"What's it about?" Francis eased himself into a higher seat across the table, knowing the Bosses were lining up on the other side of the glass, ready to second-guess him.

"The Overlords." The boy's voice was too husky for his scrawny-ass build. "They're these superintelligent aliens who just show up and act like they're going to save the earth from war and disease, but then it turns out they're running a whole other game."

"There's always a catch, isn't there?" Francis picked up the book and studied the back cover. "I read a lot myself. But usually more like biographies and history books."

"That's the past. I like to read about what hasn't happened yet."

"Hmm." Francis let that last phrase hang for a few seconds before he put the book facedown and stared at

Julian, establishing the unspoken ground rules: *Your only way out is through me.*

"So you know why we asked to stop by here today. Right, Julian?"

"Yeah. The other guy told me. You wanted to talk about Allison."

Francis took out a yellow legal pad and put it on the table between them. They both took a moment to contemplate the invisible third presence in the room.

In family pictures, she was a little heartbreaker. All wild red hair and smoky eyes, fair freckled shoulders and cloud-parting smiles. You could see why she was still getting carded at twenty-seven. She looked barely older than the kids she was taking care of in the pediatric ER. All the other doctors and nurses he'd interviewed at Bellevue made a point of saying that she didn't have to stoop much over the examining table. Everything was eye level with her. No matter how much the parents were screaming or freaking out in the doorway, she never raised her voice or resorted to baby talk when she had to put in a stitch or set a bone. She just talked to kids as though she were one of them.

Not that she was any Heidi of the hills — Heidi probably didn't have expensive black Dior underwear in her dresser or a picture of Keith Hernandez, the 'stache-wearing Mets first baseman, taped to the bottom of her mirror or E-Z Wider rolling papers in her night table. On the other hand, Heidi might not have stayed after her shift with an eleven-year-old boy who had brain cancer, holding his hand and reading inappropriate sections out loud from *Mad* and *Cracked*. And three days ago, somebody hit her so hard with a claw hammer that one of the tongs went up into her frontal lobe.

"Does your dad know you're here talking to us?" Francis asked, knowing the boy had been picked up by Sully at lunchtime outside the St. Crispin's School on East 90th Street.

Julian shook his head. "I called, but it's hard for him to hear the phone sometimes when he's working in the basement."

"He's the superintendent of the whole apartment house, right?"

The boy allowed himself a quick proud smile. "Yeah, he takes care of everything. Seventy-two apartments."

"Okay, that's fine. It's just a formal thing we have to go through whenever anybody comes in to help us. You know, 'you have the right to an attorney,' blah, blah . . ."

Francis could almost hear the sigh of relief from behind the glass. Up until a few years ago, he probably couldn't have gotten away with questioning a high school senior without a grown-up present. But then that little psychopath Willie Bosket murdered a couple of subway riders for the hell of it when he was fifteen and — *presto change-o!* — a new law was born.

"And then we usually say something like" — he dropped his voice into his best mock-*Dragnet* register — "'if you can't afford an attorney, one will be provided for you.' You know, all that bullshit. By the way, did you try calling your mom?"

"She's dead." Julian folded his hands on the table.

"Really?"

"Yeah. Long time ago. Cancer."

"When you were how old?"

"Four."

"I lost mine when I was nine." Francis said.

"For real?"

Francis rested a hand on his gut. "I had my First Communion in her hospital room four weeks before she died. . . ."

He sat back and waited. Other guys had simpler ways of getting a rapport going. But sometimes a pack of smokes and a White Castle burger weren't enough. Real scars had to be displayed. Wound psychology. You needed that shock of recognition to get a man to put his guard down.

"I still pray to Saint Christopher for my mom," the boy said softly, reaching under his collar and showing Francis part of a chain around his neck. "My father gave me a medal."

"Same difference." Francis nonchalantly pulled out the Miranda card for Julian to sign. "I know how it goes. You're always wanting something nobody can ever give you back. Sometimes you don't even know what it is. You just *want*. Sign here, please."

The long lashes fluttered and a shiny spot formed in the corner of Julian's eye. He sniffed and glanced down at the card in embarrassment.

"But it's always the same thing, isn't it?" Francis said, distracting him. "You just want what everybody else has." He nudged the card. "It's all right. You don't have to write your whole name. Just put your initials."

Trying to clear his eyes with the back of his wrist, Julian scribbled next to the warning, glad to be doing something that looked adult and purposeful.

"I see you're doing a pretty good job of looking after yourself," Francis said, tugging his attention back lest Julian start reading too carefully. "You should've seen me when I was your age. I was a mess. My shirttails were always out. My hair never got combed. My shoes were always falling apart." He chuckled knowingly. "You ever do that thing where you have to write your name on your clothes in Magic Marker because you don't have anybody to sew a label on for you?"

"Sometimes, but I still got my *papi* taking care of me. We kinda look out for each other."

Francis nodded, getting the picture. The widower and his son living together in the basement apartment. The boy carrying his father's toolbox, always breaking out the wrench and the pliers before it was time to use them.

He put the Miranda card back in his pocket, mission accomplished. "So Julian. You were working in Allison's apartment the night before —"

"*Hoo*-lian."

"Ha?"

The boy looked abashed. "My parents called me Joo-lian instead of Julio, 'cause they didn't want me to sound like every other Puerto Rican kid on the block. But then I started getting the crap kicked out of me in middle school, so my dad started calling me Hoolian the Hooligan."

"I hear *that*." Francis half saluted. "You can imagine what it was like going to Regis with a name like Francis Xavier Loughlin."

The peach fuzz mustache jerked. "Really? You went to Regis?"

"Four years."

"I think we played you in soccer last year."

"Probably." Francis humored him. "Anyway. You told Detective Sullivan you were in Allison's apartment the night before."

"Yeah. The ball cock wouldn't rise."

Francis heard what sounded like a cough behind the glass. "I beg your pardon?"

"The toilet tank wasn't filling properly. Looked like it was leaking. So actually what I did was, I tightened the jamb nut. Then she could build up some serious pressure and get a nice strong three-point-two-gallon *whoosh*. You could've flushed a cat down that sucker."

"I see." Francis nodded and reached into the canvas bag he'd brought in the room. "Hoolian, I want to ask you something. This yours?"

He dropped a Ziploc evidence bag on the table between them. It deflated with a slow *pouff,* revealing the steel claw hammer inside. The cloudiness of the bag obscured fingerprint powder on the black rubber grip and the spots of dried blood on its head.

"Guess so." Hoolian rubbed his chin thoughtfully. "I must've left it in her bathroom. Where'd you find it?"

"In the fire hose storage compartment, downstairs."

"*Damn.* How'd it get there? I thought I left it in the bathroom."

Francis shrugged, not letting on that Hoolian had just admitted the murder weapon belonged to him. "So you told Detective Sullivan that you stayed and talked to Allison awhile after you were done with the toilet."

"Yeah, you know, we hung out sometimes. We were, like, you know, friends."

"Friends?"

"Yeah . . ." Hoolian pushed up in his seat, a little disconcerted. "She was . . . a good person. We talked a lot. She was helping me write the essay for my college application."

"Yeah? Where you applying?"

"Columbia. My father always wanted me to go there."

"Good for you." Francis stuck his lip out. "I'm just a Fordham guy myself."

Slowly the hand came down from his chin, allowing Francis to focus on the pair of dark diagonal scabs.

"Still, seems kind of surprising in your type of building," he said. "People in Manhattan don't usually know their neighbors."

"Oh, I know everybody." The scabs stretched, revealing tiny cracks. "I grew up in that house since I was three. My father says I'm like the mayor, talking to people on the service elevator, going in and out of their kitchens with groceries. She'd only been there subletting about eight, nine months, but we got tight right away. We were both into *Star Trek*. . . ."

"Yeah?"

"Yeah, I came up one night to fix her sink when she was watching 'The Menagerie.' You know that one? It's the two-part episode they made out of the original pilot, 'The Cage,' with Jeffrey Hunter playing Captain Pike. You know, the one where the Talosians with the big lightbulb heads are keeping him behind the glass and projecting these crazy pictures into his mind, trying to get him to stay. . . ."

Francis nodded sagely, thinking: *This is why some men never get laid.*

"Not a lot of girls into science fiction, are there?"

"I don't know. I think her older brother got her into it."

Hoolian glanced over at the glass in the wall, gradually realizing that someone on the other side might be watching *him*.

They were certainly trying to project images into Francis's mind. Telling him to speed it up, get the damn statement, wrap it up for the mayor and the PC on *Live at Five*. Any minute, Francis Senior Himself would be in the house, ready to put his two cents in.

"So, what time did you get done fixing her toilet?" Francis asked, paying them no mind and setting up the next part of the trap.

"'Bout ten o'clock. I remember she was watching Channel Five and they say that same thing every night. 'It's ten o'clock. Do you know where your children are?'"

Francis flipped back through his notes and was disappointed to see that the answer was consistent with what Hoolian had told Sully. That fucking useless civic-minded slogan must have provided about eight hundred alibis a year.

"So how long did you stay after you fixed the leak?"

"Dunno." Hoolian pinched his shoulders. "Hour, maybe a half hour. It was hard to tell."

"Why? Didn't you say you had the news on?"

Don't lunge, he warned himself. Be patient. Remember: Time is better than a kick in the balls or a phone book upside the head. Time is better than a polygraph or an eyewitness. Time can weigh on you. Time can sit on your shoulders and play with your head. Time can make you hungry and weak. Time will give you time.

"We switched to MTV and made some popcorn," Hoolian said, faintly aware of his own words stacking up into a teetering pile. "She'd just got cable. And once those Duran Duran videos come on, one after another, man, you just sort of zone out. And then after a while, she started to get sleepy. She had to be at the hospital at eight o'clock the next morning."

It sounded almost sweet, this pretty young doctor falling asleep in front of the TV with this horny little seventeen-year-old mooning over her.

"Did she, like, have her head on your shoulder?"

"She might have." An earnest little nub of flesh bulged between the boy's eyebrows. "Why do you want to know?"

"Just, you know, it's important to get all the details right. We collect fingerprints, hair fibers. We have to figure out what belongs to who so we don't make any mistakes and lock up the wrong people."

The long eyelashes fanned out. "I still don't understand."

"Look. I have a set of facts I'm trying to make sense of. The front door of the building is locked after midnight. Okay? The only people who have keys are the tenants and the super. And your father was out that night, so you had them. The only other way to get in is to ring the front bell and wake the doorman. And that never happened. Right?"

Hoolian nodded, scratching the inside of his thigh.

"*So* . . . No sign of forced entry in Allison's apartment. No visitors buzzed in after midnight. You're the last person to see her that night. She doesn't show up for work the next morning. Your father lets in the patrolman, who finds her at ten o'clock. Help me out here."

This last part seemed to take Hoolian by surprise, like a throw from left field, a white dot out of the green getting larger and larger until it smacked him right in the mouth. "You're not thinking my father had anything to do with it, are you?"

"No. I am *not* thinking that."

They'd already checked out Osvaldo anyway. He was off on a date that night. Took a fourth-grade teacher named Susan Armenio to dinner at Victor's Café and then cha-cha-ing at Roseland, leaving an old alkie doorman called Boodha and Hoolian running the show. Maybe that got the kid mad, Dad stepping out with his mother dead and all. Maybe he just wanted some attention. You never knew.

"Then, I don't know what I'm supposed to say." Hoolian fingered his scabs, mystified. "I'm thinking I should try calling my father again. He's probably done in the basement."

"Okay." Francis sat up. "Of course, you can do that, but there's something else I want to ask you about. . . ."

He reached into the bag at his feet, took out a red photo album. He put it down in front of Hoolian.

"You know what this is, don't you?"

Hoolian stared at the book as if it were breathing.

"It's Allison Wallis's photo album. We found it in the back of your bedroom closet."

You could almost hear the blood reversing in the kid's veins. "My father let you look in my room?"

"He gave us permission to search your apartment this morning. He said, 'Look everywhere.'"

Francis watched the telltale microshifting of Hoolian's pupils.

"She let me borrow it."

Francis sighed. "Look, Hoolian. I'm sitting here, talking to you like a man. Don't you think we owe each other the respect of being honest? Why would you have something hidden in the back of your bedroom closet if you were just 'borrowing it'?"

Hoolian seemed to have lost the power of human speech.

"All right." Francis pulled back a second. "Let's try and make it easier. You guys were friends. You liked her. You did things for her. You fixed her toilet. You hoped she would like you back."

"No, man. It wasn't like that. . . ."

"*Listen.*" Francis rolled his chair around to Hoolian's side of the table: just guys talking here. "I've been there too. I would've set myself on fire for some girls when I was your age. You can't help it. Every time she looks at you, it's like a magnet trying to pull your heart outta your chest. You're dying and she doesn't even know it. Am I right?"

Hoolian hesitated, tugging on the chain inside his shirt collar.

"I'm not saying she played you on purpose, but isn't it possible she took advantage of you just a little bit?"

"*No.* She was a nice person."

"I'm not saying she wasn't a nice person." Francis got up and stood over him. "But even nice people take advantage sometimes. Look at it her way. You're this eager kid coming around all the time, to fix things and keep her company. You're a pillow for her to fall asleep on. You're *comfortable.*"

Hoolian blinked, as if he'd been slapped. *Oh yeah.* Francis moved in on him. *I got your number, son.*

"Like she didn't know how hot she was getting you."

"It wasn't like that." Hoolian shook his head, eyelashes blinking a nervous semaphore. "She had a boyfriend."

"Yeah? What was his name? Did you ever see him?"

"No . . ."

Francis inched forward, having spent much of the past twelve hours establishing that Allison hadn't had a steady boyfriend since senior year at Amherst. And that guy, a Frisbee-tossing premed named Doug Wexler, was apparently down in Guatemala at the moment, running a children's vaccination program with a couple of Maryknoll nuns.

"So, what happened?" Francis said. "You guys had a fight because she found you took her album?"

"*No,* she didn't know about that," Hoolian said too quickly, then realized what he'd just admitted. "I was going to give it back. I just wanted to see what her family looked like."

"What'd you do, use your key to get into her apartment and take it when she wasn't there?" Francis put a foot on his own empty seat and flexed forward like a sprinter.

"I think I better talk to a lawyer."

From the corner of his eye, Francis saw the doorknob turn as if one of the Overlords was about to come in the room. He shook his head, asking for more time. *Don't blow it. I'm almost there.* Time to go for the bomb.

"Okay, then, let me just ask you about one more thing."

He picked up the second evidence bag and dropped it on the table in front of Hoolian. It puffed up and then collapsed in on itself more slowly than the one with the hammer in it, breathing out odorless fumes through a tiny hole. "You know what that is, don't you?"

Hoolian shook his head, staring at the bloody little wad of cotton inside.

"You're telling me you don't know how Allison's used tampon ended up in the wastepaper basket in your bathroom?"

The boy seemed to wilt with the bag.

"Somebody must have put it there," he said weakly.

"Now how would that be?"

"I don't know, man. I never even seen one of these before."

Francis bore down on him. "Hoolian, come on. We have serology experts who can tell us that this is Allison's blood on this cotton. I'm talking about irrefutable proof. . . ."

"But I'm telling the truth." The boy's lip trembled. "I'd be afraid to even touch something like that."

"Then how the hell else would it have ended up in *your* bathroom? Can you tell me that?"

Hoolian gripped the arms of his chair, the Catholic boy confronted with direct evidence of his sins.

"*You* must have put it there," he said.

"Me?" Francis touched his chest, bemused. "After I already had Allison's family album in your closet and her blood on your tool? Does that make a lot of sense?"

Hoolian leaned forward in his chair a little, the eyelashes fluttering in panic.

"Look." Francis touched the boy's shoulder, playing Father Confessor. "Tell it to me your way. Help me understand."

Hoolian shook his head again, clinging to threadbare denial.

"Then let me help you," Francis said gently. "You were next to her on the couch. Maybe she let you touch her and pretended not to notice. Maybe she let you get a leg up. She had you going at ramming speed. Then all of a sudden, she decided she was too good for you. She tried to stop you dead in the water. And you can't do that to a man, right?"

"I didn't kill her."

"Hoolian, I'm looking at a pair of scratches on your chin. They're right in front of my face."

Hoolian touched his scabs self-consciously. Just his bad luck that he had in-between skin: not golden brown like some Latinos, but not exactly pink like a white boy's either. It was sallow and thin over the bones, almost translucent. Cuts that would heal on other kids in a day lingered on him.

"I cut myself shaving. I told the other detective that."

"Julian, look at me. All right? The time has come to put away childish things. Remember how we talked about how we both lost our mothers?"

There was a sound in the air like water about to boil. *We're almost there. Just a little further.* He'd proved the murder weapon was Hoolian's. He'd gotten the kid to admit that he'd stolen her photo album, which showed he was obsessed. His fingerprints were all over the place, naturally. And once they matched his blood to what they'd scraped from under her fingernails, they'd probably have enough circumstantial evidence. All he needed to make it a slam-dunk and remove any possible doubt was a statement.

"So you know your mother is looking down on you right now, don't you?"

Hoolian's nostrils flared and contracted. The corner of his eye was glistening again. They were on the edge of something here.

"I'm telling you, man, you have to get right with what you did."

The boy kept shaking his head. "But it's not true."

"Don't keep saying that," Francis warned him, playing this card for all he was worth. "You know she's up there and her soul is in torment, because she's afraid you won't be able to join her in heaven."

The boy opened his mouth, but only a dry creak came out.

"She didn't raise you to be a liar, did she?"

The boy looked around for something to wipe his eyes

and blow his nose with, but Francis had made a point of not bringing a box of Kleenex into the room.

"That shit is going to eat you inside. You know you've got to ask for forgiveness."

Hoolian bit his lip and shook his head again, more furiously this time.

Come on. You want to tell me. Everybody wants to confess.

"You gotta do it, brother." Francis loomed over him. "You have to get right with this. I'm giving you a way out. I know you're a good boy."

Yes, I'm your friend. Who else would be trying to put you in prison the rest of your life?

Hoolian took a deep breath, folded his hands on his lap, and stared at them, a small pale cathedral of fingers.

"All I'm asking you to do is to stand up to what you did. All I'm asking you to do is be a man."

The joints squeezed tighter, the little cathedral showing veins in the marble.

Francis crossed his arms, finding himself knotting up as well. Because what the Overlords behind the glass had forgotten was: it *wasn't* all bullshit and play-acting. Sure, you could get all righteous about it afterward, grandstanding for the press and pointing the finger at "the defendant" in court, saying, "We the People condemn you and cast you out. Begone from the sight of all good free men and women." But sometimes, in this quiet little room, before the lawyers and stenographers came in, there was a half-second when you were almost on the guy's side. Not above him or on the sidelines passing judgment. But right there in the thick of it with him, step-by-step, on his level, seeing it through his eyes. And, in your mind at least, doing the same things that he'd done. Because otherwise, why would anyone trust you enough to tell you the worst thing he ever did? You could never explain it to the so-called decent, normal, law-abiding civilians. To get someone to give it up, to lay himself before you, you had to put some soul into it, some compassion, you had to *feel* for him — if only for that instant right before he confessed. And then, of course, you could safely turn around on him and use his desperate little plea to be understood to ruin his life.

"So, what do you say?" he asked, ready to reach for a pen. "Are you gonna be a man or not?"

The kid looked up, as if he realized he'd just reached his own childhood's end.

"You said I could talk to my father."

PART II

THE WORLD'S FORGOTTEN BOY

2003

2

THE FIRST THING that threw him was the girl with the tattoo.

He'd just gotten out of the van when he saw her come strutting down the boulevard. A Queens Plaza goddess with porcelain skin and vermilion hair, a body that turned a Misfits T-shirt into elegant eveningwear. A tear in the fabric revealed a black bra strap resting on a white shoulder like a cat's paw. Old forgotten hungers began to stir inside him. Girls did not look quite this good when he went away. They weren't quite so lean and voluptuous, so thrillingly bold in the way they carried themselves, so direct in how they looked at you.

But then he fixed on the dark line circling one of her biceps. A barbed-wire tattoo. Not just any barbed wire, but razor ribbon with sharpened points of the evil kind used atop state prison walls. He stared, wondering why anyone possessing such pure lunar beauty — why any free person, in fact — would do this to themselves.

Seeing desire light up his face, she stuck out her tongue. A small gold stud lay near the tip like a pearl on pink velvet. She snaked it out and waggled it at him, enjoying the riot of shock and dismay it provoked, then walked on by, a cool kitty licking the cream from her lips.

He set down the duffel bag made of old towels sewn together with dental floss, and tugged self-consciously at his belt loops. His old clothes no longer quite fit him. His blue work shirt, which somehow had survived twenty years in the state storage system, was too tight around the collar and his Levi's were too snug. It wasn't just that he had filled out from lifting weights and eating starches, the styles had changed.

He saw a group of teenage boys with jeans slung so low that the ass pockets were on the back of their knees, eating Chinese takeout by a white Cadillac Escalade. Ultraviolet lights circled the rims, and a rapper on the speakers shouted things that you could hardly even say on a record back before he went away.

He let go of the belt loops that suddenly seemed too high on his waist, remembering himself at seventeen, buying these jeans at a Gap on East 86th Street for eighteen dollars, the private-school girl working at the register smiling shyly at him and tucking a few stray chestnut-brown hairs behind her ear.

She was probably married now, with three kids and two cars in the suburbs. And here he was, twenty years later, dumped in Queens on a late-summer night, a grown-ass man, with jailhouse muscles, trimmed eyelashes, thick black hair graying slightly at the temples, and a quarter-inch razor scar under his chin signifying this was a child who'd had all the softness bled out of him.

Something called the W train, which hadn't even existed before, rattled by on the elevated tracks, screaking and squealing like a teakettle, the passing windows casting a harsh shuttering yellow light over the boulevard.

"Say, Hooligan, you got a ride?"

Timberwolf, a double-wide-load brother Hoolian knew from Attica, had just gotten out of the Department of Correction van behind him, six foot five, 280 on the hoof, carrying a brown paper bag with his clothes inside, T-shirt untucked, and sneaker laces untied like an oversize four-year-old waiting for a grown-up to come help him.

"My cousin's supposed to come pick me up in a cab, but I don't know, man," said Hoolian, his voice rough and sandpapery from the long upstate winters. "I think maybe she might have misunderstood and thought I was coming on the four-thirty Rikers bus. Or maybe she might've got tired of waiting and been and gone already."

"Yeah, tell me about losing patience." T-Wolf yawned. "Seven motherfuckin' years I did for selling two little faggoty bottles of crack. And then they tack on another six months at Rikers for some bullshit robbery I didn't have nothing to do with. How long was your bid?"

"I was in since '84."

"*Damn,* that's more than half your life!" T-Wolf clutched his chest. "We definitely gotta get you some pussy tonight. You come to the right place."

He pointed across the twelve lanes of traffic to a "gentlemen's club" that called itself Shenanigans in festive ruby letters, just down the block from a Marine Corps recruiting station. But the mere thought of being within touching distance of a woman made Hoolian's heart start to thud frighteningly.

"Aw, man, I don't think so. What if my cousin comes for me and I'm not here?"

"You ain't probably been with a natural woman in twenty years, son. They can wait a few minutes."

"Naw, I'm a have to take a rain check. I put my family through enough already."

"All right, I hear you." T-Wolf sighed. "Guess I'm going to have to be an army of one. I'll be thinking about you, man."

"Don't think too much. Just do what you got to do."

"Heh-heh." T-Wolf rolled up the top of his bag. "You gonna think about that other proposition we were talking about, right? My nephew could use a few more good men on the block."

Riight, thought Hoolian. *I'm gonna risk my bail selling weed for some punk-ass little Hoe Avenue gangsta who wasn't even born when I got sentenced.*

"I got your number." He gave T-Wolf's meaty fist the pound. "Stay strong."

"*Peace.*" T-Wolf picked up his bag and then hesitated. "Sure you don't want to come along now?"

Hoolian squinted and shook his head, hearing the trepidation, knowing that even just seven years of head counts, lockdowns, unannounced cell searches, and regimented daily programs could make a man in size 14 sneakers afraid to cross the street on his own.

"Nah, dawg, I gotta watch myself," he said. "One slip, I'm back where I started."

"Okay, I hear you."

Slowly and reluctantly, the big man ambled off, the plastic tips of his untied Nike laces scatting and scratching on the pavement. A blue-and-white police car cruised by, eyeballing the scene. Hoolian felt anxiety crawl across his skin like insect legs among the tiny dorsal hairs. Had they been tipped off he was getting out tonight? What if they'd seen him talking to T-Wolf? No, that was crazy. They didn't have that kind of manpower. *Still.* "No associating with known felons," the judge said, setting his bail. He decided he would throw away T-Wolf's number the first chance he got.

Cars hurtled by recklessly. He looked down the street again, wondering where his cousin Jessica was. She hadn't visited in years and he wasn't sure he would still recognize her.

He fished around in his pocket for change and found a couple of quarters jammed in with the two twenties his lawyer had loaned him. Where would he go if she didn't show up? After years of hanging on by his fingernails, his 440 motion had been granted so suddenly that he'd barely had time to make any contingency plans. He'd figured he'd be lucky to see a judge before Thanksgiving. Instead, he'd found himself hustled down to Rikers and taken to a dingy little hearing room this very afternoon, almost too stunned to register Judge Santiago's setting aside his conviction but warning him that the indictment still stood.

Stomach writhing from the van ride, he found a pay phone with the words "Praise God" and "Suck Dick" scratchitied into its chrome plate covering and pumped in a quarter.

"Yo, yo, yo, whassup, y'all, this is Jes-*sick*-ahh," her voice came on after the fourth ring, a baby wailing in the background. "I can't come to the phone right now. Yo, shut the fuck up, I'm talking. Anyway, you know the drill. Wait for the beep."

He put the phone back gently, knowing she'd either forgotten about him or decided not to get involved. Could he blame her? She'd been — *what?* — maybe three, four years old when he went away.

He looked up, watching the train pull out of the station,

the wheels making a steel-on-steel grace note and a blinding spark on the tracks that made his whole nervous system shudder.

"Hey, Rico Suave." The same cop car that had passed him before was pulled up to the curb now, a young sergeant in blue shirtsleeves with his hair cut high and tight leaning out the window. "What do you think you're doing?"

He stiffened at the sight of the uniform. "Nothing."

"Go do it somewhere else. I'm getting sick of looking at you."

He hoisted the duffel bag, not looking for a problem this soon, and started up the stairs to the station, his legs knotted and cramped from being folded into a narrow seat next to T-Wolf. He stopped on the landing, trying to take it all in. After all these years of drab prison earth tones, the gaudy neon of the boulevard almost seared his eyes like jet fuel. FOR THOSE WHO KNOW THERE IS MORE, the sign for a psychic throbbed red on a nearby building. HAVE YOU BEEN INJURED? an attorney's ad asked in emerald next door.

"Can I have a token?" He stopped at the clerk's booth.

"What?" The dusky lady behind the glass wore an MTA shirt and a tiny glittering Indian jewel in the middle of her forehead.

"I said, can I buy a token please?"

"They don't sell those anymore, baby," she said. "Where you been?"

His face got warm. A man spends years studying obscure statutes and writing erudite letters to Court of Appeals judges from the prison law library, and then can't figure out how to get on the subway.

"I was away." He pulled out one of the twenties, ready to throw himself on her mercy. "What do I need to do?"

A swell of understanding raised the jewel on her brow. She took his cash, punched some buttons, and dropped a golden card into the trench under her partition without looking at him.

"Just make sure the strip faces the right way."

He nodded gratefully and hurried through the turnstiles and up to the platform, wondering how he was going to manage the next ten minutes. No one told him it was going to be *this* hard. He looked down over the railing at the street below, having a shaky moment of vertigo. T-Wolf and four other guys just off the van were outside Shenanigans, getting themselves all worked up, arguing too loudly, shouting and bumping chests as if they were more interested in attracting the attention of the police than in getting into the club.

"Okay! Okay! But what I'm asking, who put the shit in your mind? All right? Who put the shit in your mind?!"

Not me, Hoolian told himself, turning away. Some guys secretly couldn't wait to go back. It was just too hard for them, living on the outside and having to make decisions all the time. But he'd had enough time inside. He couldn't have taken another day of the boredom, the constant stress, the sense of being totally controlled yet completely unprotected. He looked up the track and, in the widening beam of an approaching train, saw the brawling mass of inmates in the Auburn mess hall suddenly parting as a little man called Pellet fell to the floor, a fourteen-inch shank buried so deep in the back of his neck that the tip came out through his voice box.

The raw-throated roar subsided and the train ground to a halt, its doors popping open in front of him. Hoolian took one look inside and, seeing no graffiti there, wondered if it was just a demonstration model not meant for regular customers.

But then he heard the familiar static goulash of the conductor's announcement, mangling the name of the next stop. Should he get on or stay off? The only address he had for Jessica was the Surfside Gardens housing project in Coney Island. He made a snap decision and got on, figuring he'd try to call again once he got there. The doors closed behind him and he took a seat, scrunching down at one end of the bench, trying not to take up too much room even though there was no one near him. An ad across the way announced, *The Whale Is Back, the Hall of Ocean Life Has Reopened*. But where had the whale gone? How had it survived while it was away?

The train rocked off, passing a broad plain of lit-up rail yards and darkened warehouses. Over on the right, the Manhattan skyline glowed like peaks and valleys of a fever chart set in glass and concrete.

At Times Square, a Hasidic family got on. The father in a white shirt, with a reddish pubic-looking beard, a black fedora, and a sleeping baby girl clinging to his chest like a little monkey. His hugely pregnant wife waddling on after him in a wig and a gray ankle-length dress, with two small boys in tow in matching yarmulkes and side curls.

Hoolian fingered his Saint Christopher's medal and thought of his own father: a widower at thirty-five, stretching a rainbow of expectations over his head, wanting Hoolian to fulfill all the dreams he'd abandoned after he'd dropped out of City College and taken a job as a janitor on the Upper East Side. His father, who read Cervantes and Dickens on the service elevator and carried the poodle ladies' groceries into their kitchens for Christmas tips. His father, who'd taught him how to caulk a bathtub, pushed him to apply to Columbia on a scholarship, and spoke only English to him at home.

He remembered that last weekend before he went upstate, when his father gathered what was left of the family for a going-away party on Orchard Beach. The Puerto Rican Riviera, Papi called it. Ray Barretto and the Fania All-Stars on the boom box. His *tia* Miriam bringing a roast pig. His uncles fishing off the rocks with bamboo poles. His cousins from Bayamón playing volleyball. And his father raising a half-empty *cerveza* at sunset and saying, "To my son, *mi hijo*. I'll never stop believing in you, *muchacho*. I'll never stop trying to bring you home."

This was a sorrow beyond dreams. Hoolian found himself seething between his teeth and furiously wiping away tears. *Goddamn you, you little* maricón. *Why're you crying now?* He slammed his fist on the bench beside him, remembering how the warden up in Attica denied him permission to go to Papi's wake. Motherfuckers never let him be, never gave him one fucking break. He punched the bench again and bit down hard on his lip, knowing such fine-tipped anguish would either lose its edge over time or eventually tear him apart.

The Hasid and his family stared at him gravely.

"*What the fuck are you looking at?*" he said.

At the next stop, they moved to another car.

He folded his arms across his chest and tucked in his chin, not looking up until the train emerged from the long tunnel and rose over the rooftops of Borough Park. So this was how everybody else had been living; clothes on a tenement line, an American flag draped over a balcony, Hollywood Tans next to Manzari Furs, a lone runner on a late-night gym treadmill, and an old couple watching television on a couch. He felt like Charlton Heston at the end of *Planet of the Apes,* seeing the Statue of Liberty half buried in sand and realizing that the world he once knew was dead.

It was after one in the morning by the time he finally reached Stillwell Avenue, the last stop in the city. The Terminal Hotel was boarded up across the street. He descended the steps and crossed Surf Avenue, looking for a pay phone to call Jessica again. All the Broke-Down Midnight People were out in front of Nathan's and Popeyes Chicken; the No Particular Place to Be People, the Runaways, the Won't Go Fars, the Overmedicated and Undermedicated, the Bottom Feeders and the people who hung around them just to have someone to look down on. And, of course, the Moonwalkers like himself: men moving down the sidewalk gingerly, trying not to bump into anyone, apologizing too quickly and looking up at the sky, trying to judge time and distance, and still not quite believing they were finally *out.*

He felt a breeze coming off the ocean and vaguely recalled there'd been a booth on the boardwalk years ago.

The moon burned an ash-white hole in the black sky. The Wonder Wheel flicked off, spoke by spoke. He walked toward the beach and found it strangely calm and faded gold in the dim lights from Steeplechase Pier. A volleyball net sagged, as if waiting for players to show up. The ocean rolled on — immense, eternal, and indifferent — the thin lip of the tide curling as it reached the shore.

He stood at the railing, trying to figure out where the horizon was, remembering how he walked backward into the waves with his father on that last St. John the Baptist Day. Almost twenty years since he'd seen the ocean. He'd forgotten how small and unimportant it could make him feel, like he was just an infinitesimal mote floating across the surface of some great all-seeing eyeball. How very little this moment of freedom mattered in the scheme of things. He used to try to delude himself that God had a game plan for him, a design that would gradually reveal itself and somehow justify everything he'd been through. But here was a reminder that God was busy. God was probably numbering the waves and naming the clouds. God was thinking just as much about a rock crab in the Atlantic or a soap bubble in Cairo. God was thinking about bacterial infections in Peru and dung beetles in Africa, about weather patterns over the Pacific Rim and tire treads coming off beside the Taconic Parkway. God didn't have time to worry about inmate number 84H5446 in the New York State correctional system.

And so Hoolian screamed into the wind. A bitter shout-out that said, *I'm still here,* to the moon, the stars, the Wonder Wheel, the foaming surf, the Terminal Hotel, the Hasids on the subway, the empty cell he left behind upstate, the screws, the lifers, the hacks and he-shes, the highest courts, the lowest snakes, the shades of his mother and his father, the unborn children of his wasted seed, and, yes, the Great Clockwinder himself. By all rights, a sound like that should have pushed back the waves and left dead kelp all up and down the shoreline.

But when it was done, the ocean was still there, gathering up stones and scattering them back randomly, making a sound like tepid applause.

3

JUST BEFORE LABOR DAY rolled around, Francis realized it was taking twice as long as it should have to find his car keys. So Tuesday morning, he finally broke down and made it to the doctor's appointment he'd been putting off since before Christmas last year.

He stepped into the little white room, took off the baseball cap with the X on the front — a souvenir from that Spike Lee movie he'd worked security on years ago — and rested his chin on a metal ledge. He found himself staring through a right eye lens into something that looked like a hollowed-out TV set but somehow under the circumstances felt more like a confessional. On a concave wall at the rear, four tiny white lights appeared in diamond formation under a glaring yellow beacon.

The technician, a young mirthless Russian blonde with a big jaw, put a clicker in his hand. "There will be flashes of light around the target, bright and dim," she said with an accent that made him want to call Amnesty International. "Every time you see one, you squeeze the trigger. Try to keep your eye steady."

"No problem."

But as soon as the visual field test began, he found himself tensing up and getting all sweaty-palmed. Some of the flashes were as clear as muzzle fire in a black alley. Others were just faint ghostly wisps, so far off to the side that he had to ask himself twice if he'd actually seen them.

"Don't just squeeze the trigger," she commanded. "Concentrate."

He tried to bear down. It had been more than a year since he'd qualified for his gun, and his reflexes weren't what they used to be. The firearms people were calling every few weeks now, wondering when he was going to make it back up to the range at Rodman's Neck. Light sparked and danced in the far upper-right corner of his eye. He squeezed the trigger a half-second late, and knew that in an actual gunfight he would have been dead by now.

"*Horasho,* the doctor will speak with you." The tech pushed a button to print out the results. It sounded like she'd said, "Horror show," but then he remembered that it was the Russian word for *good.*

"Well, you scored very well on fixation levels," Dr. Friedan said as he walked into the examination room a few minutes later with the chart, a balding chubby man in his fifties, with thick black-rimmed glasses, rapidly blinking eyes, and, most noticeably to Francis, a few obvious tufty places he'd missed shaving halfway down his throat.

"You're very good at keeping your eye steady. The technician said you didn't blink much. Most people have to or they'll get dry."

"Dryness definitely isn't my problem." Francis swiveled on his stool, waiting.

"Your false positives and negatives are another story, though."

"How's that?" Tiny dots and afterflashes from the test were still popping up and disappearing before his eyes.

"You clicked on the target three times when there was nothing there. And you missed six percent of the flashes that *were* there."

Francis rubbed his lids and shrugged, as if this were of no great importance. "What else?"

"And your gray zone threshold is . . . not great either."

"So, what does that mean?"

The doctor knuckled the underside of his jaw and handed over the computer readout.

"See for yourself."

At first, it looked as harmless as a seventh-grade math worksheet. A series of pie-shaped dots, each with a dark ring shading the perimeter. *What percentage of the graph is filled in, children?* But the more Francis stared at it, the more words he saw like *borderline, pattern deviation,* and most ominously *blind spot.* He started to notice how the shaded-in figures looked less like geometry problems and more like a series of solar eclipses. And deep within his joints and muscles, he began to feel a slight chill.

"What is this?" He handed back the sheet.

"It's your ability to distinguish subtle gradations between light and dark. You told me you've been having problems seeing at night for some time now."

"It's taking a little longer for my eyes to adjust," Francis allowed.

"Do you want my diagnosis or not?"

"That's what I'm here for."

"You've got retinitis pigmentosa."

"Okay."

The doctor gave him a searching look, waiting to see if he'd understood. "It's a genetic disease that affects the retina at the back of your eye. . . ."

"Uh-huh."

"It cripples the photoreceptor cells along the outer edge. . . ."

Francis nodded along, making the appropriate "hmms" and "aahs," signaling interest and surprise at the right moments, even as the dots and afterflashes before his eyes kept going off like private fireworks.

"Your central vision should hold for a while. . . ."

"Okay."

"But your peripheral vision is going to progressively narrow down like a tunnel." The doctor's voice became a faraway drone, heard from the end of a long corridor. "Your night vision is also going to become worse. . . ."

"And then?"

The doctor's face seemed to loom up, as if Francis were seeing him through a fish-eye lens. "I'm afraid we don't have any real treatment."

"So I'm going to go blind," he heard himself say matter-of-factly, pretending he wasn't having an out-of-body experience at this very moment.

"Well, legally blind," the doctor corrected him. "Most people can still see something, even if it's just shadows."

Everything in the room suddenly pulled back from him, the E at the top of the eye chart shrinking down to E.

"I assume you've seen other specialists about this over the years," the doctor said, not unkindly.

"I suspected something might be up," Francis admitted, trying to fight the sensation of motion sickness. "But I always thought it would just sort of go away."

Only the second part was a lie. In his heart, he always

knew something like this would happen, even before he'd started bumping into things the past couple of years. He'd sensed darkness hovering around him since he was a small boy, sneaking in at the edges, taking a little bit off the corner here and there. He'd tried to ignore it, telling himself he'd already made it through his share of close calls and near-blackouts. But in his heart, he knew it had never really gone away. The darkness was always bulging and pressing against the other side of the door, trying to get through.

"So how long's it going to take?"

"It depends on how it's been inherited." Dr. Friedan held Francis's lid open as he shined a penlight into his eye. "Some people can keep functioning for years. The majority need a cane by the time they're forty. Could be nothing's going to happen right away."

"I had an uncle was a deputy inspector who needed a Seeing Eye dog by the time he was sixty."

"*A police officer?*" The doctor pushed the lid open wider.

"My mother's brother."

"Well, that may be how you got it."

Francis felt his eye muscles straining to shut as the light focused on the rim of his cornea, a dazzling laser whiteness growing more and more intense until it felt like a finger pushing deep into the socket.

"All right, that's enough."

He panicked and pulled away, not able to see anything for a few seconds. This was what it was going to be like. He was being taken from the ranks of healthy, normal, independent people and told to go stand somewhere else. They were going to put a label on him; they were going to relegate him to special sections for the handicapped at ball games and on buses; they were going to help him find his seat and maybe give him headphones at the movie theaters; they were going to give him pamphlets to read and tapes to listen to that would help him with "the period of adjustment"; they were going to make his life more and more circumscribed until he couldn't function on his own anymore.

"Can I ask what it is you do for a living, Mr. Loughlin?" The doctor checked his file. "I don't seem to have your insurance information right in front of me."

"I'm in telemarketing," he said automatically.

"Really?" The doctor peered over the top of his glasses. "I wouldn't have guessed that."

"I can be very persuasive."

"Well, it's a good thing you don't drive a truck for a living."

"Why?"

"The loss of night vision can sneak up on you. It can go very slowly or very quickly. You're going to have to monitor it carefully."

"You saying I'm going to have to stop driving?"

"I'm saying you'll have to use your judgment." The doctor propped Francis's left eye open for a more thorough check. "Some days you'll see better than others. But I'm sure you don't want to be in a position of endangering anybody or having an accident because of your situation."

"No. Of course not."

Francis squeezed his eyes shut. All his life, he'd been the Go-To Guy. The first man you'd want into the room on a drug raid or testifying at a homicide trial. *Let Francis do it. He's an adrenaline junkie.* But now his other senses were diminishing in sympathy. His fingertips going numb, his tongue feeling dull, his hearing going tinny for a few seconds, like an old transistor losing its signal.

"You need a minute?" The doctor put aside his chart.

"No. Why?"

"It's a lot to take in. Most people would be very emotional."

He looked over the doctor's shoulder at a cross-section of the eyeball poster that one of the major drug companies had thoughtfully provided. From the side, the figure first resembled a blowfish with dozens of labeled spines coming off it. The iris, the cornea, the anterior chamber, the sclera, the bulbar sheath, the ciliary zonules. But the longer he stared, the more the shape seemed to change. The orb flared a brighter shade of orange and then pulsed and dimmed like the sun getting ready to explode.

So this was the future. One day the lights would go out and the world of visible things would cease to exist for him.

He started thinking about everything he hadn't seen yet. What about that driving tour of Ireland he'd been promising to take Patti on? Giant's Causeway. The castles in Dunluce and Carrickfergus. The so-called ancestral home in County Armagh his father was always whinging on about. Would he have to be in the passenger's seat the whole time?

Forget Ireland. What about just walking to the paint store on Court Street? He should go there right now and look at the color wheel, check out every single shade before his gray zone threshold got any lower. Or maybe he should just go out to Belmont, sit in the stands, and watch a horse run. Just to see how its muscles moved under its skin, to watch the rippling in its flanks and try to freeze-frame the half-second when all four hooves left the ground.

He thought of his uncle listening to the results from Yonkers in the kitchen of the old apartment by the Cross Bronx. His cane against the wall, letting his guide dog eat the scraps that fell off his plate, always yelling for Francis or his sister to go look for his Winstons, when the pack was sitting less than six inches from his elbow.

Not for me, thought Francis. *I'll eat my gun first.* He'd tell no one, at least for now. Less than six months from finally getting the bump to First Grade and the extra five grand a year for the pension? Screw the Braille lessons and the audiobooks. Screw the guide dogs and metal canes. Screw asking strangers to help get you across the street. He was fine. Nothing wrong with his fixation yet.

"I'm gonna be all right," he said.

"Are you?"

"Sure. I'm used to dealing with bad news in my business."

"Really?" The doctor cocked an eyebrow. "Tele-marketing must be tougher than I thought."

4

"*LONG AGO, IN a distant land . . .*"

Hoolian lay like a broken clock on his cousin Jessica's ratty-ass brown sofa, twitching in and out of consciousness, while the TV blared and a roomful of little girls played dress-up around him.

"*I, Aku, the shape-shifting master of darkness, released an unspeakable evil. . . .*"

He opened one eye and saw a cartoon demon on the screen with a pitchfork head and green lips, then drowsed off again for a few seconds as the narrator talked about a brave young warrior who stepped forth with a magic sword to oppose him.

In his half-awake state, he saw himself as the young samurai with his sword, on the steps of the courthouse in a long white robe, his hair knotted back with a chopstick, his blade curving and flashing as he laid into enemies on all sides.

"*Now the FOOL seeks to return to the past. . . .*"

He swung the sword again and the crowd gasped and parted, revealing a girl stretched out before him, gagging and pointing to a slash in her throat. His heart shrank as he saw his father behind her, cradling her head and whispering to her in Spanish, trying to keep her calm. *Lo siento, muchacha. Lo siento.*

He sat up suddenly and found a little girl with a tarnished doll's face and stringy black hair staring at him, waving a handle in his face.

"Would you do this for me?"

He rubbed his eyes, trying to get oriented, bits of sleep stinging like ground glass in the corners. It was close to four in the morning when he finally got Jessica on the phone, just coming home from a club, and walked over to her apartment from the boardwalk. Even at that late hour, he'd noticed that things seemed a little off. The heat was up too high and there was nothing in the refrigerator except for a carton of Tropicana orange juice, a few greasy containers of Chinese takeout, and a half gallon of milk three days past its expiration. Five of them were living there and sharing one cramped bathroom, with mold on the walls, a cracked mirror, and a chipped seat on the toilet. Before she showed Hoolian the sofa, Jessica mentioned he had to be quiet because she had three "babies," who needed their sleep. But now that he looked around, he saw she also had the flyest most up-to-date equipment money could buy: a wide-screen TV, a PlayStation 2, and one of those shiny high-tech stereo receivers with the little red lights that changed from a pyramid to a plateau in time with the beat.

"I can't reach the back." The girl waved what he finally recognized as a brush in his face. "Do it for me, please."

He covered himself with a blanket and saw that the clock above the TV said it was almost eight o'clock. Why weren't these girls getting ready for school?

"Come *on!*" She thrust the brush at him impatiently, six years old and used to demanding attention.

He hesitated, not sure if he could trust himself.

"Go already."

He took the brush and watched as she turned like a diva expecting her stylist to make her beautiful. A glistening black seaweed tangle confronted him. It seemed wrong to disturb it, to interfere with its wild natural splendor, to ensnare himself in any way.

"What's wrong with you?" She glanced over her shoulder. "You *stoopid?*"

Gently, he put the brush against the back of her head and slowly swept it down, realizing that he had never done this before.

"Do it harder," she insisted.

He looked around, hoping Jessica or her current boyfriend, "Exclusive," would come out and take over for him. But their bedroom door remained firmly shut and the two other little girls kept playing their dress-up game, ignoring them and shimmying like disco harlots.

He pulled the bristles through her dark strands, noticing it had been a while since the girl washed her hair.

"Ow! That's *too* hard!"

He leaned forward, concentrating, steadying her with one hand on top of her fragile little scalp, gently guiding the brush with the other, the worst of the snags already taken care of.

"Now you got it!"

He was finding his rhythm, getting the glide in his fingers. *Here I am, just brushing a little girl's hair.* Without a trace of self-consciousness, she sat down on his knee. He reached for the blanket to cover more of himself, afraid that the simple pressure of a warm body would give him an erection.

Of course, then the bedroom door opened and Exclusive strolled out, a bony-ass dude with cornrows and a build like a dislocated middle finger, scratching his nuts in beige bikini-style Jockeys. Hoolian already half suspected the man was pitching crack at the projects, what with all the expensive gear lying around. He cast a long mulish look at Hoolian and the girl as he went into the kitchen, grabbed the orange juice out of the refrigerator, and drank straight from the carton. Definitely not someone Hoolian wanted to hang with. The dude left the quart on the counter and sauntered past the two of them, hand stuffed in the back of his briefs now, scratching his ass as he smacked his lips.

"That your daddy?" Hoolian asked, nudging the girl off his lap.

"Nah, he Exclusive to my baby sister. But he jealous."

A few minutes later Jessica emerged, droopy-eyed and pudgy-kneed in a "Tupac 4 Ever" T-shirt, pink panties, and brown toenail polish.

She beckoned him into the kitchen and looked down at the floor. "There's a problem with you staying here tonight."

"Why?" He saw the little girl whose hair he'd brushed peeking at him from around the refrigerator.

"You know." Jessica trapped the big toe of one foot between two toes of the other. "My man just don't think it's a good idea you being around the kids right now."

"You're putting me on, right?"

"He very protective." She glanced toward the bedroom doorway, where Exclusive had reappeared. "He don't like another man touching my girls."

Hoolian looked between the two of them, trying to

figure out the balance of power here. "But your moms and mine were sisters. What about *la familia?*"

"I'm sorry." Jessica looked up at him with cowlike eyes. "Please don't hate me for this."

"*Don't hate you?* You're my cousin and you're putting me out on the street. What do you want me to do, *thank you?*"

"Yo, man." Exclusive came into the kitchen. "What's the problem?"

"There's no problem. I'm just talking to my cousin."

"Shorty asked you to leave. So why don't you bounce?"

"Why don't you mind your own fucking business?" Hoolian made a fist. "How 'bout that?"

He saw Exclusive freeze and look back toward the bedroom, as if he'd left his courage in there. Something about the way his cousin followed the look told Hoolian there might be a gun under the mattress.

"*Aw, forget about it, man.*" Hoolian waved in disgust. "Y'all ain't worth the trouble."

He went back to the couch and started stuffing the rest of his clothes back into his duffel bag, aware of the girl still tracking him, as if his skin were melting away, revealing a shivering shameful monster underneath covered with oozing sores and exploded carbuncles.

"Yo, I don't know what the hell you expected anyway," Jessica said. "You may be *la familia,* but I don't even fucking know you."

5

THE COFFEE SHOP menu was longer than *War and Peace,* and Francis found his eyes getting tired as he scanned each page from side to side with its tiny columns of daily specials, soups du jour, pancake breakfasts, lunchtime wraps, triple-decker sandwiches, Greek dishes, and Mexican delights. *Jesus, they really went on here, didn't they?* In a few years he'd probably need somebody to read it all for him. He closed the leather-bound book in disgust and looked up at the waitress.

"Just give me two eggs over easy and a side of bacon, cup of coffee," he said, defying Dr. Friedan's warning about the effect of diet on his disease. "And gimme an English muffin with lots of butter on it."

Across the table, Paul Raedo, the executive assistant to the Manhattan DA, ordered a plate of raw carrots and a cup of Lipton tea with honey and lots of sugar.

"And they call *me* a flake," Francis grumbled.

Paul, who'd asked Francis to join him for a late breakfast near City Hall, was a human exclamation point, a sleek guided missile in a Brooks Brothers suit. Francis sometimes felt a trifle uncomfortable discussing cases with him in the office, because Paul would bounce off the walls like a hyperactive child, close-cropped hairs poking up like hundreds of tiny nail points through his scalp, black suspenders gripping his shoulders like restraining devices. But he was a good man to have beside you at the barricades, always ready to go for the top charge, agreeing to talk plea deal only after he'd shown a defendant the gates of hell. More than once Francis had begged off going to one of Paul's famous Tuesday Night Massacre Poker Games, figuring that after a long brutal day in Homicide the last thing he needed was that kind of aggression coming at him across a stack of money.

"How are the kids?" asked Paul, closing his leather menu with a muted *pfft* and handing it up to the waitress like a sealed indictment.

"Ah, you know, competing to see who can give the old man a coronary first."

Francis was wary of people without families inquiring too closely about his children, figuring maybe half the time there was an agenda. With women, it was an occasional stirring behind the smiles, like a sniper behind shades. With men who weren't close friends, it was more often outright manipulation, an attempt to soften you up for a favor.

"Don't you have a son in the army?" Paul squinted.

"Just got sent to Korea," Francis said with a grunt, trying to ignore the way the thought made ice water seep into his stomach. "My daughter's the one with her mother's brains. Studying genetics at Smith. Says she wants to prove her father's the missing link."

A deep horseshoe grin creased Paul's face. The man had no clue. Had never even been close to married. All his girlfriends seemed to come and go within six months.

Instead, most of his free time seemed to go into planning extreme sports vacations. Where other people had family pictures in the office, there were photos of him biking across Russia, hang gliding in the Yucatán, and bodysurfing in Maui. And for reasons he'd never clearly explained to Francis, a harpoon hung on a wall opposite a portrait of General George Armstrong Custer in his Union army uniform.

"So, what's up, Paul?" he said, wanting to focus on something other than his diagnosis or his son for a while.

"I guess you heard about Julian Vega."

"What about him?" he said tightly.

"Well, you know that he's been writing letters for years from prison, raising all these side issues about witness statements and whether his lawyer was competent. . . ."

Ever since he'd left the doctor's office this morning, Francis had been having a distracting little subband of dialogue crawling underneath his regular conversation, like a cable news report, but now it suddenly cut off.

"Somebody might've said something to me," he allowed.

"So Judge Santiago had him brought down for a four-forty hearing on Rikers yesterday. And after he heard the arguments about the competency issues, he decided to grant the motion and vacate the conviction."

The waitress brought his coffee.

"Where's the fucking Sweet 'n Low?" Francis said, looking around. "Didn't these restaurants always used to have Sweet 'n Low on the tables?"

All at once, it seemed very important to him for everything to be in its proper place.

"It's right next to you, Francis." Paul pointed to the

edge of the table, just outside his field of vision. "Look, no one expects you to be happy."

"No shit, Paulie." He snatched a pink packet. "No one thought of giving me a heads-up?"

"What would you have said at the hearing? The issues didn't have anything to do with you. Almost everybody Ralph Figueroa represented is looking to get their case reopened, because he was a fucking degenerate drug addict who never told anyone they had the right to testify in their own defense. They've overturned four of his cases in the last three months."

"And it never occurred to you that I might have a problem with this? Did you forget what happened in Auburn a few years ago?"

"The judge was made aware there'd been an incident. I made sure to put a note about it in the case file."

"An *incident?*" Francis tore open the packet and poured saccharine on the smoldering black surface. "That little cocksucker tried to take a swing at me in the corridor. Good thing the COs got between us, because I was fucking ready to have a go at him."

That's some tough talk there, Helen Keller. At the time, he'd been caught totally off guard. Hurrying down the hall on a visit upstate to meet a potential CI when he'd heard a voice just outside the lunchroom, calling out, "Hey, *embustero.*" He didn't see Hoolian stepping out of line and lunging at him until it was almost too late. Not that he would have recognized the kid anyway, after all those years.

"I should've had a chance to testify about that at the hearing," Francis fumed, realizing the whole thing should have been an early-warning signal.

"The judge took the position that Hoolian already

did sixty days in solitary for it and that's enough." Paul turned his palms up as the waitress brought his tea and raw carrots. "There was no physical contact, so I don't know what else you expected."

"So, that's it? He's off the hook? Somebody from the office buying him breakfast too?"

"C'mon, Francis, don't do this."

"Don't do *what?*" The waitress put down his eggs and bacon. "Don't remind you? Is that what you're telling me?"

"No . . ."

"Do you even remember what this case was supposed to be about? Did you even look at the fucking file again?"

"Yes, I looked at the file, Francis." Paul picked up a carrot and bit it in half.

"Then do you remember the kid with the bottle?"

"The what?"

"The kid with the fucking milk bottle tied around his neck."

Paul stopped chewing and shifted a load of half-masticated carrot from one side of his mouth to the other. "What the hell are you talking about?"

"You don't remember."

"Enlighten me."

Francis glanced around the restaurant, finding himself making wider arcs than usual to see if anyone was listening. "You remember she worked at Bellevue, right?" He dropped his voice.

"Yes. She was in the pediatric ER."

"Right. *Exactly.* So just before Christmas break the year before she dies, third-grade teacher from one of the fancy-ass uptown private schools walks into the ER with an eight-year-old boy. Dad's a big lawyer at a white-shoe firm. But the teacher knows something's up, because he's got bruises on both arms and severe stomach pains every day. Allison starts to examine him and sees he's got this big lump under his shirt. And when she lifts it, it turns out to be a baby bottle tied around his neck."

"I'm still not remembering," Paul sucked his molars.

"So Allison does her thing, just the way we would," Francis said. "She goes eye-to-eye with the kid. She works him, she talks to him. She plays Monopoly with him. She gets him to trust her. And then it all comes out that his father, Mr. Big Shit Corporate Hot Dog, says the kid's been acting like a baby. Crying and wetting the bed. So if he's going to act like a baby, he's going to wear a baby bottle to school. A third-grader, Paulie. Isn't that nice?"

He stirred his coffee again, not wanting to risk asking for milk when it could be right next to him.

"All the nurses were right outside the room when she was trying to get him to take the bottle off. The poor kid's in hysterics, begging her, *'Please, please, nonononono, Daddy will be so mad. Please don't make me take it off.'* Broke their hearts. And these are tough fucking women. They've seen everything. They make *you* look like a goddamn choirgirl."

"Francis, come on . . ."

"So Allison called the father up and reamed him out. This nice girl, whose mother wrote children's books. *'You fuck-ING asshole, I am going to call Social Services, I'm going to call Bureau of Child Welfare on you. . . .'* With the Jamaican nurses in the background going, 'You tell him, girl.'"

"She get him locked up?"

"He ended up with a desk appearance ticket." Francis stirred his coffee. "*Fucker.* And, yeah, I looked at him for the murder at the time. But that scumbag was in Gstaad with his girlfriend."

"Many moons ago, Francis. Seems like the Dark Ages. Everything's different now."

"She was *one of us.*" Francis stared at him, nothing wrong with his central vision yet. "She was good people."

"Hey, Francis. Don't make me the bad guy here. It's a complicated issue. The guy went in when he was seventeen and came out thirty-seven. A lot of people are going to say we already got our pound of flesh."

"And Allison would be forty-seven. . . ."

"All right, all right." Paul put his carrot down. "No one's saying we're throwing in the towel either. This was a heinous crime. No question about it. People remember. It's not in our interest to let murderers go free before they've served their full sentence."

"Particularly if we're up for a judgeship."

"That's a cheap shot, Francis." The bristly little troops arose on Paul's scalp. "And you know it."

"So obviously it's true."

Of course, Francis had already heard the rumors. After this many years, men like Paul didn't sit around waiting for the DA to retire or die. They took their restless vaulting ambition and they went politicking. It was natural for Paul to want to be a judge. He didn't have the temperament or the social skills for the private sector — no wife to set off his intensity and give him the illusion of charm at corporate cocktail parties. On the bench, he'd be free to glower and grow cantankerous without contradiction, indulging his vengeful streak well into his sunset years.

"So where do we go from here?"

"Officially no decision's been made," Paul poured hot

water into his teacup. "We have the option of proceeding with the indictment as if it's still 1983 or letting the whole thing drop. But there's another wrinkle I need to talk to you about."

"What's that?"

"Hoolian has Debbie Aaron representing him."

"Are you shitting me?"

"I wish. Hoolian must have gone through half the lawyers in the New York bar before he got to her."

"Fuckin' Debbie A."

He pushed his suddenly foul-smelling eggs away, contemplating the ring the plate left on the table.

"You knew her when she was doing drug cases at our office, didn't you?" Paul fished the tea bag out of his cup with a spoon.

"Yeah, we called her 'Fuckin' A' because she was always trying to punch holes in our testimony before she put us on the stand."

How'd you know he was carrying a gun, Detective? Did you actually see *the money change hands? Why didn't you recover more of the drugs in the apartment?* For about three seconds, he'd thought of having a thing with her. He liked a woman who could give as good as she got. But then he realized she would wear him out with her ferocious demands for honesty and contempt for compromise — they would have been like two buzz saws going toward each other.

"We gotta tread carefully here." Paul wrapped the string around his tea bag. "I don't know if you've been following this, but Debbie's already suing the police department for malicious prosecution in a civil suit."

"That fuckup with Marty Delblanco in the two-eight?"

Francis had caught bits and pieces of the departmental gossip at various rackets. A junkie who got locked up in Harlem for raping and murdering an eighty-year-old grandmother recently freed after fifteen years on DNA evidence and recanted witness testimony. And now Debbie A. was suing on his behalf, saying the detective who'd questioned the skell had beaten him into giving a full confession. What stunned everyone was not just that the department and the city were named in the $3.2 million suit but that the detective was being held personally liable to the tune of $750,000.

"They say Deb's got a hard-on for suing cops because she was married to that detective in the nine-oh who used to knock her around some," Paul explained. "They're divorced now. She had him locked up for domestic abuse."

"But no one's talking about making Marty pay, are they?"

"Indemnification's an open question. He's supposed to have given that kid a pretty good tune-up to get the statement. It's not clear that anybody else should be responsible for that."

Francis touched his tongue to the roof of his mouth. "Motherfucker, you're not worried about that in this case, are you?"

Paul squeezed the remains of his tea bag into his cup. "We gotta stick together here, Francis."

"What're you talking about? I never laid a hand on Hoolian. He put himself on the scene."

Paul lowered his voice. "Come on, Francis. We all know this was never the perfect investigation."

"What the fuck is that supposed to mean?"

Paul rested the spoon with the crushed bag on the side of the saucer, letting the silence speak for itself.

Francis noticed the way everything on the table seemed to get very large and then very small.

"You know you weren't so fucking perfect yourself, *Your Honor.* I didn't hear about the American Bar Association giving you any citation for the way you handled some of those early interviews."

Paul cupped the back of his head self-consciously. "Well, can we just say there were certain things that both of us might've done differently?"

Francis threw his napkin down. "Sure, why not? Let's just say the whole thing was just a practice run so we could get it right the second time."

"Glad you think it's funny."

"So, what do you want to do?"

"I think we have to take the position that the indictment still stands and this is still an active investigation," Paul said, adopting the sagacious furrow and dignified chin of a man running for public office. "Nothing in the four-forty motion contradicts the underlying facts of the case itself. If Debbie A. wants to come after us, she'll have to prove there was a deliberate intent to ignore specific evidence."

"Right," said Francis, the subband of commentary beginning to crawl through his head again.

"And she's going to have a hard time proving that. It's been twenty years. I don't know where she's going to find any witnesses. . . ."

Arroyo. Hernandez. Francis was already dipping into the slipstream, trying to remember the names that came up in the original investigation. He wondered if he even had any of his old notebooks around at home.

"Francis . . . ," Paul interrupted him.

"Wha?"

Paul leaned across the table, peering out from under the mask of jurisprudence one last time. "We're sure we got the right guy, aren't we?"

"Julian Vega killed her," Francis said firmly. "The front door of that building was locked after midnight. Nobody else could've gotten into her apartment unless they had a key, like he did. His fingerprints were all over the murder weapon. No one else was seen leaving. Her blood was on his tool. . . ."

But he noticed the litany had a certain hollowness after all this time, like an agnostic's prayer.

"So has anybody talked to the family yet, let them know what's going on?" he asked.

"I made some calls to try to track them down through Victims' Services," Paul said vaguely. "But the last number I had is disconnected. They've moved around a lot since '83."

"So Hoolian's out and they don't know it yet?"

Paul looked abashed, reminding Francis that even the most calculating people in the world sometimes got the basic math wrong.

"What's going to happen if they read it in the paper first?"

"I was hoping you'd try and smooth it over with them a little, Francis." The eyebrows rose and the bristles bent back. "We want them on our side. The last thing we need is them bad-mouthing us in the press while we're going through this again. We don't want to look callous."

"Then why didn't you reach out before the hearing?"

"I didn't think there was any way we were going to lose."

Francis watched the look of genuine astonishment

spread across Paul's face, the absolute amazement that anyone could consider the same set of facts he had at his disposal and come to a different conclusion. And in that instant, he saw the totality of the man's strength and weakness. That utter certainty of his own righteousness that had made Paul a successful prosecutor and a near-total failure at every other kind of human transaction.

"All right, I'll reach out to them," said Francis. "But you're going to owe me big-time, Judge."

"Francis, let me count the ways."

"Just help me find our waitress," he said, having finally ascertained that there was, in fact, no milk on the table. "This coffee's too strong."

6

HOOLIAN WIPED HIS tired eyes and studied the subway map, eventually finding the route from Coney Island to his lawyer's office. His own flesh and blood turning him out like some scabby, flea-ridden dog. He fingered his father's Saint Christopher's medal. Wishing he'd at least had a chance to catch a shower before he got chased out. He thought he could still smell prison on his skin.

The train sliced through a graveyard, rows of low-lying tombstones darkened like a smoker's teeth by air pollution. *Land of the dead. You are now departing from the land of the dead. Please have your passport ready.*

His lawyer's office was above a Kinko's on Astor Place in Manhattan. Traffic raced around a sculpture of a giant black cube that seemed to balance itself precariously on a corner. *Where the hell is everyone rushing to?* His metabolism was still on prison time: wary, contained, hair-trigger sensitive to change.

In the waiting room, there was a confused-looking man in a lady's white rubber bathing cap. He nodded knowingly, as if he were an old friend of Hoolian's.

Beside him, a bony little Asian lady was trying to corral three wayward kids waddling across the brown carpet, and a brother with legs the size of tackling dummies was talking to himself about burning mix CDs for a party. It took Hoolian a second to realize he actually had a telephone headset inside his baseball cap.

The secretary studiously ignored them all, a lush chubby white girl with blue nail polish and Rastafarian hair, putting caller after caller on hold, a half-done *New York Times'* crossword puzzle resting next to her computer keyboard.

Hoolian stood before her, trying to get her attention and then realized he was staring too long again — just as he had with the Barbed-Wire Girl last night. *How long are you allowed to look anyway?* There was probably a rule. He held her gaze for two Mississippis and then started to turn.

"Yes?" She looked up.

"Julian Vega to see Ms. Aaron."

"Oh, Julian, come on in." Deborah Aaron peered out from behind a chipped wooden door. "I've been waiting for you."

He glanced back at the other people who'd been waiting longer, half thinking he should apologize for cutting ahead and then thought, *Fuckit.* They'd do the same to him in a heartbeat.

He stepped into the office, closing the door after him as Ms. A. gave him her hand. "Congratulations." A slight tug from her wrist brought him up onto the balls of his feet. She offered her cheek for a kiss, but he turned the wrong way and brushed her lips instead.

"Uh, thank you." He caught the scent of lilac on her skin.

"Have a seat."

Did a kiss necessarily mean a woman liked you or was she just being polite? He slowly lowered himself into a chair before her desk, carefully balancing his duffel bag on his lap. Other inmates had given him shit when she'd come to see him in prison, this tough New York lady with the china-doll face who talked too fast and always sounded like she was trying to catch her breath. They'd told him stories about other cons doing the nasty with the women representing them in the visiting room while the guards looked the other way and children pumped quarter after quarter into the vending machines.

But he wouldn't have risked anything like that while he was locked up. The woman had driven 150 miles upstate in slashing rainstorms to see him, taking his case pro bono after he'd been turned down or run the course with a half-dozen other lawyers over the years. She'd read the correspondence he'd labored over — sometimes four or five letters a day — raising both arcane Fourth Amendment issues and glaring omissions in the court record. She took it seriously when he said he'd been framed and insisted that he'd written to Mr. Raedo at the DA's office over and over asking to have his DNA tested without ever receiving a reply. Naturally, he'd fallen in love with her a little — hardly sleeping nights before her scheduled visits, looking up obscure citations and rules of evidence to impress her in the law library, his heart lifting as he heard the efficient click of her heels on the cold stone floor.

Now it was different, though. There was no correction officer watching them through a little screen window in the door. He felt a tinge of her moisture lingering on the corner of his mouth. In the clearer light of this office — a little smaller and more book-choked than he'd expected — he could see she was just holding on to a kind of careworn attractiveness. There were a few white strands in her ash-blond hair, some circles under her eyes, and her dimples were starting to become deep permanent grooves. In the next few years she'd either lapse into premature hagdom or become the kind of second-act hottie who always had younger guys eager to bring her coffee in bed.

"Sorry I couldn't stick around and give you a ride from Rikers after the hearing," she said with a strained smile. "But the babysitter had to go home early because *her* kids were sick. And I had no one covering for me. . . ."

"'S all right. I found my way."

"Oh, I'm so glad." She stopped, reminding herself to inhale. "You get a good night's sleep at your cousin's?"

"Uh, yeah. Felt good. You know. *La familia.*"

He knew it was wrong to start off the day lying to his attorney, but what else was he going to say? A part of him was still a little Nuyo-Rican boy in a *blanco* school, wanting to impress the girls.

"Uh-huh, that's great." She nodded absently. "So how you like being a free man?"

"It's a-ight." He looked around, noticing a child's finger painting next to her law degree on the wall, its taped corner flapping over an air vent. "I keep thinking you-all are going to tell me it's a joke and I have to turn around and go back."

"No, it's no joke. But we do have some serious things to discuss."

He hugged the duffel bag to his chest, hearing a hint of sternness. "So, what's the DA saying? Are they gonna let the charges drop?"

"I'm afraid I had a very testy conversation with Paul

Raedo this morning." The words went off like a string of firecrackers too close to his ear. "They're taking the position that the judge vacated your conviction on a 'technicality.'" She crooked her fingers into quotation marks. "But the underlying indictment still stands."

He fell back in his chair, knowing it was all too good to be true.

"Let's face it. We got lucky yesterday." She sat forward, leveling with him. "Your old lawyer had four of his cases overturned in the last few months. It happens sometimes, but not usually all at once. We were swimming with the tide."

Lucky? Rage started to gurgle up inside him again. If he'd been lucky, he wouldn't have been set up in the first place. If he'd been lucky, his father wouldn't have hired Ralph Figueroa. That drug-addled old bastard never told him he had the right to testify on his own behalf or that they'd been offered a five-to-fifteen plea bargain by the DA. Turned out he'd been screwing up cases for years — missing deadlines, showing up unprepared, filing the wrong papers. And taking $12,000 of Papi's life savings. The lawyer was living in a nursing home in Florida now, probably drinking out of the toilet and blissfully ignorant of the fact that four separate state judges had been forced to set aside old jury verdicts because of his gross negligence.

"I'm sorry, Julian. It's politics."

All at once he was back in the courtroom again, swimming in pure adrenaline terror and the itchy gray suit his father had bought him. The foreman reading the verdict as he felt his body go cold. *Guilty, guilty, guilty . . .* Every time they polled a member of the jury, he lost a few more degrees of body heat. His teeth were chattering by the time the guards took his arms and stood him up, so hunched over that he could barely turn around to say good-bye to Papi as they walked him back to the pens.

"All right, hold it, hold it." She could see the blood drain from his face. "This is all just posturing and jockeying for position. Everything's probably going to be just fine."

"*Probably?*" he squawked. "Ms. A., don't talk to me about *probably*. Just tell me what I have to do and let me do it."

"Look. This is an unusual case."

He noticed how she had to consciously slow herself down and pause to take a breath every few sentences, as if she were used to dealing with people who were either hard of hearing or willfully dense.

"Tell me about it. I served damn near twenty years for something they framed me for. . . ."

"Julian, I'm on your side." She put her hands up. "Okay? I'm just trying to tell you what the facts are. The reality is, this is a high-profile case. I remember it from my third year at the DA's office. It was all any of the women there ever talked about, because we were all the same age as the victim. And, unfortunately, people haven't forgotten. So now Paul Raedo is up for a judgeship. He can't afford to look like he's backpedaling."

"*Fahhkk.*" The air went out of him. "So I could wind up going back upstate? Is that what you're telling me?"

"Listen, you've been through a lot and I can see how upset you're getting, so here's what I'm proposing we do." She rubbed her pearls one by one with a kind of half-conscious tenderness. "I'll call Paul back and see if we can work out a deal for the calendar call next week. You plead guilty and Judge Bronstein would give you time served and that would be that. . . ."

"*No.*"

Ms. Aaron let go of her pearls and looked at the door nervously. She probably thought she was being so sane and reasonable. But she hadn't been at his cousin's this morning. She hadn't heard his last surviving kin declare, *I don't even fucking know you.* She hadn't seen the way that little girl looked at him from behind the refrigerator. That look was going to stay with him like a knife in the back.

"I ain't pleading to shit," he started, then stopped himself, hearing how two decades of prison life had eroded the benefits of a good education. "*Excuse me.* I am not pleading to shit. I want my name back."

She put her head down. "Julian, let's be honest with each other," she said. "You've spent more than half your life in prison already. Don't you want this to be over?"

"*Hell, yeah.*"

"Then why wouldn't you just want to cut your losses? I know how vindictive Paul Raedo and Francis Loughlin can be."

"And if I plead guilty to what they set me up for, how am I going to hold my head up? Huh? Could I get to be a lawyer like you with a felony conviction? Would I be able to get a mortgage and buy myself a decent place to live?"

Her expression had changed while he was talking. There was a pair of scissors opening behind her eyes now.

"Julian, it's time to get practical," she said. "I know how hard you've worked to keep this case alive. But there is a limit to how far wishful thinking will take you."

"What do you mean?"

"I mean, over the years, you can convince yourself that you're innocent and you've been screwed by the system.

But if we keep going in this direction, we're going to end up back in court and the facts are going to come out. And they don't always turn out to be what you want them to be."

Fury made his mind go white. "You calling *me* a liar?"

"I'm saying I don't want to see you get hurt any more than you already have been." She patted her chest for emphasis. "And, frankly, I can't afford to invest any more resources into a civil suit that isn't going anywhere." She came around and sat on a corner of the desk. "Wrongful imprisonment is a notoriously hard case to prove. You're going to have to show that the police and prosecutors deliberately ignored or corrupted evidence that could have exonerated you."

He fell silent for a few seconds, the weight of the duffel bag pressed into his lap. All the things he'd collected and saved while he was away. The dull-bristled toothbrush he needed to replace; soup cans he'd bought at the commissary and couldn't bear to throw out; the little alarm clock he'd fixed up in small-engine repair; the tube socks he'd worn doubled up when he was up to his ankles in snow in the prison yards up by the Canadian border, trying to watch fucking farm reports on the outdoor TV; the copy of *Childhood's End* he'd had in his Jansport bag that day Detective Loughlin asked him to stop by the station house. The envelope he'd been holding on to. The mementos from the life he'd thought he'd have. The *years*. They'd been stolen from him, stripped away like a mugger taking his wallet, rifling it for cash, and tossing it in the gutter. That was what made it keep hurting. That no one gave a damn. No one was keeping score. No one was trying to be fair. They'd ground his face into the dirt and had themselves a good time doing it. He'd try to move on and live with it, smiling and shrugging, go-along-to-get-along Hoolian, but it would be incubating inside him like the creature from *Alien*. Until one day it came bursting out with gnashing jaws and dripping teeth, leaving just a useless husk behind.

"Ms. Aaron, those people lied," he said coldly. "They lied and took everything I had and everything I was ever going to have. I spent the day of my father's funeral in solitary confinement. And now you're trying to tell me no one has to *pay* for that? Uh-uh. I can't live with it. If you don't want to take it to the next level and keep fighting for me, I'll find some other lawyer who will."

He saw her face fall and her hand close around her pearls. Oh, yeah, he had her pegged. From being in prison, he'd learned to see to the bottom of people quickly, to judge the level of their need and hunger in a glance. He'd already noticed the finger painting beside the law degree, and now he saw she had pictures of two kids on the credenza, a boy and a girl but no husband in sight. So she was a single mother who needed to get something out of this case almost as much as he did.

"You know, we run a shoestring operation in this office," she cautioned him. "I don't have a lot of resources at my disposal, to hire private investigators or anything like that. If you want me to keep going with this case, you're going to have to pitch in and do some real work yourself from time to time."

"That's all right," he told her. "I did twenty years in the state system. I don't mind getting my hands dirty."

"Well, all right then." She sighed. "I guess I'll get my papers ready and let the DA know we're not taking any plea here."

7

FRANCIS HEARD THE crunch of dead leaves under his shoes as he walked down West 89th Street toward the Wallis family's brownstone. This was what the change of seasons was going to amount to in a few years. The air cooling for a couple of weeks, some snowflakes melting on his face, and then — *boom* — a patch of ice on the sidewalk for him to slip on. What about seeing a sugar maple burst to life in front of a Pathmark in Rego Park, as gaudy and flamboyant as a Moulin Rouge cancan dancer tossing her petticoats? What about the sycamores in Riverside Park changing color, like a sun god was dripping fire on their leaves? He should drive out to the country with Patti tonight, just to look at the stars before they melted away.

He spotted Tom Wallis from halfway down the block, rusty hair and fair skin, sweeping up in front of the house, in pressed slacks and a white shirt with the collar buttoned, as if he'd just come home from work in the middle of the day.

"There he is."

"What's doing, Francis?" Tom put the broom aside and offered his hand.

"Good to see you, man." Francis skipped the handshake and gave him a hearty hug. "You're looking well."

It was true. Most families of crime victims got old before their time. You could see ten years pass on their faces as soon as you did the initial notification, the eyes receding into the skull right as you said the words "I'm sorry for your loss." And watching them at trial was even worse: the skin tone graying, the hair going lank, the posture slumping as they realized this wasn't about justice, but *the integrity of the process*. That these muted lawyerly compromises and confused halfhearted witnesses were all they had to address their pain.

But Tom, born five years before Allison, didn't look substantially different from the way he did that last time Francis had seen him, at the Landmark Tavern in '86, talking quietly over ginger ale and soda bread. He still had that stunned look of a young farmer seeing his first twister in the distance, the jaw just beginning to slacken, the high forehead lightly furrowed over a pair of faint, barely discernible eyebrows and that same contrast of milky-white skin and red hair as the women in the family.

"I'm glad I caught you home when I called."

"Life of a salesman." Tom touched the space between his eyebrows in the same shy, slightly self-conscious way that Francis remembered. "Gone all the time and then home on a weekday afternoon. It's been a long time, Francis."

"It has. I lost track of you guys. I used to send your mother a card every Christmas and every Easter."

"Yeah, we moved around a lot for a while." Tom nodded, only the slightest thinning of his lips hinting that he might be uneasy about this visit. "We were staying at my mom's place in Sag Harbor for a while. Then we tried Connecticut. But you know how it is. You can't stay where you were, but nowhere else feels like home."

"I hear that a lot. It's hard to settle."

"That's us, the Wandering Wallises."

"Got your mom living with you now?"

"Yeah. The price was right, so we sold the place we had in Danbury and jumped at it." Tom blinked, making no move to invite Francis in. "It's worked out nice. We cover the mortgage by renting out the top floor, and Mom's got her space on the garden level, so she gets to see the grandchildren all the time and still have her own bathroom."

"Jesus, I didn't even know you got married, Tom."

"We just had our ten-year anniversary." He fingered his gold band, preoccupied. "Terrific lady from Indiana. We've got two little girls, three and six. . . ."

He stooped down to pick up a Swedish Fish wrapper that had blown onto his front steps.

"So, what's on your mind, Francis? You said you had something important to discuss on the phone."

"I don't know if you heard about this yet. But they let Julian Vega out."

Tom stood up slowly, the wrapper making crinkling noises in his hand. "What are you talking about?"

"Believe me. I know it's fucked up. I just found out myself."

"They-let-him-out?" Tom reviewed the words, turning into an English as a second language student. "How could this happen?"

"It's a technicality. They vacated his conviction because he claims his lawyer didn't tell him he had the right to testify. It's bullshit. Don't worry about it. We're gonna put him back in."

Tom began rubbing the smooth space between his eyebrows, as if he were trying to work the idea into his head. "You mean we're going to have to go through this whole thing again?"

"Tom, I'm sorry. This shouldn't have happened."

"Wow . . . I mean, *wow*." A pink undertone began to boil up through his fair complexion. "Why didn't anybody tell us this was happening?"

"It all came up very suddenly. No one was expecting it."

Oh, Paul Raedo, the things I do for you.

"God. I don't know if my mother can handle this."

"You want me to tell her?"

Tom shook his head, his natural pallor returning only by gradual degrees. "I don't think that's a good idea."

"Why not?"

Tom took a deep breath, like he'd just ridden a child's bicycle up a long steep mountainside.

"She hasn't been herself. For a very long time."

"No?"

Francis cursed himself for not keeping up. Staying in touch with victims' families was as much a part of the job as filling out DD5s and developing CIs. Sure, some of those phone calls were torture, mothers crying, *"Why did the Lord take my beautiful baby boy?"* when you knew damn well that Baby Boy was a drug-dealing ho-slapping little gangsta with a razor blade in his mouth when he got capped. But *you had to do it.* Not only because it was the right thing to give consolation to the brokenhearted but because *you never knew.* You could be two, three years from a dead-end case, thinking it was never going to get cleared, when Grandma calls up out of the blue, says she was watching *As the World Turns* the other day when Miss Thing sashays on with her big butt and flash jewelry that reminds her of that girl Baby Boy was seeing before he got killed, who it turns out had a jealous husband just up from Ecuador.

"I know she seemed like she was going to be so strong during the trial." Tom gripped the broom. "But then she kind of went to pieces. You know, she's been trying to write the same book for twenty years."

"Uh-oh."

It figured. The ones who could hold themselves up the longest sometimes fell the hardest. He remembered Eileen sitting in the second row of the courtroom every day, this indomitable red-haired lady who never wore any makeup and raised two kids on her own in the city after her husband, the failed Abstract Expressionist, decamped to Paris with an eighteen-year-old Meredith Monk dancer.

"What happened? She sounded good the last time I talked to her."

"She sort of went downhill slowly at first and then picked up speed." Tom's mouth hardened. "Right after the trial, she started going to potluck dinners for all these support groups of parents with dead children. That was all right. But then she started having all these petty disputes with them. Complaining that people only came to the meetings when the guy who killed their kids was up for sentencing and they needed more people to come to court."

"Sure," Francis grunted sympathetically, knowing you could never take these things for granted.

"So after a while, she started hanging around with this other crowd. These New Age types. People into healing crystals and aromatherapy, you know, all that crap."

"You don't sound impressed."

"What do you want?" Tom picked up a ball of tinfoil. "I sell professional medical supplies. These people are the enemy. But then she got hooked up with the real wackos. The ones that think they can talk to the dead."

"You're kidding me. Your mother?"

Francis couldn't quite picture it. They were talking about a wised-up hardheaded New York lady, a woman of substance. A girl who got a role playing Ophelia to Richard Burton's Hamlet straight out of Julliard. An actress who worked with Cassavetes and then gave it up to raise her children. A woman who reinvented herself as a successful children's book author after her husband hived off. Francis remembered reading one of the stories, *Hello, Walls,* to his daughter, Kayleigh, a few years after the case ended and being struck by how tough-minded, funny, and scary it was all at the same time — as if the author had some special subversive understanding with her young readers that specifically excluded parents.

"Well, she was always a little . . . *manic.*" Tom tossed the tinfoil ball into the garbage with a look of disgust. "But then after my sister died, she started getting more and more depressed until she literally couldn't get out of bed some mornings. She thought these people — these *snake-oil salesmen* — could help her. They told her Allison wasn't really dead."

"Wha?" Francis heard his jawbone crack behind his ear.

"One of the 'spirit guides' told her that was another girl buried in her grave." Tom looked down at his feet, embarrassed. "Chief Missing Invoice or Something. He said a mistake had been made. Bodies were switched.

Another girl was murdered and her face was mutilated, so no one could recognize her. . . ."

"Look, Tom, not for nothing, your mother is a great lady and all, but *that was your sister.* I saw her with my own eyes." Being careful to say *her,* not just *the body.*

"You don't have to sell me. I saw her at the morgue too. But denial isn't just a river in Egypt."

"Oh, don't I know it."

Francis nodded, realizing that he still hadn't written down the date of his next appointment with Dr. Friedan.

"And then she got into the private investigators. These vultures who said they were going to find my sister for her." Tom swept at a Wrigley's gum wrapper on a step. "A hundred and fifty dollars an hour to track a bunch of ATM statements. Like they were really going to find my sister sitting in a Taco Bell in Kenosha with Amelia Earhart."

"Well, no one ever called me about it."

"The thing is, she seemed to be doing a bit better these last couple of years." Tom kept sweeping at the gum wrapper, getting more and more frustrated as it refused to budge. "Especially since the girls have got older. They've brought her out of the fog some. Particularly Michelle, my little one. They're peas in a pod, her and my mother. She even looks like Allison did at that age."

Francis turned toward the garden-floor window, thinking he'd just seen someone there from the corner of his eye.

"I really thought the sun was starting to break through," Tom said. "The other day, we were in the park with the girls at the Alice in Wonderland statue and Mom suddenly turned to me and said, 'I feel like I'm being given another chance.' And for a half-second, it was the old her again. I felt like we finally had her back. But now that you're telling me it's going to start all over . . ." He sagged. "I don't know."

"Look, none of us wanted this to happen."

"You know what the truly unbelievable thing is?" Tom said suddenly. "She *liked* that kid, Julian. Can you believe that? She met him when she was over at the building, visiting. She thought it was *sweet* the way he was always dogging after Allison. Like he seriously ever stood a chance with her."

"Probably seemed innocent enough at the time."

"They both should've known better."

Tom picked the wrapper off the step and threw it in the trash, a light burn showing under his pale eyebrows.

"Yeah, okay, I'm not arguing." Francis put his hands up. "I'm only saying anybody could've missed the signals. At the time I arrested him he looked about twelve."

"Of course. I didn't mean to go off. I just can't —"

"I know."

"— go through that whole torture again." Tom looked down and saw that a gray smudge of gum had remained on the step. "I suppose we're going to start getting calls from the media any minute now."

"You don't have to talk to them. Just direct all the calls to the DA's press office."

"You know, a part of me just thinks we should just let the whole thing drop," he said, kicking at the gummy nub.

"What do you mean?"

"I mean, it's enough already. I . . . just . . . want . . . closure . . ."

"What?"

Tom tried to work the tip of his shoe under the gum to dislodge it. "I'm saying this has been going on for twenty years. We're like professional victims. It's the only thing that defines us anymore. And I'm sick of it."

Francis stared at him, brought up short by that word, *closure*. Not something a man losing his eyesight wanted to contemplate.

"And so, what's your mother going to say?" he asked.

"Excuse me?"

"How's she going to feel if she picks up the paper next week and sees the case has been totally dismissed?"

Tom lifted his foot and saw a single elastic tendril had stuck to the sole of his shoe. "To be honest with you, Francis, she hardly ever reads the paper anymore. She's off in her own world most of the time."

Francis shook his head. "I made her a promise, Tom. I told her somebody would have to account for what happened."

"I understand that, but — ah, *fuck*." Tom tried to scrape his shoe against the edge of the step.

Francis watched him, thinking of the way certain things stuck.

"You know, I went to the wall for this case," he said. "I mean, I *really* went to the wall, Tommy. Some people might say I even went over it a little. And I wouldn't do that for just anybody. But I had a special feeling about your family."

"I know that, Francis. I know my mother trusted you."

"Yeah, well, we had some common ground."

"Yeah?"

"Yeah, you know, death in the family. My mother got hit by a car when I was nine."

"Jesus, I didn't know that." Tom looked stunned, the pinkness fading behind the eyebrows.

"Yeah, she was in a coma before she passed, but . . ."

Francis found himself playing with the antenna of his cell phone, pulling it out and pushing it in. "Anyway, your mother reminded me of her a little bit." He stopped himself. "And so when I took this case, she made me swear I'd do right by you guys."

"Oh, I remember."

"So I don't feel right, just forgetting that. I'd like to talk to her about what's going on."

"Well, she's not home right now."

Francis looked at the downstairs window again, almost sure someone had been there a minute ago.

"Well, ask her to give me a call when she's up to it. She trusted me to stay on this. We were on the same wavelength that way."

"That's great, Francis. Except for one thing."

"What's that?"

Tom grimaced down at the gummed-up end of his shoe and shook his head. "My mother is out of her fucking mind."

8

*T*HERE ONCE WAS *a woman who wished very much to have a little child, but she could not obtain her wish.* Eileen stepped away from the curtains and went back to her desk. The madwoman cackling in her hovel. Or rather, her garden-level floor-through that her son could have charged $1,900 a month for. She opened the fairy-tale book again, stirred her tea, and rubbed her thermo-stockinged feet on the hardwood floor. *At last she went to a witch, and said, "I should so very much like to have a little child; can you tell me where I can find one?"* Well, of course, that's where the problem started. Baby brokering through a witch.

"Oh, that can be easily managed," said the witch. "Here is a barleycorn of a different kind to those which grow in the farmer's fields. . . ."

"Early use of fertility drugs — and by a single woman yet!" Her mind told her hand to write large, but the letters came out small in her notebook, the latest of the bizarre side effects from the meds she was taking.

And so what happens? She went back to reading the *Hans Christian Andersen Treasury* she had propped open on the desk for inspiration. The barren woman pays her money and plants the seed, and, lo and behold, a beautiful tulip springs up. *Hmm.* Then she kisses the enfolded red and golden petals — *yes,* this is a fairy tale — they open up, and there upon the green velvet stamens — *could the imagery be any more blatant?* — is a tiny delicate maiden.

But is it a small fully formed young woman or is it still a child? Eileen stared at the actual tulip she had on her desk, as if the secret were hidden inside its pursed red leaves. No, she couldn't make up her mind. She was stuck again.

She tore the page she'd been working on from the notebook, crumpled it up, and threw it under the desk into the wastebasket already overflowing with the morning's discards. She put her pen down, her ink-stained fingers stiff from the new drugs. No concentration at all. Not even close. She padded back over to the window and hid behind the drapes again, watching the two men talk on the sidewalk. It wasn't the obvious sexual symbolism that kept stopping her, she decided. All the great ones had a powerful erotic undertow: *Rapunzel, Rumpelstiltskin, Sleeping Beauty.* It was the absence of feeling. This has to be one of the saddest stories ever told. A huge ugly toad kidnaps Thumbelina to marry her son, carrying her off to a lily pad in the middle of a stream, never to see her mother again.

But Andersen never mentions the mother's heartbreak. Never even considers it! He just prattles on about the frog and the blind mole and the swallow that appeared to be dead.

She went back to the desk and was confronted with another empty page. How could she ever have thought she could convey what it was like to lose a child? She must have already been drugged when she agreed to this deal, way back in the early Reagan years. The light blue lines on the page seemed to fade before her eyes, leaving her nothing to write on. How do you illustrate the half-life of grief? How do you write about the heart drawing back into a dark corner? The blood drying up in your veins. The ashes you can't quite spit out of your mouth. The gradual loss of sensation. The offensiveness of other people's laughter.

The poor woman must have sat by the window night after night, scattered tulip petals at her feet, waiting for the child to return, dull massive ache enveloping her like a cloud. Maybe she got really fat, eating potato chips and ice cream, watching TV test patterns. Maybe she got drunk every night and woke up every morning surrounded by empty bottles of pinot and chardonnay, wondering how they all got there. Maybe all that kept her alive were those little jagged shards of hope that kept sticking into her. Small barely discernible things. A movement in the grass, a change in the wind, a faint voice in the night, a rumor that somebody might have seen Thumbelina floating by on a lily pad or sitting at a craps table in Vegas. Maybe even two men right outside the window, mentioning her name out loud.

9

DOWNSTAIRS FROM HIS lawyer's office, Hoolian noticed an elegant caramel-colored coffee place called Starbucks by the subway entrance. Sleepy-eyed tousle-haired college girls sat at round tables, typing on laptops and reading nineteenth-century novels in the windows. Famished and tired, he stopped in and ordered a chicken Caesar salad, a slice of sweet potato pie, and a venti decaf vanilla latte with foam, thinking it sounded very debonair when the girl in front of him ordered it. He was surprised when he blew in the cup and found it barely half full.

Still, he felt like he'd achieved a minor stake in the social order by paying for a meal. He ate quickly and furtively with an arm crooked around his food. A pretty girl at the next table pulled her black turtleneck over her chin and turned the pages of *Les Misérables*. On his way out, he nodded to her and then realized he was still carrying his silverware, as if there were a corrections officer at the door waiting to collect it from him. Nonetheless, he decided this was a wonderful place and he would come back here soon, with a Signet Classic of his own.

A few blocks later, though, he saw an almost identical place on Union Square, also called Starbucks, the women inside looking a little more harried and insistent.

He walked west past the park, wavering from moment to moment, between knowing he had work to do and wanting to just stop and stare. At Mexicans unloading fruit crates in front of Korean bodegas, rising numbers on digital tote boards, ads for *Sex and the City* on buses. Women in experimental-looking shoes and men with cell phones squished to their ears gave him the evil eye, as if just by standing there in his grubby old clothes, looking up at the sky, he'd disrupted some fantasy about the glamorous lives they were leading.

"Stop acting like you in a Stevie Wonder song, *Country.*" A bicycle messenger in bright yellow spandex and goggles zipped by at warp speed, nearly rolling over the tips of his work boots.

Of course, it was *that* obvious. He might as well have been a Klingon or the Man Who Fell to Earth. The thing was, he couldn't stop staring. The city was the same, but it was different. It was cleaner, less permeable. You could no longer simply inscribe your name on its soul with a spray paint can and a blank wall. Old landmarks were gone, new ones had taken their place. The words "Met Life" were on the Pan Am building. The whole place was like a half-shaken Etch-A-Sketch screen, with some of the bold lines erased and the faint generations of a trillion previous patterns visible only when you looked very closely.

He stopped by a Rite Aid to buy a new toothbrush and a pair of nail scissors just to keep himself groomed. Then he went by the Human Resources Administration offices on 14th Street and tried to get a case opened so he could qualify for public assistance. Ms. Morales, a big-haired lady behind a little desk, told him he had a choice of applying to stay at a city shelter or trying to get into a residential drug-treatment program. When he tried to explain that he'd never been on drugs, she looked skeptical. It was easier, he discovered, to lie and say he was a junkie than to convince her he'd been locked up for no good reason. She told him to call back later to see if a space had opened up in a halfway house.

By one o'clock he was back in his old neighborhood, wondering if he'd gone too far trying to sell Ms. A. on the idea that there were still people around willing to help him. At least some of the old landmarks were still around. The bicycle store on 88th Street, the stationery shops selling the *Irish Echo* and Lotto tickets, Gus Shoe Repair, Romeo's Haircutting with the candy-stripe pole outside. He lingered for a few moments outside the schoolyard of St. Crispin's, watching the girls in their short plaid skirts do battle with the boys in their maroon blazers and gray slacks. The rectory windows looked dusty, and he wondered with a sharp lancing pang if Father Flaherty was still alive. The old priest had written his recommendation for Columbia and told Papi that his son would go far in life. A kind of smothering shame settled over Hoolian when he pictured himself running into the priest and witnessing his quiet disappointment.

Instead, he continued uptown and soon found himself staring across stately paced traffic at the familiar light green canopy with the white numbers 1347 rippling slightly in the breeze.

He told himself he had as much right to be there as anyone else. This was his house. This was the block he grew up on. This was the part of town he knew best. These were the sidewalks where he'd first learned to ride his bike. Julian, the super's son. Once more, he felt overwhelmed, remembering Mrs. Lunning from 5E giving him a Combat GI Joe for Christmas one year. Of course, now he understood that his father would've just preferred four twenties in a plain white business envelope. Back then, though, it made Hoolian feel like he was the little prince of this building, running around with an oversize doorman's cap cocked askew on his head and a taxi whistle around his neck, everyone smiling and looking out for him.

All of that was gone now. He swallowed, wondering what his friend T-Wolf was up to at that moment. Probably back on Carpenter Avenue in the Bronx, partying for the second day in a row, smoking blunts and hoisting forties, with relatives bringing over heaping plates of fried chicken and old girlfriends stopping by to check up on him. An unfamiliar anger clouded over him a moment: why hadn't Papi raised him uptown, closer to family and friends who would welcome him back? A superintendent's son wasn't one thing or another. You weren't upper class or lower class. You weren't penthouse or street, American or Puerto Rican. You weren't champagne or Malta Goya. You weren't upstairs or downstairs. You were just stuck between floors.

Hands thrust deep in pockets, he ambled casually toward the canopy, thinking he'd take a quick look, see if any of the old crew was around. Twenty-two years Papi had worked in this building. One of the only Puerto Rican supers in this part of town. *Means we have to be twice as clean and work twice as hard, little man.* Always on the job by six in the morning, white shirt and tie, charcoal slacks, hair slicked back but never greasy. Omnipresent but invisible. Discreet but dependable. Whistling for cabs. Keeping sand fresh in the lobby ashtrays. Lestoiling the marble halls. Sweeping the sidewalks. Unplugging toilets upstairs. Checking out the contractors' insurance. Making sure the service elevator was running. *Yes, ma'am. No, ma'am. I'll send the dry cleaning up. I'll have the maid brought down. I'll run this prescription around the corner to the pharmacy. I'll have the car brought round.*

Twenty-two years of keeping his eyes open and his mouth shut, of keeping his ambition back in the package room with the UPS parcels and Sherry-Lehmann wine store deliveries. And when his only son got locked up, they treated him like some smelly wetback just off the boat, virtually forcing him to quit. Of course, by that time Papi was so consumed by the case that he'd stopped turning over the sand in the ashtrays and making Valium runs for the stressed-out matrons.

The brass canopy stanchions gleamed in the sun. A rat-faced little doorman in a forest green uniform with gold braid on the shoulders clocked him suspiciously as he cruised past. So the Irish had finally gotten control of the place again.

Hoolian noticed, with some quiet satisfaction, that the black rubber mat the doorman was standing on was slightly worn, and part of the white-stamped 1347 on it had been rubbed away by hard soles and high heels. Papi would've replaced it by now.

He walked to the end of the block and then turned around to walk past the building again, his heart beginning to pound. *Come on now. Don't be a little pussy. You know what you came up here to do. Why should anybody else help you if you can't help yourself?* The doorman watched him with eyes like slits in a gun turret. *Yeah, you know I'm up to no good, don't you? What else could someone who looks like me be doing in this neighborhood?*

Or worse yet, maybe he knew. Maybe he'd heard that the old super's son had just been let out and was likely to return to the scene of the crime. One of those old cop myths that was actually true, sometimes. Hoolian must have talked to a dozen guys upstate who got caught because they kept circling around their own shit like flies.

"Osvaldo?"

He froze, hearing his father's name spoken aloud for the first time in years. He kept walking, thinking the voice must have come from inside his own head.

"Osvaldo, is that you?"

An old woman sat sunning herself on the fire hydrant just to the side of the entrance. Somehow he'd missed her the first time he walked past, in her red bolero jacket, matching skirt, and shiny patent-leather high heels. Her hair was dyed a bluish shade of black, and when she blinked, her lashes splayed over her lids like a drummer's brushes over a well-beaten snare's skin.

"My God," she said. "How long has it been?"

He stared at her until the name and apartment number came back to him. Miss Powell, 14A. With the Degas print in the foyer, the Steinway grand in the living room, and the crystal chandelier in the dining room. The original brass fixtures in the bathroom sink were always leaking.

"Come let me look at you." She raised her thin trembling arms, beckoning. "Where on earth have you been?"

He lumbered over slowly, unsure what to say. Old age had come down on her like acid rain, staining her teeth and speckling her hands with liver spots. But she still had the eyes of a girl waiting to be asked to dance.

She turned her cheek, expecting to be kissed. The dead-flower smell under her perfume made him gag slightly. But some instinct made him hold his breath. *She could help me, maybe.* She probably still had money, at the very least. For sure, she had jewelry to go with that Degas and Steinway. He put his lips to her cheek and found it was like kissing the Magna Carta.

She touched him lightly on both shoulders, pushing him back to take in the full sight of him.

"You look wonderful," she said. "Not a day older. How can that be?"

"All that heavy lifting." He flexed his arms self-consciously. "Keeps the blood pumping."

She'd always been a little loose at the hinges anyway. His father said she was some distant relative of the famous industrialist Andrew Carnegie. She'd lived here since about 1923, a shy wallflower with knobby knees and horsey gums. Legend was, her parents had thrown an extravagant Sweet Sixteen party for her back in the day, hoping to bring her out of her shell: a band in the living room, a top-of-the-line caterer in the kitchen, and engraved invitations going out to all her classmates from Spence and the boys across town at Collegiate. When eight o'clock came and went, though, nobody showed. There was just a pink party dress with no one to admire it, platters of expensive food going to waste, and musicians in rented tuxes looking at their watches.

And ever since, according to Papi, Miss Powell had hardly left that apartment except to sit outside on the hydrant for an hour or so every afternoon. Though once, when he was eight, Hoolian had glimpsed her on a swing at the Mariners' Playground in Central Park, looking up dreamily at the sky, as if she were waiting for someone to come along and push her.

"How's your son?" she asked.

"My son?"

It took him a beat to realize that his father had been close to this age the last time she saw him. Up to now, he'd only vaguely acknowledged the growing resemblance in his cell's shaving mirror, still half expecting to see his seventeen-year-old self staring back.

"He's doing the best he can," he said, playing along since setting her straight at this point would only scare her. "Trying to be strong."

"He was such a good boy." She nodded at the swish and sigh of passing traffic. "Julian. Such a pretty name for a boy."

"Got his butt kicked for having it in public school," he muttered ruefully.

"He used to come up and keep me company."

"Yes, he did."

He nodded, the doorman keeping a wary eye on him from under the shadow of the canopy, as if somebody were actually angling for his sorry-ass job.

"I used to use any excuse to get him to stop by," she said, slipping deeper into reverie. "I'd pour coffee grounds down the sink and put too much paper in the toilet, just so he'd have to come up with the snake and the plunger."

"Is that what you did?"

He shook his head. The super's son. Always eager to come up with his tool kit when Papi was too busy. Was she another one who'd taken advantage of him? He worked it around in his mind, trying to convince himself that's how it had been, so he could justify getting upstairs and exacting reparations for all the time he'd spent there without being paid.

But then he remembered how she'd let him sit at her big oak dining-room table sometimes with his calculus book, catching up on homework, avoiding the grim little motherless apartment downstairs, rush-hour light slanting through the old drapes and finding prisms in the chandelier glass, making a small rainbow on the wood while she bustled around the big hollow kitchen, keeping the servants' door open to look in on him now and then. It'd been years since he'd allowed himself to think of those long quiet afternoons, the two of them staving off loneliness until six o'clock, when he had to go start dinner for Papi.

"I never believed . . ." She caught herself on the verge of an uncomfortable utterance. "Well . . . I just thought it was a shame what happened. I knew the young lady as well. I'd said hello to her on the elevator. She was subletting, but she was lovely."

"People still talk about her?"

She looked up at him, the mist burning away a little. "Not too often anymore. It was so upsetting."

"Yeah. End of my life too." He saw her pink-rimmed eyes open wider. "Because of what happened to my son," he amended.

"Of course."

The doorman had disappeared into the building, leaving the entrance unguarded for a moment.

"So," Hoolian said, seeing a chance to help himself in a different way. "Any of the old crew still around?"

"What do you mean?"

"You know, Willie from the back elevator. Nestor, the porter . . ."

The lashes batted in confusion. "Oh," she said after a few seconds. "The older gentleman who worked in the cellar?"

"Riight."

"Julian used to bring him up sometimes, to help rearrange the living-room furniture for me. Small but strong as a bull. Didn't speak much English."

"Exactly."

He nodded again, sensing her slight unease. He knew it was too soon to be back. What did he expect, a "welcome home" banner? These people wanted to forget him, to act like he'd never existed. Look at it their way: They'd seen him grow up right before their eyes, let him into their homes, treated him almost like a son. He'd been the proof of their liberal good intentions, the evidence of their egalitarianism, the Puerto Rican boy allowed in their kitchens.

And how had he shown his appreciation? He'd betrayed them, he'd confirmed their worst fears, he'd destroyed their peace of mind and the sanctity of their homes. He'd gone and killed one of their own, a member of their class, the best of the best, a golden girl.

"He was a musician, wasn't he?" Miss Powell said, still clinging to the veil of memory. "He had this rather small feminine face but big powerful hands with long fingers. He played the piano."

"He sure did. Papi said he was in one of the best bands in Santo Domingo before he came here."

If she caught the slip, she didn't let on. "You remember, I have that old Steinway in my living room? It probably hasn't been tuned since my Sweet Sixteen party. But he came up one afternoon with the boy and, my goodness, it was like George Gershwin suddenly appeared in my apartment."

He could still see the old porter crouching over the keyboard right after they moved a couch behind the coffee table. Picking out the notes slowly, tentatively at first, like a man negotiating a spiral staircase in the dark. Wandering up and down the scale almost haphazardly, until you realized this random string of sounds was actually a melody. The left hand stirring up trouble, gradually locking into a groove. Deep pedal tones echoing off the ceiling and shimmering against the windows. Long crooked fingers stabbing and dancing, poking and prodding, plonking and tangoing, gliding and mamboing.

"Remember how we danced?" she said.

How did they end up like that anyway? Had she asked him or had he asked her? For a few seconds he was a boy again, waltzing on the old red Persian rug at dusk as Nestor thundered on, Cole Porter in one hand, Thelonious Monk in the other, the whole room threatening to fly away. They'd moved around each other awkwardly at first. Hoolian, usually sidelined by fatal self-consciousness at parties, had followed her lead, watching her perform pirouettes and arabesques that she'd probably learned in private ballet lessons in that very room. He remembered how she'd smiled, eager to delight him, and then spun over and put his arm around her waist. He'd held her gingerly, not wanting to break her, afraid of getting in trouble. But she'd persisted in falling into him, entangling his feet, engaging his arms and legs, as if she were pulling him into her own private memory. And for a few minutes, they danced as if she were still sixteen and he would never grow a day older, as if they were the envy of the whole East Side and this was the event of the season.

"I think you were thinking of my son," Hoolian said gently, knowing he wouldn't be able to suspend time for much longer.

"Oh, yes, of course."

She bared her striated teeth in a shy coltish smile and in an instant he understood that she'd known exactly who he was all along.

"So does he still work here, that porter?" he asked, a little too avidly.

"No. I thought he left before you did. Didn't he? Or maybe I'm wrong. Forgive a confused old woman."

Damn. He knew it couldn't be that easy. Of course not. Why should the rest of the world have stood still? People got older, changed jobs, had children, lost hair, invented new names. They'd turned into smears of light shooting past him.

The doorman had reemerged from the building. "Hey, buddy," he called out. "C'mere a minute, will ya?"

Hoolian excused himself with a bow and went over, again answering to the uniform rather than to the man. "What's up?"

"Why ya botherin' the old lady?"

"I wasn't. I know her."

"You know her."

"My father used to work here. This was his building."

The rat eyes narrowed, adding things up. A gristly little man in a uniform who probably thought that little bit of braid on his shoulder made him Napoleon with a taxi whistle. "You the old super's son or something?"

"Uh-huh," Hoolian answered, then immediately realized he shouldn't have. "I used to live on the first floor. . . ."

"All right, I know who you are." The doorman nodded, all bantamweight cock-of-the-walk attitude.

"I was just stopping by a minute, to check in. See if any of my father's old gang was around. Willie Hernandez still work here?"

"I don't know any Willie."

"How about old Nestor, the porter."

"There was never any Nestor."

"What're you talking about, man? He worked for my father."

"Hey, pally, lemme ask you something."

"What?"

The doorman grinned past him at Miss Powell and lowered his voice. "Why don't you get the fuck out of here?"

"What did you say?"

"You heard me."

"Hey, bro, you don't got to be like that. I just came by to see what was up."

"What's up is I'm not your brother, and this isn't your father's building anymore."

"Yeah, but there's gotta be people still here who knew him. He worked here from '62 to '84. . . ."

"Yeah, I heard about that too. The place was a shithole then."

"Yo, that's not true." Hoolian felt like he'd been kicked in the stomach. "Take that back, man."

"Your old man almost ran this building into the ground. Now why don't you get the fuck out of here before I call the police?"

Hoolian found himself gripping the nail scissors in his pocket and looking at a green vein just above the doorman's white collar.

"Why you gotta treat me like that? I never did anything to hurt you, man."

"Look, I'm not arguing with you, I'm telling you. Get off my block."

"Oh, so it's your block now? I thought I had a right to be here."

"You got a right to my shoe up your ass. What are you, stupid?"

"No, man, I'm not stupid. I went to St. Crispin's."

"Good for you." The doorman's gaze sharpened, pricked by resentment. "I guess that makes you the smartest nigger in the woodpile, doesn't it?"

Stick him. Hoolian's mind turned red. *Just take those scissors and jam them right in there, before he knows what hit him.* He pictured the doorman falling to his knees with his hand clapped to the side of his neck and blood gushing out between his fingers. But then the yowl of a passing police siren brought him back to his senses.

"Let me at least say good-bye to the lady," he said, struggling for control.

"Just wave." The doorman, blocked him. "She'll get the idea."

Hoolian raised his hand to wave. But Miss Powell already had her eyes closed and her face turned back up to the sun, retreating into Sweet Sixteen dreams of swan ice sculptures, bands playing "Rhapsody in Blue" in the living room, and young men with white dinner jackets and pomaded hair who appreciated a well-executed arabesque.

10

IT'S TEN O'CLOCK. Do you know where your children are?"

Just as the local news was starting, the former Miss Patti D'Angelo of Brooklyn walked into the living room of her Carroll Gardens row house and found her husband, Francis X., sprawled in the BarcaLounger with an ice pack on his knee.

"What happened to you?"

"Goddamn coffee table," he grumbled. "Banged myself on it, going for the phone before."

"Who was calling?"

"Nobody. I picked it up and there was just dead air."

"Hmm. Maybe one of your old girlfriends stalking you."

She eyed the ice pack and perched on the arm of his chair. Probably thinking he'd fallen off the wagon, the way he kept knocking into things lately. He knew he'd have to set her straight eventually, but every time he tried to imagine The Conversation his mind stalled out.

She'd be compassionate. She'd be concerned. She'd go to the library and do research on the Internet. She'd get on all the listservs. She'd start making phone calls about getting him into the appropriate programs and clinics for people with his condition. She'd find out what the best kind of cane was and where support groups met. And he'd hate it. Because it would be the beginning of pity.

"So how was your day?" she asked, massaging the knotted muscles in the back of his neck.

"Complicated."

"Oh?"

He felt guilty, naturally. They'd been trying to talk more lately. Neither of them wanted to have one of those traditional "don't ask, don't tell" cop marriages anymore, where they never got into what he did all day. She'd been in the game a little herself, five years as a prosecutor, so she didn't necessarily freak out if he happened to mention something about blood spatter, stippling, or septicemia. Twenty-two years they'd been together, two kids, over the river and through the woods, down into the Valley of Shadows and out into the sun again, sometimes even for vacations in Cancún. And here he was, sitting too close to the TV screen, a lump the size of a Ping-Pong ball throbbing on his knee, not telling her about the most important thing that had happened to them since the kids were born.

"Fuckin' old case, coming up again," he said. "They let Julian Vega out early."

"Seriously?"

"Here. What'm I, lying?"

He used the remote to turn up the volume. Roseanna Scotto throwing it over live with a swooshing noise to Lisa Evers standing across the street from 1347 Lexington.

"Roseanna, they say everything old is new again, and

here on the Upper East Side, memories of a notorious murder case are being revived. . . ."

"It's ridiculous," Francis said, talking over her. "They overturned the conviction because his lawyer didn't tell him he had the right to testify. Like that's anybody else's problem."

"So you're upset."

"Damn straight. I put a lot of work into that case."

There was a quick cut and Debbie Aaron's face filled the screen, drawn and severe against a background of tilting law books on a sagging shelf.

"This is a classic example of the police abusing their authority," she was saying. "The detectives in charge of this investigation settled on my client as a suspect before they investigated any other leads. . . ."

"See? That's what pisses me off." Francis waved his hand, glad to have somewhere else to direct all this agita. "She knows she doesn't have a real case, so she's just running her mouth. . . ."

"She looks good, Deb." Patti straightened her back. "I don't think she's had any work done."

"You look better."

"Hmmp." She ran her fingers through her highlights and gave him a four-beat stare.

"They made the facts fit the case against him," Deb was telling the camera.

"Bullshit," said Francis.

"You know, she can't hear you." Patti squeezed the back of his neck.

"And a number of highly irregular things happened in this investigation that need to be looked into," Deb said just as the screen switched to file footage from twenty years ago. "There's been a gross miscarriage of justice."

Francis watched the doors of the 19th Precinct swing open and saw himself at twenty-nine again, perp-walking Hoolian past the assembled cameras and microphones.

It looked so different from this angle. At the time, it was this unambiguous moment of triumph: Coming out of a grueling marathon in the box with an incriminating statement. Making up for his stint on the Farm by breaking the biggest case of the year. The Old Man himself, years from the grip of Alzheimer's, trundling along behind him, shooting the Turk an "I told ya so" grin. *So why do I look like I'm the fucking skell?* Francis asked himself. *I did all right. I went over the wall and made it back in one piece. I did my job. I made someone pay.* But there he was on the screen, tie askew, shirttail coming out, dog-faced and disheveled, as if he were the one with something to hide. Hadn't he watched this exact same footage twenty years ago, on a smaller Sony screen, with Patti four months pregnant and Francis Jr. still sleeping in the crib? And hadn't she leaned over, kissed him, and told him how proud she was?

And then here was Hoolian again, with his hands cuffed behind his back and his St. Crispin's blazer bunched up around his shoulders. In his mind's eye, Francis remembered the kid flashing a ferrety little smirk, as if he were sure he was going to beat this case somehow. But watching it now, Francis saw the little wispy mustache jerk up, revealing a pair of oversize front teeth, and he realized the boy had just been scared.

"He was so young," said Patti. "I forgot that."

"Didn't stop him from staving that poor girl's face in."

"I'm just saying it's surprising. He looks so sweet."

He caressed her thigh. Unlike Debbie A. and Paul Raedo, Patti wasn't a good hater. Never had the talent for it like other prosecutors. Because at heart, she was a *nice* person, a former fat girl who just wanted people to like her. Instead of riding out to grisly triple homicides on East 125th Street at four in the morning, she'd spent most of these past two decades mastering the art of forgiveness, immersing herself in child rearing, nurturing friendships, healthy diets, home improvements, and eventually a happening little career for herself as a personal trainer for corporate CEOs in Manhattan. In short, living what normal people called *a life*.

On the screen, there was a cut to Paul Raedo, his bristly scalp flexing in earnest concern, giving the official line from the DA's office. "Our only comment right now is that the original jury made their decision based on the evidence and we feel confident that will be borne out."

"So are they going to dismiss the indictment?" Patti spoke over him, never having been much of a Raedo aficionado.

"Fuck no. He got twenty-five to life. He should do the whole bid."

"What are you, the Ayatollah Khomeini?" She drew back. "You got twenty years out of this kid. Isn't that enough?"

"Hey, I didn't come up with that sentence. The judge and jury looked at the same facts I did. I'm just making sure no one forgets who the victim was here."

"So, what, you're going to try the whole case all over again?"

"Well . . ."

He was distracted, seeing Debbie A. given the last word. "The tragedy is a young man lost his freedom for something he didn't do."

He lowered the volume with the remote. "What am I

supposed to do? Stand there, smiling, while somebody calls me a lying sack of shit?"

"What do you care? I thought you were retiring as soon as you got the bump to First Grade in April."

He hesitated, not wanting to bring up the whole ugly threat of liability that Paul raised this morning. "I just want to make sure I don't leave any loose ends lying around."

"Why? You going off somewhere without telling me?"

"Nah, I just . . ." He started to rub his eyes and then stopped himself. "Forget about it, Patti. All right? Just never mind."

She got up. "If you're working this case again, I hope I'm not going to have to cancel Thanksgiving in Florida. I already put a security deposit on the condo, and Kayleigh is coming down from Smith with a friend."

"I'm sure it'll be done by then."

She started out of the room. "Frankie called on the satellite phone before you came home."

"Yeah?" He twisted around. "How's he doing?"

"Tells me everything except what I need to know. Just like his father. Far as I can tell, though, no one's talking about sending him over yet."

"Fucking kid'll be the death of me. I hope he's satisfied."

"I'm going to bed," she sighed, not up for the argument. "Maybe I'll see you there. I'll be the one in the flimsy nightgown."

"Yeah, I'll be up in a little while."

He watched her go and changed the position of the ice pack on his knee.

So here we are. He picked up the remote and switched to the Yankees game. Mariano Rivera mopping up against the Red Sox, another old rivalry coming around again. The Curse of the Bambino. He watched for half an inning and found he couldn't concentrate from one pitch to the next. He changed the channel and found himself watching Iraq coverage on *Fox News Live*. "America at War" and the flag, in the lower right-hand corner. Tanks in the streets of Baghdad, another convoy attacked in the desert, and still no weapons of mass destruction. *And this is where they want to send my son.*

Not much to put a troubled mind at ease there. He switched to *Star Trek* for a while. Captain Kirk strutting around with his stomach hanging out on that same Styrofoam planet, romancing green-skinned women in the days before he started playing a cop on *T. J. Hooker*. "The Cage." Wasn't that the show he'd talked about with Hoolian, way back when? Except the kid said it was Jeffrey Hunter playing the captain of the *Enterprise*. Wasn't that the same guy from *The Searchers* helping John Wayne track down the girl who'd been kidnapped by the Indians?

All right, now you've strayed a little too far off the reservation yourself, Loughlin. He turned off the set and sat there, contemplating the silence.

His eyes roamed toward the bookshelves he'd built a couple of years ago, scanning the unbroken spines of volumes he'd been collecting for all that leisure reading he was going to do after he retired. Now it dawned on him that one day in the not-too-distant future he'd have to decide which of them would be the last book he'd ever read. He looked for a likely candidate. Shelby Foote on Gettysburg. Stephen Ambrose on D-Day. Or his new main man, Ernest Shackleton on the *Endurance*. Stubborn bastard after his own heart. Tried to lead a crew to Antarctica and wound up with a ship crushed to matchsticks in the ice. That was some ballsy call he made, jumping in a lifeboat with five other guys, to try and get help over eight hundred miles of glaciers and hurricane-swept waters. To Francis, the miracle wasn't just that he managed to save every man but that he somehow made it across all that blank space without losing his mind.

Jesus, he could use a drink here.

He listened to the ticking of the kitchen clock. His thoughts breaking apart and rearranging themselves. He should turn in his papers tomorrow. He should keep acting like nothing was wrong. He should see another doctor and get a second opinion. The ticking became the tapping of a cane on pavement. Some day crossing Union Street would be as hard as crossing Antarctica. Except instead of dying trying to reach the South Pole, he'd probably just get hit by a car like his mother on the Grand Concourse.

Now there's a happy thought!

Where did he see that half-empty vodka bottle the other day anyway? Wasn't it gathering dust somewhere near the boiler in the basement, waiting to be thrown out? He didn't need to get a buzz on. Just a couple of fingers in the old Grateful Dead mug, to take the edge off a little.

Nah, don't be such a fucking morose self-pitying bastard, Francis. The old man went that way and look where it got him. He'd done better than that, hadn't he? At least for most of the past twenty years he had. Laying off the drink, devoting himself to the family, above reproach on the Job, the kind of cop you'd want handling the case if your best friend got killed. So why were his eyes turning into a couple of useless orbs? Was this payback for something specific or just the general taint of Original Sin?

He'd always had a kind of rough give-and-take with the Higher Authority, more or less getting walloped every time he lapsed. After his mother died, he figured it must have been his fault somehow, maybe because he hadn't prayed enough when she'd asked him to, so he'd tried to do penance. Five years as an altar boy kept the rest of the family in good health, he figured. But then he'd backslid in tenth grade, deciding it was all a bunch of shit, so he might as well become a dope-smoking moron. Until a car accident on the Major Deegan left his sister in a neck brace and put the fear of God back into him.

Not that he'd ever been a full-time nut about keeping a running account. Just every once in a while something would happen to whip him back into line. He'd begin running around on Patti a little just after they got married and then wind up nearly taking a bullet in the head on a narcotics raid. Or he'd start drinking again and Kayleigh would end up in the neonatal intensive care unit with a kidney infection.

But time goes by, nothing goes wrong, and you think you must be in the clear. Until your son joins the army without telling you and your retinas start deteriorating.

He squeezed the arms of his chair and started to get up, the clock on the kitchen stove still ticking loudly. *Closure*. That word that Tom Wallis had used kept bothering him. As if it were something real, something you could sleep on. He tried to be patient when people used that word, because what was the point? Closure was what they needed to believe was possible, like a benevolent God or Universal Health Care. But then you had Eileen Wallis running around after all these years, telling people her daughter was still alive. Didn't sound like she was anywhere near "closure," did it?

Could be nothing's going to happen right away. Your peripheral vision is going to progressively narrow down like a tunnel.

Stop that. He'd already decided he wasn't going to think about that. What about this case? He thought of twelve things he should've told Paul Raedo this morning.

This was never the perfect investigation. We gotta stick together here, Francis.

He realized he'd always had half an ear out for it coming around again. Not that he had any doubt about Hoolian being his man. The kid had already had his day in court, hadn't he? Defense counsel had a ball cross-examining Francis on the stand, pointing out that Allison could've easily made copies of her own keys and given them to other people. But the circumstantial evidence had buried Hoolian. So what if he hadn't testified on his own behalf? As soon as he got up on the stand, he would've choked on facts getting shoved down his throat anyway. Was it an absolutely flawless case? Of course not. But Francis had nothing to apologize for. The jury was able to connect the dots. Out just two and a half days before they convicted Hoolian for murder two. And if Judge Robbins nailed him for twenty-five to life — well, that was his hard luck, wasn't it? Ralph Figueroa had been offered a plea of man one, five to fifteen, and decided to roll the dice instead. So FEA — *fuck 'em all,* as it used to say on his Christmas card before Patti made him change it. Case closed.

He turned off the light next to the BarcaLounger and noticed how dark the room suddenly seemed. The total absence of light and discernible shapes making him aware of the settling noises of the house, the subtle creak of expanding and contracting wood. How did Shackleton do it? With no maps, no footprints to follow. How did he find his bearings in all that uncharted wilderness?

You going off somewhere without telling me?

Reflexively, Francis pulled the chain and turned the light back on so he could find his way to the stairs.

11

HUNGRY AND BONE-WEARY a few minutes before eleven, Hoolian walked into an old coffee shop that used to be called Leon's on Second Avenue. His father once had a waitress friend there named Nita who'd let him use the bathroom sometimes. Back then, it was a dowdy soup-and-burger place with a red neon sign, stale colored mints in a silver bowl by the cash register, and cheap blue coffee cups with Grecian columns on them. The new restaurant was called Café Florence; it had a plush green carpet, walnut-paneled interiors, and $8.95 tuna melts. But he took heart as he walked in the front door, noticing the same silver bowl of mints by the register.

The staff was starting to wipe down the tables, but Nita was nowhere in sight. A steak knife gleamed on the counter. Hoolian snatched it as he hurried to the men's room. Whatever the rules of survival were out here, nail scissors weren't going to be enough protection, he realized after his run-in with the doorman.

He washed his hands twice with the sweet-smelling pink soap, fussed with his hair, noticing it was too long, and then came out trying to look chill. A waitress with a face like a fallen curtain was draining half-empty ketchup bottles into half-full ones.

"Hoolian?" She turned. "Is that you?"

He smiled and put his hand up, self-consciously covering the scar on his chin.

"Look at you! *¿¡Niño!?*" She hugged him. "You all grown up. What happened to my little boy?"

She'd changed as well. She used to be taut and angular, like a tango dancer, all imperious flashing eyes and haughty-mouthed like she was looking for a rose to bite down on. But the years had softened and kneaded her, rounding off the edges, adding a few doughy pounds, putting a little of the Madonna in her weary smile.

She let go to take a look at him. "I thought they gave you twenty-five to life."

"Well, I'm out now. Least for a little while."

"*¡Bueno! ¡Que gusto!*"

Hoolian hesitated, realizing that already he was at the shady outskirts of his Spanish. The truth was, his father had taught him little and he hadn't picked up much more in prison, preferring to do his time in the law library instead of hanging with the Latin Kings and Las Neitas.

"Your daddy always knew you'd be all right. He used to say, '*¡Nos se ocupe!* That kid's stronger than I am.'"

He thought of the old man dying by himself at Metropolitan Hospital and felt poisonous fumes start to gather inside him.

"So sit down, what are you doing?" She nudged him toward an empty stool. "Where you staying?"

"Staying?"

"You got a place to go?"

He crossed his arms, holding back a wave of hunger and exhaustion. "I'm working on a few things."

"But they ain't gonna put you back in, are they?"

"Well . . ." He winced and tried to appear sanguine. "They haven't really dismissed the charges yet. But that's just technical bullshit. I didn't have nothing to do with what they said I did. That girl was a friend of mine."

"I know that, baby."

He looked over his shoulder to see if anyone else was eavesdropping. "My lawyer says I gotta try to help myself if I want to get my name back, but I don't know what the fuck I'm doing."

The corners of her mouth turned down and he realized the boy she knew twenty years ago never used to curse.

"Sorry. I been around bad people too long."

"It's all right. I'm just happy to see you."

He licked his lips, trying to ignore the gnawing in his gut. A twenty-dollar bill was trapped with a check under a salt shaker at the end of the counter. He thought about how easy it would be to grab it as soon as Nita looked away.

"Hey, didn't you use to babysit kids at our building?" He forced himself to focus again.

"Course. That's how I knew your father. I was a part-time nanny over there. Mrs. Foster in 9B."

"Lady getting a divorce?" He pictured a middle-aged woman striding through the lobby in denim hot pants and thigh-high suede boots on her way out for a night on the town.

Nita's mouth became a stern bottom line. "Too busy arguing with her lawyer about alimony and going out with married men to take care of her little girl. I swear, there were days I was 'bout this far from putting that child under my arm and taking her home with me."

"So you knew all the old gang from the building."

"Hell, yeah. I was the Don Corleone of the Nanny Mafia back in the day. And I used to go out with Willie the handyman."

"Slick brother who worked the back elevator?"

"Yeah, thought he was so fine."

Wayward Willie, his father used to call him. Because you could never raise him on the walkie-talkie when you needed him. Always horsing around with other guys in the basement or taking a little too long to put a washer in somebody's sink when the cute new maid was around.

"He was tight with old Nestor, wasn't he?"

"Who?"

Hoolian wondered if he should dare to hope. He was so famished and tired that he couldn't tell what he needed more, a good meal or help with his case.

"Nestor. The porter, who worked downstairs. Old guy who played piano. I think he was from Santo Domingo. Stooped little wiry dude. Looked like you could knock him over with a peashooter until you saw him carry a refrigerator on his back."

"Oh, *Nestor.*" She clapped her hands. "The Cha-Cha Man."

"That's right."

"Oh sure, I remember that little *bribón.* He could *play,* bro. You know he was in Cuba a couple of years and played in one of the best bands in Havana before la Revolución?"

"No, I didn't know that."

It embarrassed him to admit how incurious he'd been. Back then, Nestor was just an older man who worked for his father and played dominoes with him sometimes. It never occurred to Hoolian to ask if he'd had a family anywhere or another life. Not just because Nestor's English was so patchy. There'd been another barrier, a kind of wounded reserve to the man, as if he were some sort of fallen aristocrat refusing to speak of old troubles.

"Oh, yeah," Nita said. "We used to go sometimes after work to La Fuego up on 112th Street. They had an old Wurlitzer in the corner and after you got a few tequilas in him, he could really wail. *Tango, mambo, bolero, pachanga, merengue, bugalu,* anything. He had us dancing up on top of the bar. Why you want to know about him?"

"I think he could help me out."

An old married couple lingering in a back booth waved their check at Nita, wanting her to adjudicate some petty dispute between them.

"My father wrote me a letter in prison, saying he ran into Willie one night at a bar on Second Avenue," Hoolian explained. "And after they'd had a couple of drinks, Willie said that Nestor once kinda hinted to him there was something he never told the police. But Papi was never able to track Nestor down and find out what it was."

"And you really think that's gonna make a difference now?"

"It's the best I got so far." He foundered for a second before bucking himself up. "Check it out. Nestor was working in the basement that night. And there were only two ways out of our building. Front and back . . ."

He grabbed a napkin and a pen that had been lying on the counter, and began to sketch out the scenario. For years he'd been so pent up, trying to tell his story to anyone who'd listen — other inmates, guards, senior counselors, chaplains — that now he could scarcely keep his hand steady from the excitement.

". . . and the fire exit in the basement leads out into the alley behind the building," he pressed on, drawing lines and arrows. "After midnight, the front door is locked. You need a key to open it even from the inside." He looked over, making sure she was following him. "You'd have to wake Boodha the doorman in the lobby to open it for you. Or you'd have to have a key yourself, like one of the tenants. And the only other way out of the building was through that fire door down in the back, right past that big overstuffed chair where Nestor slept."

She touched his shoulder as if she wanted to interrupt, but now that the valve was open there was no shutting it off.

"So if he testifies he saw something or someone else go in and out of the building between like midnight and ten in the morning when they found her, then they gotta admit they framed me."

"Didn't the police try to talk to him before, though?"

"Yeah, *right,*" he said with a sneer, picking up speed to try and get around this dangerous hairpin turn. "A cop and a prosecutor who didn't speak Spanish. You know what happened. They intimidated the shit out of him. This little guy barely speaks English, wasn't in the union. Didn't even have his green card. He knows they've already set me up. They weren't going to let anything get in their way. So of course he was going to tell them what they wanted to hear. 'No, I didn't see nothing.' So he gives a bullshit statement to the ADA, blows town before trial because he didn't want to go to court to testify and then get deported back to Santo Domingo. . . ."

The more he talked, the more convincing he sounded

even to himself. Yes, a great injustice had occurred here. Someone had to pay for what they did to him. All he needed to do was get ahold of the old man and twist his arm a little to make the rest of the world see that.

"I bet he's still around," he insisted, putting the pen down and presenting her with his sketch. "He couldn't have been that old."

"Honey, he would've been sixty then if he was a day."

He registered her remark as just a minor scratch on his heart. "If I could just get to him for a little while . . ."

"Muchacho . . ."

". . . I'm sure he'd back me up. He owed my father. . . ."

"Baby." She patted his hand, not even bothering to glance at his drawing. "I think he's dead."

"What?"

"Last I heard, he was sick. He told Willie he had liver cancer and he was going back to the DR to see his family."

"But that doesn't mean he's *dead,*" he said. "Did Willie get an address for him?"

"Willie?" She snorted. "I ain't seen that *bastardo* in years. Turned out he had a wife and kids in the Bronx and another family down in San Juan. How do you like that? It took me until '86 to figure that all out. You just never know with some people."

"Maybe he got cured," Hoolian persisted, his sense of hope a match in the wind. "Liver cancer don't always kill you, does it?"

"Honey, he was half crazy to begin with."

"Are you sure?"

"Baby, you gotta eat something. You look pale."

He realized cold clammy sweat was oozing out through his pores, like he was getting a fever. "Nah, can't eat."

"How long did you say you been out?"

"Since last night." He wiped his brow. "I was counting on that fucking old man to back me up."

He stared at the emptying ketchup bottles lined up like part of a blood bank. All at once, it seemed that each terrible thing that had happened to him no longer stood alone. His mother's funeral at St. Theresa's. The interrogation room. The courthouse. The prison yard in Dannemora. His cell in Attica. They were all the same place. Even this coffee shop. They were all just illusions. He'd never really gotten out of the cage.

"You believe me, don't you? You know it's not like they said it was."

"Listen," she said, patting his hand. "You're tired. You're trying to do too much. *Echa un trago. Echa una siesta.*"

He slowly looked up, a column of steam from the dishwasher rising near the kitchen pass-through. It seemed like all this struggling and thrashing around to get his name back was just a pathetic waste of time. A side of him wondered if he should just give up and see if the DA's offer to let him plead guilty was still on the table. At least then it would all be over.

But every time he came close to setting his mind on that course, he pictured his cousin's daughter giving him that look from behind the refrigerator again. That child thought he was some kind of filthy animal. When she thought back on him, she wouldn't remember anything about the tender way he brushed her hair. She'd take her mother's word that he'd tried to do something terrible to her. And that, he surely could not accept.

"I don't feel so good." He held his fragile gut.

"I could have the cook fry you up some *huevos rancheros*. I remember how you used to like them."

He started to reach into his pocket, but she slapped his arm. "*¡Largo de aqui!*" she said. "I'll kick your ass, show me your goddamn wallet."

He gave up, touched and intimidated, as she leaned into the kitchen and gave the cook his order.

"You seriously don't have a place to sleep tonight?" She settled back on the stool.

He shook his head, not wanting to talk about what happened at his cousin's.

"*Ay.*" Nita rolled her eyes down to his duffel bag. "I'm betting you don't have a job lined up either."

"I got out too soon for them to put together a discharge plan. I'm supposed to still be there."

"Well, there ain't nothing for you here," she said, as if he were one of a long line of men who'd tried to take advantage of her.

He'd probably imposed enough already. She was a good-hearted woman who'd probably taken in more than her share of strays who'd then turned around and bit her. He'd eat his eggs and be on his way. Maybe he could catch the A train and sleep on the long ride going back and forth to Far Rockaway, until the conductor kicked him off.

"There's a little room downstairs," she said quietly.

"What?"

"A little storage room. The delivery guy crashes there sometimes. It's not the Marriott Marquis. You have to lie between shelves, with the soup cans and lard. But no one will bother you."

He stared at her, trying to comprehend. It wasn't that there was never any decency in prison. A CO might cut you a break sometimes over some pissy little infraction;

another inmate might let you use a hot plate in his cell once in a while. But you could never count on it. Kindness equaled softness, which equaled weakness, which was a sickness to be eliminated. Better to be thought of as a thief, a rapist, even a murderer, than a man, say, like his own father.

"But you have to be cool about it," she said, rising. "I don't want the owner finding you down there. I need this job."

"Thank you."

He had to resist the urge to throw his arms around her in gratitude, still not trusting the world enough to be seen touching a woman yet.

"And put back that damn steak knife." She pointed at his pocket. "I'm already sticking my neck out for you."

12

TOM WENT DOWNSTAIRS to the apartment after the news ended and found his mother holding a half-empty glass of red wine with a cigarette filter floating in it.

"Nice," he said. "Did I miss the part where Dr. Spencer said you should start mixing pinot noir with antipsychotics and Prozac?"

"Have I ever told you how much I hate those drugs?"

"And you think it's going to help if you start drinking with them?"

"I don't like the way they make me feel." Her jaw clenched. "They make my head feel full of cotton. They make me write small. They make me see things that aren't there. Did I tell you what happened the other night?"

"What?"

"I got up, thirsty, and thought I was drinking a bottle of water. The next morning I found an empty bottle of olive oil on the counter."

Tom pursed his lips in disgust. "You want to end up back in the ER again? Is that what you're going for here?"

"I'd rather feel bad than not feel anything at all."

He looked over at the oak rolltop desk she'd rescued from Sag Harbor. A tulip drooped in a vase, its petals falling off, and the scraps of discarded paper were hanging out of the wastebasket like sheared-off wings.

"You know, the least you can do is go out in the backyard if you're going to smoke." He picked up her wineglass and swirled the forlorn butt around in its dregs. "Michelle has asthma, in case you didn't notice."

"Oh, so now I'm a bad grandmother too."

He rubbed the space between his eyebrows like he was trying to smooth over a crack. Poor long-suffering Tom. Who probably put off getting married a half-dozen years to look after his crazy mother. With a twinge of shame, she remembered watching him try to play touch football in Central Park when he was young and discovering that for a few seconds she didn't like him. His awkwardness, his sheer lack of athletic grace, the way he pretended to know the rules of the game when he didn't. The way he turned pink with the slightest exertion. He didn't take to things naturally the way his sister did; Allison could pick up a tennis racket and start volleying within minutes. With Tom, everything had the potential for embarrassment. She constantly found herself comparing him with other children and then feeling guilty about it afterward. In the end, he'd shown her, though. He turned into the man of the house, taking over the finances and giving her not one but two granddaughters to justify her otherwise unjustifiable existence nowadays.

"I guess you know that Francis Loughlin stopped by before," he said. "He had some news I wasn't happy to hear."

"I'm waiting." She folded her hands on her lap in ladylike poise.

"They let Julian Vega out early. They overturned his conviction. He's free now."

She nodded, trying to maintain a dignified silence.

"I told him I thought it might be best to let it drop. We've been through enough already. But he thinks he owes it to you to keep going. . . ."

She continued nodding, finding herself unable to stop.

"I told him I was against it, but I'd pass along the message." Tom blushed a little. "He says you had a kind of understanding."

She finally held her head still and turned to him, slowly letting a sense of things collect. You wait and wait for something, and then when it happens it's as if you never expected it.

There was a little sound at the back of her throat. Just a murmur, hardly even a real word. But everything in the universe depended on keeping it there. She straightened her back, trying to remember the old actor exercise. Relax. Breathe in. Create your own sense of time. She put back her shoulders and slowly let out a breath that seemed to have notches on it. "You know, I've been thinking," she said finally.

"What?"

"Maybe there's a reason I haven't been able to finish this book. Maybe it's not the right time. I mean, rewriting Hans Christian Andersen, it's so . . . *indulgent*. Don't you think?"

"I don't know, Mom," he said weakly. "I'm not the creative one in the house."

"I've been thinking about another kind of project."

"Oh?"

"You know, I've been more interested in science

for a while now. How the body works. How the mind regenerates . . ."

"Mom . . ."

"Have you ever thought about double star systems, Tom?"

"Can't say I have." He sighed.

"Almost every star you see at night has a companion. But one usually dominates the other, so you can barely see it. What's interesting is that even if one is dying, when it gets close enough to the other it can start to draw hydrogen until it reignites again. But then it sets off a supernova explosion, and all that's left is a black hole."

"It's late, Mom. I thought we were over this."

"She was my shining star."

"I thought my girls were your shining stars." He looked at the ceiling.

"I want her to know I haven't forgotten."

"If you really think she's still alive, then why do you want to see this back in court again?" He stood up, biting his lip. "Can you explain that to me?"

"She needs a sign. If she sees the case is getting attention again, she'll know we're still looking for her. Even dying stars can reignite."

"You also said they can suck the life from each other." He went to the sink and dumped out her wineglass. "I've got an early sales call tomorrow, but then I'm calling Spencer about adjusting your meds."

"Tom . . ."

"What?"

"It's all my fault, isn't it?"

"Forget it, Mom." He plucked her cigarette butt from the strainer and threw it in the trash. "You did what you could."

13

In the middle of the next afternoon, Francis took a ride out to the NYPD's evidence warehouse in Long Island City, a dusty scaffold-surrounded four-story in an industrial wasteland strewn with truck garages, recycling centers, factory carpet outlets, and titty bars.

His heart sank when he went through the cage, crossed the scrap of Oriental carpet duct-taped to the cement floor, and saw out of the corner of his eye that the only clerk on duty was one Sergeant Brian Mullhearn.

"Gustav Mauler, word up."

"Francis X., as I live and breathe."

The sergeant took his time setting aside a tin of cold sesame noodles and wiping his hands with a paper towel. He stood up from his desk, and they gave each other the stiff long-armed handshake of old friends who can no longer abide each other's company.

Francis knew he should have called ahead, to make sure someone else was on duty.

The bright disco thump of Hot 97 on the office radio somehow emphasized the whipped-dog mood of the place.

Paint peeled off exposed pipes, mold formed on the air-conditioner vents, and a sign warning that CORRUPTION MUST BE REPORTED TO THE INTERNAL AFFAIRS BUREAU was half obscured behind a banged-up refrigerator.

"They say only the good die young, Sarge." Francis forced a smile as he extracted his digits. "So neither of us has anything to worry about, right?"

In truth, though, Mullhearn looked like one of the pieces that had been stored back among the oil drums since 1972. Limp gray hair, drowned-rat mustache, rigor mortis shoulders, a bar sponge complexion. Behind scratched lenses, his eyes were the color of pencil erasers; above them, his eyebrows were scrub marks. He moved slowly and with great effort, as if he were due overtime for each individual muscular response.

"We had us some Wild West times in Narcotics, didn't we?" he said.

"I still got the aches and pains from it." Francis touched the small of his back.

"Remember the time you fell over a third-floor railing at the Baruch Houses on Houston Street?"

"As a matter of fact . . ."

"Jesus, we thought you were dead, Francis. Five of us stood around, waiting for the chaplain to come say last rites. You weren't even breathing. Suddenly up you sit, 'Where's my fuckin' wallet?' like you'd just passed out at the counter and one of us took it."

Francis hoisted a grin. "We're all lucky to come out of it in one piece, I suppose."

"Some of us more whole than others." Mauler settled back behind his desk. "Look at me, look at you. I turn on the TV some nights, you're on more than O. J. Simpson."

"More like Homer Simpson."

"Well, you've done all right for yourself at any rate." Mullhearn picked up his fork again. "I heard you're retiring First Grade come April."

"You gotta know when to hold 'em, know when to fold 'em."

"Yeah, you always knew how to walk away a winner, I'll give you that much."

"Luck of the draw, my friend. That's all it is."

"Luck of the gene pool is more like it." Mauler let a long strand droop from the end of his fork. "I had an old man in the First Dep's office, I'd be on your side of this desk and you'd be on mine."

"Now, now . . ."

Francis sucked in his cheeks, seeing this was going to be a protracted negotiation. While he'd been on the rise these past twenty years, Mauler had been consigned to a kind of bitter civil service purgatory, a Rubber Gun Cop guarding the ancient ledger books and Great Deadly Weapons of the Twentieth Century.

"So, what can I do you for?"

"I'm looking for anything you got from the Allison Wallis case. I think Paul Raedo from the DA's office faxed over a subpoena before."

"First I've heard of it."

"But you know the case I'm talking about. You're the one with the good institutional memory, Bri. The girl doctor who got killed in her apartment by the super's son back in '83 . . ."

Mauler squinted slightly, as if he were watching a car coming up fast in his rearview. "What about it?"

"Fuckin' pain-in-the-ass granted-on-appeal bullshit,"

Francis said, playing it light. "We're reopening the case, making sure all the i's are dotted and t's are crossed."

"Oh?"

"I'm going to need everything you got on file. Bloodstain cards, autopsy samples, fingernail scrapings, any clothing they've kept around . . ."

Mauler's eyes began to swim behind his dusty lenses. "You're telling me this is an '83 homicide?"

"Is that a problem?"

"Well, fuck, Francis, haven't you got any *new* cases?" Mauler threw his napkin away, reached into a desk drawer, and slid a yellow form and an inkpad at Francis. "You can start by filling this out and giving me your prints."

"Bri, I'm in a little bit of a hurry here." Francis looked at his watch, seeing it was already quarter to three. "I was wondering if we could expedite this."

"Dude, it's all about the paper trail. If the PC himself was here, he'd have to do the same thing. We can't have people walking in and out with property and no accountability."

Before Francis could argue, the phone rang next to the Secret Squirrel on the desk and Mullhearn used the opportunity to grab it and turn away from him.

"*Yyi-eaah, what's happenin', bay-bay?*" he crooned, instantly transforming from a bitter old Irish hack to smooth-talking chilled-out Quiet Storm Mack Daddy loverman. "*You miss me?*"

Francis filled out the first few lines of the form, trying to maintain the thin membrane of civility. He looked up and saw a sign on the wall he'd missed before: RETALIATION with a red slash through it. Naturally, that was the deal here. Mauler and he had both been serious boozehounds back in the Narco days, shotgunning Budweisers to psych themselves up for raids and swilling scotch by the quart to cool down afterward. Until Francis somehow got caught sleeping off a bender in a Manhattan criminal court judge's chambers, with his pants off and his off-duty revolver missing. His father managed to quash the beef and get Francis off with a slap on the wrist. Thirty days' suspended pay and a month on the Farm addressing his "issues."

But when Mauler got jammed up for driving the wrong way down Astoria Boulevard six months later, reeking of Wild Turkey, he had no such higher power to call upon. So he ended up with a career counting pencils while Francis eventually got his shot at a gold shield.

"Bri?" Francis spoke up as he finished rolling his own prints on the form. "I think I'm all done here. Can you hook me up, maybe gimme a paper towel?"

"Hang on." Mauler held up a finger. "*Listen, sugar, call me later and we'll talk about it.* I gotta go deal with this guy. All right? I want us to both feel good."

He hung up the phone and swiveled back to Francis, immediately reassuming the form of the Bureaucrat That Time Forgot. "You were saying?"

"The Wallis file from '83." Francis looked around for something to wipe his hands with. "You should have like a barrelful of material. We collected sheets, fingerprints, carpet fibers, blood from under the victim's fingernails. . . ."

"Yeah, yeah, yeah." Mullhearn took off his glasses. "I think I remember this now. The guy wrote to us a bunch of times."

"What guy?"

"The defendant. He's got a funny name."

"Julian Vega?"

"That's the man. I must have got like twelve letters from

him. One of my little pen pals. Him and his lawyers wanted to have all that crap tested for DNA. Like every-fucking-body else upstate these days. They act like it's as easy as an EPT pregnancy kit." He nudged the phone away, an uncomfortable topic at the moment. "Piss on a stick, get a plus sign, and you're out of prison. I tell you . . ."

Francis rubbed the oily residue between his fingertips. "Wait a second. You're telling me that Julian Vega has been writing to you, looking to use DNA to prove that's not his blood we scraped from under her fingernails?"

"Well, not just to me. He wrote to the DA too. But I hadn't heard from him in a while. I thought we weren't in love anymore."

Francis took a few more seconds to work his mind around this, a whole new idea suddenly appearing like an unknown planet at the edge of the solar system.

"So did he get any of what he was looking for?"

Mauler wiped his glasses with the fat end of his tie. "Are you kidding me?"

"No. Why?"

"Have you ever looked around back there? It's fuckin' Indiana Jones land. We still got a backlog from nine-eleven we've barely made a dent in."

Francis grabbed the last of Mullhearn's lunch napkins to wipe the ink from his fingers, remembering the chaos he'd encountered the last time he'd visited this warehouse in the spring, to look for an old rape kit. A vast sprawling aircraft hangar full of potentially misfiled evidence. Towering steel shelves crowded with 55-gallon cardboard barrels. Hundreds of getaway bikes piled up at the auxiliary, like castoffs from the Tour de France. A forklift operator driving back and forth over a rolled-up carpet that turned out to have crucial hair-fiber evidence from another murder case. And most bizarrely, a collection of suburban-style barbecue grills and hibachis lined up against a wall. It wasn't like the end of *Raiders of the Lost Ark,* it was Home Depot operated by crack fiends. Eventually he'd had to give up looking for the kit and went back to get a tearful new statement from the original witness instead.

"I thought they were going to clean this up," he said, throwing the oily napkin in the nearest trash can.

"Clean it up? *Clean it up?* Are you on drugs? I mean, we keep pretty good records, but come the fuck on. People have been putting things in the wrong places since 1895. You could find Judge Crater in one of the evidence drums. So the short answer is: *No.* He didn't get what he was asking for. We just had a major roof collapse in the rain take out about five years' worth of cases. I got no idea where half that stuff is. So we told him the evidence is no longer available."

"Well, he's out now and the case is back in court, so I guess we better start looking for it."

"Ah, hahahah." Mullhearn smiled up at the clock. "I'm out of here in ten minutes, my friend. There's a very anxious young lady needs me to talk some sense into her."

Francis pictured himself getting seriously lost as he wandered the endless aisles, trying to find a couple of files with his limited vision. The way he was going, he could end up getting locked in for the night.

"Brian, I could really use a hand here. This case really means a lot."

"You know as well as I do, nothing gets pulled here after three," Mauler said.

"I would seriously owe you, my friend."

"*Oh,* so are we friends now, Francis?"

"What do you mean?" Francis checked to make sure all the ink was off his hands. "I don't get you."

"I'm saying, *do you think we are friends now?* You and I?"

"We know each other," Francis said. "There's a relationship."

"It's funny. Because I didn't think *there was a relationship.* I thought we were two guys who did some shit back in the day. And one of us got jammed up for it and the other didn't."

"Everybody's got an opinion."

"No, an opinion is editorializing." Mullhearn put his glasses back on. "This is facts. One of us got his shield because he had someone looking out for him. And the other ended up in the fucking ozone. I don't recall you getting on the phone and offering to have your old man bail me out. I'm out of here in nine minutes."

"Brian, you're gonna help me find that barrel."

"Pardon me?"

"I said, you're gonna help me find what I'm looking for."

"The fuck I am." Mullhearn dropped his food in the garbage.

"You want to spend the rest of your life feeling sorry for yourself, that's your concern. I'm not going to tell you how to get right with what you did."

Francis spoke calmly and evenly, as if he were addressing a suspect. No theatrics necessary. Just a level stare and the reasonable tone of one man telling another that a bulldozer was about to knock his house down.

"But I have a twenty-year-old homicide conviction that's just been vacated. I have a murderer out on bail. I have an indictment that needs new evidence to back it up. This is what I do, Brian. Half the bosses in the department have me on speed dial and, believe me, it's not because of my wholesome attitude and boyish charm. It's because I fucking make them look good. And they will come down on you like fucking Godzilla's left foot if I pick up that phone and tell them you're not playing."

"Jesus, Francis, do you have to be an asshole?"

"Only my wife knows for sure." He rubbed his hands together. "And she's not telling — or at least she's not telling me. Now where do we start?"

14

"COULD I PLEASE get a tall Toffee Nut latte and a slice of caramel cheesecake?"

Hoolian stood at the counter of the Starbucks on Astor Place, indulging his urge for sweetness. The girl at the register, in her black baseball cap and green apron, stared at him as if he'd just asked for a package of pure uncut heroin.

"Like sugar, don't you?"

She turned away to get his order, leaving him to wonder if he'd said something wrong.

Yesterday, Ms. A. had told him to take a break from his legal research and lighten up a little. *Enjoy your freedom.* As if she somehow knew it wouldn't last much beyond tomorrow's court date.

So he'd deposited the three hundred dollars he'd earned working odd jobs in prison and got himself a decent close-cropped haircut at Astor Place Barbers. It went nicely, he thought, with the little hipster beard he was growing to cover the scar on his chin and the respectable thrift-store jacket-and-tie combo he bought to make a good impression on the judge.

He stretched and yawned, having gotten a few more hours' sleep for once. After a long hassle with his caseworker, he'd managed to get himself placed at a halfway house in Bed-Stuy, sharing a cramped little bedroom with three other ex-cons in bunk beds. It wasn't ideal, sharing a dresser drawer with another man and a bathroom with nine others, but the rent was sixty dollars a week and the only other serious drawback was having to attend group therapy sessions to talk about his imaginary "drug problem." One way or the other, this world would make you into a liar if you weren't one already.

The girl brought him his latte and cake and he paid her seven dollars, smoothing out each bill on the counter and calculating that he had about fifty bucks left over in food stamps to last him through the end of the week.

At the moment, he couldn't think about that, though. He just needed to be away from lawyers and courtrooms and bureaucrats for a little while. He just wanted to chill awhile with Miles Davis noodling away on the stereo and pretty women talking low in the background. After all those years in a dank six-by-nine cell, a part of him leaned toward any kind of simple pleasure like a flower straining toward sunlight.

Want ads under one arm and his book under the other, he navigated his way around the islands of women at small round tables. Women on cell phones, women in dog collars, women reading books about Marxism and quantum physics, women in roller skates, women staring forlornly into laptop screens as if their troubles were itemized there, women holding hands with other women, women analyzing the minutiae of their lives, women in the shawls and babushkas of their grandmothers, women in FCUK T-shirts, women in camouflage jackets and peasant blouses. Women free to try on and discard different versions of themselves, women not yet saddled with heavy jowls, aching joints, porous marriages, and bad debts.

He staked out a table by the window and opened the paperback he'd brought along, savoring the mingled aromas of perfume, Kenyan double A, and newly washed hair.

For the second time in the past few days, he asked himself if it would really be so bad if he tried to settle out of court. His case was so long ago. Half the women in there probably weren't even born when he got locked up. Why couldn't he just be like everybody else for a while?

The girl he'd been checking out before was back at her table, pulling her black turtleneck over her chin and letting it slip off as she read her copy of *Les Misérables*. Her slender ankles twined themselves around the chair legs, and her hair was bundled up behind her head, a knot of unhappiness tempting some man to try and tug it to free her. He cracked the spine of his edition and started reading about the hungry traveler outside on a frigid night, the Alpine winds strafing his skin. Seeking refuge in a shanty, he scaled a wooden fence, tearing his clothes, only to find himself alone in a kennel with a snarling bulldog.

"So how you liking it?" he said, sneaking a sidelong glance at her.

Now that the turtleneck was off her chin, she regarded him as if she were a lady on horseback, a long aquiline nose and highborn cheekbones wreathed in a cloud of auburn curls. She went back to pinching tiny crumbs off the corner of her raisin scone.

"The book." He showed her the used Signet edition of *Les Misérables* that he'd bought from a street vendor the other day. "We're reading the same thing."

Her tongue poked against the inside of her cheek, a bulge slowly descending.

"It's long but it's good. Right? I'm getting into it."

She gave a world-weary sigh and turned back to her scone, placing a few microscopic crumbs on the tip of her tongue. She reminded him a little of Allison: squeezing just a few drops of honey into a teaspoon, licking the end of it delicately, and then putting the bear-shaped jar away so as not to be tempted.

"So, what do you think of it?"

Her fingers tapped the side of her cup restlessly. He noticed they were a little plumper than the rest of her, as if there were another woman with a healthier appetite trapped inside of her.

"It's all right," she said finally. "A little sentimental, maybe."

He wondered if she had a thing about sci-fi like Allison did as well, or if all they had in common was a hang-up about food.

"Yeah, yeah, I know what you mean. 'Sentimental.' Like he's laying it on a little thick."

She shrugged without rancor and turned back to her book.

"But, you know, I feel for the guy," he went on, still trying to get her interested.

She half turned and pulled her collar up, not quite covering her chin this time. He couldn't tell if she wanted him to stop or go on. He'd never had much aptitude for reading women in the first place, and what happened with Allison certainly didn't help. At this point, he wasn't sure if he'd be able to tell if a female was interested without her sitting on his lap and sticking her tongue down his throat.

"I mean, here he is, dog-tired, starving, been walking since sunup, willing to put cold cash on the barrel for a bed and something to eat. And these people keep kicking him out. All because of some bad rap he didn't deserve back in the day."

"How do you know?"

"What?"

"You said you just started." She finally bit off a bigger hunk. "How do you know he's not guilty if you haven't read that far?"

"You can tell by the way he's writing about him."

"But maybe you're just being fooled into, like . . . sympatheticness," she said with a slight lisp.

He looked down at the dense thicket of translated words. Maybe he *was* missing something. For years, all he'd really been reading was science fiction and parts of the New York State Penal Code. "Guess you're right." He awkwardly raised his latte in a toast. "Can't assume anything about anybody."

He put his cup down and straightened his tie, noticing his own reflection in a mirror on the wall: a man with metallic silvery glint in his hair trying to talk to a girl too young for him. Again he was jarred at not recognizing himself right away.

"So it's nice, having a place like this, where you can just hang out without anybody hassling you," he said, imitating the easy conversational tone he'd heard other people using. "They have a lot of these around town?"

"What, are you kidding?" She frowned.

"No. Why?"

"You're telling me you don't know about Starbucks. What, did you just get out of prison or something?"

"Pardon me?" He couldn't have heard her correctly.

"There's practically one on every corner. . . ."

"Yeah, but why did you say what you just said? You don't know me."

It felt like she'd just dashed hot coffee in his face.

"Forget it. Okay?"

"I just don't understand why you would say that."

She turned away and pulled her collar halfway up her nose like an old western train robber's mask.

"*Miss,* I was talking to you. . . ."

She picked up her book again and started reading, as if he'd simply dematerialized.

"*Excuse me.*" He raised his voice. "You know, it's rude not to look at somebody when they're *speaking* to you."

Several of the women at the nearby tables stopped talking and turned around, as if he'd started honking a loud out-of-tune saxophone in the middle of the delicate little chamber music they were making.

"Yo, did I *offend* you somehow?" He stared, refusing to be ignored. "If I said something, just tell me please. . . ."

They were all looking at him now, wondering who this crazy man was. They probably just thought he was some wild-eyed homeless guy in off the street, trying to get attention. They didn't know he was someone with an education. They didn't see he'd once had a future that looked almost as bright as theirs. They didn't understand how all of that could just be taken away from a person, that somebody with refinement and true deep feeling could be turned into a beast through no fault of his own, that he was less than a week out of a place where looking at someone the wrong way could get you a fork in the eyeball.

"I was just trying to have a conversation with you like a normal person," he insisted, still trying to be heard.

The day manager walked up to him, a gawky white guy with a tiny hoop in his eyebrow that was supposed to distract from the disastrous state of his pocked skin.

"I'm sorry, sir. We're going to have to ask you to leave."

"Yeah, a-ight, just hang on a second. . . ."

Hoolian put his hand up, asking only for a little indulgence, but the guy reared back as if he'd been slapped.

"Aw, come on now . . . don't be like that . . ."

He tried to make a joke out of it with a mock karate stance, but the guy started gesturing to the Asian girl behind the counter, making his thumb and pinkie into a phone shape like he wanted her to call 911.

"Hey, bro, *tomalo con calma.*" Hoolian dropped his hands. "Take it easy."

But the guy kept backing away from him, terrified. So, what was the point of arguing? Everywhere he went somebody was messing with him, trying to get him to do things he didn't want to do. It was as if they could somehow tell his settings were already on too high and all they had to do was nudge him a little to get the needle to jump into the red.

"Sir, I'm inviting you to enjoy a cup of coffee at any of our other locations." The manager pointed toward the door. "But I really do need you to go. . . ."

"All right, all right, I got the message." Hoolian

buttoned his jacket and picked up his book. "You don't have to ask me twice."

He started to edge his way out around the little tables, looking back one last time at the girl in the black turtleneck.

"You know, *sympatheticness* isn't even a word."

15

THE COURTROOM DOORS creaked open and Francis turned around, trying to find the source of the commotion.

The reporters who'd shown up to see if Hoolian's indictment would be dismissed this morning were all murmuring. Dov Ashman, that craggy old fossil who'd covered the original trial for the *Daily News* back in '84, put a clawlike hand on the ripe young pudgy knee of Judy Mandel from the *Trib*. Allen Robb, that bow-tie-wearing son of a bitch from the *Times,* started whispering to that slob from the *Post* whose name Francis could never remember. The doors clunked shut and he finally found the focal point: Eileen Wallis entering the courtroom with Tom fastened to her arm.

Jackie Kennedy herself couldn't have made a more dramatic entrance. An appropriately somber Chanel ensemble — olive rather than mourning black — wine-dark lipstick on a stark white face, the eyes hidden behind a pair of tinted glasses. The hair was still more ginger than silver and she'd kept her figure, but she walked a little stiffly down the aisle. Not that Francis would have blamed her if she was doped to the gills today; he would've emptied the medicine cabinet himself under the circumstances. But there was also something regal about her, as if grief had put her beyond the concerns of ordinary mortals.

Just her showing up today was a statement in and of itself. It said, *Hold on.* It said the ground had been disturbed. It said at least one person in this room wasn't quite ready to "move on." Yet when she stopped at the front row and started to sit down next to Francis, he saw no hint of recognition. No acknowledgment of the time they'd spent in each other's company, comparing common wounds and trying to accept unacceptable things.

"Eileen." He touched her arm as she sidled in. "It's Francis Loughlin. I'm here for Allison."

The eyes barely flickered behind the tinted lenses.

"Thanks for coming, Francis." Tom reached across her to shake his hand.

"Ah, sure, I couldn't have stood to miss it."

Though technically there were a lot of other places he could've been this morning. This was supposed to be his day off and he was already close to his unofficial overtime cap for the year. Not to mention that he had at least a half-dozen active investigations he could've been working on instead.

A side door opened and the hum of informal collegiality abruptly died away. Paul Raedo stopped shuffling papers at the prosecution table, and the old wooden pews squeaked as everyone keeled forward to get a good look. Julian Vega was just coming out and taking his place beside Debbie Aaron at the defense table.

Francis almost didn't recognize him at first. This big strapping bull with close-cropped hair and a little beard, a powerful neck sticking out of a gray wool jacket with a maroon shirt and black tie. He looked as if he could've been running for state assembly in East Harlem or at worst getting indicted for securities fraud.

"Quiet in the courtroom," Tony Barone, the court officer, snapped, his eyebrows jumping like two halves of Stalin's mustache on his forehead.

Hoolian turned to look over his shoulder and check out the crowd. He'd probably put on another ten pounds, most of it muscle, since he'd tried to go after Francis in the prison corridor. He had that hardened ex-con stance now, shoulders back, chin up, deadened eyes. But when he saw Francis, his face broke into a bitter half-smile as if he were saying, *Here we are again, amigo.* Debbie A. saw what he was looking at, frowned, and started whispering in his ear, her heels coming out of her shoes a little as she stood on tiptoe.

"All rise."

Judge Miriam "Get to the Point!" Bronstein entered, almost disappearing in voluminous black robes, dark curls framing the small pursed face of a seventy-two-year-old grandmother who still rode a bike to court every day from the Upper West Side. Francis remembered her as a Legal Aid lawyer, cranky and combative, never willing to believe a police officer could coax a legitimate confession out of a defendant without the liberal use of the Manhattan Yellow Pages upside the head. Since making it to the bench through the usual political connections (West Side Reform Democrats, Manhattan Democratic Club, etc.), she *had* made a conscious effort to be more evenhanded, but the periods of magisterial calm were often interrupted by irascible outbursts, as if everyone in the courtroom suddenly reminded her of her own notoriously disappointing children.

"Proceed, Counselors." She beckoned for Paul and Debbie A. to approach. "What do you have for me? My calendar is full today."

"Your Honor, this is continuing with the *People* versus *Julian Vega*," began Paul, who'd been second seat at the original trial. "Judge Santiago granted the defendant's four-forty motion on Rikers Island a few days ago and —"

"All right, all right, already," Bronstein cut him off. "Get to the point! Are you ready to take this to trial?"

Paul swayed back on his heels a little. He'd already warned Francis that Bronstein knew he was up for a judgeship, so there would be a certain amount of punching in the clenches this morning.

"At this point, yes, Your Honor," he said. "We're reserving the right to go full-speed ahead."

Debbie A. spoke up. "Your Honor, not wishing to waste the court's time, I want to move for immediate dismissal of this indictment."

"On what grounds?"

"Double jeopardy. It's totally unconstitutional for my client to be tried twice for the same crime."

"Nice try." The judge's eyes crinkled behind horn-rimmed glasses, perhaps seeing something of her younger self in Deb's swift astringent delivery. "But if the original conviction was vacated, it's as if the first trial never happened. Can't have it both ways, Counselor."

Francis saw Deb lean over to explain, but Hoolian shook her off, indicating he understood perfectly.

"Any other issues before we set a trial date?"

"Yes, Your Honor." Paul approached the bench. "The People would like to file a motion to discontinue bail for

Mr. Vega. We believe that after nineteen and a half years in prison, he poses a significant flight risk. Also, while he was locked up he continued to display a propensity for violence. He was put in solitary confinement for thirty days for attempting to assault a police officer. And our office has documents from the Department of Correctional Services that show he was put in the special housing unit on another occasion because of an incident involving a stabbing at —"

"Oh, that's outrageous." Debbie A. wheeled on him, chocolate-brown suit jacket snug over her shoulders. "That's not part of this court record and certainly not relevant to bail. It's just a cheap shot by Mr. Raedo in front of the press."

And an effective one, judging from the muttering out of the reporters. Francis, who'd spent four hours prying the report out of Corrections yesterday, turned all the way around and saw Dov Ashman lean over to Judy Mandel, making sure he'd heard right.

"Well, Ms. Aaron should be something of an expert in cheap shots after the interviews she's given impugning the integrity of the original investigation," Paul countered. "Her comments were clearly meant to pollute the jury pool. I'd like to ask for a gag order."

"Oh, grow up." The judge removed her glasses. "We haven't even gotten going yet and you two are fighting in the sandbox."

Francis sat back, with his arms across the top of the bench, still smarting himself about some of Deb's recent quotes. There'd been a couple of moments when it almost felt like he was the one on trial here today.

"I'm not going to revoke bail." The judge peered down. "The defendant didn't run away before the original trial, so there's no reason to sanction him. Now can we please just get to the point and set a trial date if we're going to do this all over again?"

Francis snuck a look over at Eileen Wallis to see how she was handling this. But she was distracted, fingering the clasp of her Coach pocketbook. In the pitiless courtroom light, her skin, which had remained so fair and flawless in her forties, was just beginning to show the smallest of cracks, like a vase left too long in a kiln.

"Your Honor, we'd like to begin jury selection on December second, since Thanksgiving and Hanukkah run together this year." Paul bowed his head, trying to strike a more modest tone.

"That's almost three months!" Debbie A. protested. "My client has had this case hanging over him for twenty years. He deserves a speedy disposition."

"That *is* a long time to prepare, Mr. Raedo," the judge agreed, donning her glasses again. "What's the holdup?"

"Judge, we believe there's evidence in the case file that will allow us to prove Mr. Vega's guilt beyond a reasonable doubt. Advances in DNA technology that will absolutely show that Julian Vega murdered Allison Wallis."

"Then where is it?!" Deb threw up her arms with a kind of mock-exasperation Francis recognized all too well. "My client has been asking for that evidence since 1995!"

"Yes, what's going on?" The judge turned on Paul, her irritation renewed. "Why hasn't it been produced?"

"Your Honor, none of us are naive here. We all know our archival facilities are overtaxed and understaffed. Everyone's working to capacity, even if Ms. Aaron likes to pretend otherwise. We've had people out at the evidence warehouse in Queens for the past four days. The evidence is there. It's just been mislaid."

"Mis-laid?" Deb broke the two syllables into mini-aria. *"Mis-laid?"* She raised her hands higher, making sure the press rows were getting the point. "Your Honor, *why* should my client pay the price for someone else's clerical mistakes? Presuming that's all it is. It's sounding like we might have to ask for a special prosecutor to investigate what happened here."

"Oh, come on." The judge reached for her gavel, ready to call everyone into her chambers. "Can we just stick to one set of inflammatory issues at a time?"

Francis nodded, thinking this was just why he admired Deb. Who wouldn't want to be represented by an attorney who could make any occasion a pretext for a holy war? She was one of the Tribe, a Go-for-Broke Girl, a true Hellcat Maggie. Every slight had to be answered, every plea bargain was a personal blow to her integrity.

In the meantime, he sensed the momentum from the press section changing. He glanced over his shoulder and saw Dov Ashman flipping back through the pages of his notebook, shaking his head, seeing that Paul had raised the issue of Hoolian's disciplinary record to distract from the glaring absence of the DNA evidence.

"Achh." Judge Bronstein frowned, not necessarily accustomed to being the most reasonable person in her own courtroom. "I don't see why you two couldn't have worked this out before you came here. Mr. Raedo, couldn't you have just given Mr. Vega credit for time served and let things stand after twenty years?"

"Your Honor, with all due respect, Mr. Vega has made it very clear that he's not interested in taking a guilty plea. And more important, Ms. Wallis's family is here today." Paul turned, acknowledging Tom and Eileen with a respectful nod. "Whatever so-called suffering Mr. Vega claims to have been through, he is still alive. But they haven't had a moment's peace since 1983. This was a young woman with boundless potential. And you can be sure that her mother wouldn't be sitting in the front row today if she felt the cause of justice had already been adequately served."

Francis saw Eileen start to fumble with the clasp of her pocketbook and take out a wad of folded-over yellow papers, covered in inky scrawl on both sides.

"Not now, Mom," Tom murmured, reaching over and trying to keep her seated.

Hoolian turned around to look at her as well, his bottom lip thrust out slightly. Francis told himself that it was nothing, lots of the sociopaths were good at faking normal human emotions. Still, it bothered him. How many of those guys actually *looked* at the crucial moment? Usually when faced with the victim's family, they'd stare into the mid-distance and mouth some pious nonsense about finding God and knowing the power of his eternal forgiveness.

"Enough." The judge picked up her pen. "I'm putting this on the calendar for October seventeenth. Mr. Raedo, be there or be square. That's plenty of time for you to locate that evidence."

"Your Honor, there may also be witnesses we need to locate. It's been nearly twenty years."

"If you don't have a case to put on by the seventeenth, I'm dismissing this indictment." The judge signed the papers and handed them off to a clerk. "Anything else?"

"No, Your Honor." Debbie A. nodded, knowing for once to leave well enough alone.

"Next case." The judge rapped the gavel as another defendant and his attorney sidled over to replace Hoolian and Deb at the defense table, like substitutes in a hockey game.

Whaddaya gonna do? Paul turned up his palms as Debbie A. gave Francis a sullen stare, her mouth a tidy red dash. *I know what you did, you bastard.* But what did either of them know? Lawyers. Always thinking they were above everything, never dreaming they could get any actual blood splashed up on their Donna Karan and Armani suits. Looking down on the working-class yobs and gutter grunts who were supposed to clean things up.

Why should he care anymore? He'd done his job, played his part. If somebody wanted to spread the dirt around and say he'd stepped over the line a little, let them prove it. Go ahead. Take him to court next time. He'd find his way to the stand. He gave a terse nod as Hoolian went out through the side door with Deb. Catch you later, *compañero.*

A rustle of papers distracted him. "But I didn't get to read the statement," Eileen was protesting, yellow pages trembling in her hands.

"It wasn't the time, Mom." Tom gently extracted them.

"You'll get your chance, Eileen," Francis tried to assure her. "We'll make sure of it."

"Oh, Francis, there you are." She turned, finally recognizing him, looking from the top of his balding head to his stomach. "How you've let yourself go!"

"It happens." He laughed.

She grabbed his wrist and gave it a surprisingly strong squeeze. "Remember what you promised me. . . ."

"Believe me. I haven't forgotten."

"You said you wouldn't forget my baby. You have to find her for me."

"But —"

"They buried the wrong child."

Before Francis could think of a sensible answer, Tom had his mother by the arm. "Thank you, Francis," he said, leading her out of the pew and down the aisle as the press began to surround them and follow them out, like religious icons at an Italian street fair. "We'll keep in touch."

"Please leave quietly," a court officer announced as Francis lost sight of them. "Court's still in session."

PART III

THE SILENCE OF A FALLING STAR

16

THERE'S A CERTAIN uneasy stillness to a house where men just out of prison are sleeping, a restlessness that breathes through the walls. People tend to stay on the very edge of mattresses made lumpy by the prized possessions secreted underneath. The clockwork of each body's mechanics becomes amplified and newsworthy. A loud belch in the middle of the night, a muffled fart, a stifled groan from a nightmare, all become part of the common volatile atmosphere; the use of the bathroom can become as highly contested and politicized as the Golan Heights.

On the first day of October, Hoolian woke up and lay on his side, afraid to turn over, waiting for the pearly speck of sunlight to grow in the corner of the dingy barred window. At quarter to six, he carefully descended the ladder from the top bunk and crept past his three snoring roommates with his clothes under his arm. In a few minutes they'd be lined up in the hallway outside the bathroom, banging on the door and bitching about him using up all the hot water.

He closed the door after him and turned on the light. Again, there was his father's face in the mirror above the sink, rebuking him. *You proud of yourself, bobo?* He pulled his long-sleeved jersey off over his head and checked the long dark scratches that had scabbed over across his rib cage. His chest looked oddly bare and exposed with the Saint Christopher's medal gone, and the back of his neck still felt burned where the chain had been ripped away.

The door started to open and he roughly pushed it shut with his bandaged hand.

"Yo, open up, man," an urgent voice moaned on the other side.

"Gimme a second."

"Come on, G. I ain't playing. I'm about to bust out here."

He pulled the jersey back on and opened the door. A dreadlock-wearing loudmouth called Cow, who was always trying to convince everyone he'd been the Superfly of Mother Gaston Boulevard, stepped in, instantly taking up most of the space on the tiles.

He reached into his drawstring sweatpants, fished around for a while, and finally extracted a prim little dick.

"You know, I been clockin' you, son." He casually glanced over his shoulder as he sprinkled into the bowl, his face swollen, almost feminine-looking like an overseasoned geisha girl's.

"Yeah, how's that?"

Cow smirked at the dressing on the back of Hoolian's hand. "I say, I know what you been doing, acting all shady."

"Niggah, say wha?"

"You're not like you say you are."

"Man, just take your piss and get the hell on outta here." Hoolian found himself trying to tug his sleeve down over the bandage. "I'm trying to get ready for work."

He'd only just started the job at the supermarket, but he'd made up his mind to be the first one there every day.

"Knowledge is power." Cow pulled up his waistband and turned away from the bowl without flushing.

"Motherfucker, you don't know anything about me."

Cow planted himself in front of the door, blocking him. "I checked you out on the 'Net at the library, booyy. I know you didn't do no twenty for breaking any Rockefeller drug laws."

"Why don't you mind your business?"

"You been lying at every group therapy session you been to. You ain't no junkie." He reached for Hoolian's sleeve. "Let me see your arms. I bet you never even picked up a needle."

"Man, get your hands off me." Hoolian pushed him away. "Did I ask you to touch me?"

"Yeah, I knew you were a fucking liar the moment I laid eyes on you, G."

"Yeah?" Hoolian suddenly grabbed a fistful of the bigger man's shirt. "Well, I been checking you too, *pendejo*. And I hear you weren't no majorweight heroin dealer. I hear you were in for sodomy one with a little girl in a stairwell. You want me to bring that up at the next group meeting?"

Cow tried to smile as his piss fermented loudly in the toilet.

"Maybe we best avoid each other's company awhile." He gently tugged his shirt from Hoolian's grip.

"Damn right." Hoolian poked him hard in the flabby chest to make sure the point had been made. "Now why don't you go play with yourself somewhere else? I need to finish getting ready for work."

17

"TOP OF THE morning." Francis shook off the rain and flashed his tin at the uniform officer guarding the door. "What's the word, Johannesburg?"

"She's still in the bathtub." The patrolman looked about twelve. Parochial-school acne, snub nose, the jittery eyes of the paperboy caught looking through the neighbors' windows. "Hope you got a strong stomach."

Francis slapped his gut as he sidled by. "Inspectors have used it like a trampoline."

He noted his time of arrival on his pad and scanned the door for signs of forced entry.

"So I'm guessing you got a good look at her," he said offhandedly. "Chalk fairy hasn't been here as well, has he?"

"Who?"

"One of those morons thinks it's a good idea to draw a line around the body."

"I didn't touch anything."

"Good. Dangerous business mixing fine art and foot patrol."

He nodded, put the pad in his back pocket, and shoved

his hands into his front pockets, making sure he wouldn't touch anything. Had to be doubly careful these days about stepping on evidence. *Slow down. Take your time.* He stepped through the little foyer and into the living room like an elephant on a tightrope.

He scanned the room, still trying to get used to having to look around for things other people could spot right away.

Somebody's first grown-up apartment. One of those cramped $2,200-a-month Upper East Side shoeboxes with no doorman, seventy-year-old plumbing, and a partial view of an airshaft. He noticed the subtle quickening of his pulse, the internal Geiger counter that went off when he first entered a victim's home. A potted fern hung under the Venetian blinds. A plump blue upholstered chair with an antimacassar sat at the far end of a shawl-covered coffee table, with a thin-necked halogen lamp leaning over the side like a mother looking over her daughter's shoulder. He went around the side and saw a brown teddy bear leaning back against the cushions in an old-fashioned nurse's apron with a Red Cross hat.

He was conscious of himself as a big man moving through a young woman's apartment, a musky unwelcome presence like a derelict in a beauty parlor. If it were his daughter's place, she would've told him to get the hell out already.

Moving his head in the four-square motion that was becoming second nature, he quickly scoped out the pine IKEA bookcases on the right side of the room, the shelves lined with CDs and volumes arranged by size. Never knew when somebody would have a copy of *Final Exit,* the suicide manual, and — bang — there's your motive and method before you even see the body. Instead, there was

Angela's Ashes. Pride and Prejudice. The Human Stain. Atonement. The Dispossessed. Every other title seemed freighted with extra meaning these days. *The God of Small Things.* He paused on the last one, intrigued. What every homicide detective needs watching over him. The God of unreliable witnesses, mitochondria testing, spatter patterns, cell phone dumps, tox screens, DNA swabs, polygraphs, fingerprint kits, trace metals, ecchymotic suck marks, and stray carpet fibers. There ought to be a shrine to the God of Small Things in Homicide. Just before he turned away, he noticed the book on one side of it was the *Physician's Desk Reference;* on the other side was a tattered paperback called *The Illustrated Man.*

He glanced back at the teddy bear in the nurse's uniform, and the light in the room seemed to dim. He shrugged it off and kept looking, seeing no obvious signs of violent struggle. The cable box was still perched atop a small Sony TV in the corner, and a slender bud vase with a red tulip remained undisturbed on an antique end table.

He turned left, the Geiger counter inside him clicking more rapidly as he sensed himself coming closer to the body. Somehow he knew before he saw it that a kitchen pass-through would be in front of him. Had he been in this building before? Through the window he saw, first, boxes of high-fiber cereal and then a little bear-shaped honey jar. Didn't mean anything, he told himself. Lots of people had them. His eye moved to a dense mosaic of Polaroids on the front of the refrigerator. Again watching where he stepped, he went around the side entrance and squeezed into the tiny kitchen to get a better look.

Kids. About three dozen pictures of fucking kids. With gaps in their teeth, scabs on their mouths, IV needles in their arms, cleft palates, neck braces, butterfly stitches, and gauze pads on their ears.

No, the victim couldn't just be any kind of nurse or doctor. Of course not. It just had to be one who worked with kids.

Thump. He stared at the dripping faucet, resisting the urge to turn it off before it'd been dusted for prints.

He heard the furtive mutter of male voices nearby, the sound of men working in a woman's apartment. They could've been fixing an air conditioner or replacing a light switch. He left the kitchen and went around into the bedroom.

The shades were down, but the bed was made, its soft pillows fluffed and piled, a thick downy quilt folded in half. He turned toward the maple dresser and felt his heart jump when he saw a picture of a mustachioed player in a Mets cap. But then he realized it was just Mike Piazza, the current catcher, not Keith Hernandez, who played first base twenty years ago. Still didn't mean anything, he cautioned himself. Plenty of girls watched sports nowadays. He checked out the other pictures on the dresser. The common element in each one was a smallish doe-eyed girl with straw-colored hair. Something of a jock herself, maybe. In one of the photos, she was golfing with an older couple, grandparents perhaps. In another, she was pirouetting on ice skates before a cheering crowd. The victim, of course. There was something proper and a little Victorian about her face that made Francis think of a dusty old locket found in the back of a dead relative's drawer. But there was a sort of scrappiness there that kept her from seeming too pure and virginal, a determined set to her mouth, a competitive way she thrust out her chin.

The red light of an answering machine blinked frantically on the night table.

"Francis X.!" A voice cried out from the bathroom. "No justice, no peace, baby!"

"Jimmy Ryan, word up." He moved into the doorway.

His old partner, now in Crime Scene, was kneeling over the rim of an ancient claw-foot bathtub, a steel-headed gerbil in a tweed sports jacket burrowing for clues. Thirty-five years on the Job, but *he* wasn't having to slow down because of some goddamn infirmity. Even after he won 6 million dollars playing Lotto ten years ago, Ryan wouldn't even let the word *retirement* be spoken in his presence. He was too used to the ringing phones, the late-night takeout, the ID flip-books, the moment in the lineup room when the witness began to chew his lip in nervous recognition. He knew that he couldn't trust himself at rest. Men like him had their going-away racket on a Saturday and started forgetting their grandchildren's names by Thursday.

A ropy black guy in a navy suit stood over him, black tie tucked elegantly into his shirt, snapping Polaroids.

"Rashid Ali, meet your new best friend," said Jimmy. "Mr. Francis X. Loughlin. Second-sharpest detective in the Manhattan North Task Force. I'd say he's number one if I wasn't thinking of coming back myself."

The black guy lowered his camera to give him the once-over, disdain dripping off him like Spanish moss. *Oh, here we fucking go,* thought Francis. *Let the butt-sniffing begin.* Rashid's eyes lingering a beat too long on the American flag and Deadhead pin on the lapel of Francis's coat. He took his time evaluating the package, knowing Francis would be supervising him on the case.

"How you doing?" said Francis. "You from the one-nine squad?"

"That's how I'm living."

"My old stomping grounds."

Now it was his chance to check out his blind date. Black guy in his mid-thirties, all gym-buffed and hard-angled. A trim dagger of a beard, deep sculpted cheekbones, V-shaped torso. Even his shaved head had angles, or were they just dents?

"How you get along with my main man Gary Wahl?" Francis asked after his old sergeant.

"The captain?" Rashid wrinkled his nose, as if he'd just caught a whiff of kitty litter. "A little friction here and there. We smoothed it out."

Figures this is what I'd get. Francis shook his head. Harry Hard-On. With a Muslim name, no less.

"So, what do we got?"

Rashid moved aside, giving Francis a full-on view.

"Damn."

He needed a step back to take in the whole thing. An angry red fireball had exploded on the tiles above the bathtub, spindly veins of blood dripping down into the grout.

Even after twenty-five years on the job and maybe close to five hundred bodies, murder had not completely lost its savage power, its ability to make him feel personally affronted, told to step up or get out of the way. He forced himself to slow down again, to recompose, inhale, exhale, concentrate.

Everything rippled out in circles from there. The girl in the curly-rimmed tub looked a little smaller and darker than she did in her pictures. There were conspicuous henna streaks lending a touch of red to her hair. One arm was hanging languidly over the side, fingertips lightly brushing the talons of the claw-foot. She could have been relaxing after a long hard day at work, except the tub was empty and she was wearing only a black bra with no underwear. Her left knee was crooked up in front of her, exposing and spreading her labia as if she were posing for a lewd truck-stop calendar.

He hissed as he went into a half-squat to assess the damage more carefully. Blood still wet in her nostrils said she hadn't been dead long, and a crack in her lower lip said she'd been punched full in the mouth at least once. Her throat had been slashed twice. Once ineptly, as if the knife had gotten stuck, and then again more deeply on the second try, sending a fine misting spray all the way up onto the ceiling. Thicker blood puddled around her collarbone.

"So, what do you think?" Jimmy Ryan asked. "He started off hitting her in the face and then he cut her throat?"

"I don't know." Francis slowly raised his eyes and saw a bloody clump of hair and brain matter on the towel hook. "I'm thinking maybe he stunned her first, by knocking her head against the wall. If she was conscious while he was punching her, her hands might've been more up in front of her face. Who called it in?"

"The attending on her shift at Mount Sinai," said Rashid. "She was supposed to be covering for one of the other doctors at six last night. Never showed. She's one of those never-late types. So they knew something was up right away. Left about a dozen messages on her machine here and beeped her about a hundred times. This morning they called the building, and the landlord let himself in."

Francis stood up slowly, a diver trying not to get the bends. "What's her name?"

"Christine Rogers," said Jimmy.

"Okay," said Francis.

He decided he had to treat this like any other new case for the moment, no jumping to conclusions. *Tabula rasa. All I know is what I don't know.*

He gave the newbie a sidelong glance. "Ever handle a big press case before?"

"Why?" asked Rashid. "You think this is going to get more play than if it was at the Edenwald Houses up in the Bronx?"

"Is that a note of sarcasm I detect?"

Rashid smirked.

Yeah, you know better, brother. You know that no matter what I say, it does *count.* A black girl probably won't have the mayor and the police commissioner giving press conferences about her homicide. A black girl won't lead all the local newscasts tonight and get the headlines in all three tabloids tomorrow morning. A black girl won't have six detectives squabbling over her case, where for once the victim looks like somebody who could've lived in their neighborhood, been in school with their kids, maybe even gone to their parish.

"Detective Ali just got his gold shield in January," Jimmy said meaningfully as he ducked out into the bedroom.

"And what were you doing before?" asked Francis.

"Brooklyn North Narcotics." Rashid drew himself up. "We did a lot of buy-and-busts. A few of our cases hit the paper. We did the Blood Money Sex gang over in Brownsville. Top story on *Live at Five* with Sue Simmons, front page of the *Daily News* the next day. So, yeah. I know how to handle the media."

"Fine, I just want to make sure we're on the same page about leaks," said Francis.

"I won't be talking to anybody."

"Good." Francis glanced again at the girl's hands, the nails short and unpainted. "So you want to get some bags on those?"

"What?"

"I said you wanna put some bags on her hands. Exchange and transfer. She may have the perp's blood or skin under her nails."

Rashid pulled a couple of Ziploc bags out of his pocket.

"Not plastic, come on." Francis frowned. "Paper. Use the brown paper bags."

Rashid glared at him. "Why you gotta talk to me like that?"

"Like what?"

"Like I'm bagging your groceries."

Francis looked up, his eyes eventually finding a stress fracture in the ceiling.

"Listen," he said. "No disrespect. But you gotta give the skin a chance to breathe. Otherwise, the evidence can degrade."

"I know *that*. You don't have to lecture me."

"Well, excuse me, but just because you got balls the size of grapefruit and can walk into a crack house full of Tec 9s wearing five thousand dollars worth of gold, that doesn't mean you know everything there is to know about running a homicide investigation. All right?"

Rashid crossed his arms in front of his chest, like

a rapper posing for a magazine cover, defensive and unapproachable. "So I got to be the bitch. Right?"

"Oh, for the love of Christ . . ."

Francis sighed and looked back at the girl, the old tub seeming to grow larger as it held her. Now that he was focusing, he could see there were definitely traces of sticky-looking blood under the nails and what appeared to be a reddish strand of hair wrapped around a finger joint, possibly pulled from her attacker's head. So she *had* fought back, after all. *All right,* he thought. *I got you now. I know where you were coming from.*

"So, what else you-all want me to do?" Rashid fidgeted with his camera.

"Just follow the steps. Check the drains and traps in here and the kitchen for blood and hair. Jimmy will bag the brush on the sink, see what we can find in the bristles. Get the answering machine tape and call TARU about helping you get her phone records. See if she's got a cell phone. Check out her e-mails. Then run this address on the system to see if there's any parolees living in the building or complaints from any of the neighbors."

"Got any dry cleaning you want me to pick up while I'm at it?"

"What?"

"Nothing. Just wondering what you're going to be doing while I'm running around."

"I'm going to call in to the Chief of D. so he doesn't start driving us crazy, asking for updates every five minutes, and then I'm going to check to see if there's any film in that security camera I saw in the elevator."

"There isn't." Rashid shook his head. "It's empty. Placebo cam. I already checked it out. That would've been too damn easy."

"Hey, hey, my man Rashid. You're way ahead of me."

Rashid sucked his cheeks in and raised the camera once more, not ready to play the tension off so easily. "What*ever,* man."

"All right, let's finish up in here and let the Crime Scene guys handle the rape kit." Francis took out his steno pad to sketch the bathroom's layout. "Remember, keep an open mind. Nothing's irrelevant. Anybody could do anything."

"Hey, Francis!" Jimmy called from the other room. "You want me to blow your mind?"

Francis followed the sound of his voice, one foot in front of the other, the short path between the two rooms a potential minefield. "What up?"

He did the four-square search, the fact of not seeing Jimmy right away triggering a spasm of tightness in his chest. Was he that bad already? Gradually his eyes adjusted and found Jimmy across the room with a limp scrap of paper in his hand.

"So I'm looking around in here and I see she's got a night table with a drawer in it and I'm thinking, *What the fuck?*" Jimmy shrugged. "Maybe she's got a diary or an address book that's got a couple of useful names in it."

"Abso-fucking-lutely," said Francis.

"So I'm rummaging around in the drawer, and I see she's got a bunch of newspaper clippings lying around in there underneath some other crap. And I'm thinking, *That's weird.* For a woman, I mean. I leave a newspaper on the bathroom floor, most times my wife is ready to call the marshals. . . ."

"Jimmy. Can we get to the point this fiscal year?"

"So then I take a good look and what do I find?"

He held up one of the clips and Francis took a step

forward, not quite trusting his eyes. "Are you fucking with me, Ryan?"

"Déjà vu all over again. Am I right, Francis?"

"What is it?" Rashid trailed into the room.

"Girl was collecting stories from the newspapers about this guy that Francis made his bones locking up in '83. Just got out because his conviction was overturned."

"What'd you lock him up for?" Rashid asked.

Francis stared at the page-five headline from the *Post* that Jimmy was dangling in front of him.

"Killed a lady doctor."

He felt a touch of coolness, as if the top of his skull had just come off.

What did they say déjà vu was? Just a mental glitch, a lapse in sequencing, a rerouting of information from short-term to long-term memory storage, so it only *seemed* like something had already happened. He reached into his pocket to get a pen for taking notes and then realized he was already holding one.

"You all right, Francis?" Jimmy eyed him. "You look a little peaked."

"I'm fine." He clicked the pen. "But Jimmy, do me a favor."

"Wha?"

"Next time you ask if I want my mind blown, wait until I say yes, will you?"

18

ILEEN WAS TRYING to get the girls dressed in matching corduroy jumpers for school when Tom came in the room.

"What's going on?" He put his coffee down with the weariness of a man who'd waited until he was forty-six to give his mother a grandchild. "I already laid out clothes for them."

"They wanted these. They said they wanted to be alike today."

"*Oops, I did it again!*" The girls started jumping on their beds.

"Since when?"

"It's just a stage they go through," said Eileen, trying to get Stacy, the eldest, to settle down for the brush. "Your sister was the same way at this age. Always wanted to wear what I was wearing."

"Nice for *you* to think so, anyway," he muttered. "Hey, what happened to your lip?"

"I banged with the bathroom mirror." Eileen touched the mark under her nose. "Don't get old. There's no future in it."

He was still staring at it when Stacy dropped in his lap and threw her arms around him. Of course, then her little sister had to get in on the act, competing for lap time. Surrounded by women with needs, her son's lot in life. So much easier for Daddy. Daughters never appreciate their mothers the same way. There's always an edge, some resentment brewing, a simmering jealousy. She remembered how her skin broke out when she was first pregnant with Allison, and her own mother, never a soft touch herself, announced she must be having a girl. Daughters always steal their mother's beauty.

"How'd you manage to get up here so early anyway?" he asked, glancing over at the Little Mermaid clock. "I didn't hear you come upstairs when I was down in the kitchen, making coffee."

"I was here already. Stacy was calling out in the night. I don't know how you two managed to sleep through it."

"You heard her from downstairs?"

"I couldn't sleep. Another lovely side effect from the new combination I'm taking."

She was scaring him again. She could see it by the way he was ignoring the girls and focusing on buttoning his cuffs.

"Maybe you want to take it down a notch," he said. "Sometimes these things need a little fine-tuning."

"I don't mind being a little more awake."

He touched his brow, a little disconcerted. No doubt thinking, *Mom's acting up again. Gotta start keeping tabs on Mom. Keep things from getting out of hand. Keep the madwoman in the basement.*

"Where's Jen?" He looked around. "I thought she was getting up."

"M'lady's indisposed. She's said she's feeling unwell again."

He seemed to accept that with a stoic half-smile. Poor Tom. After all the drama in his life, he probably thought he was getting a solid-state truehearted midwestern girl who'd keep the house running without a hitch, and not yet another complicated female with faulty wiring.

"I gotta finish getting dressed." He tugged on the thin end of his tie. "I'll take the girls to school before I drive out to Morristown. Let them wear whatever they want."

19

As the automatic doors swung open and Hoolian walked into Met Foods, he felt a cold ripple of apprehension, half expecting Lydia, the pretty cashier who always smiled at him, her handcuff-size earrings winking in the fluorescent store light, to suddenly point a long curly silver-painted nail in horror and start screaming, *"¡Asesino! ¡Asesino!"* Murderer.

Instead, she just waved and went back to helping one of the local bag ladies count out her change, penny by penny.

He went to the time clock to punch in. Next to the Department of Labor clipboard for listing on-the-job injuries was the calendar he'd been looking at every day since the store manager had agreed to give him a shot part-time. His life was all about numbers now. Sixteen days since his last court date. Another sixteen until his next one. Ten days since he filled out the application here, writing *no* in the space where it asked if he'd been convicted of a felony. Not a lie, he told himself; the conviction had been "vacated." Twenty-four more days until he officially got in the union, making it harder to fire him.

Every hour was a struggle. Yes, there were fleeting pleasures. The change of seasons in the air, the shrinking yolk of the sun, the collars coming up, the hemlines going down, the late-summer radio anthems muffled behind closing car windows, the little dogs on the street wearing sweaters, mysterious shiny pieces of cassette tape hanging from the tree branches like Christmas tinsel. But for every one of those, there were misread signals, dreadful misunderstandings, moments of spurting-nozzle anger and unintended consequences, deep black holes threatening to swallow him up. It wasn't at all the same, being out, as he thought it would be. The ants never stopped crawling across his skin. He touched the back of his neck, still feeling the mark left by the clasp getting ripped off.

"Yo, Jools, I need to talk to you. Right away."

He flinched and spun around to find Angel, the store manager, watching him from the elevated booth, where he spent most of the day surveying his retail kingdom of ten aisles, plus produce and deli.

"¿Qué pasa?" Hoolian braced himself.

"Just take a walk with me, amigo." Angel came down the short set of steps. "No one else needs to hear this."

He grabbed Hoolian's arm and pulled him toward a quiet alcove near the basement stairs. Hoolian felt the weight of the new Leatherman knife he'd been carrying in his pocket, hoping this wasn't the kiss-off that he'd been half expecting. He'd desperately wanted the respect of this fastidious little man, who reminded him so much of his own father in his pressed white shirt and necktie. How guilty he'd felt after their first interview, where he'd played up the fact that both their families were from neighboring towns near San Juan but neglected to mention he'd just gotten out of prison.

Ever since then, he'd been waiting to get pulled aside — just like this. Of course, he should've taken the initiative, knowing his name could be back in the newspapers any day now. Every day, he told himself that he was going to go down to Angel's office at closing time and confess, but every night he'd come up with another reason to put it off. It wasn't his fault, he told himself. It was Angel's responsibility. Angel should've known who he was already from all the press; he should've checked the references more carefully.

"I do something wrong?" He nervously rubbed a thumb along the smooth side of the closed-up knife.

"*¿Qué mosca te ha picado?*" Anybody say you did?

"Nah, just . . ."

He was aware of himself tic'ing and twitching. Not knowing how to lock his knees, steady his eyes, or relax his shoulders.

"Looks like that spot's gonna be opening up at the deli counter next week." Angel dropped his voice into a conspiratorial murmur. "Still interested in the extra hours?"

"Oh." His hand came out of his pocket. "What happened to Charlie?"

"I caught Charlie sleeping in the stockroom when he was supposed to be wiping down the meat slicer. I think the kid's on the pipe."

"Well, I ain't ready to take over. I just got here."

"Nah, don't gimme that." He clapped Hoolian on the shoulder. "I got my eye on you, *hombre*. I see how you're waiting at the gate when I come to open the store every morning. I see how you keep the aisles clear just the way I told you to. Just keep doing what you're doing. . . ."

Angel's voice trailed off and Hoolian realized the manager was staring at the knife he'd taken out of his pocket without realizing it.

"What you got that for, bro?"

"I was just going to go downstairs and start cutting open some boxes," he explained innocently.

"There you go, my man. That's what I'm talking about! Don't let me stop you." Angel grinned. "You're an animal, amigo. I wish I had a hundred like you."

20

WHAT DID THEY have to do that for? She was so good."

The nurse at Mount Sinai, a satiny throw pillow of a girl named Tracy Mercado with olive skin, a gravy boat smile, and dyed-blond tresses, was weeping. Fat hot-looking tears streaked her makeup, looking all the more substantial for having sat in the corners of her eyes awhile. Francis shot Rashid a cautioning glance, warning him not to get too close or say anything falsely comforting. Grief uncorked needed a chance to breathe.

"Tracy, we need to ask you a couple of things," Francis said after a decent interval. "When was the last time you talked to Christine?"

"I don't know." She choked up, trying to get a grip. "I think the day before yesterday. She'd just worked like three twelve-hour days in a row. I warned her she was seriously pushing it on the Libby Zion rules. All she was going to do was go home and sleep."

He gave Rashid a subtle headshake. She was going to be no help at all in establishing time of death.

"Did she happen to mention if she was expecting any company? A boyfriend or anything?"

"No. She wasn't seeing anybody, far as I could tell." The nurse worked a bent knuckle into the corner of her eye.

"Would you know for sure?"

"Would I *know?* Yeah, I'd know. I was her fucking best friend."

Sunset Park. Francis placed her accent. A girl from around the way. He could picture her getting up early to catch the N train while everybody else in the house was still sleeping.

"I'm kind of surprised, you say she was your best friend." Rashid cocked his head to one side. "I thought the doctors and the nursing staff didn't usually get along in a hospital like this."

"Aw, Christine wasn't stuck up like that," Tracy sniffed. "I mean, she was from East Armpit, Wisconsin, but she was a homegirl. You know how I'm saying? She was always just kickin' it with the regular staff, reading Kohl's catalogs in the break room and goofing on *The Ricki Lake Show* with the rest of us."

"She have static with anybody else around here?" Francis asked. "Hospital security? Custodial staff? Patients?"

"Oh, she wasn't afraid to get in somebody's face when she had to. She'd tell you straight up if you were full of shit, pardon my language. Insurance company, hospital administrators, cardiologists. She'd tell off any senior staff member for not doing enough tests. And people whose kids had AIDS? Forget about it. They start missing appointments for their drug cocktails, she be all over their shit. Up in their grill, calling them night and day, shouting in the phone, 'What's the matter with you? Don't you know what's going to happen?' I saw her put her coat on at the end of her shift and walk right over to somebody's apartment in the Schomburg Houses. Miss Figure Skating Champion. Knocked right on those people's door and dragged the kid over here herself to make sure she got the protease inhibitors."

"Any fallout from that?"

"Nah, they knew she was right."

He cut his eyes over to Rashid, knowing they'd need help from other detectives in securing the ER records; it was going to take days to comb through all the logs, making sure they had the names of any parents who might've given her a hard time.

"Tracy, there's something else we've got to ask you about." Francis lowered his voice. "And we're going to be depending on your discretion, because if any of these details got out to the media, it could seriously hurt our investigation."

"A-ight, I hear you." Tracy squared her shoulders, eyes minesweeping from Francis to Rashid. "G'head."

"We found some articles in a desk drawer that Christine was collecting about an old case. . . ."

Tracy started nodding before Francis was done with the sentence.

"Yeah, yeah. That girl who was a doctor at Bellevue, like twenty years ago."

"Hang on, you know about this already?" Rashid said.

"Know about it?" Tracy put her hands on her hips. "She wouldn't shut up about it. She was obsessed with that shit."

"We're talking about Allison Wallis, right?" Francis

asked, making sure he wasn't just feeding her setup lines.

"Yeah, right. Allison. Whatever. The one they had articles about a couple of weeks ago. With the guy who just got out of prison, said he didn't do it."

Francis tried to give Rashid a sidelong look, but he didn't have the range for it.

"What was she obsessed about?" He began taking notes in longhand, trying to get her exact words.

He could already imagine Debbie A. hammering him for going down this road too soon. *Did you even consider other possibilities, Detective?*

"Well, as soon as they had the article about it in the newspaper, we were all over it, passing it around," said Tracy. "I mean, she was a girl our age, working in an ER with kids. Even if it was twenty years ago, you still think, *mi dios,* that coulda been me. But Christine wouldn't let it go."

"Whaddaya mean?" asked Francis.

"She kept talking about it and talking about it. I saw her cutting out that story in the paper, about whether they were going to let the kid go or try him again. She was like, *'Damn,* what if he didn't have nothing to do with it? What if he was in prison for twenty years and he was just like this innocent guy?'"

Francis heard a tiny pop within his eardrum as he turned to Rashid. The newbie was right there with him, stride for stride.

"You have any idea why she was so interested?" Francis asked coolly.

"No. I was like, *qué pasa,* girlfriend? You going out with that guy or something?"

"Was she?" asked Rashid, anticipating Francis's question.

"Nah." She started to bat the idea away and then caught herself. "Well, not that I heard of. It was just a thing she was talking about. Far as I know."

She looked toward a doorway with an odd squint, like she'd just discovered a new unfamiliar attachment for an old appliance.

"What?" said Francis.

"It's nothing. We're a big-city ER. We got people coming and going all the time, with crazy shit. They crawl across the border from Mexico or get off the plane from Africa, with diseases you never even heard of. Eyes turning green, worms coming out of their butts. It's like *The Exorcist* some days. And then you got the guys from the rehab center around the corner, trying to walk in and steal drugs . . ."

"So?"

"So I mean Christine was kind of an easy mark with guys from the neighborhood. I'd be like, 'Girl, cut that shit out. You encouraging those lowlifes to keep after you.'"

"Anything bad come out of it?" Rashid asked.

"Nah . . . 'Cept the other day, she asked if I'd walk her back to her block. And she kept looking over her shoulder like someone was following her."

"She say who that might be?" asked Francis, still trying not to jump to any unwarranted conclusions.

"No. But this is New York, yo. Lot of freaks out there."

21

BY THE NEXT morning, the media carnival had moved on and Eileen decided that it was safe to go back over to the East Side.

A big black Hefty bag sat in a dented garbage can outside Christine's building, a twisted little yellow piece of Crime Scene tape sticking out the top, discarded coffee cups stuffed in with it, probably by the reporters and camera crews who'd been there yesterday.

Someone had set up a small memorial by one of the trees. A red votive candle dripped tears of wax by the short black fence meant to keep dogs out. Daffodils, carnations, and roses lay in bunches on the sidewalk, still wrapped in cellophane from the Korean market up the block with the price stickers left on. There was a blurred Polaroid of Christine, from the left, not really her best angle, Eileen thought, showing too much tooth and gum, smiling as she held up one of her patients, a tiny apple-cheeked black girl with a huge IV needle in the back of her hand and bright red devil-dot flashes in her eyes.

"To Dr. C.," said a child's scrawl on a three-by-five

index card next to it. "I know your with the angles now. See you soon. Love, Adelina."

Eileen looked around, noticing at least two dozen other snapshots and letters just like it, maybe even a few more than there'd been for Allison. There seemed to be almost the same amount of flowers, but then again you couldn't be sure: she was getting here late and there were always a couple of heels in a neighborhood not above stealing them.

Most of the mourners would forget soon enough anyway. They'd move on to their own little dramas and crises, their diet plans and lottery schemes, their romantic delusions and secret vices. Until finally it would just be a girl's mother mourning. Other people would say they understood, would make the appropriate gestures and mouth the right words at the funeral, would probably even come by the house a few times and listen for a while. But then their eyes would start to drift. The warm smiles would come too quickly, the pat on the hand would be a little too insistent, and then would come the darting glance at the clock. And eventually the unspoken question hanging in the air: *Aren't you over this yet?* Not because people were impatient or cruel but because they were afraid to get too close. They didn't want to get what you had.

She took a Kleenex out of her pocketbook and dabbed under her sunglasses. Don't let them know. They wouldn't understand. It's none of their concern.

But then she looked at Christine and the girl with the devil-dot eyes, and she went to pieces on the sidewalk, with birds singing in the trees. Children passing her on their way to school tugged at their parents' sleeves and asked, *What's wrong with that lady?* She gasped for air. It wasn't supposed to happen again. History couldn't be repeating.

This awful feeling couldn't come twice in one lifetime. It was too much for the mind to take. She wasn't made to survive this. Now she wasn't sure she deserved to.

She became aware of being watched, a pair of eyes boring into her spine. She turned and wiped away the blurring tears, just as a yellow cab cruised past, with a pale red-haired girl staring out the window at her.

22

WITH THE LOSS of peripheral vision, Francis was learning to infer things indirectly. So when he walked into the 19th Precinct that morning, he knew before he even saw them that the victim's family had arrived. The other detectives in the squad were moving a little too briskly for this time of day, speaking just a little too courteously on the phone, being just a little too fastidious about their paperwork.

Finally, he spotted two older petrified-looking white folks sitting by Rashid's desk.

"Detective Loughlin, this is Mr. and Mrs. Rogers," Rashid announced, with pointed formality. "They came here straight from La Guardia."

"I'm sorry for your loss." Francis nodded, surprised to recognize them as the seventyish couple from Christine's golf pictures. "I have a daughter of my own."

The man, gangly and awkward in a heavy flannel shirt and thick glasses, jumped up like he was greeting a long-lost relative. "Roy Rogers. I was on the Job myself. Thirty-three years, Wisconsin highway patrol."

A fraternal handshake and a cowboy star name. As if

Francis needed some further incentive to take this case seriously. He'd been working until one in the morning, running back and forth between here and the task force office uptown, coordinating with the half-dozen other detectives involved so far, working the phones, checking in with the ME, combing through Christine's address book and hard drive, interviewing as many of her colleagues and patients as they could round up, and trying to ignore the calls from various bosses every hour looking for updates to give the PC. By the time he got home, he was so wired that he couldn't sleep, driving himself and Patti crazy with his tossing and turning. And then, of course, the six A.M. phone call from his old friend Jerry Cronin, now chief of Manhattan detectives, telling him that the homicide had made the front page of the tabloids and word had come down from on high that City Hall would be monitoring the progress of the investigation step-by-step, with the mayor personally getting involved in paying for the parents' plane tickets and hotel room in the city.

"I guess you didn't expect us to be so old." The father settled back in his seat, a worried glance over at Rashid, telling Francis that these three hadn't been having a warm bonding experience before he got here.

"It hadn't occurred to me."

Francis watched the mother chain-smoking by the open window. She had the long drawn-down face of a woman who'd spent her whole life waiting to be disappointed. He knew without looking that the manila folder on her lap would be filled with things she'd been up all night collecting — crayon drawings from kindergarten, fourth-grade report cards, National Certificates of Merit, Polaroids from high school graduation, letters from college, civic citations, copies of a medical degree, holiday greetings—in short, anything that attested to the fact that this was someone who mattered, damage had been done, there was a hole in the universe.

Francis was moved, as he always was by the parents of dead children, but he also noticed Mrs. Rogers looked nothing like her daughter.

"Christine was our miracle baby," the father spoke up, as if he sensed the confusion. "We prayed for her. We'd been trying for years, before they had all these fertility drugs and treatments. We'd just about given up hope and then God blessed us and let the adoption agency bend the rules when we were both in our forties."

"Our friends used to call us Abraham and Sarah." The wife used the end of one cigarette to light another. "And now we have nothing."

Her husband grabbed her arm and squeezed, as if he'd just been pierced.

"No other children?" Francis asked, looking over at Rashid to make sure he was taking notes.

"No, there's no one." The wife stubbed out the dead end on the window ledge. "Two nieces in California who barely know us. That's it. Once we go, that's the last of us."

"It's a bitter, bitter thing." Roy Rogers shook his head. "This morning on the plane, I turned to Ruthie, I said, 'Honey, I hope once we start to go downhill, we get to the end fast because there'll be no one to keep us from wandering into the traffic.'"

Francis waved away the odor of smoke blowing back into the room, feeling a little touchy about the prospect of walking into traffic himself these days.

"Listen, I know how hard this is. . . ."

"But you need to get moving quickly." The father

nodded a bit too vigorously, wanting to cling to the illusion of manly professionalism. "Of course."

"We pleaded with her not to move here," the mother interrupted. "But she just *had* to go looking for trouble."

"I'm not sure what you mean by that," Francis said.

"She was just a girl who loved to mix it up," Roy Rogers explained. "Always was that way. She used to love to ride in my cruiser and work the siren when she was little."

He showed Francis a picture of Christine at about eight, a state trooper's hat falling over her eyes as she tried to reach the steering wheel.

"You encouraged her," Ruth snapped. "This was a girl who could've done *anything*. She was in the finals for the state figure skating championship, for goodness' sake. She had a full scholarship at the University of Wisconsin. She could've been a sports doctor or a pediatrician in Green Bay. But, no, you had to go get her all hopped up about looking for things that should've been let be."

"I'm still not following you here." Francis looked from husband to wife and then back again.

"My wife thinks I encouraged her to go looking for her birth mother here." Roy stared glumly at a *Daily News* headline on the next desk. "But she always wanted to work in a big-city emergency room. She said, 'Daddy, every week it's like being in the middle of a TV show.'"

"Wait a second." Francis put his hand up. "Run that by me again. She came to New York because she was looking for her birth mother?"

"No, that's not how it was." Roy scowled at his wife. "It was just something she kind of got interested in once she came here. That's just the kind of girl she was. Once she got hold of something, she couldn't let it go."

Francis found himself picturing how the blood dried

under the girl's fingernails. "I'm just curious. Who was her mother?"

"I think she might've been some kind of student or teacher, something like that." Roy gave his wife an uncertain look. "We did the adoption through an agency in Milwaukee that isn't around anymore. It's not like nowadays, where you get to know where the birth mother got her bachelor's degree before you decide to go ahead. We were told her name was Phelps, but who knows? Christy looked into it a little once she got here, but I don't know how far she got."

"I'd like to see any papers or correspondence you still have from that adoption agency." Francis scratched the back of his ear.

"I'm not sure what we'd still have," said the father. "Why would you need it anyway?"

"You never know what's going to turn out to be important."

"*We* were the only parents she ever knew." The mother gathered the mementos on her lap, as if someone were trying to take them away from her.

"I know that, ma'am." Francis gave her a deferential nod. "No one's trying to say otherwise. But I think we're all after the same thing here. So we have to look at every angle. We're going to need any letters or e-mails you got from Christine the last few months. The names and phone numbers of any friends you may know about. . . ."

"Anything you need," the father piped up, desperately trying to stay in the loop.

"Did Christine, by any chance, ever mention an individual to you by the name of Julian Vega?"

"No," the mother said sharply. "Who the hell was he?"

"Some of her coworkers said she'd been talking about him a lot. And we found she'd been collecting newspaper stories about him." Francis looked at the father, humoring him. "Obviously that's not something we'd want to get out."

"Oh sure, I understand," said the father. "But who was this Julian? I don't think I've ever heard of him."

"Sir, I'm afraid he's a guy who just got out of prison for murder," said Francis.

The lines around the mother's mouth instantly sank so deep that it looked like she had the jaw of a marionette.

"But how did that happen?" asked the father.

"Unfortunately, these cases don't always go the way we'd like them to," Francis said.

"And what makes you think Christine knew him?" Roy hunched forward, elbows on his knees.

"She might not have. We're trying not to jump to any conclusions."

"Those strays again," the mother muttered, resentfully flicking ashes out the window.

"Excuse me?" Rashid arched an eyebrow.

The parents gave each other a recriminating look.

"She had a soft heart," Roy said. "When she worked at an inner-city clinic in Chicago, she was always inviting some poor child over to her apartment or going to visit some family in the projects. I suppose she wasn't good at what you call boundaries."

"Soft head is more like it." The mother shut her marionette mouth and then opened it, tired of keeping her harshest opinions to herself. "She could've stayed in Madison and married that boy who was going to be a cardiologist. . . ."

Francis cricked his neck to catch Rashid's eye for a

half-second, making sure they heard the same tumblers falling into place. *Taking in strays. No good at boundaries. A soft heart.* They'd just nailed down that Hoolian was working for a supermarket in the neighborhood. Was it that much of a stretch to think he'd managed to wangle his way into Christine's apartment on a delivery run or something, selling her some sad-sack tale of woe about his innocence?

"Mrs. Rogers, we're going to do everything we can to get the guy who did this to her," Francis said.

"Fine," the mother said, stubbing out her cigarette on the sill. "Then can you tell me what I'm supposed to do with the rest of my life?"

23

HOOLIAN WAS WAITING in front of Met Foods when Angel arrived to open up that morning.

"You're an animal, *compañero*." The manager smiled admiringly as he reached into his pocket. "Better watch my back around you."

"You said you wanted me to come in early, right?"

"*Tanto majo*." Angel tossed him the keys. "You lift the gate today. Way you're going, it's probably gonna be your store soon."

A little before ten, Francis parked across the street from the supermarket and left a yellow police business placard on the dashboard. He'd decided to play behind the beat a little, as if he were just following up on Allison's case. No mention of Christine Rogers at all. He turned off his cell phone and locked the car door, not wanting to hear from any bosses at the moment. Everybody knew how to run an investigation these days, from the lowliest patrolman up to the mayor's special assistant for coordinating catered events.

He crossed the street, looking carefully both ways,

noticing that it took a fraction of a second longer now to see cars coming from the side.

Stomp or slash. Angel wasn't particular, as long as that cardboard got flattened. The boxes that were thick and tightly glued needed to have their sides razored. But the thinner ones you could just jump up and down on, crushing them with your feet and getting all of your ya-yas out. Hoolian always liked working in basements anyway, being close to the warm pumping guts of a building, feeling like he was the secret engineer keeping all the systems running smoothly. He remembered the long hours playing hide-and-seek around the storage cages and boiler room with Nestor. The two of them chasing each other around the dim narrow hallways, garbage barrels, and slop sinks of their little rabbit warren when the old porter wasn't working in the incinerator room or running errands on the service elevator.

He finished flattening the boxes and then loaded them one by one into the compactor, enjoying the pure mindless exertion of physical labor for a few minutes. He pulled a lever and a flat broad iron lowered on a piston, crushing the cardboard with a series of satisfying pops. What was left was a solid brown chunk, as if a child had kneaded a piece of pumpernickel dough into a cube. Then he went to the giant spool in the corner and reeled off four feet of twine to thread through the machine so he could tie the pieces up for easier handling.

Francis stood in the doorway, waiting for his eyes to adjust. The walls, shelves, and floor of the storeroom were painted gray, so objects emerged only slowly from the darkness, like shapes in a developing photo. There was Hoolian, snipping off lengths of twine and tying hunks of crushed cardboard together. Gradually, Francis discerned muscles moving under the dainty-looking store smock as Hoolian tossed the pieces across the floor like bodies going into a sandpit. Without the courtroom suit on, he looked a little more like the ex-con that he was.

"Well," Francis said. "Somebody's been eating their Wheaties."

The detective looked older and somehow smaller, standing there in his three-quarter-length leather coat with an American flag on the lapel. In Hoolian's memory, Loughlin had always been a towering slab about to fall on him. Now he was just a middle-aged guy losing his hair so that you could see the raw pinkness of his forehead and the nasty peaks of his eyebrows.

"What happened to your hand?"

Hoolian stepped back a little, remembering that the last time he'd been this close to Loughlin was in a prison hallway.

"Got it caught in a subway door."

"Really? In a subway door? I can't quite picture that. There's rubber everywhere."

"I was leaning against it with my hand and then the door opened real sudden and it got stuck. The rubber must've worn away there."

"I never heard of that."

Hoolian resisted the urge to hide the hand behind his back. "What are you doing here, man? How'd you find me?"

"You're out on bail, aren't you? Your lawyer has to keep the court informed about where you're supposed to be at all times, in case you don't make your trial date."

"That's a bunch of bullshit, man."

Loughlin kept looking at the dressing, like he could actually see blood spreading across the gauze. "Must've hurt like a bastard. Where'd you go to get it fixed up?"

"Emergency room, St. Vincent's. What's it to you?"

"I was thinking you might've stopped by Mount Sinai or Metropolitan. That's a lot closer, isn't it?"

"I was going *downtown* on the train." Hoolian flexed his fingers, trying to appear unfazed. "Look, I don't think you should be here. You got anything to say to me, you should say it through my lawyer. Otherwise, it's ex parte."

"Ex parte?" Loughlin stuck his lip out, pretending to be impressed in that familiar unnerving way. "You really must have been hitting the law library when you were upstate."

"It's *improper* for you to be talking to me outside of court. How's that?"

"Oh, I got you the first time. But this is still an active investigation and I am still the primary."

"Yeah. So, what do you want?" Hoolian put his shoulders back and shook out his arms. "You wanna finish that beef we started upstate?"

"Nah, I'm ready to let that go." Loughlin reached inside his jacket and pulled out a long Q-Tip in a clear plastic wrapper. "Can't keep licking old wounds."

"What the fuck is that?"

"It's a swab stick for DNA."

"Man, get out of here with that crap." Hoolian swatted the air between them. "You could've called my lawyer's office and we would've made an appointment at the lab to give you a sample."

Loughlin shrugged. "Look, I don't know how they handle specimens there. People try all kinds of things. I've seen guys tape squirt sacks under their dicks so they can use somebody else's piss in a drug test. But on my watch, I'm going to make damn sure everything is done according to Hoyle."

"Well, I'm not doing shit until I call my lawyer."

"Hey, bro, I thought you wanted this. What are you afraid of?"

"I'm not afraid of anything. I just don't trust you. You're the cocksucker who set me up in the first place. Why couldn't they send another detective?"

He went into a dark adjacent room to get more boxes and noticed that Loughlin stumbled as he tried to follow him.

"It's still my case," he said.

"They must not be giving you anything else to work on, you got all this time to fuck with me."

Loughlin looked strangely distracted for a moment, as if he'd been eavesdropping on a snatch of conversation in the other room.

"Lemme ask you something, Hoolian."

"It's Julian. Call me by my right name."

"O-kay, *Joo*-lian." He made his lips into a little circle of contempt. "The judge allowed your four-forty motion because your lawyer allegedly never told you that you had the right to testify in your own case."

"Yeah. I was a kid. How would I know?"

"I'm just kind of curious then. What exactly would you have said if you got up there?"

Hoolian put a box on the floor and stomped on it,

knowing he shouldn't be letting the cop rev his motor again. "I'm not gonna get into that with you. That's what I got a lawyer for."

"Come on now, amigo. Just you and me talking, off the record."

Loughlin almost tripped over a recycle bag full of Poland Spring water empties; Hoolian wondered if he'd been drinking.

"Fuck you. I'm not a little boy anymore." Hoolian stomped another box, the coil in his head starting to glow red. "You can't play me like that this time."

"Who's playing anybody? I'm talking about what your public sworn testimony would've been. If you wanted to say it in court, what's the big secret?"

"You wanna know what I would've said?"

He heard a whistle rising in his ears as he looked down and saw the cardboard hadn't collapsed correctly.

"Yeah."

"You really want to know?" He took out his knife and started ripping at the sides.

"I can't wait."

"I would've told everyone how bad you flaked me, you piece a shit."

This room was even dimmer. Francis tried to stay attuned and alert to how Hoolian's voice was moving around the space, coming at him from different angles.

"Is that *still* your story?" He waggled his eyebrows, the merry Irishman not letting on that anything was amiss.

"You and me both know what you did."

Francis saw a silvery flash in the dark and realized Hoolian was holding a blade.

"And did *I* put your fingerprints on the murder weapon?" he said coolly. "Did I *beat* you into confessing you used your key to go in and out of her apartment when she wasn't there?"

"You put me in that box all day and kept my father from seeing me. I asked for a fucking lawyer."

"So, that would've been your testimony? That I *set you up?*" Francis smiled like he had a dog licking his face. "Dude, who do you think is going to be more credible to a Manhattan jury? Me with more than twenty-five years on the Job and a half-dozen commendations, or you with twenty years in the can?"

"What the fuck you smiling about, man? You think that's funny?"

Metal winked less than a foot from Francis's eyes.

"I seriously think you might want to be more careful waving that blade around," he said, trying to follow its movements through the grayish light.

"What?" Hoolian held the knife up in front of his own face. "Oh, you afraid of this now? You call this a deadly weapon?"

"Doesn't look like a loofah to me."

"A . . . ?" Hoolian looked confused. "So, what, you're gonna shoot me because I'm cutting boxes?"

Francis tried to judge the distance between them. "You don't want to be seen threatening an officer."

"Oh, yeah, like I'm really threatening you." The blade's gleam blinded Francis for a second.

He tugged back the side of his jacket, so he could reach his Glock more easily. "You're making me a little nervous here, Hoolian. Don't be talking wild. I heard about what you did up in Attica."

"Yeah, what the fuck you know about that?" Hoolian made a quicksilver slit in the darkness.

"I know Fat Raymond lost a kidney because of that shiv you stuck in him," said Francis, refusing to be intimidated.

"Because that *hijo de gran puta* wouldn't stop his girlfriend from blowing smoke in my father's face in the visiting room. And my old man had a fucking tank of oxygen for his emphysema."

"How long did they put you in the bing for that?"

"A month. I missed my father's funeral."

"Poor Hoolian. Always the victim."

"He died by himself, man. I never even got to say good-bye to him."

"And whose fault was that supposed to be?"

"Far as I'm concerned, it was yours." The knife was shaking in Hoolian's hand. "Treat a man like an animal long enough, he'll become an animal."

"I'm telling you to put that blade down, Hoolian. I got my eye on you."

"And I got my eye on you." Hoolian forced himself to close the knife up before he did something stupid.

"Yeah, how's that?"

"I been doing my homework." Hoolian jabbed a finger, the whistle still rising in his head. "I know all about you."

"Sure you do." Loughlin grinned again, goading him.

"I know you got brought up on disciplinary charges back in '81."

"Pardon me?"

"It was right there in the case file, asshole."

"What are you talking about?" Loughlin gave him a molelike squint.

"*The case file.* They didn't just have my record in there, they had yours."

"Yeah, right."

"It's true. How would I know otherwise?" A voice in Hoolian's head was warning him to stop, that he wasn't helping himself, but he ignored it. "My lawyer FOIA'd your ass to see what else we could get. She thinks you got disciplined for 'testilying.'"

"Knock yourselves out." Loughlin shrugged. "*I'm* not the issue here."

But Hoolian was on to him. He'd been to the great universities of fear — Elmira, Auburn, Attica, Clinton— and had studied with the masters. He'd learned the language and customs, the symbols and signifiers. He could tell the difference between mere woofing and dangerous growling, and right now he *knew* he had this man scared.

"And she's gonna hear about you showing up like this with a Q-Tip," he said, the whistling in his ears starting to drown out the calm warning voice. "That's not right, man. It's just more harassment, pure and simple."

"You think so?" Loughlin asked. "I just see an officer doing his job. You don't want to give me a DNA sample and clear your own name, that's fine. We'll just keep bringing you back to court."

"You want my DNA?"

"That's what I came for."

Just seeing the man standing here, still trying to bluff and pretend he wasn't spooked, made bile gather at the back of Hoolian's mouth.

"You really just want a sample?" he asked, feeling himself start to go off the rails.

"Absolutely." Loughlin twirled the swab stick. "Ready when you are."

"Well, all right then . . ."

Don't do it, man. You're only hurting yourself. Hoolian ignored the voice, sucked in his juices, and let fly the thickest, most acidic gob of spit he could gather right into the middle of the detective's face.

"There. Is that enough for you to work with?"

"Now I remember why we used to call you Fuckin' A."

Francis crossed the street to his car, still wiping his face with a handkerchief and talking on his cell phone.

"And how are you, Francis?" Debbie A.'s voice crackled through the static. "I'm surprised to be hearing from you. Outside of court."

"Your client tells me you're pulling up *my* file. What the fuck is that about?"

"Context me, Francis. I've got a client in my office."

"My fuck-ing departmental hearing in '81." He shouted to be heard above the traffic. "Total bullshit, Deb. I've lost all respect for you."

"Don't blame me. That letter was in the case folder at the DA's office. Obviously, your friend Paul Raedo must have put it there back in 1983."

"Why the hell would he do a thing like that?"

"Maybe he thought Julian's lawyer would find out about it. He probably thought he'd have to bring it up to the judge beforehand and try to defuse it as an issue."

"No way," he insisted. "You've got somebody on the inside helping you with a favor."

"If you want to delude yourself, Francis, be my guest," she said, voice rising even as the signal grew weak. "But tell me something. What are you doing talking to my client anyway? I don't want you anywhere near him —"

He hit the Off button just as a minivan came flying out of his blind spot, horn screeching, its shiny front grille rushing right at him.

At the end of the shift, Angel called Hoolian into his office and held up the card that Loughlin had left, the words "Manhattan North Homicide Task Force" printed in bold black ink on an eggshell backdrop.

"*¿Qué hubo?* You wanna tell me what this is?"

Hoolian felt his mouth go dry, as if he'd used up all his spit on the detective. "*Lo siento,* man. I'm sorry. I thought maybe you knew."

"How would I know if you didn't tell me?"

"It was in the news before you hired me," Hoolian said lamely, knowing he was just making it worse.

"And that makes it okay for you to lie? Because you know all I read is the sports and business?" Angel slapped the desk with a three-week-old copy of the *Post* that Loughlin had obviously left as well. "I hate this tabloid shit."

"You asked if I was 'convicted.' And I'm not. Anymore."

"That's weak, *compañero*. You knew what was up. The application says 'have you *ever* been convicted?'"

Hoolian hung his head in shame, realizing, of course, that it was Papi's voice he'd been ignoring right before he hocked in Loughlin's face.

"I kept meaning to speak to you on this. I just wanted to show you I could do the job first. . . ."

"You tied my hands, *hermano!* I took a chance hiring

you. And this is how you thank me? That cop just told me he wants to subpoena all your time cards and get the receipts from all the buildings where you did deliveries. You mind telling me what *that's* all about?"

"No idea." Hoolian tried to swallow.

"Mierda." Angel squeegeed his eyes with the heels of his palms. "Do you know what Corporate is going to say when they find out about this shit?"

Hoolian looked over at Angel's computer monitor. The screen saver showing a red brick wall coming closer and closer, as if the viewer was in a car about to crash into it.

"I know I made a mistake. Let me make it up to you."

"How?" asked Angel. "What are you going to give me? Your word?"

Hoolian watched the screen saver hitting that same wall over and over. How many times? When was he going to stop hitting that same wall?

"Here. I paid you through the end of the week." Angel pulled open the top desk drawer and took out a seafoam-green check for him. "Don't worry about missing Friday and Saturday. I've got you covered for those days."

Hoolian studied the check dolefully, seeing that in fact Angel had tacked on a hundred extra dollars beyond the two days' pay.

"I feel bad about this, man," he said. "It's all been a big mistake. It's not like you think."

The screen saver hit the wall again and a web of virtual shattered glass spread across the monitor.

"Claro que sí," said Angel. "Now you tell me."

PART IV

I HEARD HER CALL MY NAME

24

THREE DAYS AFTER he wiped a generous dollop of Julian's DNA off his face, Francis went back to Bellevue, a place that always filled him with bubbling dread, not only because Allison Wallis had worked in its ER but because he'd been there himself twice as a patient. Once after a bullet grazed the side of his head during a drug raid — Patti showing up, white-faced, three months after their honeymoon. And then again, twelve years later, when a sudden bout of pneumonia put him in an oxygen tent, with Francis Jr. in the doorway, saying, "Please don't die, Daddy."

Today his business was up on the ninth floor, where the medical examiner's office had a lab for processing crime-scene evidence from rapes and homicides.

The elevator doors parted and David Abramowitz stepped up to greet him. "Hey, Francis, what's the good word?"

"Doctor Dave, you been working out?" Francis squeezed the forensic scientist's biceps through his lab coat and was surprised to feel a muscle the size of a regulation softball inside the sleeve.

"I've been hitting the gym a little more. And your friend Paul had me out playing paintball a couple of times this summer."

How things change. When he'd first run into Abramowitz a few years back while working a triple homicide up in Inwood, he'd made the guy for a typical lab rat: all buggy eyes, long arms, Ichabod Crane throat, swollen-looking brain casing under nebbishy black curls. But since 9/11 and the Queens airline disaster a couple of months later — when the ME's office had stepped up and developed revolutionary techniques to process the remains of more than three thousand victims at once — science had gotten studly. Dr. Dave, Ph.D., had become the Man. He'd gotten LASIK and ditched the horn-rims; he'd developed shoulders like a horse and a neck like a thigh; he'd grown a groovy little jazz pharaoh beard that somehow worked for him; he'd learn to swagger and speak up when asked his opinion about a case. *I don't care if she told you she had sex with only one guy that night, Detective. She's lying. . . .*

"Listen, I want to prepare you for something." He dropped his voice into a manly grumble as he guided Francis through the lab area. "The result we got is not quite the one you expected."

"Whaddaya mean?"

Dr. Dave put a finger to his lips, cautioning him, as they passed hip-looking young techs working with bio-hazard hoods, spinning centrifuges, and big screwdriver-size Pipetman tools. So this was where the action was these days. Even the machines seemed set to rock 'n' roll, swiveling and shimmying as he walked by them. DNA samples lit up in fluorescent shades of red, blue, and yellow on blackened gel screens, like flashy pieces of modern art. Every surface gleamed, reminding Francis how ancient and crusty-looking most precincts were by comparison.

He followed Dr. Dave into his office and closed the door after him, slightly irked by the blond-wood furniture and the photos of firefighters on the walls with their arms around Dave, thanking him for a job well done in helping put their lost brothers' remains to rest.

"Something very strange has happened." Dave settled behind his desk. "And we need to talk about it."

"Shoot."

"And I want to be very clear about the sequence of events that's occurred here." Dave picked up a sheaf of papers. "So there's no misunderstanding."

Queasiness rolled over Francis, as if he'd just heard an airline pilot announce that the FASTEN YOUR SEAT BELT sign had been turned on.

"Yeah?"

"Monday morning, we took autopsy samples from a brand-new victim named Christine Rogers, including fingernail swabs and a hair fiber she'd had clutched in her hand."

"Right."

"Next day, you dropped off a saliva sample for analysis from a Julian Vega and asked me to compare it. I have a photocopy of the voucher right here."

"Yeah, I remember." Warily, Francis sat down and took the photocopy Dave was offering. "You setting me up for something here?"

"I'm just trying to be clear about the chain of custody, because it's very important in this case." Dave shuffled his remaining papers, studiously avoiding Francis's glare. "Two days later, a Detective Ali from the Nineteenth

Precinct came in with fingernail scrapings and part of a bloody pillowcase that had apparently either been missing or misfiled at the evidence warehouse until he found them. Both pieces were labeled as being samples from a 1983 victim named Allison Wallis. Would you like to see a copy of that voucher?"

"No, that's not necessary," Francis said. "I know he did that."

At the time, he'd been so pleased that he offered to take Rashid up to Coogan's on Broadway and give him the "attaboy have a couple on me" in front of half the squad. But Rashid had begged off, saying he had to go study for night school, and now Francis wondered if something had gone terribly wrong out at the evidence warehouse.

"So then you asked me to do another comparison, between the blood that was found under the fingernails of your 1983 victim Allison Wallis and what was found under the fingernails of your 2003 victim Christine Rogers. Your theory, of course, being that we would find a match for Julian Vega's DNA on both these ladies. Since both of them appear to have scratched their assailants."

Francis put the photocopy he'd been given facedown on the desk. "David, I feel like you're trying to wall me in here, brick by brick. Just tell me what the hell's going on."

"I know how you like to be methodical in laying out a case." Dave pulled on his beard, refusing to be hurried. "And that's what I'm doing here."

"Why? Am I the one under indictment or something?"

"No, but you're not going to like what I'm about to tell you: there was no match for Julian Vega's DNA under Christine Rogers's fingernails. In fact, there was nothing with a Y chromosome at all."

"Shit."

He experienced disappointment as a sharp cramp below the rib cage. Immediately he began fumbling around in his mind for an explanation. Hoolian had been more careful this time. He'd had twenty years to review his mistakes. Maybe he'd worn gloves and a condom on Sunday night. Maybe he'd wiped the place down for prints and thrown away anything he might have left saliva on.

"But for sure you must've found a DNA match for him under Allison's fingernails in '83," he said hopefully.

"No."

"What?!" His vision suddenly narrowed with the rush of blood to his head. "We already proved it was his blood type they found under her nails. And he had visible scratches on his face."

"ABO typing is broad-side-of-the-barn stuff these days," Dave explained. "More than one out of every three people have type O blood, which is what they found. They could just as easily have matched you or me to the original crime scene. With DNA, the chances of finding another donor with a matching profile are a trillion to one, unless there's an identical twin."

Francis had a sudden dropping sensation.

"So whose blood *was* it under Allison Wallis's fingernails?" he asked as calmly as he could.

"Well, that's a very good question," Dave said, nodding. "Because again, I noticed there was no Y chromosome involvement."

"You're kidding me. It wasn't even a man's blood we found?"

"Well, here's where it *really* gets strange." Dave fussed with his papers. "I mentioned that your friend Detective

Ali also brought in part of a pillowcase that was labeled as having the victim's blood on it."

"Right."

"So just to keep things straight for our filing system, I compared the sample from under Allison's fingernails to the blood on the pillowcase, thinking one would be from the assailant and the other would be from the victim."

"And?"

"They were the same."

"Come again?"

"They were identical. That's not the strange part. It sounds like your crime scene was quite a mess back then. There was blood all over the place. It's very likely Allison touched her own wounds and blood got under the cuticles. I've certainly seen it happen."

"But?"

Francis felt himself drawing up to meet a scientific caveat.

"But then I realized there was something familiar about the electropherograms I was looking at."

"The . . . ?"

Dave presented him with a stapled stack of three charts. Francis turned the pages, seeing graph peaks sticking up here and there like stalagmites.

"Doc, I have not a fucking clue what I'm looking at," he confessed, noticing a series of small boxes under the peaks with numbers in them.

"Oh, you masters of the soft sciences." Dave allowed himself the briefest twitch of a smile as he reached across the desk with a pen.

"Okay, I was a C student in bio at Regis. I admit it."

But I'd like to see you running around West Harlem at four in the morning, looking for some fucking angel dust–smoking psychopath who's just cut up his wife and shot three cops, Francis thought.

"This is a report converting DNA into numbers on a chart. To come up with a profile, we look for variations at thirteen different locations on twelve different chromosomes. Basically, you get one set of genes from your mother and one set from your father. The numbers you see on the chart represent how many times the DNA segments are repeated at each location. And all the little variations help account for the fact that I'm not sitting here talking to a carbon copy of your father."

They call that evolution? Francis wondered which number on his chart was making him go blind.

"Then we look at something called the amelogenin locus, which tells us gender identification." Dave made a circle on one graph with his pen. "When you see a single peak like this, it's a woman." He made a second circle on another graph. "When you see two peaks, it's a man."

"Okay."

Francis began to flip back and forth between the three pages. The first page, clearly marked "Christine Rogers, 2003," had a graph with a single peak near the top and the number 103.01 displayed underneath it. He turned to the next page, tagged "Allison Wallis, 1983," and saw an identical graph with the same peak and the same 103.01 below it. The third page was exactly the same as well.

"I don't understand," he said. "I can't see any differences between these."

"Exactly." Dave sat back, satisfied that his job was done.

"You're showing me that both these victims twenty years apart had the same *female* DNA under their nails?"

"*And* it matches the blood found on Allison's pillowcase."

Francis stared at the last chart, the stalagmite peak turning into a long jagged spike pressing into the top of his skull.

"You fucked up."

"I did *not* fuck up." Dave squeaked forward in his seat. "We run a clean shop here. This is one of the most advanced professional offices of its kind in the world. I personally checked these samples when you brought them in. The one from Christine Rogers was almost still wet to the touch. The two from '83 were dry and crusty. There was no mistake here. The chain of custody was never broken."

"And so you're seriously telling me you found Allison Wallis's blood under Christine Rogers's fingernails?" Francis found himself doing the pan-and-scan around the office, as if someone else were standing nearby who could explain it all to both of them.

"What can I say?" Dave turned his palms up, Francis noticing how soft and white they looked from being snug in rubber gloves all day. "You asked me for a match and I found you one. It happens to be female. Beyond that, I don't know. . . ."

"But why can't you definitively tell me that this is or isn't Allison Wallis's blood? That should be the easiest thing in the world."

"It would be if your Detective Ali brought me a larger sample to work with." David shrugged. "But all he had were those fingernail scrapings and the pillowcase with her name on it from 1983. He couldn't find that bloody tampon that was supposed to be in the original case file, so I have nothing else to compare it with."

Another flush of adrenaline made Francis's vision narrow a few more degrees. It was just getting worse and worse here. He pictured that little bloody stub of cotton crammed in with other dead people's things in a barrel on a high shelf, secretions dripping in the heat and cross-contaminating one another.

"God*damn*." He twisted his neck. "What about the hair that we found wrapped around her finger?"

"Doesn't have a root, so we can't get nuclear DNA out of it, and it's not long enough for us to send out for mitochondrial testing. We'd have to do a consumption test. Which means we'd need permission from both the prosecution and the defense, because afterward there won't be any evidence left."

"*Fuck.*"

Eels wrestled in his gut. He'd seen some bizarre things in twenty-five years of police work. He'd seen a 350-pound gangster pull a pork chop out of his suit pocket in the middle of a trial; he'd seen a Chihuahua hanging by its neck from a shower curtain rod in a tenement bathroom like it had committed suicide; he'd seen a guy on angel dust who'd peeled his own face off and fed it to his German shepherd; he'd seen a man fall twenty-five floors and land on his back on top of a car, somehow ending up with his palate under his ass. But he'd never come across a murderer who'd saved his victim's DNA while he was in prison so he could leave it at another crime scene.

But what were the other options? The eels thrashed and the jagged peaks in his head sharpened. That Allison Wallis was still alive, as her mother thought, and going around killing other girls? That she had some identical twin that nobody had bothered to mention? Each scenario was more ridiculous than the one before it, but the common element in all of them was that he'd sent the wrong man to prison for twenty years.

But that was impossible. That was Antarctica, a whiteout, a place you could never come back from. That was the sun fading and the sea freezing up. He pictured himself standing at the edge of a precipice, a howling icy crevice opening at his feet. Snowflakes spiraled down into the bottomless void. Once you started to fall, there'd be no saving you, no bringing you back. No rope could reach that far. The walls would close in and trap you there forever.

"So, what do we do now?" he said.

"We?" The jazzbo beard dipped.

"Yeah, 'we.' You're gonna have to testify about what happened in this case too."

"Well . . ." Dave waggled a ballpoint between his fingers. "Obviously, first you want to start looking at female suspects. . . ."

"I still don't believe this," Francis said. "Has to be a mistake."

"Then the other thing we have to do, if you're so sure there's been an error, is eliminate your 1983 victim Allison as the person whose blood we found under Christine Rogers's fingernails."

"And so how do we do that?"

"Unless you want to start digging up bodies, I'd suggest you try to get comparison DNA from a member of her family. Any of them still around?"

"A mother and a brother," Francis said.

He remembered hearing back in '84 that the father had keeled over from a heart attack at fifty-seven, trying to play soccer with the eleven-year-old daughter from his second marriage. Another middle-aged man in Paris done in by young women and heavy sauces.

"Mom's better." Dave made a circle on his graph. "Then you can see which number in the genetic profile came from her directly."

"I was afraid you'd say that."

"Why, is that a problem?"

"Mom's a little in and out on the whole reality issue," Francis said. "She thinks Allison is still alive."

"Now *that's* interesting. Any chance of it?"

"Jesus Christ, Dave, I saw the body myself." He massaged his eyes, noticing how tender and sensitive they were to the touch. "I'm not sure how I'm going to finesse getting a sample off her."

"Better do it soon," Dave warned him. "I got a call from Deb A. this morning asking for the test results off her client's DNA. I put her off, but you know it's all going to end up in the case file eventually."

"Yeah, I know."

Francis brooded, wondering how he would even broach the subject. *Sure, happens all the time. We always ask the family of victims to give samples twenty years after a case is closed. Nothing to be alarmed about.*

"I'm just asking myself." He closed his eyes and saw afterflashes. "What happens if it turns out that we *did* find Allison's DNA under Christine Rogers's nails?"

"Then it might be time to forget the genetic analysis," said Dave. "And invest in a decent Ouija board."

25

DRAWING HIM. The girl on the train was drawing him.

Hoolian felt something tugging at his attention as the 1:56 pulled out of Syosset early Sunday morning, just after he finished his first night's work washing dishes at the West Side Jewish Center. But then he got distracted, reaching for the second half of his round-trip ticket. The conductor, a mildewed tub of a man in a blue uniform, round and damp in all the wrong places, punched the holes as the car heaved forward and then looked across the aisle, where the girl was sitting.

"You're not allowed to have your feet up on the seat like that," he said.

The sketch pad remained defiantly up on her bent knees, blocking Hoolian's view of her face. The fierce sound of pen-on-paper scribbling attested that a feat of artistic derring-do was in progress.

"Ma'am?" The conductor bent solicitously at the waist.

She ignored him with a kind of fizzing impatience. More lines were drawn, an angle shifted, the small feet in sporty red socks flexed impertinently and remained firmly on the seat. Only after satisfying herself for the moment did she hand her ticket over the top of the pad.

"Thank you." The conductor bowed and moved on, acknowledging defeat.

But she was already drawing again, shoulders tensed in steely concentration, the occasional sustained hiss of felt-tip on the pad telling Hoolian that a long arching line had been drawn.

He started to turn back to *Neuromancer*, having finally given up on *Les Misérables* a couple of weeks ago. The pen paused. He glanced over and brown eyes flicked on top of the sketch pad and then dropped out of sight again.

A cop. Maybe she was working for the police as some kind of undercover sketch artist. Following him around and trying to catch him in the act. The conductor departed, his blue cap tilted at a jaunty cockeyed angle, and let the door close behind him, leaving the two of them alone in the car.

Her focus felt like a compression of air. He nervously faced forward, hearing the dry squeak and pivot of her felt-tip.

He shouldn't be on his own with a woman. He remembered from studying the map that it was a long way between stations on this line and the ticket taker would not be returning soon.

The brutish churn of wheels on the tracks got louder. He started to gather his things up in his duffel bag. This girl was trouble for him; he could feel it. He wouldn't even have to do anything wrong this time. She could just point and scream and they'd haul him off in cuffs at the very next stop.

But then the sketch pad tilted back and he saw her gnaw on her pen in a familiar way, resting it in the corner of her mouth like a cigarillo. The waitress from the bat mitzvah.

He'd noticed her while he was standing in the kitchen doorway a few hours back, marveling at the scale of the reception. A hundred and fifty guests in evening clothes cruising steam tables that groaned with the weight of brisket, boiled chicken, and guinea-pig-size baked potatoes. He was lucky to be there. After he'd been fired from the market, Ms. A. had wangled him a tryout with the catering company; a friend of her cousin's agreed to give a poor boy a break, on the condition that Hoolian keep a low profile.

The deejay was cranking out *Fiddler on the Roof* tunes for the grandparents and new jack hits for the kids — *"It's gettin' hot in herrre, so take off all your clothes"* — while crews of Rebecca Epstein's thirteen-year-old friends gyrated like little Lolitas in their spangly outfits, hotsy-totsying their hips and twitching their pert booty-licious butts like there were small frisky animals trapped in the back of their dresses. The boys, however, moved like they were made of spare parts, clumpy clueless junior Frankensteins in undersize blazers, barely staying afloat in the sea of raging hormones.

Their parents sat around the linen-covered banquet tables, getting tanked on Moët and Cristal, oblivious to the adolescent bacchanalia behind them.

Hoolian had opened the door a little wider, watching the bat mitzvah girl's father, a real estate developer, short and proud, with a robust chest and a prominent brow asserting eminent domain over a retreating hairline, hugging relatives, giving toasts, and accepting white envelopes presumably stuffed with cash and checks for his daughter. The mother, a busty little battleship in a bright pink sheath, collecting bags of swag from Macy's and Gucci.

And then after a few too many speeches, the two of them hitting the dance floor, risking slipped disks and muscle spasms as the deejay spun "I Want You Back." The father draping his jacket over the back of a chair, with the cash envelopes secreted in its pockets, the swag sacks nearby, just about five yards from where Hoolian was standing.

The dangling sleeves seemed to sway in time with the music. *Oh, baby, give me one more chance.* Was God trying to tell him something? Saying, *Listen up, Hoolian. Don't tell me about your hurt. Don't tell me about your pain. This is who I look out for. Only the strong survive, so snatch them goodies, dawg. That's why I put them there right in front of you.*

But then she'd come over to stand beside the chair. This girl with eyes big as tambourines and coal-black hair. She looked right at him, as if she knew exactly what he was up to, taking the tiny measurements of his soul right before she hurried off to give the rabbi's wife her Diet Coke.

"How are the hot dishes?" she asked over the sketch pad.

"Say what?"

"I heard Marco yell about these hot dishes before."

"Oh yeah."

He winced, remembering that predinner meltdown; the captain of the crew, screaming in the middle of the kitchen about needing three hundred hot plates ready for the Orthodox wedding reception next door in two hours, where the table centerpieces were each named after a settlement in Gaza. *Those dishes need to come out piping hot!!*

"So, what did you do?"

"Wasn't enough room in the dishwashers, so I had to do the rest by hand." He flexed his left hand, noticing the bandage had gotten wet even though he'd been wearing rubber gloves. "Then I stacked them on a steel cart and wrapped the whole thing in about ten yards of Saran Wrap to keep the heat in."

"Very clever."

He nodded. If twelve years working in prison kitchens around psychopaths and sharp knives didn't make a man resourceful, nothing would.

The brakes gave a fatigued squeal and the train listed a little.

"Zana." She leaned across the aisle to shake his hand, almost spilling out of her seat.

"Christopher," he said, using his middle name.

He took her hand gently, as if he were handling a frail bird, and then quickly set it loose, still not sure he had the timing down.

"What are you drawing?" He tried to see over her pad.

"Only your face."

"Yeah, right."

She had one of those tricky European accents that went flat and low when you least expected it to, so you couldn't be entirely sure if she was putting you on or not.

"No one's asking you to model previously?"

He turned away, deciding that she was, in fact, ridiculing him. Seconds later, though, he heard the pen sliding and swiveling, each little mark making a distinct sound.

"Keep your head straight." She directed him. "It's better when you don't know I am watching."

"You seriously drawing me?"

"Don't pose." She pouted. "Too much self-consciousness."

"I wasn't posing."

"No?" Her voice dropped again, as if she was reaching under his shirt and threatening to tickle him.

"No, this is just the way my face looks."

"I don't believe you. This is an alligator face. This is not you."

"How do you know? Maybe I'm just a crocodile knows enough to keep his mouth shut."

She shrugged, her eyes playing over his features like a jungle gym. "It's not the same thing — crocodile, alligator."

"Both cold-blooded."

"Crocodiles have longer noses."

"Why're you-all drawing me anyway? Don't you have anything better to do?"

"You have an interesting face."

He scratched the tip of his nose and turned away, thinking she could have recognized him from one of those old pictures. Ms. A. had told him to keep his head down and his collar up whenever there were photographers around so there wouldn't be so many new shots of what he looked like now. But someone with a discerning visual sense could easily subtract a little hair and add a beard to one of the old images, like a child playing with an Identikit.

"You like an artist or something?"

"Parsons School of Design." She put her pad aside and

looked at him plainly. "When I'm not the waitress at a bat mitzvah."

By all rights, she shouldn't have been pretty at all. She was too damn wan and hollow-cheeked — almost consumptive-looking. Her neck too skinny to hold her head up, her brown eyes way too big for the rest of her face. But there was something about her you couldn't quite ignore. A kind of casual fatalism that made her seem almost glamorous. You could imagine her lighting a cigarette and taking the time to blow out the match while you were driving a car off a cliff.

"I'm just surprised you use a pen. I thought most artists used pencils first so they could erase their mistakes."

"Why should I erase my mistakes?" Her eyes went back to the pad. "In life, you don't erase."

"But what if you really mess up?"

She shrugged. "You draw around it. Or do it again, so it looks deliberate. Sometimes the picture comes out better that way."

"On paper at any rate." He palmed his chin, covering his scar.

"Yes," she conceded. "Sometimes it's better on paper."

"So, what're you into?"

Her mouth shrank down to a small insouciant O, as if he'd asked her to take off a piece of clothing.

"I mean, are you into comics or anything?" he said, catching himself.

"Of course," she said, capping her pen matter-of-factly.

"Like what?"

"Mr. Art Spiegelman. Genius."

He nodded, not sure who that was.

"Mr. R. Crumb. Genius. Mr. Joe Sacco. *Safe Area Gorazde.* Total genius."

"Uh-huh."

She ticked off the rest of the names in a bored singsong voice like a seafood restaurant hostess seating late-arriving guests. "Mr. Jaime Hernandez and Gilbert Hernandez. *Love & Rockets.* Genius. Mr. Eric Drooker. *Flood!* Genius. *Eyeball Kid.* Genius . . ."

He was lost, not knowing any of these people. Either they'd all started publishing while he was away or had been too adult for him to read before he got arrested.

"What about the Marvel and DC guys?" he asked, trying to get back on more familiar turf.

"Oh yes. Mr. Frank Miller, *The Dark Knight.* Genius. Mr. Stan Lee and Mr. Jack Kirby. Utter complete dope fly genius. I would have the children of their children just to pass on the seed of their genius."

"Seriously?"

"What do you think?" She let her shoulders slump in a way that left him utterly bewildered.

"I just haven't met that many girls who like the same things I like."

"Oh? And where have you been?"

He plucked at the underside of his chin. "You know. Different places. Different times."

"Hmm, very mysterious."

Every time he thought he'd figured out how to tell if she was kidding, the emphasis in her tone shifted a little.

"You draw also?" she asked, almost tipping out of her seat again as the train went around a bend in the tracks.

"Me?" He reached out, ready to catch her. "No, not really. I'm just mostly a fan. You know how I'm saying?

Though sometimes I think I got stories. Just like crazy ideas. Nothing I've ever written down."

"So tell me."

"Nah, I'm embarrassed. You'll think I'm an idiot."

"*Proceed*," she demanded, like some impatient bureaucrat. "There are no mistakes."

Easy for her to say. She looked like she was about twenty-four. What did she know about losing your freedom, about crushing boredom and despair, about making up stories when you couldn't sleep because the men on the upper tiers wouldn't stop screaming, about the smell of wet stone and diarrhea, about the fluttering doves of fear and anxiety going from cage to cage as word got around that another man had hung up or cut himself?

"Okay . . ." He cleared his throat. "So, like, mankind has cured all the major diseases. Right? There's no more cancer, no more AIDS, no more diabetes. Nothin'. People don't even go bald anymore. The only thing left is fear."

"Hmm."

"So they try to develop a vaccine to inoculate people against it. Kind of like the old polio vaccine, where they give you a little of whatever you're most afraid of and then you don't get it again. Only what happens is, the vaccine backfires, starts an epidemic. Everybody goes crazy with paranoia and starts trying to kill each other."

She sighed. "Where I am from, we call this realism."

He paused, trying to figure out what she meant. But the tambourine eyes shivered high above the hollow cheeks, giving nothing away.

"But then there's one kid who never got the vaccine, because they thought he was going to die when he was young —"

"I thought they cured everything."

"I don't know, maybe he was born with a bad heart or something," he said, slightly irritated by the interruption. "*Whatever.* He survives while everybody is going crazy and killing each other in the streets. During the day, he scavenges for food and at night, when all the zombies come out, he hides in the Metropolitan Museum, with all the armor and samurai swords to protect himself. . . ."

"And then what?"

"I'm not sure." He touched the side of his face. "I never get past that part of the story."

"Maybe he meets a girl," she said.

"And how would he do that? Everybody else is a zombie."

"Maybe she's been hiding in another part of the museum, watching him the whole time. . . . Maybe they fall in love and try to start over the human race."

He studied her, noticing that with each wash and drain of light through the windows, her face changed a little.

"I hadn't really thought about it being a love story."

"Who says this is a love story? Maybe they all die in the end."

"Wow." He almost laughed. "That's kind of heavy. Don't you think?"

"To me, it's most plausible." She shrugged again. "But I'm from Prishtinë."

He knew that she was telling him something important. There was just a subtle difference of intonation, a certain way her voice went up a little when she said the name of the place. The problem was, he had absolutely no idea what she was referring to. No clue where Prishtinë might be.

"I guess it must be kinda rough there," he mumbled.

"When I went back to my father's house last year,

all that was left were the bees in the backyard, buzzing around where we used to have the honeycombs."

He nodded, pretending to understand. It had been twenty years since he'd read the newspaper regularly. For long periods, he'd just shut down and acted as if the outside world no longer existed, so he could just focus on survival. He'd been away for AIDS and crack, missed five presidential elections, been only dimly aware of the Berlin Wall coming down. Was it possible there'd been a third World War while he was gone? The accumulated weight of what he didn't know began to hang on him like an orangutan.

"So, what's your drawing like?" he asked, embarrassed, eager to get the searchlight off himself.

Without any great ceremony, she handed him the sketch pad across the aisle.

"Whoa, check it out."

She'd drawn him a little younger than he was, with longer hair and untrimmed lashes, as if she'd intuited what he used to look like. She'd given him a smaller beard that would've left his scar exposed and an unbroken nose that made him smile a little, knowing that his actual face probably didn't measure up.

But what struck him most were some of the even finer details. The crease in his brow, the folds of his neck, the triangulation of his nose and mouth. She must've been scoping him out for far longer than he realized, observing him intimately.

Maybe he should get her phone number. Maybe he should leave her alone. Maybe he should ask where she was getting off. Maybe he should move to another car before something bad happened.

"Hey, what are these?" he asked, noticing a series of

arcs and dashes she'd drawn around his head like shards from an explosion.

"Edges."

"Edges of what?"

"Of where you might begin and end, but I'm not sure. You can never tell when you first meet someone. A big man turns out to be small, a weak man turns out to be strong."

"But are you going just to leave all those marks on? Or are you going to fix them later?"

"I leave them on, of course, so I can remember. Because this is when it's best, when nothing is definitive. Everything shimmers. I wish it could go like this always."

The train's horn sounded a warning blast, telling middle-of-the-night workmen to get off the tracks.

"You're a trip," he said, giving the pad back. "You know that?"

"And you are not?"

"I don't know what I am," he said. "You want to get a bite when we get back into town?"

26

O N MONDAY MORNING Francis stood in the doorway of the Manhattan North Homicide Task Force, watching a northbound Broadway local roll by the windows. That deep reverberation from the el tracks sometimes made him think of dead souls going past the office, glancing in to see if anyone was working on their cases.

The place itself was nothing special. A pale green room with a checked floor, nine beat-to-shit desks, a couple of autographed pictures from the cast of *NYPD Blue,* and a corkboard collection of police patches from Culpepper to Nutley, N.J. Eleven-by-eights of the PC and his deputies overlooked a set of Arts and Crafts wood blocks spelling out the name of one of the most elite detective squads in the city, and therefore the world. Any murder that happened between 59th Street and the tip of the island — whether it was in a Fifth Avenue penthouse or a Washington Heights shooting gallery — was within its jurisdiction, and even after ten years, Francis still got a little charge out of having a front-row seat at the circus every day.

This was where he was always meant to be. God

knows, he would've had trouble fitting in anywhere else. How would he ever find another tribe to belong to, people who spoke the same language? The stories and humor here never translated; normal people didn't think it was funny, a little skell bitching about how somebody almost cut his "gigolo" vein in a fight or half-wit hit men using Idaho potatoes as silencers. He watched the silver subway cars turn into trickles of mercury in the sun, a moment of somber reflection interrupted only when he turned his eyes and saw a young detective named Steve Barbaro pawing through the box of phone records on his desk.

"What the hell do you think you're doing, Yunior?" he said, moving his Rolling Stones lips-and-tongue mug out of harm's way.

"Skumpy wanted me to make sure you hadn't made any of these calls already," Yunior said with a nod toward another detective two desks away. "No sense in redundancy."

Francis looked around at the four other detectives who'd come in early to work the Christine Rogers case, wondering why none of them had bothered to defend his turf for him.

"You couldn't have just asked?"

The kid shrugged. He was probably going to be a decent detective one of these days, but he needed a little seasoning. Skinny Italian guy who went to Dartmouth and thought he had to prove he could bark and bite like the Big Dogs.

"This is what the chief wanted too," Yunior said.

"Since when?"

"Ask him yourself."

Yunior jerked his thumb toward the lieutenant's office, where Jerry Cronin Himself, now chief of Manhattan detectives, had commandeered the desk and started making calls. Francis realized he must have missed seeing him out of the corner of his eye when he walked into the squad room.

"What the fuck, JC?" He marched into the Fish Bowl without knocking.

"I gotta go." The chief put the phone down and looked up. "Good morning, Detective."

"Do I look *redundant* to you?"

JC gave him a sour-ball squint. The years had just made him smaller and tighter. His hair had turned into a wafer-thin discus on top of his head, and his skin looked rope-burned, marking him as the perfect high-blood-pressure candidate. He seemed to spend most of his days fretting about the commissioner's mood swings, his dream of holding court in a corner booth at P. J. Clarke's, with Sinatra sending over a bottle of Hennessy's, long forgotten.

"We thought the Christine end of things could use a fresh set of eyes," he said.

Francis shut the door behind him, aware of everyone in the squad room watching the two of them through the glass.

"There a problem, JC?"

"That's some report you got from the ME's office." The chief shook his head. "A match for the same *woman?*"

"It's gotta be a mistake." Francis turned and saw Rashid Ali walk into the squad room with a new box of medical records. "All three samples look like they could be from Allison Wallis, and we *know* that's not right. As soon as I get a comparison swab from the mother, it'll get straightened out. I already have a call in to her."

"Eh . . ." The chief curled his lip.

"Wha?"

"I gotta call from Judy Mandel from the *Trib* this morning, wants to know why we've got the same guy working both cases."

"I didn't talk to her," said Francis. "She's the one racked up Dick Noonan from the Six-oh about the thing with the teacher and the bomb on the school bus. . . ."

"We're thinking you might want to take a step back."

"A step back?"

"Some people are a little concerned about the way this case is developing," JC said. "They think you're a little too close to it."

"Is this you talking, Jerry, or somebody a little higher up the food chain?"

"You're the detective. You figure it out. They just want to make sure no one can accuse us of having tunnel vision."

"Come again?" Francis cupped a hand behind his ear.

"They don't want it to seem like there's a vendetta. Looks a little funny. Hoolian gets his conviction overturned and, bang, right away you're looking at him for another murder."

"Excuse me, Jerry, I'm not the one making the connection." Francis splayed a hand over his heart. "Christine's friend at the hospital said she was 'obsessed' with Hoolian. Her words, not mine. Anybody think I planted those newspaper clips in her drawer? For crying out loud, Crime Scene found a video in her VCR with stories about Hoolian from the local news taped on it. And Rashid just showed her super a Polaroid, and the guy says he's seen Hoolian on the block the last few weeks. So don't tell me I've got blinders on."

"Well, if the DNA's telling us it's a woman, why aren't we looking at that?"

"We *are* looking at women." Francis insisted, a little stridently. "We're cross-referencing the staff lists at both hospitals, to see if there were any females who worked with both Christine *and* Allison. We're going back over their phone records, recanvassing both their buildings separately, reinterviewing both their families to see if either of the victims had a problem with a woman."

He glanced back out at the squad room and felt a throb in his temples when he saw Yunior was still standing at his desk.

"All I'm saying is a little church-and-state separation can't hurt," said JC.

"So, that's it? You're cutting me off at the knees? Jerry, I've known you twenty-two years."

"Then we can afford to be honest with each other." The chief lowered his voice. "If it turns out you fucked up that case in '83, you better believe you're not going to be number one on the borough list to make First Grade come April."

Francis turned his head again, aware that until about a quarter-second ago the whole squad room had been watching the two of them. It didn't matter if he'd lost a little peripheral vision. You put five of the best detectives in the city together in a room and none of them are looking right at you, you can be damn sure you're under suspicion.

"Boy, you got some pair of balls on you," he said.

"C'mon . . ."

"No, you c'mon. You think you'd have a driver and an assistant chief's pension if I didn't walk in a room and get a statement out of Julian Vega?"

"Hey, who was the one who let you walk in the room in the first place?" JC's ears reddened. "Way I remember it, the Turk wanted you out writing traffic summonses on Staten Island after your little stint on the Farm. I got you that shot, my lad. So don't talk to me about gratitude."

"*Fine.* Then we're in it together. So don't be trying to cut and run on me, you miserable fuck."

Over the chief's shoulder, Francis saw a shroud of wax paper fly up in the wake of a passing train and then drift back lazily over the arches of the West Side Highway, disappearing from his line of sight a second before it should have.

"You know, you really shouldn't call the assistant chief 'a miserable fuck,'" JC said quietly.

"All right, I misspoke. You *ungrateful* fuck."

JC crossed his arms. "Jimmy Ryan's back in the task force for this. He's gonna be the primary on the Rogers case, and Steve Barbaro's gonna be helping him out. And nothing's going to change that."

"Then I guess Oz has spoken." Francis took a deep breath, filling his lungs for ballast. "But you gotta let me follow through with Eileen Wallis."

"Why's that?"

"Kill two birds with one stone. We're gonna need to ask her if there were any women Allison was having a problem with, *and* we're gonna need to get a DNA sample from her to eliminate Allison as a donor. I'm the one who has the relationship with the family. You send Ryan and Yunior, she'll jump out the fucking window. Then you'll know what bad press is."

JC sucked his teeth. "You already put in a call?"

"I was about to take a ride, you want to come along."

"Fucking Francis. You're like one of those real estate

developers, borrows so much money from the bank, they can't afford to let him go broke. How did I get so tied up with you?"

"I guess it was written in the stars, my friend."

A southbound train passed outside, drizzling track dust on detectives' cars parked below the el.

"Just do me a favor and keep an open mind," said JC.

"I'm wide-open, baby. I'm looking at the whole goddamn canvas. I'm receiving on all wavelengths. I'm living seventy-millimeter IMAX Dolby Surround Sound. I contain multitudes. My name is legion."

"Well, good." JC sat back, satisfied for the moment.

"But I'm telling you right now," Francis said from behind his wrist. "The same guy killed both these girls."

27

HOW DID IT go at the catering hall last night?"

Hoolian looked up as Ms. A. walked in at lunchtime and found him in the dowdy little wood-paneled conference room she shared with the immigration lawyers down the hall, surrounded by cardboard boxes of trial transcripts and the 1983 New York Telephone records that she'd finally pried out of the DA's office.

"Ai-ight," he said. "I met a lady."

"Uh-oh."

"It's all right. It was cool. She was waitressing at the bat mitzvah. We talked on the train for a long time and then we went and got a slice at Sbarro on 34th Street."

"You tell her what your deal is?" She sat down on the edge of the conference table.

"Nah. You think I should have?"

"Kind of hard for me to say," she equivocated, a dating expert in courtroom pinstripes. "It *is* a tough sell."

"Tell me about it. 'Yo, I just got out of jail after twenty years and I'm still under indictment. Wanna go out with me?'"

"It *would* give me pause," she admitted, her right leg swinging slightly.

He noticed she looked more put together today. Not just the pinstripes and pumps and the skirt rising above her knee when she crossed her legs, but a little more makeup and mascara. She wore a white silky blouse with one button discreetly open at the top, revealing a silver necklace on a bare collarbone. Her hair was a slightly more vivid shade of yellow. Why hadn't she looked this good when she went to court for his case?

"So, what do you think I should do? Should I tell her?"

"Jesus, Julian, I don't know. If you tell her right away that you've been in prison for killing a woman, you're going to scare her off for sure. But if you wait, it's going to seem like you were hiding something."

"Yeah. That's how I was thinking too."

"I guess I'll have to think about it a little. I hadn't expected it to come up so soon."

She donned a pair of glasses and saw he'd been taking notes on a legal pad. "So, what are you looking for?"

"You asked me to pitch in a little. So I was trying some of these old phone numbers Allison called after I left her apartment that night."

The glasses were a second pair of eyes, he realized. For once, she was looking at him not just as a lawyer but as a woman, trying to figure out what somebody else would see in him.

"Oh, I should've told you not to bother," she said. "Most of those numbers are disconnected. I checked already. It's been twenty years. Everybody hasn't just been in a state of suspended animation."

Was she trying to say that he had? Her flippancy stung

him a little, until he noticed that Brooklyn hadn't even had an area code of its own before he went away.

"Yeah, sure, I figured. I just thought I'd give it a shot anyway. . . ." He flipped through the pages, avoiding her eye for the moment. "Did you notice Allison kept calling these same two numbers after I left her apartment that night?"

"Yes, I did notice that." Ms. A. nodded. "I should've told you. She called her brother in Manhattan twice and her mother out in Sag Harbor twice."

He put the records down, a little disconcerted. "But that's good. Isn't it? Proves she was still alive when I left."

"It also indicates she might have been pretty upset over something that happened while you were there and maybe wanted to talk to somebody about it." She angled her glasses.

"Oh."

He leaned back, with an uncomfortable twinge in the side of his neck.

"The prosecution could still say you went back downstairs, got your house keys, and let yourself back in after she was asleep," she said. "Same as you let yourself in when you stole her photo album."

"What does that have to do with anything? They didn't put me away for twenty years for taking an *album*."

"Hey, I'm on your side." She reached down, patting his arm. "Remember?"

He looked up at her uncertainly. My lawyer. The one who got me out of my cell. *You wouldn't be here if it wasn't for her, homey.* On the other hand, she *had* been a prosecutor. And in his mind, that was like being a vampire or in the Mafia. You could act like you'd changed, but you never really stopped looking for blood.

"You know, there's something else we need to focus on," she said, beginning a new tack.

"What's that?"

"Who else could've done this murder. Your first lawyer tried to throw up some smoke screens, but he never developed a real alternative to sell the jury."

"Because he was a lying old drunk who never gave a damn about me."

"That may well be, but if this case goes to trial again, you better have another answer." She fixed him with an unsettling stare. "Come on. You've had twenty years to think about it."

"That's not my yob." He flashed a grin, trying to charm her with his old *Chico and the Man* bit.

Her face drooped like an unironed dress.

"Look, why am I supposed to do the police's job for them?" he said. "I've been in a cell since '84. How should I know who she was seeing or talking to?"

"Well, who else had keys to her apartment?"

"In the building? I already told you a hundred times. Just the super and the doorman."

"And so they questioned your dad about where he was that night?"

The question almost knocked him sideways.

"Why you wanna talk about that?" he said woundedly.

"I saw the detective had in his notes that your father said he was out on a date that night with a woman named Susan Armenio," she prodded. "Did you ever meet her?"

"No." He folded and unfolded his arms. "I don't think he went with her again. He was never with anybody except my mother."

"Well, what time did he get home that night? He told the police it wasn't until about four-thirty in the morning. Was that true?"

"If he said it, it was true. That man never lied about anything."

He saw her features sharpen, making her look less like a china doll and a bit more like a hawk. "But did you see him or hear him when he came in?"

"What are you trying to say?" He found his fingers curling into a fist.

"I'm just asking the question. He must have been in and out of tenants' apartments all the time with his key."

"No." He shook his head, like a child resisting the approach of a medicine spoon. "Don't be talking like that."

"Why not?"

"He didn't have nothing to do with what happened to that girl."

"How do you know?" She cocked her head to one side suspiciously. "Did he ever discuss what he did that night in detail with you?"

"He didn't have to discuss it with me, all right?" He tightened the fist, digging his nails into his palm. "That man was a fucking saint. Always made sure I had money in my commissary account. Took the Columbus Circle bus every other weekend to come up and see me upstate, with those damn bitches smoking their cigarettes. So don't you be saying anything bad about him."

"Okay, take it easy." She patted the air, trying to soothe him. "I was just trying to look at the angles you might not have considered."

"So now I considered them. And there's nothing there.

The subject's closed. Unless you want me to find another lawyer."

"Well, then, you're not leaving us much to work with." Her shoulders slumped. "We can't find the porter. The DNA evidence hasn't come back yet. And you still don't have any other alibi witnesses. I have to tell you, I'm getting a little nervous here. We've put ourselves pretty far out on a limb, refusing to make a deal when we had the chance. It's not going to be easy to turn back now."

Hearing her revert to her old habit of talking too fast made him hunker down a little. "So, what're you hearing from the DA anyway?"

"Not much the last few days. But they may be preoccupied with this other murder that's been in the papers."

"I don't know about that."

She looked at him strangely. "The girl from Mount Sinai." She paused, waiting for a glimmer of recognition. "I don't know how you could've missed it. It was all over the news the last few days."

"What can I tell you?" He yawned into his fist. "I've been busy, trying to work on my case and bring in a little money."

"Right." Her eyes rested on his fist, registering that he still had the bandage on it. "You thought any more about suing the supermarket?"

"Ha?"

"You said you cut your hand working in the stockroom. We were thinking about filing a claim against them."

"Nah, it's all right." He dropped his hand to his side. "I thought about it. The manager gave me a job and I wasn't straight with him. I got what was coming to me."

Her eyes lingered on the dressing, like lipstick on a

collar. He realized this whole conversation had been like a second date; she was still feeling him out, testing him and trying to decide whether he was trustworthy. She knew there were things he hadn't told her yet and there would come a time when she couldn't ignore them anymore.

"You know, I'm thinking about what you said before." She took off her glasses. "I'm thinking maybe it *is* too soon for you to be getting involved with anybody."

"Why?"

"You've just got a lot going on. We still have plenty of work to do on the case, and things are really unsettled in your life. It's not the best timing."

"So how long *do* you think I should wait?"

"I don't know." She raised her chin thoughtfully. "Probably until the indictment gets dismissed."

"Which could be months or maybe even never. Right?" He dropped his voice. "Ms. Aaron, can I tell you something? I've never been in a real relationship with a woman. Did you know that?"

"Well, uh . . ."

"Thirty-seven years old. Does that seem right to you?"

"No. Of course not."

"Then tell me what I should do." He reached for her sleeve with his bandaged hand.

Reflexively, she drew her arm back. And then smiled in apology, embarrassed by her own reaction.

"Go easy, Julian," she said. "You might want to break it to her slowly. A girl could have a few problems of her own."

28

THE DUCHESS! The Duchess! Oh my dear paws! Oh my fur and whiskers! She'll get me executed, as sure as ferrets are ferrets!"

The six-year-old ran away from Eileen, screaming with delight, a little redheaded moppet flushed out from behind the bronze rabbit with the pocket watch.

"'Off with her head!' said the Queen." Eileen crept up on her. "Off with her head!"

The baby sister, who was three, yet another redhead with alabaster skin, toddled after Eileen, yanking on the back of her shirt.

"A-ha!" Eileen whirled around. "Behead that Dormouse! Turn that Dormouse out of court! *Suppress him!* Pinch him! Off with his whiskers!"

Could this be the same woman who'd staggered into court less than a month ago in a near-catatonic daze with her son propping her up? Francis stood behind the trimmed hedges, watching Eileen skip through the shrieking munchkins swarming the Alice in Wonderland sculpture in Central Park.

"Mercy!" Giggling, the six-year-old scooted under the

hood of a bronze mushroom turning the color of a scuffed penny loafer in the midafternoon sun.

"'No, no!' said the Queen." Eileen gnashed her teeth and clawed after her. "No mercy! Sentence first! Verdict afterwards!"

The child squirted out past the Mad Hatter, her grandmother capering after her in tennis shoes, with the three-year-old hanging on to her shirttails, coming to an abrupt halt only when she spotted Francis stepping out from behind the benches.

"Looking pretty spry there, Eileen."

She slowly straightened up and shooed the children back to their babysitter, a hefty lass in a "Legalize It" T-shirt networking with the other nannies on the benches.

"I have my good days and my bad days," she said guardedly. "This *had* been a good day."

"Not anymore?"

"I'm always happy to see you, Francis, but you don't always have good news for me."

She still had that dry husky Grand Dame voice that made it easy to picture her bellying up to the bar at Farrell's with a bunch of firemen or dragging a mink across a marble floor after a Broadway opening.

"Did you follow me here, Francis?"

"I did," he admitted. "But only because you didn't return my phone messages."

"Well, shame on me then. Manic depressives have the worst manners, don't they?"

He looked at her sideways, surprised to hear her get off a line at her own expense. From hearing Tom describe how tenuous her grip on reality was, he'd figured on treading lightly today.

"Coffee?" He reached into the bag for the extra cup he'd brought along. "I remember you take it black, like me."

"No thanks." She looked after the girls. "I don't need anything else keeping me up at night."

"Still don't sleep well?"

"They say that's a side effect of some of these antidepressants. Dry mouth, constipation, loss of sexual desire, micrographia, hallucinations . . . As if any of that wouldn't make you depressed all over again. But, no, I don't think I've had a good night's sleep in maybe twenty years."

They watched her granddaughters clamber up on top of the mushroom and nestle their way into Alice's lap. The statue had a serene expression and half-closed eyes, as if the model had just decided to rest a moment on the cusp before adulthood.

"You know, I used to bring Allison here all the time." She watched light glitter off the nearby sailboat pond. "It all goes by so fast."

"Tell me about it." Francis started to sip his coffee. "I've got one in the army and another in her sophomore year at Smith who was always trying to get me to read *Alice in Wonderland* at bedtime."

"Kayleigh, wasn't it?"

He drank his coffee too fast and burned the roof of his mouth. "I can't believe you remember that."

Patti was barely pregnant when this case started. He'd felt self-conscious even mentioning that they were expecting again to a mother who'd just lost her child.

"Ah." She tapped the side of her head. "There's a few gumballs left in the machine. They didn't all roll out at the bar."

He touched the tip of his tongue to his scorched palate,

watching a duck sail across the pond. He found himself counting the number of seconds until he could no longer track it. How could she possibly recall a name she hadn't heard in twenty years, yet still be going around telling people her daughter was alive and well?

"Those were special days, when it was just Allison and me," she said. "Feeding ducks in the park. Going to see the mummies at the museum. You never want them to grow up."

"Where was Tom?"

"Oh, that was when he was either off at boarding school or spending summers with his father. Terrible what happens to boys when a family falls apart."

"That it is." He nodded, remembering his own father's complaints about the burden he'd been after his mother died.

"We used to play hide-and-seek around this statue." Eileen watched her granddaughters slide down and crouch under the mushroom, waiting for her to start the chase again. "That was her favorite. Even when we were living in a tiny walk-up on Broadway and 98th, it could take me twenty minutes to find her. And then she'd turn up in the clothes hamper. Or behind a curtain or under the bed. Some place I was sure I'd already looked. Like she could just make herself disappear and then reappear, like the Cheshire cat without her smile."

He felt the hair on his wrists start to rise. "Eileen?"

"She was everything to me, Francis. *Everything*. We were so close that we talked three times a day on the phone. We even wore the same clothes. But she was better than me. I mean, really better. I was almost envious sometimes. To be a writer is such a paltry thing compared to a doctor.

After she was gone you know how many people wrote to me?"

"No idea."

"Almost a hundred. And she'd only been at Bellevue a year and a half. They came out in droves, with these unbelievable letters about how she'd saved someone's life or their job. But you know what the terrible thing is?"

"What?"

"That I *hated* all these people, in a way. I mean, I was jealous of them. Because every minute they had with her was a minute I didn't get." She tried to smile, but her lips wouldn't stay up. "I know how crazy that sounds."

"That's all right," he said, humoring her. "You didn't happen to keep any of those letters around, did you?"

"No. Why?"

"Ah, no big deal. We're just looking to tie up a couple of loose ends."

"Could you be a little more specific?"

"Allison never mentioned having trouble with any of the women she worked with, did she?"

"There's a problem with the case, *isn't there?*"

Her eyes suddenly flared so intensely blue that it was as if Francis were seeing clear through the back of her head to the sky behind her.

"Nah, not a problem really. We're just looking at a couple of inconsistencies. . . ."

"Because she's not dead," she said. "It's what I've been saying all along. . . ."

"Oh boy." He hitched up his belt, knowing he was in for it. "Eileen, I know how badly you want that to be true."

"No one would listen to me." She jabbed a finger at him. "But she's still out there. I knew it. . . ."

The Mad Hatter stood behind her, his teeth bared in a

rictus grin. Tom was right. She really had slid into full-blown delusion. There'd probably be no easy way to get her to come in for a more formal interview or give them a DNA sample.

"I mean, when I first heard she was gone, I couldn't handle it." The words spilled out like marbles. "I went over to her apartment and I slept in her bed. I wore her pajamas, just so I could still smell her. I went through all five stages — denial, anger, bargaining, depression, and acceptance — and then I'd start them all over again. It wears you down, grief. It really does. Having to wear this mask of 'normality' all the time. It's exhausting. You have to stop and think how to answer every time someone asks you how many children you have. The only part of the day I looked forward to was being alone in the shower. So I could scream with the water running."

Francis nodded. The mask of normality. Not exactly an unknown concept to a boy who'd lost his mother at nine or a man losing his eyesight.

"You know what's strange, Francis?"

"What?"

"The *anxiety*. For years, I'd get panic attacks whenever I walked past a coffee shop or a movie theater where I'd been with her. But why? The worst that can happen already happened. Hasn't it? I buried my own child. So after that, what is there?"

Francis said nothing, thinking about Shackleton facing the white sea.

"And of course, in the end, there's the *guilt*."

"The guilt?"

"You keep asking yourself, what did I do that was so bad? Why are you punishing me? It must be something I did."

"I'm not sure it works like that."

"Don't give me that, Francis." She glared at him. "You can't fool me. I remember how you said it yourself for what happened to your mother . . ."

"I told you about *that?*" He cringed. He must have really fallen off the wagon, commiserating with her around a bottle of Jameson's. He thought he never got down on that level with anyone, except maybe at the Farm.

"You were very kind," she said. "I haven't forgotten. But most people go on with their lives, don't they?"

"I suppose they do."

He watched an old woman with a torn down coat and a shopping cart rattle by, carrying a raft of cans and a long stale-looking baguette.

"Well, I *didn't,*" Eileen said. "I just kept waking up in the middle of the afternoon with more and more empty bottles around me. I thought I was losing my mind. At one point I decided I was going to have myself committed, but then I realized I'd have to go to Bellevue first. Right around the corner from where she worked."

"I can see how that might've bothered you."

"So instead I just took all those pills and ended up in the emergency room."

The woman in the down coat started tearing off pieces of bread and throwing them at the blackened pigeons milling around the steps.

"Jesus Christ, Eileen, I never heard about that," Francis said. "You couldn't have picked up the phone and called somebody?"

"And told them what? That I was about to OD on Valium and cheap merlot for the third or fourth time?" She smiled, tired of her own drama. "Tom was always finding me and dragging me to one hospital or another to get my stomach pumped. I used to joke that's how he got interested in selling medical supplies."

The birds jostled for scraps like a bunch of addicts fighting over a few stray crumbs of crack.

"And then one afternoon I was in Fairway and I heard her."

"She *spoke* to you?"

"I was right in front of the pomegranates and she said, 'It's okay, Mom.' She must've been right behind me. But when I turned around, she was gone."

Francis started shaking his head. "Eileen, come on. . . ."

"It was her, Francis. Sure as I'm standing here, talking to you."

His scalp started to contract.

"And then it happened again, about a month later. When I was coming out of the Apthorp Pharmacy on Broadway. That time, she was watching me from the bus shelter across the street. It was raining. By the time I got to her, the bus had pulled away. She left me standing there, soaking, watching her through the back window."

"And you're sure it was Allison?"

"Well, I don't have any other daughters out there, far as I know," she said in an earthy rasp, as if she were the sensible one in this conversation.

Francis held back on the commentary. One thing he'd learned from being a detective was how to keep his mouth closed and his mind open. You could spend seven hours in the box, listening to some drooling lunatic babble on about microwaves from Uranus and JLo bearing his two-headed love child and then casually mention how he'd tossed the gun he'd used to kill his cousin off the Willis Avenue Bridge.

On the other hand, this was a woman he'd cared about.

Someone who reminded him of what he'd lost in his own life. Hearing her go on this way, he pictured her turning into someone like the pigeon lady with the baguette and the stuffing coming out of her down jacket.

"Just the other day, I saw her in a cab. She calls me on the phone sometimes too. To hear my voice. . . . But she never says anything —"

"Let me ask you something, Eileen," he gently interrupted. "If Allison really was still alive, why would she pretend to be dead?"

She looked startled, as if the question had never occurred to her.

"Things got between us," she said quietly.

"Such as?"

"You have children of your own, Francis. They've never pushed you away?"

He thought of Francis Jr. halfway across the world, on an army base in Korea. Signed up four months after 9/11 and never said a word to his father about it ahead of time.

"We were talking about Allison," he reminded her.

"There were things going on in her life that she knew I didn't approve of."

"What are we talking about here?" asked Francis. "A boyfriend? Drugs?"

"I'm sorry, Francis." Her eyes began to get glassy. "I can't talk to you about this. You couldn't possibly understand."

"Oh, don't worry about me. I've been to beyond and back."

The glass started to melt and leak out of her eyes. "They have secrets, you know."

"Who does?"

"Children." Tears ran down both sides of her nose.

"When they're young, they seem so open to you. But they always keep parts of themselves hidden."

"Eileen." He produced a handkerchief from his breast pocket and gave it to her. "I have to tell you that what you're saying doesn't make any sense. Allison is gone. We have no choice but to accept that. The best we can do is to make sure what happened to her never happens to anybody else."

She took a moment to absorb what he was saying, blowing her nose and watching her granddaughters climb down from the mushroom, the pair of them tired of waiting for her to start the chase once more.

"It won't happen again," she said abruptly.

"What?"

"I'm saying, you're right. *I won't let it happen again.*"

"Eileen?"

Nimbus clouds seemed to drift across the sky-blue eyes. Useless, he realized. She was probably too far gone to be of any real help. The pigeons flew off, having picked the paving stones clean. The best he could do here today was get a sample of her DNA without being intrusive, so they could at least clear up the confusion at the lab.

"You just have to *act* sometimes." Her jaw locked. "A thing doesn't stop just because you pretend it isn't happening."

"Because *what* isn't happening? You've lost me here, Eileen."

She glanced over, the clouds clearing a moment, coming back to her senses with the rebuke.

"I'm sorry, Francis, but I've been neglecting the children." She shook herself, gave him a fleeting smile, and folded up his handkerchief. "What would you like me to do with this?"

29

THE BUZZING IN Hoolian's mind that had started about halfway through his conversation with Ms. A. was just starting to die down when he turned from the Starbucks counter and saw that same curly-haired girl with *Les Misérables* sitting at a centrally located table with her ankles twined balletically around a chair leg.

He gave her a wide berth as he navigated back toward Zana by the window, balancing two lattes and a slice of caramel cheesecake on his tray.

"Ah, my Mystery Man returns." Zana put down her sketchbook. "You are trying to make me into the Fat Chick."

"Hope you're in the mood for something sweet."

He glanced back at the curly-haired girl, changing his mind and half hoping she'd notice that in fact he was there with another woman today.

"My *nene* would kill me if she saw me eat this. She'd say, '*Zana, ndale! Ndale!* In America, everyone wants to be skinny-skinny supermodel.' But I tell her what Sir Mix-A-Lot says."

He looked at her blankly.

"'I like big butts and I cannot lie . . . ,'" she chanted.

He smiled, pretending to know what song she was referring to. Twenty years of popular music he'd missed, except for snatches drifting out of other people's cells. Whole trends had come and gone without leaving a trace and he was still trying to adjust to the fact that they weren't selling vinyl in most record stores anymore.

"G'head then. I like a woman with a little meat on her bones."

She put her fork aside and let her gaze roam free across his face again. "So, please, can I ask you something?"

"Sure."

"Why didn't you give me your phone number before?"

"I dunno." He jogged his shoulders. "Isn't it usually the man that calls?"

He'd already thought through the scenario of her calling the halfway house and getting Cow or one of the other lowlifes he lived with on the line.

"I'm wondering, is there somebody you don't want me to talk to maybe?"

"Yeah, my roommate. He doesn't take messages."

Her eyes seemed to get bigger, as the rest of her face got smaller. "I don't know about you."

"What don't you know?" he said, trying out the playful teasing tone he'd heard other men use on women.

"How come you're a man this age who has a roommate and isn't married?"

"Guess I never met the right lady."

She puffed out her lips and sulked. "You sure you're not a big-time liar with a wife and seven children somewhere?"

"There's nobody else, far as I know. See any ring on me?"

He held up the unbandaged hand and tried to look innocent. But he knew full well that if she hadn't been new to the country herself, she might have asked some of these same questions sooner.

"But where have you been all this time that you don't have a normal job or a special lady friend?" she asked, clearly having reviewed some of their earlier conversations. "Why you haven't seen *Nightmare on Elm Street,* one, two, three, four, five, or six?"

"I told you. My father died and I was upstate, studying the law," he replied, strictly adhering to the facts. "I didn't get out to see a lot of movies."

"There's something else you haven't told me." She turned her fork over. "I feel this in my *zemer.*"

He put one hand over the other, covering the gauze that had started to feel damp while he was talking to Ms. A.

"Well, what about you?" he asked, trying to reroute her. "You're always asking me the questions. How come you don't have a boyfriend?"

"Oh, don't start on me, please," she said. "I am the refrigerator magnet for bad men."

"Hmm, what's that say about me?"

"I don't know." She pinched her bottom lip. "That needs to be determined."

"You didn't leave somebody behind in, ah . . ."

"Kosovo." She rolled her eyes.

"Yeah, what happened there anyway?"

"Ucchh, Americans. The rest of the world doesn't exist for you until it flies an airplane into one of your buildings."

"All right, I'm an idiot. Tell me."

"No one who wasn't there could understand," she said.

He massaged the scar under his beard, having thought the same thing when he was in prison about 150,000 times. "Try me."

"You heard of 'ethnic cleansing,' haven't you?"

"Uh, yeah, of course." Once more, he realized he was trying to stand up in the deep end of his own ignorance.

"You cannot believe it's possible for human beings to act this way, except in history books. And then you come home one day and your neighbors are in your house, stealing your mother's jewelry. They killed our cat and sprayed its blood on the walls to drive us away. That was a totally animal thing."

"We're all animals," he said, dropping the bandaged hand down to his side self-consciously.

"Yeah, sure. Okay. Of course. This is another banality. But it's one thing to know it and another to see it."

He liked the way she talked to him, all bright-eyed and intense, like they were both students at the kind of highbrow university he never got to go to.

"Oh, I've seen it." He picked up his latte. "From time to time."

"How? Are you a secret Kosovar?"

"No, but I've been . . . around." He took a sip. "You know."

She studied his face over the rim of the cup, examining each feature one by one, to see if she'd missed anything the first time she'd drawn him.

"I guess people could do anything." He dabbed his mouth with a napkin. "Under the right circumstances."

"No, I don't think so."

"Why?" he asked. "You don't think somebody who's basically an all right person can get pushed into a corner and do something they wouldn't normally do?"

Her eyes moved a fraction of an inch, as if she were just noticing something behind him.

"Sometimes," she allowed. "But there are some things that should disqualify someone from the human race."

"Like what?"

He realized he was testing her a little, trying to see where her edges were. The undefined time was ending. The hard lines were forming.

"The soldiers who did this thing to my cousins," she said. "They weren't human."

"Why, what'd they do?"

Something small and shaky in her voice made him sit up a little, like a dog hearing the word *bone*.

"They stopped the car and they take my cousin Edona out to the barn and two of them rape her. Slap her face and ask each other, 'Why you treating this whore so good?' Then they came out and shot her little brother in the head, so he wouldn't grow up to revenge on them."

"That *is* fucked up."

"Someone who does this is totally disqualified from being human," she said, the color draining from her face even as she made it sound like she was just talking about somebody getting thrown out of a soccer game. "This is not even animal."

He sensed he was coming up to one of her edges.

"Anything like that happen to you?" he asked, pushing her.

"No, of course not." She shook her head too vigorously. "They only burned our house down and made us walk five days in the rain to the border. We were the lucky ones."

"You call that lucky?"

"The lady in the next tent died and left three children,"

she said. "We only lost our home. It's not so bad. By comparison."

He didn't believe her. He could almost smell that there was something else she hadn't told him. It was in the air like the ozone after a lightning strike. "But the rest of your family made it out okay?"

"Yes. Everyone is intact. Why are you still asking?"

"I don't know. Just sounds like you dropped a beat somewhere."

He still had that thing, that upstate instinct. Once you'd been ripped down the sides, you could see where other people were stitched up. She was starting to open up to him without even knowing it. A core was half exposed, something warm and fragile that he could crush as easily as a trembling little sparrow. The thought of such power, such dominance excited him and then disturbed him. He had to stop and ask himself exactly what it was that he wanted from her.

"Maybe it's better not to talk about these things." She started tearing her napkin into little cannonballs.

"I'm sorry. Did I upset you or something?"

"No, just, there are complications, always. Like I say, you don't erase mistakes. You draw around them."

"I still don't understand."

"Why should you?" Her fingers spread across her sketch pad, like she was covering the front of a dress. "It's impossible for anyone else."

"How do you know?"

"What?"

"You keep saying that, but how do you know?" He put his unbandaged hand over hers. "I might be the one person who gets you."

He registered the pulse of tension under his palm and

the flicker of longing on her face. She wanted to believe in him, wanted to think he was a better person than he actually was.

"You shut me down," he said, "you're never gonna know."

The curly-haired girl put her book down, eavesdropping. Hoolian shot her a warning glance, to mind her own goddamn business.

"You're a sweet man." Zana quickly took her hand back and swept the shreds of her torn napkin into her cupped palm. "I worry for you."

"Why?"

"Because the world is a very bad place for sweet men."

30

*D*ENIAL. ANGER. BARGAINING.

Okay, stop there. Let's talk deal. It's not that dark yet. Just hold back the night a little; a few more hours of daylight is all it would take.

Francis dropped off Eileen's DNA with Dr. Dave, left a message for Tom Wallis to check up on his sister's female acquaintances, typed up his notes, and then headed home. Amber rays slanted through the Brooklyn Bridge harp strings, making bright strobe flashes on his windshield. A stretch of pink was showing under gray clouds, like a glimpse of a girl's midriff under a thin sweater. He found himself constantly adjusting his mirrors to compensate for blind spots, trying to make sure he didn't get sideswiped. The chipped diamond sparkle of the East River was lost on him these days because he couldn't afford to take his eyes off the road.

— *Come on, God of Small Things, just get me home in one piece. I'll take it from there.*

— *Still a fine one for playing the angles, Loughlin, aren't you? Just one more drink and I'll quit. Just let me clear this case and I won't bitch about the next three. Just get me through this door alive. I promise I'll believe you until the next crisis.*

He wended his way down Sackett Street, the sun just beginning its slow descent over the old rotting piers of Red Hook and the fuming grumble of traffic on the BQE. Without his quite admitting it, he'd begun to notice himself tensing up with the coming of night lately, paying more attention to following the same route home, becoming just slightly more aware of double-parked cars, of children running after balls in the street, of how long it took the city to fix the broken light in front of the house.

He locked the car and saw the curtains move in the neighbor's front window. The lady who lived there was the widow of a firefighter who'd died at the Trade Center. She had Jesus on a half shell near her front steps and honored her husband's memory by hardly ever speaking to Francis. Whether she was carrying on the great tradition of interdepartmental rivalry or silently asking God why he'd take her good man and let Francis live, he couldn't say.

He got the mail and went up the stoop, quickly shuffling the letters to see what aggravation awaited him. An oil bill, Con Ed, Patti's seed catalogs and yoga brochures, another bill from his father's nursing home upstate, and something from the Jewish Guild for the Blind. Probably a fund-raising solicitation. He started to put his key in the door, idly wondering how they got his name in the first place. Who would they go through? DMV, Detectives' Endowment Association, doctors' offices? The key ring slipped from around his finger just as he remembered seeing pamphlets for the guild and Lighthouse International in Dr. Friedan's waiting room.

I need this? He tore the letter in half and stuffed it in

his pocket, then bent down, looking for the keys, hoping the angry widow wouldn't look out and see him fumbling around like he was already blind.

The house was as quiet and dark as a mausoleum as he let himself in. He missed the kids blasting music at each other — Slayer versus the Indigo Girls — and Patti clanging around the kitchen, chatting to her girlfriends on the phone and getting dinner ready. He remembered she wouldn't be home until nine tonight because she was working late with clients at the gym again.

He started turning on lights and making as much noise as he could, a habit he'd had since he was ten, coming home from school to an empty house. He found the remote in the living room and put on CNN. Just in time to hear about a roadside bomb killing three soldiers outside Mosul. Jesus. He listened, with a grappling hook in the middle of his chest, waiting to hear if there was any word about more troops being called up from Korea. Fucking kid. Had to show the old man he couldn't pull rank anymore. *Got you there, Dad. Never fought in a real war, did you?* The boy had struggled to find himself. Never a good student like his younger sister, and not much of a prospect on the Bishop Ford baseball team. He'd been easy pickings for the local army recruiter, who'd told him he could make something of himself, defend his country, and get more pussy than Snoop Dog all at the same time. But for what? Weapons of Mass Destruction? Get the fuck out of here. That was the story of another underachiever trying to one-up the old man.

But what could you do about it now? You start a fight, you finish it. And if what was behind it was a little shaky, well, that just meant you had to fight harder. Besides, the guy they were after was an asshole, gassed a hundred thousand of his own people. The case against him needed a little help? *So what?* You knew he was up to no good anyway. They all were. Sometimes you just had to fill in the missing pieces for everyone else to see the whole picture. Didn't mean you were wrong, did it?

He turned off the set, not able to take the agitation, and started up the stairs. Thinking about reopening plea negotiations with the higher authority. *Okay, here's what I'm putting on the table. You keep my boy out of this war and I'll give up my driver's license in the next six months. I'll take five degrees off my vision and a chronic pain condition to be named later. I'll even start going to confession again. Forgive me, Father, I have sinned. It's been thirty-three years since my last confession. . . .*

You sleazy bastard. What right do you have to a better deal? How about showing a little gratitude? You could have been dead a half-dozen times over the years. Falling down that flight of stairs at the Baruch Houses. That kid stepping out from behind a Datsun on Lenox Avenue and dry-clicking three times on you with a Browning, the barrel maybe a yard and a half from your face. Almost falling down an airshaft on 132nd Street, chasing a rapist over a rooftop.

Sometimes those moments seemed more real than the fact that he was here, in this stolid old house, with this spectacular woman, who'd forgiven him for all the spectacularly stupid things he'd done. More real than the fact they'd had two children, who used to sit on his lap watching old John Wayne movies long after they should've been in bed on a school night. Maybe he was actually lying at the bottom of that airshaft, and this was all just a dying man's dream.

He stopped on the landing, resting for a moment. He

wondered if this would still be a good house for him in a few years. A fair number of steps, but so what? He was losing his eyesight, not his legs. The more immediate problem would be all the little scars and dings he wouldn't see until Patti pointed them out. Constant vigilance being one of the hidden costs of owning an old house. You had to look out for chipped wainscoting, nails sticking out of the floorboards, towel racks coming away from the walls. How would he be able to handle a hacksaw or an acetylene torch when he needed a Seeing Eye dog just to get a quart of milk from around the corner?

He put his jacket on a hanger in the bedroom closet and went into the bathroom to wash up. A cool glob of water pinged on his scalp as he stood before the sink, a direct hit on the bald spot, reminding him that it was supposed to rain on and off again tonight and he still hadn't found that leak in the roof. Dripping since April. Where was the water getting in? He figured he'd have about forty-five minutes to get up there and have a look around before it got too dark.

You keep asking yourself, what did I do? He patted his head with a washcloth, brooding on what Eileen said. *It must be something I did.*

Not me, sister. He didn't have anything in the record that he couldn't stand up to. Well, nothing he couldn't really live with. He went through the litany again, just to reassure himself. You've been a good husband (after a couple of early stumbles out of the blocks), a good provider, a good father, *a good cop.*

It wasn't as if this Hoolian thing had been lodged in his brain like a splinter all these years. Everybody had a couple of calls that might have seemed a little questionable when you looked back on them. But it was what it was.

You live the life you live, and it's up to somebody else to add it up and give you the bill at the end.

Those were savage times and he was the man for them. Two thousand murders a year in the city: babies shot to death in their cribs, lawyers stabbed on the subway, doctors slaughtered in their living rooms. You don't send for the Jesuits. You send someone who's willing to man the barriers. Life and death, it's not for the quibblers and hairsplitters. The state penal code never helped a broken heart. The Fourth Amendment never comforted a family that lost a loved one. Sometimes you had to put your precious little guidebook aside and operate in the gray-zone threshold.

Did you actually see him put the gun in his pocket, Officer? No, I observed the outline through his jacket. *Did you actually see him exchange the money for drugs?* Well, how the hell else do you think they got in his pocket?

Each time he'd told himself he wasn't going to do it again, knowing he was coming closer and closer to crossing the line and not being able to get back. He was a good man, a good cop. So why the hell had he done it? They probably already had enough to make the case. Hoolian's fingerprints on the murder weapon, the keys to the victim's apartment in his pocket. But at that crucial moment, when no one was looking, he'd found himself picking up that bloody tampon that had somehow ended up on the floor near the fire hose, as if it had been dragged there, stuck to the bottom of the murderer's shoe, and he deposited into the bathroom trash can inside Hoolian's apartment less than twelve feet away.

Over the years, he'd replayed that scene in his head a half-dozen times, asking himself why it had happened. Each time all he could recall was how scared he'd been.

Of course, he was afraid of getting caught, but it was more than that. He must have been afraid *not* to do it, he realized now. He must have been afraid of failing, of everyone seeing that, in fact, he was not the man to be entrusted with the Job.

He opened the medicine-cabinet door and closed it. *Fuck it.* Just like in a war, you couldn't always wait for absolute proof. And besides, they were all guilty of something, weren't they?

But in twenty years since then, he'd never stepped over the line again. Something about hearing that kid's father cry out when the judge said, "Twenty-five to life," had put the fear of God back into him. He'd been put on notice.

Whether he wanted to admit it or not, he'd changed after that. Not all at once, but by degrees. Stopped drinking and fucking around, started spending more time with the kids and making amends to Patti. And made damn sure he never locked another man up without giving him a fair shake. By every measure, he'd done his penance. So why did he still keep feeling this heavy hand resting on his heart?

He left the bathroom and saw the answering machine blinking on the night table. Too soon to be hearing back from Dave at the ME's office, so his thoughts wandered back to Eileen again. *Children have secrets.* Whatever that meant. He wondered if he was missing something along the sides again. Same blood twenty years later. *Come on, God of Small Things, give us a hint.* A partial print on a water glass. A bloodstain on a carpet fiber. A speck of Hoolian's DNA on one of Christine's washcloths. Not that he was angling for any particular result this time. *I'm through playing God,* he told himself. The hours are no good and the benefits are lousy. *Just help me get it right this time.*

The phone rang before he could press the Playback button. He snatched it off the cradle, hoping it was Rashid calling with good news from the warehouse, and growled, "Yo." But there was only a hiss cresting and fading, like snow falling in a stiff wind.

"Anybody there?"

He looked down at the caller ID box on the phone and saw the word "Unavailable."

"Look, whoever this is, I don't need your shit right now. I'm off the clock. You got a beef, call me at work with all the other assholes."

He heard the pressure of a light breath coming through the line and noticed the room suddenly seemed chillier.

"All right, fuck you then."

He hit the Off button and tossed the phone on the bed. Then thought better of it and tried to *69 the number, without success. *Okay by me. I ain't afraid of no ghosts.* He went to the window to see how much daylight he had left. The glass under his fingertips was cool and lightly fogged, as if someone had just been breathing on it from the other side. Clouds hung low over the river, bits of gray matter half shading the Manhattan office towers. And from the other room, he heard water dripping from the ceiling and splattering in the sink at odd intervals.

31

HOOLIAN WATCHED THE rain come down like a hundred thousand fishing lines and then crouched before Zana's bathroom again, still trying to hang the door for her.

"Whoever did this before must've been smoking angel dust," he said. "Look how the hinges are lined up wrong."

"Hmm." She stood a few feet away, hands tucked under her armpits, watching him with those wide brown eyes, probably hoping he wouldn't make things worse than they were already.

She lived on the second floor of an old unrehabilitated building in Red Hook, a waterfront neighborhood cut off from the rest of Brooklyn by the expressway. Cranes and cargo loaders loomed like dinosaurs along the piers. The streets had cobblestones and names like Pioneer, Verona, King, Beard, Coffey, and Visitation Place, and there seemed to be someone lingering in a warehouse doorway every block or two, suggesting he do things that probably weren't in his own best interest. Even in the rain he could see part of the Statue of Liberty through her window, and every once in a while a tugboat sounded its horn as it passed through Buttermilk Channel nearby.

Zana had done what she could with the place, hanging brightly colored scarves in the open doorways, lighting candles everywhere, covering holes in the walls with black-and-white cartoon panels she'd drawn of stark little figures wandering intrepidly into canyonlike alleyways and paintings of babies in jars, which on closer examination turned out to be the same woman at different stages of life, always suspended in formaldehyde.

"You don't have a drill by any chance, do you?"

She went into the other room and came back with an electric Black & Decker, a quarter-inch bit already in it.

"Why is it that you got all these tools around and no idea how to use them?" he asked, plugging it in and watching the wall outlet carefully to see if sparks came out.

"He was a carpenter."

"Who?"

"The man I was with previously. My husband."

"Your *husband?*" He almost dropped the drill. "What's that? How come you never mentioned him before?"

"He's irrelevant to the circumstances. We're no longer married."

"Uh-*huh.*"

He gunned the drill twice and looked at her, trying to figure out what to say. He felt like he'd just caught another man going through the things in his cell. He turned and started boring a new hole in the jamb, busying himself before he did something stupid.

"He was from my town," she explained. "My parents knew his parents. You know how it is. They thought he could take care of me after what happened back home.

But then we come to America, and he can't even take care of himself."

He put the gun down and blew sawdust out of the hole, trying to see how deep it went. "How do you mean?"

"He is big-time asshole," she sighed. "There's nothing more to say about it."

Drugs, he figured, trying to stay cool. That seemed to be the answer to about one out of three questions that came up on the outside as well as inside. "At least he left you some of his tools." He picked up the tape measure she'd given him, pretending he wasn't that bothered.

"Among other things . . ."

She looked out the window, more interested in the weather than in this topic.

"So you divorced now?"

"Naturally." She waved at someone outside. "I see him with as little frequency as possible."

"You must've been young."

He held a hinge up to the jamb and made a mark for where the second screw would go, telling himself that this was how mature people on the outside dealt with these things.

"Everyone is young. This only excuses so much."

He picked up the drill and started making another hole. He thought of all the other things he should've been doing right now to help himself. He should've been doing more research; he should've been looking for more alibi witnesses. At the very least, he should've been looking for another job or writing more letters to his father's union, to see if he was entitled to any benefits. But here he was again, Hoolian the sucker, unable to resist a woman in need.

"So how long you lived here anyway?" he said, releasing

the trigger and letting the shrill whine die away. "Doesn't seem like you have a lot of family or friends around."

"Just a few months," she said. "Before, I am up on Pelham Parkway in the Bronx, but that was almost like being back home. All these people who know my family— I couldn't stand it. I had to move. My mother cries and cries, but I say, '*Meme,* why you bugging? We're in America. *Shtendosem.* Chill.'"

"Yep. Can't blame someone for wanting a clean start."

"So you think you can fix this door? This would be good, to have privacy."

"Yeah, I think it'll be all right." He measured the distance between the upper and lower hinges, glad to have his hands occupied. "But who did this work over here? I see somebody just tried to put on some wood putty. It still hasn't dried."

"My husband. Everything he does is off by a few inches."

He turned around slowly. "I thought you never saw him after you moved from the Bronx."

"He comes over sometimes. But only by necessity."

"I see." He let the tongue of the tape measure snap back into place and dropped it on the floor.

It dawned on him that there were a couple of other rooms in the apartment she hadn't shown him yet. He sniffed and glanced into the bathroom, as if he could pick up the scent of another man living there. His muscles gathered in as he thought of what he would do if it turned out he was being played for a chump again.

"Well, next time you see him, tell him he should leave a tool alone if he doesn't know how to use it."

But instead of listening to him, she'd abruptly left the room, drawn by the sound of keys in the front door.

The jangling went straight to his nerve endings as the door closed. He heard her giggling and talking to someone in a high playful voice she'd never used with him.

He got down on one knee and tried to line up the lower hinge, realizing he'd been used again. He should just walk out and leave her without a bathroom door, he told himself. Let some other fool deal with her problems. Or he could start running his mouth and sticking his chest out when his rival walked in, knowing he had a drill in hand as a weapon. But instead, he decided he'd finish the work, the way Papi would have, just to show up his rival. Say, *see,* this is how a man would do it. And then turn around and walk out, like the gunfighter riding high in the saddle.

"Hey, you wanna get me a screwdriver so I can finish this shit?" he called out, dropping his voice a half-octave to let the interloper know he was here.

"A moment, please," Zana answered, before she started whispering conspiratorially to her guest.

It was too much, he decided. He couldn't stay. He hadn't survived things that would've killed other men ten times over just to be treated with this much disrespect. He half rose from his crouch, bracing for a head-on collision.

But then the curtain between the two rooms moved and instead of the stoned oaf he'd expected, a little boy emerged, no more than four or five years old. He moved with lurching eager haplessness, as if the arches of his feet weren't fully formed and the size of his head was pitching him forward. His eyes were a little too big for his face and his skin had that familiar, potato-pale sallowness. Hoolian looked back at Zana behind him, confirming the mother-son resemblance, only then registering that the kid was bringing him a flathead screwdriver with the point aimed down at the floor.

32

THE MOON WAS packed in heavy clouds when Patti came up through the hatch and found Francis on the roof in near-total darkness, his flashlight slowly moving across the tarred seams.

"Crime Scene Unit?" she asked.

"That leak above the bathroom sink again. Driving me crazy."

She went over and huddled against him. "You're cold. You weren't out here when it was raining before, were you?"

"I caught some of it. It's supposed to rain more later."

He turned toward Manhattan, the lights as dim and blurry to him now as underwater lamps. He remembered how he used to love to come up here and look at them, knowing that each illuminated window was part of the city's vast genetic code, a pattern that only gods and urban planners were meant to understand.

"Don't you think it's kind of hard to find a leak in the dark?"

"The best time to look is right after it rains." His beam

wandered aimlessly. "Water could be coming in from anywhere."

A passing bus below sighed, sagging with the loneliness of late-night riders.

"So, what's going on?" she asked.

"You know how I been going nuts about this weird-ass thing that happened at the lab?"

"Yeah, you were looking for Julian Vega's DNA and found samples from the same female on both victims instead."

"Exactly. So I got a sample off Eileen Wallis, just so we could eliminate her daughter, Allison, as the source." He skipped telling her about the subterfuge with the handkerchief, knowing that as a former prosecutor she'd bust his balls for it.

"But why do you need to do that? She's dead, isn't she?"

"Of course, but we still have to go through all the steps to make sure nobody screwed up and mislabeled the victim's blood."

"And?"

"I just got a call from David Abramowitz at the ME's office on my cell." He took a deep breath, still trying to absorb what he'd been told. "The results came back. Eileen Wallis is the mother of the woman whose blood was found at both crime scenes."

"*What?*"

"You heard me right. It's her daughter."

"Wait." Patti touched his shoulder. "Explain this to me."

"Okay. There was blood under the victim's fingernails in the '83 homicide, like she scratched her assailant. So at first, we thought that might be Hoolian's DNA. But when we compared it with some blood of Allison's that was left on a pillowcase, it turned out to be a match, both from her."

"I'm with you so far," said Patti. "She bled all over the place."

"Fine. It happens. The problem is that Dave had already done a comparison with DNA scraped from under Christine's fingernails just the other day. I'd asked him to do it, thinking it would turn out to be Julian in both cases and we could nail him that way. Instead, the scrapings matched the female DNA on Allison's pillowcase."

"Uh-oh."

"Right. So then we realized we needed to go back and be sure that the blood that was labeled Allison's on the pillowcase really belonged to her in the first place. Otherwise, we're just proceeding from a false premise. So we get a sample from her mother, and what do we find? Not only is it her daughter's blood on the pillowcase, it's also her daughter's blood under Christine Rogers's fingernails."

"Wait a minute, wait a minute." Patti waved her hands. "I thought she had only one daughter. I didn't know she had any others."

"She just told me she doesn't."

"Oh *shit.*"

There was a loud pop and they both jumped. Boys' laughter echoed up from the bodega on the corner, and Francis realized someone had just set off a small firecracker on a metal garbage can lid.

"I'm lost, Patti," he admitted. "I am totally fucking lost."

"But how is this possible? You're telling me that you

found Allison Wallis's skin cells under Christine Rogers's fingernails, twenty years after her funeral?"

"It does appear that way."

"And what's the margin for error?" she said, starting to think analytically again after all these years away from the DA's office.

"None, unless there's an identical twin."

"Somebody's messing with you," she said.

"That's a given."

"I mean, somebody's *really* messing with you. I've never heard of anything like this."

He nodded grimly. "I've got this kid from the one-nine I'm working with, Rashid. He's back out at the warehouse tonight, looking to see if he can come up with anything else that has Allison's blood on it. His sister is friends with a girl who works the lobster shift. But truthfully, I don't know what I'm going to do if he finds another match that proves it's Allison's DNA under Christine's fingernails."

"You sure you buried the right girl back in '83?"

"Oh for Chrissakes, Patti, now you sound like Eileen Wallis. . . ."

"Why, what's she saying?"

"'Allison's not dead'. Somebody else's out in Cricklewood."

He swung the flashlight beam, and it left a trail in the darkness like a trout moving through black water.

"There's gotta be another daughter." Patti shook her head. "Unless the brother's a woman in drag or something."

"I've stood next to him at a urinal. He's got everything I got."

"Then Eileen's lying to you."

"Why would she do that?"

"Who the hell knows? You told me she was crazy."

"Yeah, but what am I going to do? How do you find somebody who's not supposed to exist? If Eileen had another daughter that she isn't telling anybody about, the girl's probably got a different name, a whole different identity. Finding her is going to be like finding somebody out there."

He pointed his beam out toward where the Manhattan skyline used to be, the coded pattern changing and evolving moment by moment.

"Are you a real detective or what?" Patti nudged him. "You're looking for a suspect and you already have the mother's DNA. What do you think you're going to do? Feed it through the state and federal systems and see if you get a hit. If you're talking about somebody who's killed two people in the last twenty years, there's a good chance they got arrested for something else at least once."

He put the flashlight under her chin, illuminating her from below like the Lincoln Memorial.

"Pretty sharp, lady," he said.

"A lot of things become much more obvious in this world when you have a vagina."

He nodded, acknowledging the universal truth of this even as he began to fall into despair again. "Problem is, I don't know what we do if we come up empty on that. I guess we could do a system-wide search of marriage licenses and birth records, to see if Eileen was married before or gave a kid up for adoption without telling anyone. But the thing is, if she's lying now about having another kid, she probably lied then and used a different name."

"Then I don't know how you're going to figure it out."

He swept the beam through the air, no longer able to see more than two feet in front of his face. Darkness had snuck up on him. He'd come up here thinking maybe he could catch a few last minutes of daylight, but then the night suddenly collapsed in on him.

"Francis," she said quietly. "I want to ask you something."

"What?"

"Does this mean you put the wrong guy away?"

He saw the light flicker slightly and shook the flashlight, hoping the batteries weren't dying.

"You don't know that and neither do I," he said too quickly. "I still think Hoolian had something to do with it. It's too much of a coincidence, Christine talking about him all the time and collecting stories about his case."

"So, what are you saying, that it's a . . . *conspiracy?*" she asked, like she was about to tell him to go sleep off a hangover on the couch.

"I don't know what it is. I'm just saying I didn't send any innocent guy to the can for twenty years."

"Sound awfully sure of yourself, for somebody who doesn't have all the facts yet."

"Hey, I did my job," he insisted. "I gave the case to the DA and he gave it to the jury and then *they* decided on the evidence. That's all there was to it. I was just part of the process."

She took his hand and squeezed it tighter than he would have liked.

"Let the chips fall where they have to," he said. "I can handle it."

"I hope that's so, Francis."

He let go of her hand. "I'm gonna sleep *fine* once this is over."

"Okay. I'll have to take your word."

He heard her moving away from him, going back toward the hatch and the ladder.

"Coming down to bed?" she called out.

He took a step and almost stumbled over that tar bucket he'd meant to take down while the sun was up.

The darkness gave him no quarter, no hints where to turn. It wiped out Manhattan, blotted out the stars and swallowed the neighbors' windows. It was alive with the menace of unseen things: car alarms, ambulance sirens, low-flying airplanes, squealing brakes, ranting derelicts, shattering glass.

"I can't."

"What?"

"I said, I can't. I can't move from where I am."

"Why not?"

"Because I can't find my way down from here, baby," he said. "I can't see a fucking thing."

33

SEE, THIS IS how it was."

Hoolian spread the subway map out on the hardwood floor as Zana's son, Eddie, sat on his lap, still playing with the screwdriver.

"So every Saturday morning, when those other kids were still sleeping, my papi would get me up real early with buttered rolls and *café con leche* and take me riding on the trains."

The heavy little head rested back against his chest and he started to trace the long colored lines with his finger.

"We tried to take a different line every time so it would be like an adventure. Sometimes we'd go looking for ghost stations."

The kid looked back over his shoulder and wrinkled his nose.

"You don't know about those?" Hoolian asked. "There are these abandoned stations that everyone has forgotten about. So, like, if you turn your head real fast when the downtown six goes around the turnaround loop, you can see they built this beautiful grotto under City Hall, with brass chandeliers and this fancy Guastavino tile on the walls. My father said if you were on the train late at night sometimes, you could see the ghosts in their party clothes dancing and drinking champagne."

The boy scrunched up his face again, trying to imitate cynicism, but his eyes were shining.

"But my favorite was always St. John the Baptist Day," Hoolian went on, knowing the kid was in his thrall. "See, every summer, Papi would take me on the F train out to Coney Island to go on all the rides and all that. But at the end of the day, we'd go down to the beach and join all these other people gathered along the shore to walk backward into the ocean. It was like this cleansing ritual to wash bad luck away."

He fell silent a moment, remembering. The old man had never been that big on tradition, but it broke his heart not being allowed to walk backward into the water with his son one last time. The state made Hoolian start his sentence before *el Día de San Juan Baustista* that year.

"Eddie." Zana came in from the kitchen with a sponge. "*Ba.*"

"No, *Meme*," he said, pleading for time.

"Go," his mother insisted. "Make like the trees and beat it."

He turned and hugged Hoolian, as if it were part of some nightly routine the two of them had been doing for years. Then he jumped up and scampered to the bath, with no inkling he'd just torn a chunk of insulation off a grown man's heart.

"So how come you didn't tell me you had a kid?" Hoolian looked after him, wondering how it had happened so fast.

"This is not appealing to many men."

Hoolian heard the bath start to run and he drifted into the kitchen to help her finish washing the dishes.

"I appreciate that you allowed him to assist you," Zana said. "This is good for him to see a big man working. Not like his father, who is completely a bum. He likes you."

That's understating it, Hoolian thought. The kid had jumped all over him, bringing him tools and water, making unsolicited suggestions about how to plane the corners and shim the hinge sides, staring up in awe when the door swung open cleanly for the first time.

"So who watches him during the day?"

"My neighbor Ysabel has a little girl, 'bout the same age, so we trade off. She's my dope fly homegirl."

She smiled shyly, revealing a small space between her two front teeth. Yet somehow it brought her whole face to life and it thrilled him a little, knowing she'd just shown him something she didn't show most people.

"Yeah, I used to help my papi out when I was his age. That's the only way I learned to do anything with my hands."

"Haven't you ever wanted your own?"

"Oh, sure." He picked up a rag and started drying dishes. "I think I'd make a hell of a father. They say you pass down whatever you get to the next generation."

"So why haven't you done it?" She passed him a plate.

"What?"

"Had children, at your age? What's holding you back?"

"I dunno. Just never worked out."

"I don't believe this." She turned off the hot water and faced him. "You are either gay man or you are in love with another woman. No one is nothing."

"I'm not gay," he said, crossing his arms in front of his chest and then uncrossing them, lest he look effeminate.

"Then what are you? You are telling me there was never anyone?"

"I don't want to get into it."

"I knew it," she said.

"It was a long time ago."

"She hurt you?"

"I don't know why everything has to be somebody's fault. Sometimes things just happen."

He took a sponge and attacked the dinner table with the coarse side, going after tomato stains and dried spaghetti strands.

"No, I don't think this is so," she said. "Someone is always the victim."

"Well, I'm trying to learn not to look at things that way."

He finished wiping the table and went into the other room, hearing that Eddie was out of the bath and watching *Sesame Street Visits the Firehouse* in the back.

Pale yellow light from a half-dozen votive candles snapped and retreated at shadows, giving the living room a kind of eerie warm subterranean aura marred only by the sound of Fireman Bob singing "Waiting for the Bell to Ring."

"Do you still think about her?" Zana stood in the doorway.

"Sometimes." He sat down on the fold-out couch, looking for his work boots and trying to decide if it was time to go. "And then sometimes I don't want to think about her at all."

"So you are still in love with her?"

"What makes you say that?"

"It sounds that way."

The candle before him stuttered, a small orange blade digging at the dark.

"She's dead."

She started across the floor and then stopped halfway. "For real?"

"Yes. For real. A long time ago. Seriously messed me up."

"But what happened?"

"Something really fucked up. Would you mind if we didn't talk about it?"

The flame before him wavered. He was sure she would press him now. And then he would either have to lie to her or tell the truth and ruin everything. Candle wax guttered into the saucer. A part of him longed to give it up and get it over with. His heart was only going to end up punctured and shredded anyway. But the other part yearned to pretend just a little while longer.

"But someday will you tell me?"

He made a sound deep in his throat, not yes or no. He half hoped she would hear the warning in it and know enough to stay back.

"Well, I think it's sad," she said.

"What?"

"To have such a good heart and no one to give it to."

"Who said I had a good heart?"

He heard the bare soles of her feet peeling off the floorboards, one at a time. She should go to the door now and open it for him. That instinct that got her out of wherever she was from was kicking in here. She knew the truth without hearing all the details: he was too damaged to be any good to anyone. He put on his boots and stood up, ready to make his excuses and go.

But instead, she stopped in front of him, blocking him and staring up at his face. He felt the warmth of her body nearly touching his and an almost painful longing threatened to pull him apart. He tried to hang on, telling himself this couldn't be right. It must be a trick, another setup. What could she be seeing in him? He was supposed to be alone. He was supposed to be untouchable. Love was supposed to pass him by. The candles crackled and Mr. Monster in the next room cried out that his house was on fire. The rest of his insulation was melting.

He put his arms around her gingerly, sure she would push him back. Instead, her knee came up between his thighs and he felt a combination of joy and terror rise up inside him. Her hand came to rest on the back of his neck and her body pressed into him, imprinting him with the shape of her desire. Twenty years of keeping his guard up and never letting it down, of mistrusting all pleasure and always expecting the worst, of struggling and striving to keep his most powerful urges under wraps.

And just like that, she snuck her tongue past his lips and undid him as easily as a child undoing a shoelace.

34

FRANCIS LOOKED UP at the ceiling, a grown man a few months shy of fifty. An almost First Grade detective with twenty-five years on the job and a half-dozen commendations. Injured three times in the line of duty and never missed more than a month of work. He'd even killed a guy once. A parolee named Arturo Cruz jacked up on coke and Cuervo who'd charged him with a Stanley knife right after he'd stabbed his estranged wife to death. Francis, fourteen months out of the academy, pulled the trigger twice and dropped him in the hallway of an Avenue C tenement. Not his happiest memory, but you do what you have to do and fuck the begrudgers and second-guessers. Since then, he'd locked up psychopaths, throat-slicers, child molesters, capos, gangbangers, wannabes, and cut-price contract killers. He'd done a three-month-long undercover operation on a majorweight heroin dealer in Loisaida, who'd then been heard swearing on a wiretap that he'd have Francis's head severed for testifying against him. Instead of asking for protection, he went to court the next day and laughed in that fool's face.

But now he was here, in his own home, in his own bed, next to the mother of his children, scared of the dark.

"You must think you're pretty slick," said Patti.

"What do you mean?"

"The way you covered up. Moving furniture around. Leaving the light on in the hall. Having me drive when the lighting's bad. I thought maybe you were drinking again."

He tried to spoon her. "I didn't mean to lie to you, hon."

"No, of course not. You just neglected to mention the fact that you're going blind."

She sat up and turned on the reading lamp.

"How long?" she said, shining it in his eyes and giving him the third degree.

"I don't know. I guess I'd been noticing it awhile before I went to the doctor —"

"*No*, Francis. How long until you can't see anymore?"

He saw she was studying his eyes closely, as if she could actually see the bony spicules accumulating.

"Not for a long time, probably. It's not like flesh-eating strep or anything."

"But you had an uncle who had this, didn't you? You told me he was always yelling at you for stealing his lighter when it was right in front of him."

"Yeah, but he was a royal pain in the ass. I'm not going to be like that. You know me. I can take care of myself."

"So is that all?" she said. "Have you got anything else you want to lay on me? Brain cancer? Liver failure?"

"No. You're just going to be married to a blind man. Like Ray Charles without the music. I think that's probably enough, for the moment."

"Fuck you, Francis. You think that's funny? What'd you do, tell your friends at Coogan's before you told me?"

"No, I haven't told anybody. I figured if I didn't say anything, it wouldn't really be happening."

"I'm *your wife*." She pulled the covers off him. "I'm the one who's going to have to fill out all the insurance forms and take you to the doctors. Didn't you think I had a right to know?"

He heard the rain pelting the windows and listened for the leak in the bathroom, dreading each little splat in the sink.

"So are you going to leave me now?" he asked.

"What?"

"I'm just saying it's an option. You didn't sign up to be the helpmate for the handicapped."

She propped up on an elbow. "You really think I'd do that?"

"You get out soon enough, no one's going to accuse you of abandoning ship. God knows, you could've done it a hundred times before and no one would've blamed you."

"Jesus Christ, Francis, I'm not your mother."

He grimaced as if she'd raked her nails across his face.

"I guess I had that coming."

"I'm sorry." She pinched the bridge of her nose. "That was uncalled-for. All I meant to say was, you're not going to lose me."

He put his arms around her in quiet gratitude. But at the same time, he wondered how long she'd really abide him. You could say all the right things, make all the loving supportive gestures, but at the end of the evolutionary day, the male of the species was supposed to take care of the female. Soon enough she'd start to notice that even the simplest things they used to do together were becoming an ordeal. A night at the movies. A romantic dinner in a dark restaurant. A stroll in the park at dusk. Pity would bind them together awhile, but eventually the cord would start to fray. She'd lose patience. It would get on her nerves always having to drive, always needing to point out when something was smoking on the stove, having to make excuses when he walked by old friends on the street without recognizing them. Gradually, they'd begin to grow apart, becoming strangers in adjacent spaces, one light and one dark.

"So you really haven't talked to anyone on the Job about this?"

"No."

"So, what's going to happen the next time you have to drive at night?"

"I'm still getting around pretty good," he said. "In fact, *you* didn't know anything was wrong until tonight."

"And what about if you have to draw your gun?"

"I can't remember the last time I had to do that. . . ."

He looked up again, thinking how he used to be able to see all four corners of the ceiling while he was flat on his back; the turn-of-the-century detailing around the border, the vent above the closet, that odd little vestigial fixture for the old gas line by the window. But now everything was black except for a small circle of light the bedside lamp made over his head.

"Look, I'm not *that* irresponsible," he said.

"So when are you going to tell them?"

He tried to take a deep breath, but his lungs felt like they'd shriveled to the size of dried apricots.

"I always said I was going to turn in my papers right

after I got the bump in April." He caressed the back of her hair. "An extra five thou a year, and last I heard those New England colleges weren't lowering the cost of tuition."

Everything after that was beyond the edge of the map. What exactly was he supposed to do with himself once he retired? He'd been trying to think about it practically these past few weeks. Those corporate-security jobs he'd wanted to apply for on Wall Street were out of reach: not much call for a surveillance expert with a progressive eye disease. He wouldn't even be able to get a blazer-and-slacks gig making people show their IDs in the lobby. The circle of light over his head closed in a little. He certainly wouldn't be spending a lot of time playing golf with other ex-cops. And forget that sailboat he'd talked about buying a few years back. He probably wouldn't even be much use helping Patti out with the garden in the backyard.

"Don't you think you should tell them sooner?"

"Absolutely not."

"Why not?"

"I'm in the middle of two major cases, Patti. What do you want me to do, walk away?"

"Sure. There's other people in the squad who could take over."

"*No.* They're mine. These are my cases. I'm responsible."

"That's just your ego talking."

"You say that like it's a *bad* thing." He put a hand over his heart, like he was offended. "That ego's been very good to me."

"Don't be an asshole."

"All right." He raised his hands, starting over in earnest. "You asked me before, how I was going to feel if it turned out I locked up the wrong guy. Right?"

She nodded cautiously, wary of entrapment.

"So I'm just trying to make sure everything's done right. I'm not letting anybody take the files off my desk and start criticizing the way I ran these investigations."

She sat up abruptly and hugged her knees. "Francis, is there something else you haven't told me?"

"No. Like what?"

"I know you. I know when you're holding out on me— at least, I thought I did. Did something go on between you and this guy Julian that you haven't told me about?"

He looked up and saw that the circle of light over his head seemed to have shrunk a little more.

"What are you asking me here, Patti?"

She let the question sit awhile. He heard the leak in the bathroom starting up again. This was what you got for sleeping with a former prosecutor.

"I'm asking, did you do something you shouldn't have done back then?" she said in a low deliberate voice.

He forced himself to look at her, knowing he was scaring her a little. In twenty-two years, he'd asked her to put up with a lot. He'd made her stretch and accept things in her life that she should have balked at and maybe thrown him out for. And each time, somehow, she'd moved back the walls and found space in her heart to accommodate him. Like making special ramps and access points for the handicapped. But this was too much. She couldn't hear what he had to say and still love him. If she tried to make herself large enough to take it in, she'd break. And so he decided he wouldn't ask her to.

"Baby, all I'm saying is, let me finish what I started. Okay? Don't take me out of the fight. If something went wrong in this case, let me be the one to fix it. You know there'll be no living with me otherwise."

"There's already no living with you."

She rolled over and turned off the light. They lay next to each other in the dark, the rain like a jackpot hitting the storm windows.

"Francis?" She gave him a gentle tug under the sheets.

"What?"

"Just try to be a good man, all right?"

35

TWENTY YEARS IN state prison didn't do much for most men's lovemaking skills. Most of the action Hoolian had seen involved either porn mags or the visiting room, where guards would routinely have to break up under-the-table hand jobs and furtive humping. Not having connections with live women on the outside, Hoolian couldn't set up conjugal visits. Instead, his first month at Attica, he'd found himself alone in the showers with a big buck called Dirty D., who'd stood under the needle spray, staring at him and soaping his dick over and over until Hoolian asked, "What's up, man?" And then that old booty bandit just bowed a leg to soap inside a crevice and replied, *What do you think is up?*

He'd barely managed to get out of that one with just a broken nose and a chipped tooth; fortunately after that, he'd come under the protection of a drug lord named Ronnie Raygun and a few other gang guys he was giving legal advice to. Meanwhile, that need never went away. It always seemed to come up at the worst times. First thing in the morning, last thing at night, daydreaming in the kitchen, seeing the shapes of breasts and buttocks in clouds over the exercise yard. How many times had he almost sawed off a finger or put a nail through his knuckle because he was distracted in woodshop? It seemed like whole years would pass when he'd done nothing but fantasize about women and the only reliable source of information he had about pleasing them was a book passed around the cellblock called *Lesbian Sex Secrets for Men.*

So he was on a hair trigger the first time Zana touched him. No sense of rhythm or restraint at all — just disgraced himself immediately.

"Are you okay?" The way she touched his shoulder afterward and smiled in subversive sympathy just made it worse.

"Yeah, it's been a while."

"I can tell." She half smiled and started to turn away, her thin shoulder blades vibrating a little. "Don't worry about it. . . ."

"Are you laughing at me?" he asked.

"No, of course not."

"Yes, you are." He felt himself start to dissolve in an acid bath of humiliation. "Why don't you look at me?"

"I'm looking for my shirt."

"I'm saying, look at *me.*"

He suddenly grabbed her and pushed her down on the sofa bed, forgetting about her kid sleeping in the next room. She bucked and tried to kick him off.

"What are you doing?"

He had something to prove now. He grabbed her ankles and buried his face between her legs. Her back arched, like she had a scream caught halfway up in her chest.

"Noo, not like this . . . ," she gasped.

He felt her squirm and grab a fistful of hair from the

back of his head. He braced himself, sure she was about to start hollering for the police. But before he could get his hand over her mouth, she rolled over a little and slid a cushion under her ass.

"There," she said, presenting herself on the platform. "Much better."

Tentatively, he began to nose around, an explorer getting oriented. Everything looked and smelled just a little different than he expected it to. Not bad at all, but more . . . human. He understood instinctively he shouldn't jerk around or move too quickly. Patience was the one thing he had, and gradually he began to find his way. His tongue coming out to touch and probe. His fingertips learning the dynamics of her body. There was more music in her than he'd expected. He heard a sharp intake of breath and thought he might have hurt her. But then she closed her thighs around his ears and put a hand on the back of his head.

He tried to concentrate on the places that seemed to amuse and sometimes even delight her, slowly inscribing a secret alphabet with the tip of his tongue. After a few minutes, he noticed things becoming more humid. The arch of her foot touched the small of his back. She said things he didn't recognize. *"Shume mire."* A hum started to rise from the back of her throat.

He steadied himself on her thighs, dwelling on the letter O, gradually enlarging it into widening circles. She grabbed the back of his hair with greater urgency this time, wrapping her legs around his shoulders and then raising her hips to meet him again and again, riding the waves until finally she stayed at the top of the arc as long as she could, the scream stuck in her chest seeming to hoist her up toward the ceiling.

When she finally came down, he was ready for her. He kissed her neck, her shoulders, her mouth, her collarbone, before she firmly took hold of him and put him where he'd always wanted to be.

And then all of a sudden, he was inside the mystery. Not just a man on the outside, making up myths. So the fucking finally began. First they tried to fuck their way around things they hadn't told each other yet. Then they tried to fuck the hands off the clock. They tried to fuck away bad memories. They tried to fuck like money and religion and national borders didn't matter. They tried to fuck past soreness and exhaustion. They tried to fuck like they were movie stars and not just two lonely people in a tenement apartment on Coffey Street. They tried to fuck like neither of them would ever fuck anybody else again.

Then they moved away from each other a little and listened to the rain going down into the storm drains under the windows. The city sleeping. The city snoring. The city rolling over on its side.

"You okay?" Hoolian asked after a while.

"Yes. I am . . . quite . . . sufficient."

He lay on his back and looked up, hearing a foghorn in the distance.

"How long?" she said finally.

"How long what?"

"How long since you've been with this other girl?"

"Ssshh." He threw his forearm across his brow. "Was I that bad?"

"No. Just very . . . *aggressive*."

"And is that good?"

"Usually I would prefer not to be fucked so vehemently, but . . . it's okay."

He heard truck wheels sluicing rainwater into the gutters.

"Twenty years," he said.

"Pardon?" He realized she was starting to fall asleep.

"I said, it's been twenty years since I tried to do that. . . ."

He could wake her right now and tell her everything. About the shanks and the showers, the flocks of geese flying past the guard towers, the way the vans smelled when you were getting transferred from one facility to another, vaguely aware that every time you went through a new set of gates, you were becoming more like the other men you were doing time with and less like people on the outside.

But then she curled up beside him and put her head next to his, so he could feel her cheek touching his ear and her warm breath on the side of his face. He couldn't do it. There was something too sweet and hopeful about this moment that he couldn't bear to disturb.

I don't want better. I don't want worse. Just keep it this way for a little while.

Once he told her, she would never lie so plainly naked beside him in moonlight, with the boy sleeping in the next room, the end of his loneliness almost in sight. She would never ask him over for dinner at a moment's notice or imagine him again as a surrogate father for the son he now realized he'd always wanted.

She would hear the whole story and she would pretend to believe, but then she'd ask him questions and wonder what else he hadn't told her. She'd flinch a little the next time he touched her and think of what she'd heard about men who'd been in prison. And then she'd stop returning his messages. And soon he'd find this was no longer a working number.

Water dribbled in the drains. The tugboat sounded its horn more faintly this time. Tomorrow he'd go back to being what he was. The sun would come out and reveal everything in a stark pitiless glare. All he wanted now was to stay this way for just a little longer, to dream awhile, at least until the rain let up.

PART V

COMPLICATED SHADOWS

PART IV

COMPLICATED
SHADOWS

36

A BUNCHA GUYS SITTING around an uptown office with their ties hanging down, like the tongues of panting hounds.

"Gotta start working the phones and computers today," Francis said to "Yunior" Barbaro, Rashid, and gray old Jimmy Ryan. "Make sure we're putting that DNA sample from under Christine's fingernails into every state and federal data bank we can find, see if we get a hit."

"We've been doing that since last night." Yunior swiveled his chair around defensively. "You think we're not going to check if the doer's been arrested before?"

"I'm just saying, think outside the box. Start calling around to different states to get birth records too. See if Eileen had another daughter she hasn't told us about."

"Yeah, good fuckin' luck," said Yunior, checking his cell phone.

It was one of those newfangled Nokias with all the bells and whistles that could give you the time, the date, instant text messaging, museum-quality pictures, and weather patterns in Indonesia, but couldn't get a call from one side of the street to the other in certain parts of the city. Like

Yunior himself, it was a shiny new model trying just a little too hard and somehow still not quite getting the job done.

"Hey, we know we're looking for a woman," said Francis. "We know she left a sample at the '83 crime scene as well. And we know she's related to Eileen Wallis."

The lieutenant on duty, Joe "Bodega Coffee" Martinez, ambled into the squad room. He was a doughy amiable guy Francis knew from back in Narcotics, when Joe was always disappearing right before a raid, saying, "I'm a go get coffee for everybody from the bodega on the corner." These days, his two ambitions were to keep the squad running smoothly and to eat at every high-quality steak house from one end of the country to the other — sort of like that old Burt Lancaster movie *The Swimmer*, with sirloins instead of swimming pools.

"Any word about the Big Dig?" Rashid looked up.

"That's a nega-tory," said the loo, patting his stomach. "Nobody wants to exhume Allison's body unless we really have to. Can you imagine how that's going to play in the *Post*?"

"Well, if Loughlin had bothered to check the toe tag before they planted the wrong girl, we wouldn't be running around now." Yunior snapped his cell phone shut.

"Hey, fuck you, Yunior. You'd need an extension ladder just to get up high enough to kiss my ass."

"Oh, here we go." Jimmy Ryan clapped his hands. "Katie, bar the door."

"Legend in his own mind," Yunior muttered.

"Ivy League pussy." Francis smiled with all his teeth.

"Come on, guys," said the lieutenant. "Can't we all just get along?"

Rashid shot him a look.

"Look," said Francis, letting the static fade for the

moment. "JC was just telling me to keep an open mind, don't get a hard-on for one guy, so let's freestyle it a little."

"What do you mean?" said the loo.

"Middle of the night last night I got to thinking." They didn't need to know about his little caper up on the roof and the bedroom interrogation afterward. "I'm just riffing here. All right?"

He was pleased to see that they all still subtly leaned toward him a little, like the actors in one of those old E. F. Hutton ads. *When Francis X. talks, people listen.*

"So I'm not completely writing Hoolian off, I'm just asking: Christine Rogers's parents said she was adopted. I-ight?"

Rashid nodded cautiously, confirming that Jimmy, Yunior, and the lieutenant knew it as well.

"Anybody checking out who her biological birth mother was?"

"*Shit.*" Yunior's face swelled up like a wad of bubblegum under his ninety-dollar haircut. "You're not serious."

"Course, I'm serious," said Francis. "We know there's some blood connection between these two cases and we have no idea who her real mother is. So we gotta look at everything."

"But people spend years trying to chase that crap down. You ever hear of confidentiality laws covering adoptions?"

"Then you better stop wasting time and start talking to Legal Affairs about getting around them," said Francis, waggling his eyebrows while the phone on his desk started to ring. "Not that I'm telling everyone what to do, God forbid."

"And why doesn't this guy do it?" Yunior eyed Rashid. "He's the one from the precinct."

"*Allahu akbar,* brother." Rashid gave him the Black Power fist. "Servants to the same master."

"Still doesn't make any fucking sense." Yunior turned back to Francis. "Allison was twenty-seven when she died in 1983. Christine turned the same age in February this year. That means she would've been seven years old when Allison was murdered."

"'Since these mysteries are beyond me, let's pretend we're organizing them.'" Francis started to reach for the phone. "Bet you never learned who said that at Dartmouth . . . *Hello* . . ."

"Francis Loughlin?"

"'At's my name. How can I help you, young lady?"

"Judy Mandel from the *Trib.*"

"Uhhh-huhh."

The rest of the task force scurried away as if a RADIOACTIVE sign had just been put around his neck, somehow sensing it was either the press or the brass on the line.

"I catch you at a bad time?"

"As a matter of fact . . ."

"Then I'll be quick." She sounded like the kind of high-strung girl who constantly had to remind herself to say please and thank you. "I'm working on a story about the link between the Allison Wallis and Christine Rogers cases."

"Are you now?" Francis switched the phone from one shoulder to the other, not about to fall into the old trick of confirming a story by agreeing with its premise. *And when did you stop beating your kids?*

"And who said they were connected?" He tried flipping her.

"Come on. We're both grown-ups here."

"Well, that's kind of presuming we're about to have a real conversation."

Somebody had talked. His eyes searched the room for likely suspects. Couldn't be Ryan. The only reporters he dealt with were the old Irish ones, guys who looked like they chased parked cars and shaved with the sidewalk. The lieutenant was a possibility, since he was such a steak whore. A filet mignon at Sparks could mean a week's worth of columns for an enterprising writer. Rashid was unlikely, since he was relatively new to the game. But Yunior was a possibility, since he always seemed to have some lissome young freelancer on the hook.

"Okay, if you don't want to talk to me, I'll just go with what I have," she said. "I'm going to feel bad, though, running a story that says you guys blew two cases without any comment from you."

The one train ran past the windows again, sending a light tremor through the squad room.

"You get permission to talk to me from Public Information?" Francis asked, taking care not to raise his voice.

"I thought we could keep this on background."

He slipped a discreet finger under his collar, knowing he didn't have a choice. "So, what is it you want to know anyway?"

"How'd you end up finding DNA from somebody who's been dead twenty years on the body of a victim from last week?"

Another train passed going the other way, rattling an empty Diet Coke can on the windowsill.

"Ah, that's bullshit." He laughed. "Somebody's putting you on."

"And why would they make up something like that?"

"I don't know what goes through a defense lawyer's mind," he said, still trying to smoke out her source. "I'm just saying, you're way out in left field here. What else you got?"

"I know you started off looking at Julian Vega for the Christine Rogers homicide."

He started fidgeting like a crackhead, pulling apart a paper clip and straightening its metal bends. Lots of ways she could've found out, he realized. The super at Christine's building could've tipped her off after they'd shown him a photo array with Hoolian's picture in it. Or somebody from Crime Scene could've dropped a dime. Even Hoolian himself could've worked out that something was up after Francis tried to sandbag him at the supermarket. Though why he would've told the press, Francis didn't know.

"We're looking at a lot of people," he said, twisting the ends of the clip together. "Doesn't mean anything."

"Then why've your guys been back and forth between the ME's office and the property clerk like a dozen times, trying to prove it's his DNA at both girls' crime scenes?"

"We're at those offices all the time. This is Homicide. We got a lot of different cases there."

Could Dr. Dave at the lab have given him up? Unlikely. You didn't get a lot of forensic scientists spilling their guts to the press after hours in the local watering holes.

"No offense, but I think somebody's spinning you, miss. One thing you learn on this job, everybody talks to you for a reason."

"Excuse me, am I interviewing you or are you interviewing me?"

"I'm just saying, everybody's got an agenda. Even innocent little lambs like you and me."

Two desks away, Yunior glanced over and wrapped the end of his Hermès tie around his finger.

"So, what's your explanation for why you couldn't even find Julian Vega's DNA under Allison Wallis's fingernails at the '83 scene?"

"All I can tell you is that this is an ongoing investigation." Francis started rearranging papers on his desk, just to keep his hands occupied. "We're not going to give out anything that's going to jeopardize the case."

"I see," she said. "So how *do* you explain that it was the same woman's DNA that you found at both crime scenes twenty years apart? Did you mishandle the evidence?"

"Absolutely not." He could feel the tension start to rise up the back of his legs. "This is pure fiction. Excuse me, *science* fiction."

She was cornering him and she knew it. Cutting off all means of egress. He gnawed on the inside of his cheek, knowing he had to deflect her. As soon as this information hit the papers, the freaks would start coming out of the woodwork in their tinfoil hats and ballet slippers, eager to help with the investigation.

"Look, I hate to see you get it all wrong when we're on the verge of making an arrest here."

Rashid, who'd been walking by with another box of files, did a double-take.

"When is *this* going to happen?" she said, brought up short.

"Any day now." He hunched over in his chair, like a crafty old poker sharp. "Just have to pound a couple of nails for our probable cause. You know how it is. Nobody wants to go off half-cocked."

"Well, what are you talking about? A week? A month?"

"You want, I could give you a heads-up. Fair's fair."

Jimmy Ryan gave Francis a knowing smirk as he walked by, taking in the whole sucker's play in a glance.

"You're not just playing me, are you?" Judy Mandel was saying in an anxious voice, like she was stuck at an intersection with everyone honking at her. "If I hold back this DNA story and it turns out to be true, I'm going to kill myself."

Can't have that. He gave Jimmy the all-clear sign, safe for the moment. "And if you run it and it turns out to be bullshit, you're gonna be out on the ledge as well. So, really, it's six of one, half-dozen of the other."

"Goddamn it."

He could almost hear her chewing on a number two pencil over the phone line. He pictured the brass end dented between her tiny teeth.

"I just want to say that if I don't hear from you by the weekend, I'm running it anyway," she warned him.

"Knock yourself out."

As soon as she hung up, Yunior turned to Francis with his palms flat on the desktop, like the champion of the Dartmouth debating club. "Saint Augustine," he said.

"What?"

Black specks floated before his eyes. He tried to blink them away.

"That's who said, 'Since these mysteries are beyond me, let's pretend we're organizing them.'"

"Jean Cocteau, the surrealist." Francis picked up his *Bartlett's Familiar Quotations* and heaved it at him. "Know who your sources are, asshole."

37

HOOLIAN CREPT OUT of Zana's bedroom that morning and found Eddie sitting cross-legged on the plank-wood floor, watching *SuperFriends* with a kind of wide-eyed wonder that most regular American-born kids probably wouldn't have had for such a cheesy cartoon. "Thanks for saving me, Aquaman!" A slimy gray creature swam out of a giant clam just as it slammed shut on the orange-shirted blond-haired Protector of the Seas. "Too bad I couldn't do the same for you!"

He sat down beside the boy. "Can't be out of the water for too long, right?" He tried to remember the character's ground rules. "But he's got that special telepathy lets him talk to fish."

Without a word, the kid crawled into his lap again and curled up against him for warmth. "He's gonna get away, you know." Hoolian put his arms around him, like they'd been doing this for years. "Can't hold a slippery man for long."

When the show ended, he went into the kitchen, sorted through the pots and pans, and made oatmeal for all three of them with too much brown sugar and Log Cabin syrup on top, and served it to Zana in bed. She sat up and fixed him with a grave stare. "You're not going to do this all the time, are you?" Did that mean she was afraid he would do it again, or he wouldn't? He shrugged, caught a shower without getting his bandage wet, and then changed back into the clothes he'd been wearing. He walked with mother and child to Eddie's day care program on Van Brunt Street and then accompanied Zana to the elevated station at Smith and Ninth Street. How long could Aquaman stay out of the water anyway? Was it an hour, a day? After a while, everything had to return to its natural habitat.

He rode the train with her into the city, the two of them holding the same metal pole, surrounded by the crush of bodies, catching each other's eye for just a moment here and there, remembering things from the night in the flicker of track lights going by, sharing a secret while the rest of the crowd read their morning papers, buttoned up their leather coats, and listened to their headphones.

So this was how normal people did it. They touched each other, put their clothes back on, and blended into the rest of the world. But in their heads, they kept that little hum going, and every now and then maybe they smiled to themselves. Somewhere under the river, he realized how badly he wanted this.

How long could he go on pretending he could breathe on land? Soon she'd find out who he really was, his secret identity. She'd want to get away and protect the boy from him. And that would kill him. He wouldn't be able to take it. Something had changed between his fixing the bathroom door last night and watching Aquaman this morning and it frightened him terribly, because it meant he had that much more to lose. He'd begun to fall in love not just with her but with *them,* with the thought he could be someone hanging around their kitchen at night, someone who knew where the lightbulbs were, someone who could figure out how to get the heat working on a frigid February evening and buy the boy his first bike. Someone who would take them to Orchard Beach on the Fourth of July and handle the barbecue. He wanted it all and more. He wanted sex and gratitude and late nights watching reruns together. He wanted everything he'd missed. And he was afraid of what he'd do if he didn't get it.

They got off at Union Square and paused at the top of the stairs. Zana raised her chin and stood on her toes, so their brows touched.

"How come I never met no one like you before?" she said.

"I don't know. Just lucky, I guess."

38

THE RADIO AT the evidence warehouse was blasting, and Brian Mullhearn was singing along at the top of his lungs when Francis showed up with Rashid, Yunior, and Jimmy Ryan in tow.

"Some stupid with a flare gun . . ."

Francis stepped up to Mauler's desk and put a hand on either side as if he was about to flip it over.

"Are you acute, Brian?" Francis asked.

"Wha?"

"I'm saying, do you consider yourself an *acute* observer of human nature?"

"I'm not following you." The eraser-colored eyes moved under a dull watery film.

"I mean, when we were both working Narcotics, we had a chance to do a lot of observing, right? All those hours in the surveillance van with the binoculars, you learn a lot about people. You see how they roll up on each other. How they pretend to be friends when they're holding on to grudges and how they wait for a chance to get over —"

"What's your point, Francis?" Mauler turned down the radio.

"I got a call from a reporter yesterday. She had a story about our cases that came from you."

"*Bull*-shit." Mauler tried to look past him. "Jimmy, will you tell this asshole to start taking his meds again?"

But Ryan shook his head, not willing to get between them. The two civilian employees in the office — an Indian guy with a silver crescent moon around his neck and a pregnant black lady — busied themselves at the file cabinets.

"You're the one who knew we were trying to pull all the old Allison Wallis evidence."

"So what? Your friend Detective Ali over here has been showing up like every other day for a week and a half. Why aren't you grilling him?"

Rashid gave him a mellow sated smile, knowing the words had fallen about a yard and a half short of their target.

"No, Brian, he's actually got a career to look forward to," Francis explained. "You, on the other hand, are sitting on your ass here, vouchering newspapers from the Christine Rogers crime scene and you're the one who's got a girlfriend he knocked up, works filing at the crime lab."

Mauler took off his glasses and looked down as he wiped them with the fat end of his tie, having no ready reply.

"You're gonna be a resentful little bitch because you and me had some garbage in the past, either speak up like a man or shut your fucking mouth. All right? You don't go leaking to the press, to settle someone's hash. That's two homicide investigations you fucked up. Is that how you show respect to the people you work with?"

"I don't know what you're talking about."

"Look at me, Brian."

Mauler's chair creaked as he leaned back.

"I said, *look at me.*"

Francis pushed aside an old mechanical Rock 'em Sock 'em Robots toy set that had been sitting on the desk between them.

"You see me looking right or left? You see me doing *anything* except staring at what's right in front of me?"

"It's got nothing to do with me, Francis."

"You just keep saying that, Brian. Because it makes me good and mad. Because I don't give a shit about anything else right now. I'm not eating, I'm not sleeping, I'm not spending time with my wife. And I *really* love my wife. So when I put that much work into my cases and someone trashes them I tend to get a little intolerant."

"You're way out of line here." Mauler met his eye with some effort. "This is just a witch hunt."

"No, since you're so concerned about definitions, a 'witch hunt' would be when IAB investigates you for those washer-dryers that went missing from the warehouse last month and then pulls your cell phone records to prove you called that girl at the paper." Francis pushed a form at him across the desk. "A *punishment* would be when they go after your pension. Big difference."

"I'm calling my rep," said Mauler.

"Do it from the pay phone on the corner." Francis looked past him and signaled for the civilians to come take over the file. "Just get the fuck out of my sight."

39

IN HIS DREAM, he was on a beach with Zana and Eddie, who'd somehow been transformed into a pair of colorful kites flying low above some telephone lines. He looked over his shoulder and ran toward the sea, trying to keep them aloft and untangled with a ball of twine in his hand. But then he realized he'd forgotten how to swim. He charged into the surf anyway, knowing it was the only way to keep them airborne. And as the water began to rise up over his chin, starting to drown him, he let go of the string and saw them sail off into the sun.

The superintendent, a bony old guy in a graying Afro and a "Live at Lincoln Center" T-shirt, came out onto the landing and squinted at Francis pounding up the stairs with Rashid and five guys from the Warrant Squad.

"What's up, gentlemen?"

"We're looking for a Julian Vega." Francis caught his breath and showed him the papers that Paul had somehow induced a judge to sign at midnight.

"Never heard of him." The super winced at a flashlight beam pointing in his face. "He a singer?"

"The director of his halfway house says he's got a girlfriend, name of Zana, lives in this building. We got probable cause to search any of his things that he has here."

"Oh, that Ukranian girl. She drew my picture."

"That's the one." Francis adjusted the radio and gun on his equipment belt. "He's supposed to be staying with her."

"Third floor, in the back." The super yawned. "You lock him up, let me know. I'm kind of sweet on her myself."

The sound of the front door flying open woke Hoolian from his dream. He yanked back the covers, disoriented, and saw that Eddie had climbed into bed between them during the night.

"Come on, Hoolian, let's do this the easy way." He recognized Francis Loughlin's voice and thought for a half-second that it might be part of his nightmare. But then the cop stepped into the bedroom doorway and aimed a piercing flashlight beam at his face.

Out of instinct, Hoolian grabbed a book that had been lying on the bed and winged it across the room.

It seemed to fly in slow motion, its pages flapping like a seagull's wings, giving him just enough time to register not only the size of his mistake but the fact that Loughlin wasn't getting out of the way.

The book clocked the detective on the side of the head and fell open on the floor. It was as if he never saw it coming.

"I'm hit!" Laughlin yelled as he ducked out of view. "Look out!"

It triggered instant hysteria. Hoolian heard a stampede of boots on the hardwood floor and another officer yelling, "Gun! He's got a gun in there!"

"Don't shoot!"

But they couldn't hear him amid the shouts of *"Ten-thirteen!"* and blasts of static as they radioed for backup.

The boy sat up next to him, confused and frightened. In a panic, Hoolian pushed him off the mattress and then shoved him under the bed, for his own protection. Then he snatched up his clothes and duffel bag and lunged for the half-open window.

It was a crisp night and the metal bars of the fire escape felt like dry ice sticking to the soles of his feet. His heart pounded. Now that he'd committed himself to running, there'd be no turning back. If he stopped, Loughlin would surely shoot him in the back and plant a gun on him to prove it was self-defense.

"You're telling me you don't know any Julian?" Francis touched his head and saw he wasn't bleeding. A child's illustrated book about steam engines lay open at his feet.

"Kush eschte?" Hoolian's girlfriend pulled down the little T-shirt to cover herself and then put her arm around the bug-eyed child who'd just scurried from the bedroom. "I only know Christopher."

"Right." He headed for the window Hoolian had just gone out. "You see him before us, he's got some explaining to do."

*   *   *

The moon swathed in gray clouds was as dim as a dead fish's eye. Hoolian waded waist-deep into the weed-choked lot, still in his bare feet. He heard the police somewhere above and behind him coming out on the fire escape and talking on their radios. The nearest subway was about a mile off, he realized. A chill wind came in off the water, carrying the faint scent of old barges, industrial waste, and seaweed. He turned right with the duffel bag and clothes under his arm and saw the lights of the Red Hook Houses, the famous sprawling projects with forty or fifty buildings, in the distance. It gleamed like a forbidden city, with laws of its own. If he could get there ahead of the police, they'd never catch him.

Everything was submerged in pea-soup darkness to Francis. He might as well have been in the middle of the jungle at midnight.

"You all right?" Rashid came out to join him on the fire escape.

"Yeah, I'm good." Francis stared, trying to get a fix on things. "We getting any backup?"

"Might be a while. Housing's got a caper going over at the Red Hook Houses, looking for a rapist with a chopper and everything." Rashid pointed in the general direction of the projects. "You wanna wait?"

"And lose him now that we finally got something on him? Fuck that." Francis started to feel his way toward the ladder. "Get a couple of the other guys back here and stay in touch on the radio. I'm on channel three."

As soon as he put his weight on the first rung, the ladder shot down to its full extension and he felt his lungs fly out of his chest as he tried to hold on.

"Sure you're okay?" Rashid asked from above him.

"I'm fine," Francis snapped. "Why you gotta keep asking me?"

He climbed down and then jumped the last few feet to the ground, almost twisting his ankle. *"Fuck."* He found himself in a thicket of tall damp weeds. What was he thinking, stumbling around in the dark, forty-nine years old and going blind? He tried to stand up and feel his way back toward the fire escape ladder, but it had merged with the night and disappeared. He wasn't sure he could've chinned himself up that high anyway.

He heard something move in the weeds ahead of him and cautiously swept his beam across the lot. The field of forgotten things. His eyes slowly adjusted, picking out old tires, sparkling shards of broken bottles, empty Budweiser cans, scattered bricks, a caved-in television screen, cereal boxes, a collapsed birdcage, and a large 1950s-style GE refrigerator with the door hanging off. The weeds shivered again and he became aware of another presence nearby, breathing heavily.

"Hoolian?"

Hoolian recognized Loughlin's voice as he crouched behind the refrigerator, hiding from the beam. The cop had probably come to finish off what he started. Probably had all the rest of the squad in on it too, to cover for what he did. By the morning, there'd be DANGEROUS EX-CON GUNNED DOWN in the headlines.

"Hoolian, come on out. I'm not mad at you, G." Francis patted the Glock at his side, keeping the flashlight steady in his other hand. "We can still talk about this. You're not in that much trouble yet."

Nothing. He could see nothing beyond the hazy little aura his beam was making. Everything else was indigo ink on black paper.

"I know you just freaked. You didn't mean to hurt anybody."

Three feet. Loughlin was less than three feet away now. He'd walked right past the refrigerator. The flashlight beam came around again, strafing the weeds and revealing a hand-size hunk of cinder block within easy reach. Hoolian found himself looking from the stone to the back of the cop's head, noticing how Loughlin's bald spot glowed in the moonlight.

Who would know? They'd never be able to prove anything. No witnesses at all. I could split his head open. Then I'd take his gun and finish him off, like he deserved.

The cop suddenly turned. For a full second, he seemed to stop and look right at Hoolian, who froze, standing halfway, his lungs pinned to his spine. He held his breath, terrified the wild thumping of his heart would reveal his location. But the cop kept looking at him blankly, his beam only an inch off Hoolian's face.

"Hey, Rashid." He keyed the radio mike on his shoulder. "Any of you guys helping me search this lot?"

Slowly it dawned on Hoolian that this man really could not see him. Somehow he had become invisible. It was meant to be, he realized. They'd been brought together under the cover of night for a reason. This was his chance to collect justice, to avenge his life. The brick was right there. The cop turned again, presenting his pate once more as an unprotected target.

So why couldn't he make himself do it? The command got stuck halfway down his arm. *What's the matter with you?* He tried to send the hot impulse down again, but it just came back cold. *¿Qué pasó? This man took everything from you. And he's about to do it again. Break his head open.*

He should've noticed it before, Francis realized. That lurking presence. That peculiar heat in the air. That panting that he hadn't distinguished from the lap of water on the nearby pilings or the throb of blood in his own ears. It had crept up and caught him unaware. He caught the odor of wet fur just as he turned.

The dog was snarling, gathering everything it had behind its jaws, as it came out of the weeds. It looked from Loughlin to Hoolian and then back again, like it was something the two of them had conjured together with their enmity. Then it bared its teeth and made a throaty burr, one of those muscular pit bulls you heard about in prison sometimes: the kind drug dealers would train as attack dogs. Hoolian had seen a couple of them wandering the streets and scavenging the lots in daylight around here, abandoned by owners who couldn't control them anymore.

More than once, he'd had to pull Eddie back from petting them, warning the kid that once these animals locked their jaws on you, they never let go. They'd tear the muscles right out of your leg if you tried to pull them off. He dropped his duffel bag and started to run for the projects.

Francis almost tripped over a waterlogged mattress, with the dog right behind him. God was trying to make him give up another bargaining chip. *No, don't help me. I can do it myself.* He stepped on a lightbulb lying in the weeds, shards almost cutting his ankle. *Let me find my way out on my own. Nobody else put me here.*

He felt the dog's hot breath on the back of his leg. No way could he outrun it. He pulled his gun and turned, ready to blow the animal's head off, praying he wouldn't hit one of the other cops searching the area. He steadied his grip and aimed at nothing. No clue where the attack would come from. But the weeds had stopped moving. He realized the dog had veered off, somehow having lost his scent. He walked out into the street and hunched over, sucking wind and ready to throw up from the exertion. The rhythm of his breath matching a *sup, sup, sup* sound drawing nearer. He looked up and saw light shafting down from the sky, the Star of Bethlehem searching the courtyards of Red Hook Houses. Gradually he tracked it back to the police helicopter hovering above the projects.

What is it? Hoolian's chest was bursting and his bare feet were sore from slapping the cobblestones. He got to the projects' entrance and saw there were already police officers flooding the courtyards. The helicopter was circling overhead. He sagged against the wrought-iron fence, knowing it would be only moments before they picked him up. He looked back toward Coffey Street. By now they would've told Zana who he was. They would have showed her a warrant and maybe even old pictures. They would have made her understand that he was a liar, a criminal, a danger to her and her child. *You're lucky you got away from him in one piece, lady.* When he tried to think of how he could answer and explain himself, saying how he would never do anything to hurt her, terrible ache welled up inside him.

It was useless to keep running. You could stay out of the water for only so long. The whir of blades grew louder and the beacon of light from the sky finally found him leaning against the fence, looking up at the sky with open arms.

40

"FRANCIS, YOU ARE a miserable son of a bitch."

Deborah Aaron, in a ribbed turtleneck and jeans, spotted him talking to the duty sergeant after she'd pushed her way through the media locusts outside and walked in the front doors of the 19th Precinct.

"You couldn't just pick up the phone like a human being. I would've brought him in any time you wanted. Monday, Tuesday, Wednesday. But *noo*. You always have to be running your little power trip."

"Nice to see you too, Counselor." Francis signed the log book and gave it back to the sergeant. "You're looking very relaxed."

"Obviously, you thought you were going to catch me going away early for the Columbus Day weekend, so you'd get Julian to yourself. Unfortunately, I had to drop off some papers this morning and my little one had a second-grade dance performance that you're making me miss. I was up all night sewing his turtle costume and trying to write a brief for Judge Del Toro. Thanks a lot."

"Whaddaya want me to do, Deb? Coordinate with his teachers?"

"You're the one who's always bitching about not getting a heads-up."

He turned his back on her and headed for the stairs without bothering to see if she was following. Even though the building had been gutted and rebuilt from the ground floor up since '83, somehow the place had quickly reacquired a banged-up, old-school feeling, as if the energy field from certain long-forgotten crimes had forced its way up through the foundation.

"You must really be desperate," she said. "Barging in on my client with a half-assed warrant and searching his girlfriend's apartment."

At the top of the steps, he threw open a door and made it seem incidental that he was holding it for her. "After you, Counselor."

In the corridor on the way to the Detective Bureau, there was a Wanted poster with the ghostly black-and-white image of an unnamed passenger in the backseat of a livery cab. The picture, taken with a hidden camera, was of a small-eyed young man in a Timberland sweatshirt with the hood up, who would soon pull out a .22 and shoot the driver, a Mr. Sandeep Singh, of Jackson Heights, Queens, in the back of the head, spraying skull fragments all over the windshield. No witnesses so far to ID him, no reward offered. A grim reminder to Francis that he actually still did have other cases.

"And I don't appreciate you calling up Judy Mandel and the rest of the working press and making me run the gauntlet out there."

Deb tracked him into the squad room and through the warren of desks, rubber soles squeaking on the wooden floor, an odd feature of the precinct contributed by its grateful well-heeled citizens.

"Hey, I don't know who tipped them off about Hoolian being here." Francis shrugged. "I'm not his publicist."

A plastic barn owl stood on top of a file cabinet, keeping a watchful eye on a sleeping figure in a holding cell across the room and reminding Francis this precinct had always been a little too slow for his tastes. A half-dozen girls just a little younger than Christine and Allison would have been stared down from the Missing Persons posters on the wall. "Highway to Hell" blared from the radio and a copy of *The South Beach Diet* sat next to an open salad container on a detective's desk.

"You at least get him something to eat?" Deb asked.

"Would you?" Francis gave her a backward glance.

"Sleazy intimidation tactic."

"Hey, it wasn't exactly *The Sound of Music* when you were prosecuting."

She sucked in her cheeks, knowing just as well as he did that she used to badger starving defendants relentlessly and make their lawyers cool their heels for hours in corridors that were like tuberculosis wards.

"I never had you pull a guy off the street twice without probable cause."

"How do you know it's without probable cause? You got a police band radio or something? I didn't think you were that much of a buff anymore."

He saw the insult cut more deeply than he'd meant it to, then remembered a half-second later that she'd had to have her husband, the detective from the Nine-Oh, locked up for beating on her.

"Look, we had a signed warrant to search his property," he explained, trying to get back on a more professional basis. "It was his decision to assault an officer and run out the back."

"Yeah, assault with a Dorling Kindersley Eyewitness Book," Deb snorted. "Like that's really going to stand up in court if you try to charge him for it. What were you looking for anyway?"

"Obviously we think he had material in his possession that's relevant to a case we're working on. You can figure that out, Deb."

"Like what? You think he's been holding a dead girl's blood twenty years so he can sprinkle it around a crime scene?"

"Okay, we brought him up here to play Pin the Tail on the Donkey."

"Wouldn't be any stranger than some of the rumors I've heard about this investigation." They stopped outside the interrogation room. "I hope you're proud of yourself, Francis."

"Whoosh." Hoolian clapped his hands in relief when his attorney finally walked in. "Beam me up, Scotty. I've had it."

He'd been in this room since six this morning, trying to keep from crying or breaking down while Ms. A. was tied up. Everything physical had changed about the precinct; only the fear was the same. That one-hundred-blue-jays-screaming-in-your-head, about-to-piss-in-your-pants terror he remembered so well.

"You doing all right?" Ms. A. squeezed his shoulder.

"Yeah. But I think I done enough talking around here already."

Wearily, he started to his feet as the black detective who'd been with him the whole time pushed off the wall.

"Good afternoon, Ms. Aaron." He offered his hand and smiled, all sweet and silky playa charm now. "Rashid Ali. I've heard good things."

"Not from your partner, you haven't."

"Then he doesn't appreciate a truly *fine* attorney."

Hoolian looked around, realizing that he had not, in fact, seen Loughlin since he'd arrived at the station. One more thing different from the last time.

"You mind telling me why you brought my client in?"

"Fucking bitch," said Paul Raedo, coming over to join Francis at the glass.

"Is that any way for a future state supreme court judge to talk?"

"I never got along with her, you know," Paul muttered. "Always shoving her tits in the DA's face when they were on the same elevator. Like *that* was going to get her into Homicide after only three years."

Actually that didn't sound like Deb's style at all, Francis had to admit. She was more the diligent, industrious grind, hyperconscious of scoring most of her points on the merits and hardly ever trading on her looks.

On the other hand, Paul was in the Top Ten on Francis's Shit List these days. Letting Hoolian get out of prison in the first place; neglecting to contact the victim's family; getting his ass publicly scorched by Judge Bronstein; and worst of all putting those papers in the case folder about his disciplinary hearing in '81. Francis had been trying not to obsess about it too much because — *well,* because what could he do at this point? But one of these days, after all this was over, he was going to pull Paul over and say, *Dude, get your knife out my back, I hate sleeping on my side.*

"Think I should go in and lay the good news on her?" Paul raised his eyebrows, backing up the close-cropped hairs on the crown of his head.

"Nah, let my man Rashid keep going. He's doing all right."

Detective Ali put the swatch of khaki linen that he'd shown Hoolian earlier back on the table, with three dark overlapping blots of different sizes and slightly different coloration on it, a series of dark moons half eclipsing one another.

"What am I looking at?" Ms. A. asked.

"Well . . ." Ali yawned. "As I'm sure you know, there's been a lot of talk about the chain of evidence in this case. People are getting some crazy ideas. So yesterday we decided to take one last run out to the warehouse and see if we could come up with something besides a pillowcase."

"And so this is . . . ?"

"This is part of a slipcover from Allison Wallis's couch. The one, in fact, she was lying on when they found her."

"Which you should've had in the first place." Ms. A. snapped. "And more important, which *I* should've had in the first place."

If Ali was bothered by the fact that she was addressing him like a lazy sales clerk, he wasn't letting it show. "We all strive for perfection, Ms. Aaron. Only some of us achieve it."

"Where are you going with this, Detective? My client's been in here a long time. If you're going to charge him for resisting arrest or some other nonsense like that, let's go to the arraignment and get it thrown out. I looked at that warrant you got Judge O'Brien to sign. He must have been half asleep."

"So the first stain we're looking at is blood." Ali ignored her and touched the material with a shiny buffed fingernail. "The forensic examiner was able to determine it was a female. Mostly likely the victim herself."

"So stop the presses and hold the back pages." Ms. A. put her hands on her hips. "You found the victim's blood at her own crime scene. Congratulations, Francis." She stared right at the one-way glass. "That's the first thing you've done right in this case."

"*Welll* . . . not so fast." Ali drew the pause out like a drumroll. "We've still got two other blots to deal with."

"I can't wait."

The detective smiled and pointed to the second-biggest stain. "Now this one here is blood too. Except it doesn't belong to the victim. We had the medical examiner analyze it last night and come up with a DNA profile. And guess what? It matches the saliva sample your client Mr. Vega so generously provided for Detective Loughlin a few weeks ago."

Ms. A.'s eyes crept over, reminding him how furious she'd been about his spitting in Loughlin's face.

"Excuse me, Detective, but *So What, Part Two*?" she said, without dropping a stitch. "My client stated in the original interview that he'd been doing work in the victim's apartment, fixing her toilet before he sat down on the couch to watch TV with her. Obviously, he could've cut himself while he was working with tools."

Hoolian watched, impressed; the only signs that she

was thrown were the little fanlike lines radiating from the corners of her eyes.

"Good point." Ali nodded. "Only one thing."

"What's that?"

"The last stain here." His finger hovered over the largest blot. "Would you like to know what it is?"

"I'm sure you're going to tell me."

"It's Mr. Vega's semen. As you can see, it's quite a sizable amount. And it's touching both his bloodstain and Dr. Wallis's bloodstain."

In a tiny twitch, Hoolian saw a three-act drama unfold on his attorney's face: shock, hurt, betrayal. Then she shut down for a moment, to try and process it. With anybody else, it would barely register as a pause. But coming after her usual breathless fusillade of words, the silence was deafening.

"Oh, I get it," she said finally.

Her mouth twisted into a bitter smile as she turned back to the one-way, shifting all her anger from Hoolian to the men on the other side.

"You guys thought you'd bring my poor client in here, threaten him with arrest over these phony charges, and shove this crap under his nose to try and get a rise out of him before his attorney arrived."

"Nobody forced him to answer any questions after he said he wanted his lawyer," Detective Ali said. "We were just sharing some information, hoping he could help us out. If he wanted to make a statement about why his semen would be mixed up with Dr. Wallis's blood, that's up to him."

Ms. A. kept staring at the glass, continuing the wordless showdown with Loughlin and whoever else was watching.

"If you're not going to charge my client, I'm taking him home," she said. "It's obvious that you wouldn't be trying to sucker punch us if you found anything of substance during your raid this morning."

Ali sat on a corner of the table, barely moving. In his tab-collar shirt with French cuffs and cobalt blue drip of a necktie, he could've been a *GQ* model waiting to have his picture taken.

"Ah . . . There *is* one other thing I forgot to mention."

"He's not talking." Ms. A. shook her head. "You have any more questions, pick up the telephone and call my office for a real appointment. Detective Loughlin and Mr. Raedo both have the number, I'm sure."

"That's fine." Rashid half smiled. "We were just wondering why Julian was seen hanging around 294 East 94th Street, that's all."

Ms. A. looked nonplussed.

"Where that other lady doctor lived," Hoolian muttered.

"I don't understand."

"The building's superintendent ID'd Julian here from a photograph. Said he'd seen him on the block. Acting 'suspicious.' His words, not ours."

"I already done fucking told you, G.," Hoolian erupted. "I did deliveries in the neighborhood."

"Julian, shut up."

She said it cleanly and nonchalantly, like she was backhanding a tennis ball over a net.

"This conversation is over." She hooked Hoolian under the arm and pulled him up. "I'll see you in court."

They walked out the door, leaving Ali with his hands in his pockets.

In the squad room, a half-dozen other detectives were back at their desks, trying to appear busy, though they'd obviously just been lined up at the glass, listening to every word. Ms. A. steered by a row of green file cabinets, where Loughlin and Paul Raedo had their backs turned, pretending to study a case folder.

"Very nice, you guys," she said. "Trying to hang two murders on my client when you can't even prove one."

"So we're not going to charge him for assault and resisting?" Francis asked.

"I just heard from the DA." Paul shook his head and put the cell phone back in his pocket. "He wants to let it drop. He's concerned that it looks like part of a continuing vendetta against this guy. And, uh, he also had some questions about the way I filled out the warrant." Paul looked sheepish. "He thought we might get hung up with the judge on some of the procedural issues."

"Fuckin' bullshit," Francis muttered. "In the old days, you didn't get a pass for throwing crap at a New York police officer. You got an attitude adjustment."

"So, what do you think?" Paul jerked his head in the direction of the empty interrogation room.

Francis ground his jaw, already second-guessing himself for not going in there to raise the temperature a little.

"I think we got the guy's blood and semen at the first crime scene. And somebody ID'ing him as being near the second one. *Something* is up."

"I guess you're right." Paul nodded. "Up until yesterday, I was ready to write him off because of this Bizarro World thing with the DNA. But now I don't know what's going on."

"Neither do I," Francis admitted. "My brains are

coming out of my ears. I'm almost starting to wonder if we did bury the wrong girl."

"So, what do we do now? We don't even have an operating theory, do we?"

"You mean a way of squaring the fact that we got Hoolian's semen at the first crime scene, the super recognizing him from outside Christine's, and then the same woman's blood in both crime scenes?"

"Any ideas?"

"Not really." Francis sighed. "But he has to be tied up with it somehow. Though why he wouldn't just open his heart and blurt it all out, I don't know. Maybe he really has been keeping some of her DNA around. I mean, he stole her photo album. Maybe he's been hoarding something, like one of those fetish objects. You know, people get into weird shit with women's shoes and all that."

"Well . . . I don't really know about that kind of thing." Paul's eyes wandered sideways. "Did the guys ever find that duffel bag anyway?"

"No, we did a grid search of the lot in daylight and couldn't turn it up. Not that it would've done us much good if we were going to have a problem with the warrant."

"So where do we go from here?"

"We just gotta keep our options open. We've got a couple of plainclothesmen keeping an eye on Hoolian's halfway house for the next couple of days, so he probably won't try anything. Rashid's going back over the case folders inch by inch, to see if there's anything else we missed. Yunior's checking birth records to see if Eileen had another daughter she didn't tell us about, Jimmy Ryan is recanvassing Christine's neighborhood, and we got three other detectives reinterviewing every patient and staff member she ever saw at the hospital."

"And what are you doing?"

"I'm going home for a few hours to get some sleep before I go completely nuts. I just need to clear my head a little."

"You're going home?" Paul stared at him as if he'd just announced he was going to spend the weekend molesting Girl Scouts.

"Don't look at me that way, I burned through all my overtime for the year the last few weeks. I'm fucking exhausted."

"Uhhh, I don't know, Francis." Paul shook his head. "You've changed on me."

"What do you mean?"

"I'm beginning to think you and I aren't quite on the same page anymore. My father never used to worry about his overtime cap. He did whatever it took."

Francis stared at him, thinking he had to be kidding. Everyone knew Paul's father was a corrupt old Narcotics detective known as "Shake 'Em on Down" Raedo in the pre–Knapp Commission days. But Paul just stood there, glaring at him, his bristles standing up like porcupine quills. *No*, Francis thought. *We're definitely not in the same place anymore.*

"Don't sweat it, Your Honor. I'm just across the bridge."

"Yeah." Paul turned his back on him. "I'll be sure to call you when the next girl gets her face beat in."

41

"HOOOLEEEYAAN!!"

One joker at the rear of the pack kept chanting his name over and over in a nerve-needling falsetto.

"Hooo-leeee-yaaaaannnn!!!"

It was like an emery board on his eyeteeth. He put his head down as Ms. A. pushed him past the snake-slither sound of cameras and the wall of taunting voices outside the precinct.

"Hey, Julian, over here!"

"Julian, why'dja kill her?"

"Did they get you good this time?"

"Miss Aaron, is your client under arrest again?"

She raised a bag in front of his face and tried to hail a cab as they closed in around him like schoolyard bullies, shouting questions and taking pictures.

"My client is the target of an ongoing smear campaign by the police and the district attorney's office," she called out. "He was not formally charged today and, as you know, his earlier conviction was dismissed."

"Hooooleeeyaaaaannn!!" The falsetto turned brawny and mock-operatic. *"Hoooleee-oooleee-ooo-leee-yaaannnn!!"*

He bared his teeth and turned around as a dozen shutters clicked, immortalizing his snarl for the next day's paper; he'd look like the ape about to be put to sleep for mauling the zookeeper.

"Debbie, were they asking Julian about the Christine Rogers case?"

A yellow cab finally pulled up and she reached for the handle. "We're not going to have any further comment at this time. I'm asking you to respect my client's privacy and direct all your questions to my office."

"What'd she say?"

"Where's her office?"

"What're you doing this weekend?"

She yanked the door open and pushed Hoolian into the taxi. "Astor Place," she said, sliding in after him and pulling it shut, one last *"Hooleeeeeeee —"* following them as they eased away from the howling scrum.

The driver, a Sikh wearing a turban and a luxuriant black beard like a mink covering the lower of half of his face, checked them out in his rearview.

"You are on TV?"

"Now we are," Ms. A. said grimly.

"I thought I recognize you. You are *Fear Factor*?"

"Does this partition close?"

Before he could answer, she shut it herself and turned to Hoolian. "Is there something we need to talk about?"

"What?"

"A little spot of your blood on the couch *maybe* I can explain away." She held tight to the Nantucket basket on her lap. "But your *semen*?"

The taxi fishtailed as the driver went around the block and headed downtown on Lexington.

"Do I really have to spell it out?" Hoolian reached for a strap to steady himself.

"Yes. I'm definitely going to need a little help."

He stared out the window and said nothing until they hit a red light right near Bloomingdale's.

"It's so clean around here now. There used to be so much more garbage on the streets."

"Talk to me," she said. "I need to know the truth here."

"She touched me."

Neither of them said anything for a few seconds as the engine idled at the crosswalk. In one of the store's windows, a birch-white female mannequin in leather and shades posed in front of a sign that read, I WILL OBEY THE FASHION POLICE.

"You're telling me that Allison Wallis, a mature woman, almost ten years older than you, with a medical degree, initiated a sexual encounter with you? That's what you're giving me to work with?"

He felt himself being surveilled on all sides by female pedestrians watching him through the cab windows. Each of them seemed to meet his eye for a second and then hurry away, gripping her bag a little tighter.

"That's what I wanted to tell the detective back in '83, but I didn't know how to say it."

"She groped you. While she was having her period? You're seriously expecting me to believe that?"

"Why not?" He crossed his arms.

"Jesus Christ, Julian —" She stopped, trying to get a grip. "Do you know how much time I've put into this case? Do you know how many nights I've missed being with my children?"

"I never lied to you."

"I'd like to believe that's true, but you are really scaring me here. My knees are shaking."

He shrank down in the gray vinyl seat, feeling the loose change spilling out from between the cushions. The things people left behind by accident.

"All right," he said. "It's like I told you. I'd come up to her apartment sometimes to fix things and we'd hang out and talk."

"About *what?*" she said fiercely.

"Just about stuff. And sometimes she'd be stressed-out about things that happened at the hospital and her back would be in knots. So I'd rub it for her sometimes."

"Hmm." She nodded and sniffed, deciding to stay calm for the moment.

"And so like it got to be a regular thing. We'd sit there, watching television, and I'd rub her shoulders sometimes. That's it. Both of us acted like it wasn't any big thing. Though now that I look back on it, I'm like, *Damn, what was up with that?*"

He gave her a sidelong glance, to see if she was buying it.

"Go on," she said cautiously.

"So that one night, her toilet wouldn't stop running and I had calls all over the building because my father was out and the regular handyman was off. So *I* was the one running around, fixing things and trying to keep all these women happy. I remember Mrs. Condon in 7A had a leak in her sink and Mrs. Rosensweig in 4D had a problem with the pilot light in her oven. And like by the time I was done, I was *seriously* stressing. And that's when she offered to rub my shoulders for once."

"Oo-kaay." She made her mouth into a small tense circle.

"And then one thing led to another and we wound up kind of holding each other a little," he said. "You know, just like a brother-sister thing at first. 'Oh, you're always there for me. You're really my friend. I love you so much. . . .' And then, it sort of started to go a little further."

The light turned green and they began to weave through the thicket of cars blasting traffic reports and block-rocking beats.

"Julian, we are waaay past the euphemism stage. I need you to be really explicit with me."

"All right, I got *hard*. There it is." He sat back. "She knew what was up and so did I." He scowled, not having meant to play with words. "You know how it is when something is happening and you pretend it isn't? And then after a certain point you can't pretend anymore?"

"Yes," she said stiffly. "I think I've heard of that."

He didn't like that she was still trying to hold herself above him. Knowing damn well she must have royally screwed up a few things in her life if she'd ended up representing people like him and raising two kids on her own.

"So that's what it is," he said. "And I was just this little *espina* who'd never even had a lady close enough to breathe in his ear, so I couldn't hold out for long. Understand?"

"You ejaculated on her right away."

He cringed at the clinical sound of it and looked up at the smudged partition to see if the driver had heard. "You don't have to say it like that."

"I need to be completely sure what we're talking about this time." The groove between her nose and mouth lengthened. "There's no margin for error here."

"Yeah, that's what happened," he mumbled, trying to

find his voice again. "But she'd been into it. *For real.* It only took me 'bout seven or eight years to figure that out. I was pretty naive then."

He wondered what Zana was going to think once she heard this story.

"And afterward?"

His eyes darted past her. "She kind of started getting upset, I guess."

"Oh?" She made the word drip like an icicle from her lips.

"I mean, at first she was okay. Like she just wanted to forget it and act as if it didn't really happen. But then she started getting all nervous, like she was worried somebody was going to find out."

"Did she say who?"

"No, she was just like, 'You really have to go now. You can't be here anymore.'"

He hated that she was going over everything he said with a fine-tooth comb, trying to catch him out, like the detectives.

"And why didn't you tell Loughlin any of this in the first interrogation?"

"I was an uptight little Catholic *chico* who'd started shaving a month before that." His voice cracked. "I didn't even know what words to use. I could've said a whole Mass in Latin easier than I could've said 'dick' or 'pussy.'"

"What about your lawyer from the first trial, Figueroa?"

"He knew the whole fucking thing. I told him *exactly* how it was. But he was like you. He wouldn't believe me. He said, 'That's terrific, Julian. Now keep it to yourself.

You're never getting anywhere near a witness stand with that story.'"

Condescending old hack. Hoolian could still see him in his Court Street office, light mustard stain on the cuff of his suit jacket, spines peeling on the out-of-date law books on his shelf, acting all gruff and avuncular when all he really wanted to do was cash his clients' hard-earned checks and get stewed on his private boat in the Florida Keys.

"If it's all true, why the hell didn't you tell me any of it before?"

"First thing you said: 'Only answer the question that's been asked. A good witness knows, never wise up a chump. Only focus on the issues relevant on appeal.' Which were" — he ticked them off with his fingers — "was my lawyer incompetent? *Yes*. Did he tell me I had the right to testify? *No*. Why hasn't the state come up with the DNA evidence we asked for? And why didn't they chase down all the witnesses who could've cleared me?"

She nodded, conceding each point as the color drained from her face. "Yeah, but what about them finding your blood *and* her blood on the slipcover?" she asked.

"Like you said. I was doing a lot of work in the building that night. I guess I might've sliced myself cutting some tubing and some of it might've got on her couch when we were together. How *her* blood got on the slipcover, I don't know. That must've happened after I left and someone else came in and attacked her."

"Oh my God." She rolled down her window, needing fresh air. "I'm telling you, Julian. You better not be lying to me. If you are, I'm not the one who's going back to prison. You got twenty-five to *life*, in case you forgot."

"Do I sound like I'm lying?"

She lapsed into sullen silence. All around them, people were starting to leave town early for the long weekend. Men and women with suit bags and attaché cases, hurrying to Grand Central, casting worried looks up at the sky, and passing the Graybar Building's canopy, where for once even the carved rats on the suspension cables looked like they were trying to abandon ship. Going back in for another five years probably wouldn't have scared him so much just a few days ago, before he got involved with Zana and her kid. But being on the outside tainted you. It made you forget how to live in confined spaces.

"What about this other thing?" she said quietly, like she was carefully tugging at a conspicuous thread hanging from his sleeve.

"What?"

"This other woman they were asking you about. The intern from Mount Sinai."

"What about her?" he said evenly.

"Are you going to tell me why the super ID'd you hanging around outside her building?"

"I worked nine or ten blocks from there. I never even made a delivery in her building. If I did, there would've been a slip for it and they would've been shoving it in my face."

"Then what about your hand?"

"Yeah, what about it?"

He opened and closed a fist, aware of how she was watching his every move now.

"What did you really do to it? I know you didn't cut yourself in the stockroom. You didn't even look at me when I suggested you file a claim."

He thumbed his lip and thought awhile. "What happens if I tell you the truth?"

"Depends." She made sure her seat belt was buckled. "I'm an officer of the court. I won't suborn perjury. If you're going to get on the stand and lie about something you've done, you're on your own."

"I think I might've hurt somebody."

She shut her eyes and drew her knees together. It seemed for a few seconds not entirely impossible that she would try to push him from the moving cab.

"Okay," she said, slowly trying to unknot herself. "Now you're *really* going to need to make me understand this."

"Attorney-client privilege still holds, right?"

"Julian. *Cut the shit.*"

He edged forward in his seat, making sure the driver had the partition closed and the radio all the way up.

"So I was on the subway after work, right? And homeboy starts looking at me."

"Where was this?" she snapped, ready to pick his story apart.

"All the way from 86th Street to Grand Central on the four train. I'm like, '*Damn,* brother, do I know you from inside or something?' Then at 42nd Street, he follows me off the train with his friends and starts, like, 'Say, man, whatchoo lookin' at?' And I was wearing this Saint Christopher's medal my father gave me."

"You trying to tell me they jumped you for some twenty-dollar chain?"

"That gold meant a lot to me." He touched his chest, where the medallion had been. "So me and homeboy got into it coming off the platform."

"You started fighting?"

"For real. I think homeboy must've had a razor, because my hand got cut pretty bad. There was blood running down my arm. So I pushed him —"

"Onto the tracks?" She audibly caught her breath and held it.

"Nah, down a flight of steps, but it was a pretty long flight," he admitted. "Down to the number seven platform. He like fell in slow motion." He put his arms up like he was flailing. "It took him a while to hit bottom. And then all his friends went running down after him."

"Was he all right?"

"I dunno." He started toying with the lock on his door. "I ran upstairs and out the terminal. That's why I was afraid to tell you about it. I was afraid I might've broken his goddamn neck."

She watched him raising the knob up and popping it down with the flat of his palm. "So you could've killed him? Is that what you're telling me?"

"I don't think so. I checked the newspaper the next couple of days, and there wasn't anything about it. But I mighta fucked him up pretty good."

"Shit." She put her head back. "And then you lied to the police and your attorney about it?"

"I panicked, a-right?" The driver turned, hearing him raise his voice. "I thought they'd lock me up again for assault or reckless endangerment before I even got to go back to court," he whispered. "And then everybody would think maybe I'd done what they said I did in the first place."

"And you expect me to believe this just coincidentally happened at the same time this other girl was killed?"

"Nah, this was like almost a week before. You even saw me with the bandage on then. Don't you remember?"

Her confidence was shaken, though. He could see it in how she turned away from him, smoothed the wrinkles from her pants and started rubbing her lips over and over, trying to reestablish the time sequence in her mind. "I have to tell you, Julian. I don't know what to think now."

"Well, I'm telling you the truth."

"I see. So it was only yesterday you were lying?"

He looked out the window and felt the desolation of the long holiday taking over. How eerily deserted the canyons of Manhattan seemed at times like these. Even in neighborhoods where people didn't go out of town, it was as if a neutron bomb had hit, leaving only the buildings still standing, casting long shadows. He saw the empty sidewalks, green lights for absent pedestrians, ghosts in the window displays, and up ahead, the Met Life clock tower stark against a graying sky, the hands still strangely stuck at 9:15.

"I guess maybe I don't look like such a good guy now," he said.

"Yeah? Where'd you get that idea?"

42

ALLISON'S EX-BOYFRIEND, Doug Wexler, had an old picture of himself on the credenza. It showed him as a lean, mop-haired postgrad playing Frisbee with a bunch of little kids in a Guatemalan village. Francis noticed that the photo was slightly bigger than the others in the oak-paneled office, including the portraits of his family and the shots of the buildings that were part of the real estate empire his late father had bequeathed to him.

"I've been kind of half expecting you to call," said Doug, now a jowly, slightly dissipated middle-aged version of the guy in the picture, wearing an old Lacoste shirt and chinos to the office on a Saturday afternoon. "Ever since I saw Allison's case coming up in the newspapers again."

"And why's that?"

"I don't know. I just had a feeling that certain things weren't quite settled the first time."

Francis, a little more alert after a few hours' sleep, looked at the picture just behind Doug again. It was a measure of his desperation and confusion that he was here in the first place, back at square one, interviewing the original victim's former boyfriend to see if there was something crucial they'd missed in '83.

"You were out of the country for her funeral, weren't you?" said Francis. "I don't remember seeing you there."

"I was living in a village where they didn't have indoor plumbing, let alone telephones." Doug ran his fingers through his thinning blond hair. "I didn't hear about it until like a month afterward."

"Must have been a shock."

"Oh my God." Doug's jaw drew in, making a stubbly little croissant under his chin. "My ex-girlfriend gets killed in an apartment building owned by my father? I never even told my wife about it until just a few years ago."

"Remind me how that happened again." Francis flipped open his steno pad nonchalantly. "How'd she end up subletting in one of your father's units after you'd broken up with her?"

"Not much to it. We stayed friends after we broke up and I knew she was coming back to New York after we graduated. So my father was managing all these co-ops and rentals, and I gave her a number to call. And that was that."

"Did you ask your father to give her a break on the rent?" asked Francis, still not quite sure what he was fishing for at the moment, but certain a new approach was needed after yesterday.

"I didn't get that involved. I just passed it on, as a favor to a friend. At the time, I didn't even think I was going to go into real estate. I thought I was going to save the world. . . ."

His eyes drifted wistfully across the office, past the Turkish rug and Oriental vases, the framed civic citations and pictures of his father receiving awards from various mayors, and the sixty-fifth-floor view that made the intricate sprawl of downtown Manhattan look like the circuitry of a computer chip.

"I felt terrible about it afterward. Especially because I missed the funeral. My father sent a huge flower arrangement and paid for the limos out to the cemetery. He was devastated."

"Why? Did he know Allison?"

"Well, no, but . . . ," Doug sputtered. "She was killed in one of his apartments. By the son of one of his employees."

"Anybody talk about suing him?"

"Why do you ask?"

"You said he sent flowers and paid for limos to the cemetery. I'm sure he was a very decent generous man, but somebody got killed in his building by the son of one of his employees. Sounds like he could've been liable."

"Well, I never heard about any lawsuit, but I wasn't involved in the business at the time." Doug pushed up on the arms, as if he was trying to make himself look big enough to belong in the seat. "And unfortunately, my father isn't around for you to ask him about it."

"If Allison's family had actually filed suit, though, you'd think you'd know about it. Wouldn't you?"

"Probably. There'd be papers around."

"Seems strange," Francis said, realizing he hadn't had reason to give it much thought before. "I know Tom and Eileen Wallis pretty well. They're not greedy, but you know, money is money."

"I always thought they were a little odd myself."

"How's that?" Francis looked up from taking notes.

"Oh, you know, Allison didn't always get along with them when she was alive."

"Since when?" Francis heard himself sounding indignant, almost proprietary, like he was upset about being told something he didn't know already. "I never heard that before," he said, trying to sound more neutral. "I thought they were close."

"They were. Maybe a little too close, if you ask me."

"Whaddaya mean?"

"God, they were always going at it hammer and tongs." Doug massaged his temples, like he still had the headache.

"About what?"

"About everything." Doug frowned. "Food, clothes, you name it. They had some *serious* control issues."

For some reason, Francis found himself picturing the little bear full of honey on Christine Rogers's kitchen counter.

"Sure you're not confused about this?" said Francis. "It's a long time ago."

"Trust me. I haven't forgotten. She'd talk to her mother on the phone and then be hysterical for hours afterward. Nothing you could do or say would console her. That's one of the reasons I stopped going out with her. You know what it's like when you're seeing someone and you just realize at a certain point that there's this thing standing between the two of you that you're never going to get on the other side of? That's how it was. Like something was in front of the sun."

Francis set his pad aside. "I gotta tell you, Doug. This doesn't sound right to me. I worked this case a long time. I interviewed the people who worked with her, kids she treated, other people in her building. And none of them described what you're talking about."

"Well, they can say whatever they like." Doug sighed,

leaning on his elbows. "But I was there when she'd starve herself or lock herself in the bathroom. A couple of times she had these cuts on her arms and wouldn't tell me where she got them."

"No shit," said Francis, trying to recall whether he'd seen marks like that on the body and just assumed they were made by her attacker. "Do you have any idea what *that* was about?"

"No. It was way beyond what I was equipped to deal with when I was twenty. I remember once she said, 'I wish I could just disappear sometimes.'"

"Those words exactly?"

Francis had the uncanny sensation that someone else had just walked into the room, just outside his line of vision.

"Well, I don't know about 'exactly,'" Doug said. "She was a funny girl. Sometimes you got the impression she just didn't like living in a world with grown-ups."

"What makes you say that?"

"Because the only time I remember her really happy was working with kids over at the clinic in Springfield. We had a thing where we'd volunteer to help do intake at one of the local hospitals two days a week. And after we were done, I'd be out in the parking lot, ready to go for a beer or something. And she'd still be hanging around with the kids inside, playing with dollhouses or building Lego castles in the waiting room. That's who she was comfortable around. I'm not judging her. I'm just saying it wasn't so easy to be in a more mature kind of relationship with her."

"I'm not sure I follow you here."

"Well, I don't want to get too graphic but —" Doug dropped his voice. "She was a little, um, weird about the physical side of things. You kind of got the sense she'd rather be playing Monopoly."

Francis scratched the side of his jaw.

"Yeah, I know what you're thinking." Doug shook his head. "But it wasn't just *me*. She didn't have a lot of boyfriends, period. Before or after, as far as I know. It's like something else was taking up that space in her life."

"Like what?"

"No idea. After college, I only saw her once in a while, when I was in town to visit my folks. But all she ever wanted to do was watch *Star Trek.*"

"Yeah, she was into that, wasn't she?"

"I used to tease her that her tastes never developed past the age of twelve."

There was that déjà vu brownout again. *Star Trek.* Francis tried to follow the string of associations back to the point of origin. "The Cage." Captain Pike. The guy from *The Searchers.* The girl who disappeared. It was like a trail of Christmas lights. One blink, yes. Two blinks, no.

"You know, I saw her a few years ago." Doug sat forward abruptly.

"Who?"

"Allison's mom. Eileen. I was in a restaurant and tried to say hello, but she looked right through me."

"Maybe she didn't recognize you. I hate to tell you, Doug, but none of us are getting any younger."

"No, that wasn't it. She knew who I was. I introduced myself." Doug looked back at the pictures on his credenza. "But she didn't want to see me how I am now. Because she knew Allison would never be this age. Some people just never adjust."

43

MISS, CAN YOU help me, please?"

Eileen was in the children's department at Bloomingdale's, trying to buy the girls winter coats at the Columbus Day sale. They need to cover up in layers, their mother, Jennifer, was always saying. Under the quilt herself today with one of her mysterious flus. The poor thing was having more and more trouble coping. *Layers. We all need layers to protect us.* Something to trap the air between.

She was going from rack to rack, trying to find the right sizes so the girls didn't look like they were being swallowed up in giant down potatoes again, with their little stalklike legs sticking out the bottom. Don't let them get swallowed. *You have to protect them. You have to hold on.*

"Excuse me?" She waved to a slender salesgirl heading to the stockroom with an armload of red sweaters. "Can you help me find something here?"

"Ask Karen. She's over in Juniors."

Eileen wended her way around frilly nightgowns and flannel skirts. Had they changed the layout here? Wasn't it just the other day she was buying a Sunday coat for Allison? Navy felt with a soft velvet collar she liked to rub on her cheek. Weren't they playing this same song, "Dancing Queen," on the sound system?

A cloud of red hair drifted out from behind a row of party dresses. Her heart gave a fierce start. It's her. It's not her.

"Hello . . . I need assistance. . . ."

Everything comes back. Plaid skirts, dying stars, certain fairy tales. You need to stay strong. Don't let them get swallowed. Our skin isn't enough to protect us. We need more layers.

She saw the sign for the Juniors section and turned left. The clothes were too big for the girls here. They were still so small. How could they defend themselves? Their mother couldn't protect them. She was huddled under too many layers herself, a sweet Indiana girl in the big city, afraid to look at what was right in front of her.

The cloud of red hair went past a row of jeans. Eileen felt that tilt in her stomach and that old familiar tension in her hamstrings, the queasiness of seeing a child hang too far out over the edge. A small-boned girl with tiny hands disappeared around a line of blouses. Playing hide-and-seek with her. Eileen found herself starting to follow. It can't be. It can be. Dying stars can reignite.

She caught up just outside the dressing rooms. Out of breath, an old woman shouldn't have to run. She reached for a thin delicate wrist. *There you are, I'll never let you get away again.* She seized the fragile bones and squeezed. The girl, who turned around, had somehow been transformed. The eyes were brown. The skin was copper. The child wasn't there anymore.

"Oh, I'm sorry." Eileen let go and backed away. "I don't know where my mind went."

44

As soon as Hoolian walked in the kitchen at the Elmont Catering Hall that night, he could see things had changed.

Zana was leaning against a stove, smoking a cigarette and talking to one of the other waiters. She brushed her hair back from her ear, turning her wrist out slightly, and gave the other man the same smile that Hoolian had thought she would give only him from now on.

He hung up his jacket near a cutting board and cleared his throat, making his presence known.

"Yo." He gave her a confident little wave, meant to show he was cool about her talking to another guy.

She put her head back and laughed at something the waiter had just said, blowing a trail of smoke at the ceiling and keeping her elbow tucked in protectively against her ribs.

The kitchen was a steam room, full of hot plates coming out of the Hobart dishwasher, butter sizzling in skillets, prep cooks laying small strips of salmon on pumpernickel, and lobsters thrashing around in boiling pots. In the main room next door, the deejay was doing a sound check for the wedding reception, playing "Celebration," with the bass turned up so loud that the bride and groom atop the wedding cake in the corner vibrated.

"Hey, you get any of the messages I left?" Hoolian came over to touch her shoulder. "I've been trying to get you on the phone for two days now. There's some things I think I need to explain to you."

The man she'd been talking to turned around, a tiny gold stud winking in a meaty pink earlobe.

"You mind?" he said.

He was a pumped-up white boy in a rented tux, with a redwood neck, a shaggy mullet, and ruddy shiny features that looked slightly bloated by steroids. In spite of his size, Hoolian sensed something a little soft at the core of him, as if he were only an actor trying to play a tough guy.

"I wasn't talking to you." Hoolian put his shoulders back.

Zana nervously pinched the cigarette between her thumb and forefinger and brought her elbow in closer to her body, as if she were trying to demonstrate a certain kind of European sophistication.

"Since when do you smoke?" asked Hoolian. "You don't do that around your kid, do you?"

"Please, it's not necessary to embarrass me."

"Why? 'Cause I'm trying to speak to you?"

"It's not a good time." She dropped her eyes.

"Well, can we talk afterward on the train? There's some things you need to understand about what happened the other night."

"I have a ride." She glanced over at the guy with the mullet.

"Hey, can you gimme a little space here, Big Man?" Hoolian forced a grin. "Everything's copasetic."

Zana hesitated, tapping the butt of her cigarette before she gave a cautious nod. "Is okay, Nicky."

The big man made a point of wandering only a few feet away, checking his bow tie in a polished samovar as the bartenders started unstacking the crates of champagne.

"So I guess you're upset, huh?" said Hoolian. "You must think I'm some kind of monster, right?"

She put her feet together and adjusted her posture with a resigned formality that he found both poignant and mildly intimidating.

"I didn't say anything."

The cigarette came up near her ear, trembling a little.

"You think I did all those things they said I did, don't you?"

"No, I'm believing you instead," she answered. "Who lies about his real name."

"I was building up to it." He rubbed his hands together, feeling grubby. "I didn't want to scare you off —"

"Tell me," she interrupted. "How many years were you in prison?"

"Almost twenty."

This was clearly not the time to equivocate about bad lawyers and missing witnesses.

"And that's all they give you for killing two women? It's not very much." She turned down the corners of her mouth, as if she were personally offended.

"That was only for *one,* and I didn't fucking do it." He pounded the side of his leg with his fist. "If you read all the way to the end of the story, it said they threw out my original conviction. They made a mistake."

"Then why are they arresting you again?"

"They just want to nail me for *something* because they know they were wrong in the first place and don't want to admit it. Look. It's all just bullshit. They flaked me. I'm the victim here."

She dropped her cigarette into a half-empty champagne flute, extinguishing it with a bitter hiss. "Please, I'm just wanting to know one thing."

"What's that?"

"Were you going to hurt me too?"

She spoke so softly that he almost didn't hear her. *"What?"*

"Isn't that what you were going to do?"

"No. Of course not. Are you crazy?"

"I left my son alone with you. I was going to let him take the train with you."

"Ah, shit." Shame quick-seared him. "He took it bad?"

"The police are in his bedroom. What do you think?"

"Damn."

"I left Kosovo because there were police in the house. And now this? Maybe it's my fault."

"No, it's not your fault. . . ."

The dishwasher opened behind him, releasing a humid fog that engulfed him. How many times could this keep happening? When was he going to get out of this repeating nightmare and find the way back to the life he was meant to have?

"Look." He reached for her. "I'm not the bad guy here —"

"Don't touch me!" She jerked back. "Just get away."

Nicky came lumbering back over, his cummerbund like a weight lifter's belt around his midsection. "Everything okay?"

"Yeah, man, we're fine." Hoolian waved him away. "Just step off. I'm not done with the lady."

"Looks like she's done with you."

"What do you got, telepathy? I didn't hear her ask for you."

"You're scaring her."

"She's not scared. Zana, will you tell this fool what's up?"

She looked away, wiping her hands on her apron.

"All right, there you go." Nicky rested a hand on Hoolian's elbow. "She wants you to let her be."

"Hey, *maricón,* why you feeling me up? You wanna be my boyfriend or something?"

"Easy there, amigo."

"Oh, you speak Spanish now?" Hoolian swatted the hand away. "*Chinga tu madre.* Understand that?"

"You want to fuck my mother?"

"Yeah, I wanna fuck your mother. I fuck your sister, I fuck your grandmother too. *Cara de crica.*"

"Who you calling pussyface?" The big man shoved him back into a stove. "Bitch."

Hoolian heard a loud alarm bell ringing in his ears. He grabbed two hanks of mullet hair, yanked them as hard as he could, and smashed his forehead into the middle of the man's face. He saw little sparks and flaming cinders floating before his eyes. When his vision cleared, he had a splitting headache and Nicky was slumped against a counter, with blood streaming from his nose and wounded rage brimming in his eyes.

Just in case anyone else wanted a piece of him, Hoolian grabbed a skillet off a nearby stove and waved it around, ignoring the way the handle burned his hand. Immediately, everyone else in the kitchen fell into a respectful silence. He noticed how two of them ran out while others started moving knives out of the way.

Their fear invigorated him, gave him a sense of power and authority he hadn't known since he got out of prison. It was almost a relief, to see the veneer of things fall away, to know that once you took away the flowers, the bow ties, the wedding dresses, and the table settings, all the symbols of fake polite society and gentility, it was still a matter of who was willing and able to give out a good beating.

But then he saw the way Zana was looking from his face to the skillet and then back again. It was as if she were seeing him get smaller as the weapon he was holding got bigger.

He realized it was too hot to keep holding. He put the pan down just as Kevin, the professionally charming owner of the catering company, rushed into the kitchen.

"Christopher! What are you doing?"

"Nothing." He felt his palm throb with the burn.

Kevin looked at Nicky holding his nose. "You didn't have to come in tonight," he said, trying to smooth it over as fast as he could. "We could've covered for you."

"Well, I'm here now."

"It's okay, we'll reimburse you." Kevin took a deep breath, making eye contact with everyone in the room to make sure nobody else was hurt. "You should've been informed."

Hoolian touched the bump rising on his forehead and realized it was still slightly damp with Nicky's blood. "Sure? I can stick around to help with the cleanup afterward."

"That's all right. I think we have enough people."

Just over the manager's shoulder Hoolian saw a lobster struggling to get out of a boiling pot, a bright red claw reaching slowly over the edge.

It stretched for the light, straining against its rubber band, making one last desperate attempt at escape.

But it had been sitting in the pot too long. It never stood a chance. Its insides were already cooked. With a heavy scorched heart of his own, Hoolian watched the claw go limp and lifeless over the side.

PART VI

BEGINNING TO SEE THE LIGHT

45

O N THE TUESDAY morning after
Columbus Day, Francis went to a meeting at the district
attorney's office and found Tom and Eileen Wallis already
staring down Paul Raedo and Doctor Dave across a conference table.

"Francis, what is this I'm hearing?" Tom pinched the
fold of skin between his eyes. "You said you were looking
out for our family. Instead, we're getting dragged back and
forth to court again, we've got the media calling the house,
and now I'm hearing some crazy story about my sister's
blood showing up in some other victim's apartment."

"Tom, Eileen, I apologize." Francis took a seat under
Paul's harpoon. "We're going to get to the bottom of
what's going on as soon as we can. Apparently, there's
been some mix-up with the DNA evidence in this case
and we need to get it straightened out before the defense
gets ahold of it and uses it to muddy all the waters."

"I don't understand any of this," said Tom, running his
finger back and forth across a crease in his brow. "First,
you let out my sister's murderer before the end of his
sentence. Then this other girl gets killed and it's somehow

connected to Allison. And in the meantime, this guy Vega is still not back in prison?"

"If I may?" Dr. Dave interrupted. "There are a couple of aspects to this that we need to go over very carefully. We've already established there's a definitive DNA link between your family and the woman whose blood we found at the Christine Rogers homicide. So the first thing we need to know is if you have any other sisters."

"Of course not." Tom rolled his eyes. "What kind of insane question is that?"

"We're just looking for logical explanations about whose blood this might be," said Dr. Dave.

Francis cut a look across the table. "Eileen?"

She'd been sitting there silently, in her black suit and tinted glasses, the elegant sphinx.

"I know this is a hard thing to talk about." He prompted her, thinking she might have doubled up on her meds since the last time he saw her. "But we really need to know. We're all grown-ups in this room. We all understand that things happen before and after people are married. So you need to tell us the truth. Did you ever have another child that you maybe put up for adoption?"

She took off her glasses and looked at him, no clouds in the blue eyes today.

"Francis," she said. "If I'd had another baby, I think I might've noticed. I haven't always been the most observant of parents, but that probably would've gotten my attention."

The men each took a share of one great shrug.

"Wait a second, wait a second." Tom stopped rubbing his forehead, leaving a raw red spot. "How is it exactly that you guys established a link between this newer DNA you found and our family? I don't recall giving anyone a sample."

"I gave it to them," his mother said.

"You what?"

"Detective Loughlin came to see me last week when I was at the playground with the kids," she said. "And so I happily gave him what he needed. In a handkerchief. I'm sorry, honey. I probably should've mentioned it to you."

Tom's Adam's apple went up and down and he turned to Francis, as if he expected an explanation. But Francis was looking at Eileen, trying to figure out what she was up to. Was that the slightest hint of a knowing Cheshire cat smile on her face?

"Well, then, the bottom line is we don't have any choice," said Dr. Dave, picking up a pencil and slowly turning it. "We're going to have to order an exhumation."

"You're going to dig her up?" The red mark on Tom's forehead began to fade.

"I'm afraid we have to," said Dave. "It's the only way we can definitively eliminate your sister as a donor for this more recent sample."

Francis gave Tom a sympathetic nod, knowing what it was like, trying to keep a broken family together.

"Tom, I understand how you feel. . . ."

"You *don't* understand how I feel, Francis. Are they digging up somebody in your family?"

He gave his mother a long-suffering headshake.

"Tom, believe me" — Paul stretched a hand out — "if there was any other way . . ."

"But what about this other story that came out over the weekend?" Tom protested. "The one that said you just found something else that connected Vega to my sister's crime scene? Why aren't you following up on that instead?"

"We are," said Francis. "We still think he's connected to it, but we're at a little bit of an impasse because of this other DNA. So we have to try and clear up where it came from."

"Ucchh." Tom threw himself back in his seat. "It's so sick. I can't believe we have to go through this all over again. It's like you're yanking the stitches off the same wound over and over."

"I'm all for it," said Eileen.

Francis felt a tiny crystal crack in the air. He looked around and saw Paul, Tom, and Dave all similarly brought up short.

"You're all going to see I was right all along," she said. "That's not her."

"Mom . . ." Tom flushed.

"I'm serious. The truth is going to come out."

"See what you did, Francis?" Tom pressed his finger into the tabletop until the cuticle turned white. "You encouraged her. Does she sound sane to you?"

"Doesn't matter," Dr. Dave murmured.

"What do you mean, 'It doesn't matter?' This is going to turn into an even bigger media circus, when I'm trying to protect whatever little shred of dignity my family still has. I'll petition the court to keep it from happening. . . ."

"Don't bother." Paul started shuffling papers.

"What do you mean 'don't bother'? Who are you to tell me?"

"It's the final decision of the chief medical examiner. We don't need a family's permission to exhume a body if it's buried in the five boroughs."

Francis studied the reaction of mother and son. Tom

giving his mother a look somewhere between mournful exhaustion and disgust. And Eileen staring serenely into space, ignoring him, like the smiling figurehead on a great ship oblivious to the spraying crests and dark squalls up ahead.

"So why'd you even bother calling us down here?" Tom asked.

"Common courtesy," said Paul.

46

HOOLIAN, UNSHAVEN AND red-eyed from a sleepless night in a city shelter, showed up at Nita's coffee shop around lunchtime. One side of the restaurant was filled with young mothers with deep circles of their own under their eyes, struggling to shovel the occasional spoonful up to their mouths when they weren't trying to soothe their screaming infants. Relaxed older women in running shoes and denim jackets watched them from across the aisle with wry jaundiced amusement.

"What are you doing here?" Nita intercepted him at the bowl of mints by the register.

"I got thrown out of my halfway house," he said, clutching the duffel bag he'd retrieved from the lot in Red Hook this morning. "They said I was having 'a negative influence on the atmosphere' because of all the bad press."

"What happened?" She looked at the bump he still had on his brow from head-butting Nicky. "They arrested you again for this other girl?"

"No, Nita, listen, I swear I had nothing to do with any

of that. They're just out to get me. It's a setup, to cover for what they did. . . ."

He saw her lids grow heavy; the more he talked, the less she wanted to hear from him.

"Look, I just need a place to stay for a little while. They had me down at the Bellevue shelter last night, and it was just too scary. All the guys in the other beds staring at me and the guards talking about me behind my back. I was afraid to go in the bathroom. It was like being in prison again, except worse because I don't even have a cell to hide out in. I was just out in the open, where anyone could get me."

"Well, you can't stay here again." Nita tucked a pen behind her ear. "My boss found out about it last time and almost fired my ass."

"Then maybe I could go home with you, just for a couple of nights. I'll sleep on the floor, I'll sleep in the tub. I don't care. . . ."

"No, baby, I can't do that for you."

He waited for her to explain, but she didn't. Not even an excuse that her apartment was too small. She just didn't want to be alone with him.

"Then I don't know where I'm gonna go tonight." He flapped his arms. "I can't go back to that shelter. I'll wake up with a shiv in my chest."

"But what happened to your case? I thought you were going to go prove you didn't kill that first girl and all that."

"I tried, but I got kind of sidetracked. Things came up. I got a job, met a girl. Shit happens. . . ."

It was his own fault, he realized. If he'd been able to maintain that same 24/7 sense of vigilance he'd had in prison, he would've been all right. But no, he had to let his guard down. He had to let himself get seduced by an illusion. He'd forgotten he was still in the cage.

"Who was the girl?" she asked.

"What?"

"You said you got mixed up with a girl." Her eyes narrowed on the little flesh-colored Band-Aid that had replaced the gauze on the back of his hand. "That's not this other doctor they're talking about in the news, is it?"

"*No.* Shit. Nita. Listen to what I'm trying to tell you, will you? I know everybody who's been in prison says they're innocent. But I'm *really* innocent."

A bell rang from the kitchen pass-through and a cook appeared in the slot, pointing down at a garden burger on a bed of wilted lettuce.

"You gotta help me, Nita, I'm serious. You remember me from back in the day. I was a good boy. They got all these crazy ideas about what went on between Allison and me. Maybe you can just tell them that after I left her apartment I came downstairs and played checkers with you."

"You want me to lie and say I was with you when she got killed twenty years ago?"

"We used to hang out sometimes, didn't we?"

She shook her head, the net of lines slowly tightening over her face as if someone had pulled a drawstring on them. "I'm sorry, baby. I can't do that for you."

"Shit."

He hunched forward and held himself. It felt like he had hot oil leaking from his guts.

Another waitress rushed up to the register and frantically started punching in numbers. A lady with twins in a double stroller cruised up with a check and a fifty in hand, forcing Hoolian to step to the side.

"Well, could you maybe front me a little cash 'til I get paid again?" he asked, raising his head up. "I'm between jobs, but I'm good for it. You know that, don't you?"

"Julian, I'm barely scraping by on tips myself. Haven't you been talking to your father's union to see if you're due any benefits?"

"I been trying, but those motherfuckers won't return my letters or phone calls."

"Then I don't know what to tell you. . . ."

The cash drawer shot open with a jolt and the lady with the double stroller put her hand out for change.

Something. He needed *something* to hold himself together. He was getting so scared and paranoid that he no longer trusted his most basic perceptions from one moment to the next or his ability to react to things rationally.

The waitress started counting out singles and putting them in the lady's outstretched palm. *Two, three, four . . .* It was inevitable. He was going back upstate, no matter what he did. He was just a dog, low and feral, only dreaming of being off the leash.

He thought of just grabbing the money out of the lady's hand, knocking her down, and shoving the stroller out of the way as he ran out of here. Knowing full well he'd be caught by the time he reached the subway. But at least then it would be over. They would arrest him and send him away again, and that would be that. His destiny would be fulfilled. People would nod their heads sagely and say, *Well, of course.* And maybe then he could finally stub out that last little glowing ember of hope that had kept him from slipping all the way into darkness, like the guy in that old War song.

But then he felt a tug just below his waist, and looked

down to see Nita stuffing a pair of folded twenties into his pants pocket.

"Get out of here," she murmured as the bald-headed manager hurried by. "And don't come back no more. You used me up."

He pushed the money the rest of the way into his pocket, grabbed a fistful of stale mints from the silver bowl, and left.

47

FRANCIS EASED OFF on the brake, following the morgue wagon past the tombstone multitudes and out through the grand Gothic archway, leaving the eternal peace of Cricklewood Cemetery for the bumper-to-bumper hip-hop-and-holler cacophony of Fourth Avenue.

"So you were talking to Scottie Ferguson about this, huh?" He adjusted the rearview.

"He was standing there, videotaping the backhoe, and he asked me a simple question." Paul fidgeted in the passenger seat. "You want me to say, 'It's business as usual'?"

"I just hate to think anybody's trying to pass the buck here." He turned the wheel, remembering how Paul had been pointing at him at the graveside.

"Nobody's passing the buck, Francis. Don't be paranoid."

He followed the ME's van down toward Fort Hamilton Parkway, headed for the Brooklyn Battery Tunnel. Huge rattling oil trucks and minivans shot out of his blind spots on either side, veering dangerously close and cutting into the lane in front of him without putting their signals on.

"Paranoid is not necessarily a bad thing in this case," he said, looking quickly over his shoulder. "Can you imagine what would happen if it got out to the press that we dug this girl up?"

"Hey, look out, you're about to hit a traffic cone."

"I see it." Francis swerved.

"I'm just saying there's no need for us to turn on each other."

"Absolutely, Judge. If one of us goes down, the rest of us do."

They stopped at a light before the tow bridge, the Gowanus Canal rippling its green scales below them. Back in the eighties, Francis had been on a barge with Harbor Patrol when they dredged out a corpse, everyone saying they were surprised it didn't have fins after a few days facedown in that toxic brew. Now they were flushing out the greasy old vein, and supposedly there were already blue crabs and jellyfish down there, a whole new ecosystem beginning. This city. You could never really say any part of it was dead for good.

"So, what do you think?"

Francis watched the morgue wagon idling in front of them. "You mean if it turns out that the girl we dug up isn't Allison?"

"I've got to tell you, I'm scared." Paul pumped his leg up and down, as if he had his own pedals. "What if it turns out the mother's been right all along that it's somebody else's remains?"

"Let's not get ahead of ourselves. Could be a lot of other explanations."

"Like what?"

Francis, listening to the vibrations of the engine, said nothing.

"What's up with her anyway, the mother?" asked Paul. "She was always a little spooky, but what was that business about giving you the DNA in the handkerchief? I thought you got it from her on the sly."

"I thought I did too. But I guess she was way ahead of me."

"So you thinking she knows more than she's been saying?"

"I've had a hintch for a while." Francis stepped on the gas as the light changed.

"A what?"

"A hintch. It's halfway between a hint and a hunch."

"So, what is it? You still think there's another daughter?"

"I was just looking at a box of medical records from St. Luke's-Roosevelt from about a year and a half ago, when Christine Rogers was doing her residency in the ER there."

"Yeah, and?"

"Could be nothing. But she was on duty the same night they brought Eileen Wallis in for eating half a bottle of Valium and chasing them with a couple of glasses of Bordeaux."

He heard a loud thump from Paul's side of the car but didn't dare to look over.

"You're shitting me."

"I shit you not." He moved the mirror once more and saw Paul looking nauseous. "Listen, it's a big hospital and she wasn't the doctor who treated Eileen that night. But it's definitely bothering me. I got Rashid and a couple of the other guys trying to run down the staff and see if anybody saw these two talking to each other."

"And what if they did? What would it mean?"

"I don't know. Fuckin' weird coincidence, if that's all it is."

They crossed over the bridge, the suspension shimmying as the tires rolled over the ironwork. It had been there from the start, Francis realized. Maybe not even a *hintch,* but a very slight *hitch.* He'd seen it for probably less than an eighth of a second twenty years ago when he'd asked Eileen if she wanted to view the body. A kind of momentary blankness that came over her. As if she were erasing one face before she came up with a more appropriate one to show the world.

"I'll tell you one thing we are doing, though," he said.

"What's that?"

"I called up Dr. Dave at the ME's and asked him to run Eileen's profile against Christine Rogers's DNA."

"What?!" Paul's seat vinyl squeaked. "You think *they're* related?"

"Anything's possible, man. She was an adopted girl, looking for her mother in the city. I'm still wide-open."

"Oh shit." The whole balance of the car seemed to shift with Paul sinking down into his seat. "Now you're really fucking scaring me, Francis. You got anything else you been holding back on me?"

"Nothing that comes to mind immediately."

Two lanes were closed for construction ahead of them and cars began to merge recklessly. He lost sight of the morgue wagon behind an Access-A-Ride minibus for the handicapped.

"Don't go nuts on me, Paul. I got no proof of anything.

I don't even have a theory yet. It's just something to keep our eye on."

"Hey, Francis."

"What?"

"I think you just missed our exit."

48

EVEN MORE JITTERY after spending a night trying to sleep on the A train, Hoolian showed up that morning at the offices of his father's old union, Local 32BJ, just north of Canal, where the streets splayed out like the extended blades of a Swiss Army knife. With a certain amount of wheedling and brandishing of old letterheads and IDs, he managed to talk his way up to the twentieth floor, where the East Side delegates had their offices.

He wound up outside a gray cubicle, its flannel walls adorned with a "Justice for Janitors" poster and a pennant for the Coqui Soccer Club in Puerto Rico.

A heavyset man in a boxy suit sat behind a large desk with an old green doorman's cap resting on the far right corner. He had a lumpy omelet face, glasses as thick as a World War I pilot's goggles, and a ring that looked like it had been detached from a set of brass knuckles on his left hand. If he ever took his jacket off, Hoolian was sure there would be half-moons of sweat under his arms.

"Uh, Mr. Tavares?"

"Who wants to know?"

"They sent me up here from Payroll. They said you might be able to help me out."

"Yeah, who'd you talk to down there?" The delegate's eyes didn't stray from his computer monitor.

"Carmen. She said I had to catch you before ten in the morning or after four in the afternoon, because the rest of the time you were out talking to the membership."

"I'm going to have to have a word with Carmen."

"Don't give her a hard time." Hoolian stepped into the cubicle and grabbed the back of a chair, trying to keep from getting swept out too quickly. "I've been bombarding her, trying to get a meeting. I just wanted to know about my father's pension and benefits package."

"What about it?"

"He worked in an A building on the East Side for twenty-two years, most of them as the super. I was trying to find out what the family was entitled to."

"He still alive?"

"No. Died from emphysema and diabetes a few years ago."

"Mother?"

"She's been gone longer. Since '70."

"Then you got *nada,* my friend. There, that was easy."

Hoolian squeezed the back of the chair with both hands, trying to take it in stride. This one little nugget of pride that he'd been protecting had just been stepped on and ground into dust. He looked at the doorman's cap on the desk and had to bite the inside of his cheek, to keep from crying. Twenty-two years of service had no meaning, no value, no legacy that could be passed on to him.

"Come on, amigo." The delegate picked up his phone. "You want a long sit-down, talk to your shop steward about setting up an appointment with me. Are you even in the union yourself?"

"No."

"Ayy. Why am I talking to you then?"

"I just thought . . ." His voice trailed off as he kept looking at the doorman's cap with its gold braid over the bill. "I just thought you could help me for old times . . ."

"*Vete a bañar.* This is Local 32*BJ,* amigo, not the Salvation Army. Who the hell's your father anyway?"

"Osvaldo Vega."

"For real?"

"Why, did you know him?"

"No, but . . ." Uncertainty inched across the delegate's well-mapped face. "You serious? Osvaldo was the Man."

"I know. . . ."

"No, I mean, he was like the Jackie Robinson of Puerto Rican supers." Tavares fumbled to hang up the phone. "Before him, it was almost all Irish running the A buildings below 96th Street on the East Side."

Hoolian half smiled, pleased to hear Papi spoken of with the respect he deserved.

Tavares angled his glasses. "So you're the kid who just got out of the can?"

"Basically."

"The thing with the girl who got killed in the building that was back in the papers a few weeks ago?"

"Yeah, but they set me up. . . ." He was so sick of hearing himself say the same words over and over that he was beginning not to believe them.

"I have a brother who's been in and out of state prison a few times himself," Tavares said grimly, tugging at the ring that seemed destined never to come off his pudgy finger. "Can't stay off drugs."

"That wasn't my problem," Hoolian snapped. "My problem was the union wouldn't help my father find a decent lawyer."

"Hey, bro." Tavares put his hands up. "I'm not saying the union was perfect back in the day, but there wasn't much we could've done anyhow. The bylaws are damn specific. We can only shell out for Class E and D felonies. You get charged with murder, *compañero*, that's a whole 'nother ball game. We had troubles of our own."

Hoolian nodded, remembering the stories his father used to tell him about corruption at the local. But what was the point of bringing any of that up now? *Put the ass on your lip,* they used to say upstate. *Put the ass on your lip and keep kissing it.* Nobody gave you a fucking thing in this life because you made them feel bad. They either helped you because they were scared of you or because it made *them* feel good.

"I wish I could help you out, my friend, but my hands are tied. We can't give you any benefits and we can't get involved with the case. I don't know what else I can tell you."

Hoolian picked up the doorman's cap and studied the inside stitching, hearing a window start to open a little in Tavares's voice. "Well, could you maybe try and help me find somebody who used to work for Papi?"

"Who's that?"

"It's a long shot. Guy's probably dead now anyway. Old Dominican porter named Nestor. I don't even think he was in the union."

"What makes you think he wasn't in the union?" Tavares sat up, defensive, his pride challenged.

"I doubt he was in the country legally. I always thought

my father was just paying him off the books to help out in the basement."

"That doesn't sound like what I heard about Osvaldo. Far as I know, he was a member in good standing 'til the day he died. Never hired scabs and honored every strike we had. Not a bad little organizer either, when it came time to get the vote out. I don't think he would've put anyone on the payroll who wasn't in the local. It's up to the building's management to figure out whether they're here legally."

"No way is this guy alive." Hoolian put the cap aside, changing his mind and deciding he didn't want to get suckered again. "He was probably sixty when I knew him. And he was telling people he had liver cancer."

"You never know with some of these old porters. They're tougher than cockroaches. If the cleaning fluids and carbon monoxide fumes don't kill them, nothing will. Survival of the fittest."

No. They weren't going to play him anymore. No one was going to fool him into thinking things could turn out right. *Leave me alone. Just let me stay in my little dark box with the bars around it.*

"So why do you want to find him?" the delegate asked.

"I thought he could help with my case."

"What do you mean? Like as a witness?"

"I'm saying it's a long shot." Hoolian nodded.

Tavares started to reach for the phone, then pulled his hand back. "You know, there's no percentage in us getting involved. We don't gain anything from being associated with a criminal case after all the shit we've gone through with the reorganization."

"I hear you."

"Twenty years is a long time, though." Tavares scowled, working a finger into his ear. "And we didn't exactly step up to the plate the last time, did we?"

"I didn't say anything."

Hoolian tried to arrange his features into the shy diffident expression he'd seen his father wear around Christmastime, when the tips were given out. Keep the ass on your lip. Don't let it fall off. He realized now that the old man had been a master at hiding his true feelings.

Tavares removed the finger, studied it, and reached for the phone. "What'd you say this porter's last name was?"

49

JUST BEFORE MIDNIGHT, Dr. Dave walked into a bar near Bellevue called the Recovery Room, ordered a Guinness draft and punched the Doors song into the jukebox with the line "CANCEL MY SUBSCRIPTION TO THE RESURRECTION. . . ."

"I'm thinking you got something to tell me," said Francis, waiting for him in a back booth.

"You're killing me with these hours, Francis. Nobody comes back with DNA results in less than a day. It's unheard-of. Backs up the whole system."

"So, what do you got?"

The doctor watched the sandstorm raging inside his glass, the head of the stout slowly settling. His eyes looked small and irritated from having stared at polymerase chain reactions and gel screens nonstop since they had brought the body in. Jim Morrison droned on in the background. Another one who wasn't supposed to be buried in his own grave, Francis remembered. Probably fat, bald, and living in a condo in Florida, playing golf twice a week with Elvis and cursing every time "Light My Fire" came on the radio.

"There wasn't a lot left after twenty years." Dave turned his glass. "Mostly bone fragments and hair. But we got enough."

"And? Is it Allison?"

"What I can tell you is this." Dave held a finger up, refusing to be rushed. "I can definitely tell you that it's a female. I can tell that she was also the daughter of Eileen Wallis. I can tell you that she was probably between twenty-one and thirty years old and that she was no taller than five foot three. She had no signs of osteoporosis and had never been pregnant. Her actual name is not for me to determine."

"So it's *not* the same woman whose DNA was under both girls' fingernails?

"It was not."

"So it probably *was* Allison buried in the right grave?"

"That I don't know. The DNA we got out of the coffin does not match the sample on the pillowcase that was labeled 'Allison Wallis' at the warehouse. It's possible it was a filing mistake. But what I can say for sure is that the woman in the coffin and the one whose blood we found at both crime scenes definitely have the same mother."

"Fuuuck." Francis tipped a wedge of lime into his club soda and watched the bubbles fizz up. "You're telling me Allison was killed by her *sister?* The mom's still saying she never had another daughter. And there's no match for this girl, whoever she is, in any of the DNA data banks."

"I don't care. I have my gels. The same blood was under Allison Wallis's fingernails and Christine Rogers's. And so all I can tell you is that it's the sister of that donor who we dug up."

"And what about that other thing I asked you about? Did you compare Christine Rogers's DNA to Eileen's to see if they're related?"

"They aren't related, Francis. Different families."

"Then I'm tapped out."

Francis finished his club soda and put the glass down. Oh, to have a real drink now. Just to be able to have the clamps off his skull for a few minutes. He'd been more himself when he was drinking. Looser, funnier, not so hemmed in by caution. Braver too. He wouldn't be skulking around, avoiding the dark places, if he were still boozing it up. No sir. He'd be bold and reckless, the way he was in the Narcotics days, first man through the door, consequences be damned, willing to do whatever it took, other men watching him with that bleary-eyed admiration again.

Oh shaddup, Francis, you were an asshole. Only thing almost as bad as a blind man with a gun is a nostalgic drunk.

"Shit, I don't know what I'm doing," he said. "Maybe my daughter's right."

"About what?"

"The other night, she called home from Smith, told me I'm becoming a dinosaur. Says, 'Patriarchal modes of thinking are obsolete.' Can you believe that?"

"Well, I can't say our mode of thinking is getting us anywhere in this case."

"No, I suppose there's no argument there," Francis conceded.

He studied the dead lime lying at the bottom of his glass. *Come on, God of Small Things.* Help me out. I didn't have a drink just now when I could've used one. Open my mind a little wider. Let me think outside the lines. The longer these cases went on, the more you got locked into just one way of looking at them, getting stale and unimaginative from staring straight ahead all the time, missing the side views.

He shut his eyes. For a few seconds he went dark, imagining he was already blind. Waiting for the afterflash to stop, making himself still, and letting the visible skin of the world fall away.

Eventually he noticed the sounds around him becoming more defined and nuanced. He found he could distinguish the clinking of wineglasses from the heavier clunk highball glasses made. He recognized the thin tap of stiletto heels passing, with the cloddish stamp of a man's rubber soles close behind. He realized he could pick up cues about age, regional differences, and even romantic expectations, if he listened hard enough for pauses in conversation. But when he tried to focus on one voice in the booth right behind them, he found he couldn't quite tell if it was male or female.

"Francis? You all right?"

He opened his eyes and saw Dave staring at him.

"Jesus, I thought you were having a seizure."

"No, just going off-road a little," he said, studying the Guinness foam as it settled halfway down the glass. "Dave, let me ask you something."

"What?"

"Are you sure genes never lie?"

"Am I *what?*"

"I'm not talking about a mistake on paper. I'm asking, does DNA ever get it wrong?"

"I told you, one in a trillion times. What're you drinking anyway?"

Francis watched the tracks of brownish residue sinking

down the sides of Dave's glass, reminding him of the gel screens he'd seen at the lab. Something was ebbing away inside him, leaving him with a bleak clarity.

"I think you better let me get the next round," he said.

50

IT WAS LIKE music in a dream. Soft cloudy chords drifting and dissolving in the moist air. It was only as Hoolian got closer that a song started to take shape. An incandescent trill at the high end of the keyboard sweeping down into a dark moody thunderhead. An urbane stroll through the middle range suddenly tripping into a wild rampage over the black keys. And then quickly shifting right back into the elegant melody, like a drunk straightening his tie on the sidewalk after getting thrown out of a four-star restaurant.

The card with the union bug that Mr. Tavares gave Hoolian got him past the doorman and down into this basement. So now he turned the corner and made his way past the musty storage cages, following the sound of one of his father's favorite songs meticulously deconstructed and put back together by a mad scientist.

"Night and day, you are the one . . ."

This was one of those Upper East Side buildings that kept its lobby and hallways pristine, while its past moldered down in the cellar. He walked by the wire-mesh cells of ancient rocking horses, dismantled four-posters, Old World Victrolas with big sound horns, wardrobe boxes, gilt-edged mirrors, tarnished silver tea services, decommissioned dining-room tables with their legs off, mounted moose heads, tongue-tied Persian rugs cinched in twine, antique lamps with shades like flappers' dresses—all sitting in six-by-nine bins, long-forgotten inmates in a secured facility.

". . . and this torment won't be through . . ."

He stifled a cough from the dust, knowing he'd chase his quarry away by making too much noise before he walked up on it. The boiler rumbled next door, a steady toiling flame. Twenty years he'd been waiting.

He went around the corner and then stopped, watching the old man stooped over a Wurlitzer upright in a storage bin. An abrupt hiked shoulder sent a spasm down his arm and into an arthritic-looking claw. It was hard to believe someone so gnarled and decrepit was making such soaring sprightly youthful music.

Water flushed through one of the overhead waste pipes and the old man threw his head back, relishing the sheer pleasure of playing for himself and no one else.

"¿Qué hay de nuevo, Nestor?" Hoolian called out to him from under a bare swinging bulb. "Remember me?"

The old man froze, his hands hesitating over the keys, the unresolved melody left hanging in the air. Then he turned, peered out, and slowly smiled with crooked brown teeth, as if he'd been sitting in this very cage since 1983, waiting for Hoolian to find him.

51

O RIGINALLY, THEY WERE all supposed to meet again in court today, to decide whether to go forward with Hoolian's indictment. Instead, they were back up in the sixth-floor conference room at 100 Centre Street, Paul Raedo sitting under the portrait of Custer, a young homicide prosecutor named Margaret Eng under an Ansel Adams nature print, and Francis within easy reach of Paul's harpoon. Hoolian sat brooding across the table, sandwiched between Debbie A. and the brand-new witness.

"I have to say, I'm very skeptical," Paul began brusquely. "I spoke to this witness back in '83 and he had nothing relevant to say. Why is he coming forward with a different story after all this time?"

"Mr. Vega asked him to." Debbie swiveled in her seat. "Mr. Arroyo has known the defendant since he was a child."

The porter was on her right, a shrunken courtly-looking old man in a threadbare checked jacket. Francis reckoned he'd probably retrieved it from a wealthy tenant's Goodwill pile back in 1962. A white straw Panama hat sat on the table before him, with what looked like a bite taken out of the brim. When he smiled, he revealed a state of civil unrest in his mouth, little brown teeth turning against one another. In fact, everything about him seemed a little like battered bamboo, except for his hands, which were wide long-fingered spans with tendons like suspension cables.

"Yeah, yeah, yeah, but why only now?" Paul asked. "You're telling me he's been sitting on this twenty years?"

"Mr. Arroyo had concerns about his immigration status." Debbie glanced back and forth between the new witness and Hoolian, both on her left. "He was worried that if he testified, he could get deported back to the Dominican Republic."

"Am I hearing an element of coercion here?" Paul leaned back under Custer, a thumb under his red suspenders as he gave Margaret Eng a sidelong glance. "Is this guy suddenly changing his tune because your client showed up and intimidated him at his workplace?"

"Just let him tell the story," Francis snapped.

The rest of them looked at him like he'd fired a gun at the ceiling.

"Well, come on," he said. "He's not a sworn witness yet. Let's hear what he has to say. Give him a Queen for a Day."

He felt Hoolian's eyes boring into him from across the table. Francis had deliberately chosen a seat just a little to the right so that they wouldn't have to face each other directly yet. He, at least, needed a chance to work up to it.

Paul grimaced and then quietly conferred with Margaret Eng. She tossed her black mane, adjusted her horn-rims, and gave a curt nod.

"All right, Queen for a Day," said Margaret. "He gets a pass for the time being as long as he tells us the truth."

Debbie started to translate, but the old porter put his hand up.

"Is okay," he said, a slight lisp whistling through gaps in his teeth. "I unnerstand, a little."

The porter looked across Debbie A. and flashed a smile at Hoolian. From the corner of his eye, Francis noted that Hoolian didn't smile back, preferring to concentrate on the task of folding and unfolding the corner of a press release left lying on the table.

"You can bring in the office translator once we're done here so you can ask your own questions and get a full written statement, without Mr. Vega or myself in the room," Debbie said. "Mr. Arroyo already told me the whole narrative when he came to my office with Mr. Vega this morning."

A knot of tension was forming in the middle of the room, the six of them staring at the same whorl in the lacquered wood as if it were drawing them all together.

"Long and short of it is, Mr. Arroyo was working in the basement that night," Deb explained. "He saw someone come down the fire stairs and go out the entrance to the alley behind the building well within the time frame of Allison Wallis's murder."

"Bull*shit*." Paul's suspenders stretched like slingshots.

"Do you want to hear what happened or do you want to show off your vocabulary?" Debbie asked.

"Keep going." Francis made a rolling motion with his hand. "What time would this have been?"

"About two-thirty, quarter to three in the morning." Deb looked at the porter, confirming. "It fits right in with the frame that's been established."

"How you figure that?" asked Francis, making her work for it.

"Nine-thirty, Julian comes to Allison's apartment to fix her toilet. Ten o'clock, they start to watch television. Channel Five, MTV. They start to get comfortable, and that's when this little encounter between them takes place."

"You mean it's when he tried to rape her." Paul leaned forward on his elbows.

"When they tried to have *consensual* contact." Debbie wagged a finger. "There's no testimony to contradict it."

"Course not." Paul smirked. "He's alive and she's dead."

"In any event, there's no question that it didn't work out," Deb said quickly.

Francis smiled, recognizing the Moment of Acceleration, that familiar way defense lawyers and their clients raced over shaky parts of their story, as if no one would notice them.

"She pulled back," Deb said, slowing down slightly. "He wasn't ready. She wasn't ready. Whatever. They both got scared. It's a disaster. There's blood and semen on the slipcover. She freaks out, asks him to leave."

Francis snuck a glance at Hoolian, to gauge his reaction. But Hoolian was biting his lip and looking down, not daring to meet the eye of either of the women in the room.

"After that, there's a series of phone calls to her mother in Sag Harbor and her brother in the city," Debbie said. "Obviously, she's got something on her mind."

"Yeah, the fact that the super's son just tried to jump her," Paul said.

"Neither of them mentioned that," Deb countered.

"Tom thinks they talked about where they were going to go for their mother's birthday dinner, which was coming up. Eileen didn't remember anything specific about her conversation, except that Allison seemed 'agitated.'"

"Come on, Deb, you know that happens in sex assaults," Paul interrupted again. "Sometimes people wait until the next day to report it. Except this time, he had a key to her apartment so he could let himself back in later the same night."

"Welll . . . not quite . . ." Deb rounded on him. "We're thinking someone else could've had a key."

"How? It was only tenants and the super who had keys."

"She could've had a copy made and given it to somebody, who could've let themselves in the front."

"What about the doorman? Don't you think he'd notice?"

Hoolian and the porter looked at each other and laughed.

"What's so funny?" asked Francis.

Hoolian stopped smiling abruptly and looked over, reminding Francis of the very first time they'd laid eyes on each other. The deer hearing the hunter in the woods. They both froze a little, still not quite ready to acknowledge each other.

"Everybody knows Boodha was so deep in the bag by midnight, you could stick a cherry bomb up his ass and he wouldn't wake up." Hoolian turned back to Nestor, trying to pretend he wasn't bothered. "Ain't that right?"

"*Ay* . . ." The old man threw his head back, with a hacking bark. "*El borracho bufón.*"

"Yeah, fine, but this is all just total speculation." Paul

waved them off. "I expected more from you, Deb. I thought you came here to talk about something real."

"I did. Mr. Arroyo saw your murderer leave the building just before three in the morning."

"Who's this supposed to be, and why didn't he tell me about it when I interviewed him twenty years ago?"

"I do," the porter spoke up. "But you no listen."

"*What?*" said Paul. "Look, I went through the case file. You think I'd deliberately ignore something like that?"

Francis noticed Margaret Eng putting her head down and starting to take copious notes. No fool, this one. She knew potentially exculpatory evidence for a civil suit when she heard it.

"I say, '*Pelirrojo! Pelirrojo!*'" The porter pounded his fist on the table. "But you still no listen."

"What is this, Debbie?" Paul motioned like he was shoving garbage over toward her side of the table. "What's '*pelirrojo*'? We talked to this guy once and then he disappeared on us."

"Because you scared him away, telling him he had to come to court and answer questions. He had a family here and no green card. Now he's got one."

Francis stared at the old man, thinking he must be a pretty hard-bitten character. Letting his boss's son do twenty years for a crime he didn't commit, just because he was worried about deportation.

On the other hand, who was he to talk? Up until his last conversation with Dr. Dave, he'd done a pretty good job of ducking and weaving himself, to avoid what was right in front of him.

He angled his chair and tried to make himself look Hoolian straight in the eye. He wanted to see if anything remained of that boy who'd been in the interrogation room twenty years ago.

Where was the weasely little shifting of the pupils? The fluttery eyelashes. The drumming fingertips. All the little telltale signs of guilt. How did this bearded, justifiably pissed-off, old-before-his-time *man* take his place?

It was too much. Both of them turned away at the same time. Neither of them ready for full-on confrontation just yet.

"What does that mean anyway? *Pelirrojo?*" Paul glanced at Margaret Eng, who was busy taking notes. "Remind me."

"It means redhead," Hoolian said softly, staring down into his own lap.

"Yes, I know." Paul threw his pen down. "The victim had red hair. So what?"

This time, Francis set him straight. "Paulie," he said quietly, looking away. "I don't think this guy is talking about the victim."

52

Hoolian came down in the elevator forty minutes later with his lawyer and Nestor, still trying to absorb and integrate everything that had just happened.

The dim marble lobby was full of grim-faced family members moving slowly through the metal detectors, white-shirted court officers barking orders, and, of course, all the young men in trouble, on their way to court. Strutting around in their FUBU shirts and fresh-from-the-box Nikes, all chesty attitude with no idea of what a bid in state prison was actually going to do to them.

"Way out's over there." Ms. Aaron pointed to daylight beyond the revolving doors. "We're done for the moment."

Hoolian followed her out onto the sidewalk, with Nestor close behind.

"So, what happens now?" He shielded his eyes from the sparkling mica.

"We file a motion to get the indictment dismissed." Ms. A. put on her sunglasses. "The police and prosecutors do whatever it is they do. And eventually we'll try to mount our civil suit, provided Mr. Arroyo here doesn't disappear on us for another twenty years."

Nestor smiled at her with his crooked teeth.

"Claro," he said with a slight bow. Of course.

She pursed her lips, clearly not charmed by his courtly older gentleman act. "Sir, I want to ask you something."

He tipped back the brim of his battered Panama. *"Cualquier cosa."* Anything at all.

"You claim to be very fond of Mr. Vega."

"Sí."

"And you mentioned to me earlier that you thought his father was a great man for hiring you and keeping you on the payroll, even when you didn't have your green card."

"¡Ai!" He nodded at Hoolian. *"Yo dar las gracias."*

"Then why on earth would you let his only son spend twenty years rotting in prison?"

The old man kept smiling and nodding, as if he hadn't understood a word she'd said.

"Hey, Ms. A.?" Hoolian piped up. "Don't be too hard on him."

"Julian, this man could've come forward with this evidence at any time."

"Yeah, I was mad at first too," he sighed. "But people have circumstances, you know."

"Circumstances?" Her eyebrows jumped over her tinted frames. "What kind of circumstances justify letting a seventeen-year-old boy go to jail from 1983 until now?"

"Look, when I found him down in the basement last night, I was mad too. I was like, 'I'm a kill you, old man. You ruined my life.'" Hoolian popped a fist into his palm. "But then . . . I don't know. It's different when it's somebody you grew up around. Tell me, how am I gonna hate someone who used to let me run the service elevator when I was six?"

"He certainly didn't do much to look out for you after that."

"I know." Hoolian gritted his teeth. "But what am I gonna do? He was scared. He got all spooked by Mr. Raedo and left the city. He didn't know what was going to happen to me."

"I'm sure he heard once you got locked up," Ms. A. said, still indignant on his behalf.

"He had his own shit to deal with. He thought he was dying of liver cancer. His son died of a drug overdose. His wife left him. People have their own lives, I guess. I stopped expecting anyone to look out for me a long time ago."

The old man's eyes glimmered in silent appreciation.

"You're a forgiving soul, Julian." Ms. A. shook her head.

"No, I'm not," he corrected her. "I'm still *all* fucked up about it, but I'm no fool. When I found that old man, I knew I had a choice. I could either break his neck, or I could try and get him to help me."

He wrung the back of Nestor's neck half playfully and felt the old man stiffen a bit.

"I knew my father would've told me just to use my head."

"You're still a better man than I am, Gunga Din," Ms. A. said, turning back to Nestor. "But, Mr. Arroyo, I still don't know about you. I'm glad we have your statement so we finally know the real story, but it's a little late. You'd think someone who'd experienced that kind of pain in their lives might show a little more compassion for someone he knew. And don't pretend you don't understand. I think your English is a lot better than you let on."

The porter smiled and tipped back his Panama. *"¿Qué quiere de mí, yo soy solo el pianista?"* he said.

"What does that mean?" Ms. A. looked to Hoolian for translation.

"He says, 'What do you want from me, lady? I'm only the piano player.'"

53

As THE NIGHT began to soften and a fine mist settled over Riverside Park, men in shirtsleeves alighted from the brownstones on 89th Street, noisily dragging trash cans to the curb for early-morning pickup. Tom Wallis was among the last of them, lugging his two barrels like there were bodies inside and then clapping his hands as he went back up the stoop and into the house, satisfied with a job well done.

"All right, that's it." Rashid, in the driver's seat, lowered his binoculars. "He's got it all out there."

"Lights on in the house?" asked Francis, sitting beside him in the Le Sabre parked a half block away.

"Just on the third floor and first floor."

"Then Eileen and him are both still awake. We better wait awhile. I don't want to tip our hand and let 'em see what we're up to."

They sat in silence for a while, listening to the riotous wail of uilleann pipes and electric guitar on the CD player until Rashid couldn't take it anymore.

"'I was born to play the funky ceílí'?" He ejected

the disc and held it up to the dome light. "What kind of fucked-up shit is that?"

"Black 47 rule. And we just got through a half hour of Biggie Smalls and Dr. Dre bitch-slapping ho's and smoking blunts."

"All right then, let's not listen to anything. Let's just sit here."

"Fine."

They waited until the upstairs light went off, and then Francis took the binoculars.

"Say, man, you think it's weird we don't talk more?" Rashid finally asked.

"Why, what's on your mind?"

"I'm just saying you're pretty closemouthed, G. You mad at me or something?"

"No. Why do you say that? You one of those oversensitive guys watches Oprah and cries at card tricks?"

"That's what my wife says, man. But she don't know. She got a mouth like a MAC-10. But I was telling her the other night. 'I don't know what's up with this guy I'm working with. He got a nasty attitude. He won't even wave to me when I see him across the street.'"

"When was this?"

"It's happened like three times. I was right there on Broadway outside the office and you acted like you didn't see me."

"Sorry." Francis lowered the glasses, not able to see shit in this light. "No disrespect."

"I'm just saying, I'm having a seriously hard time getting synched up with you. I feel like you got a whole house party going on in your head all the time, and I'm not invited. This is some lonesome-prairie shit, sitting here. If you're still pissed about what happened at the crime scene, you should get it off your chest. I don't deserve the silent treatment, son. I'm voluble. I like to talk."

"Hey, Rashid, you know how you can tell you have a good relationship with your partner?" Francis interrupted. "It's when you *don't* have to say anything. You can just anticipate what the other guy is thinking. I mean, you and I, we could sit here and we could talk about whatever you talk about when you spend eight hours in a car with somebody. We could talk about the case or tax-deferred Treasury bonds or the Yankees or whatever. But in the end the way we're gonna know we're really getting along is when we can spend eight hours together and not say a word to each other."

"Wow." Rashid sighed. "Your poor fucking wife."

"Brother, you don't know the half of it." Francis gave him back the glasses. "That woman's a saint for staying with me. Every day I thank God for clouding her mind until I could get her up the aisle."

Rashid stewed a few more seconds. "I just want to say one more thing, all right? I'm not going to be the one getting out of this car and going through that garbage can. I'm telling you that straight-out. This is your show."

"Okay, chill. I'll do it. I'm not afraid to get my hands dirty."

A little man with a large German shepherd strolled into the well of light before the Wallises' house and dropped a weighted bag into one of the barrels Tom had brought out.

"Dang." Rashid hissed in disgust. "You sure this shit is even protected under the Fourth Amendment, going through people's trash?"

"What're you trying to be, a constitutional lawyer?"

"Matter of fact, I am. While y'all are out drinking at Coogan's or whatever, I been taking night classes at Fordham Law. So I'm not looking to get jammed up for doing a search without probable cause."

"Don't worry about probable cause. They got their garbage cans right there on the sidewalk for morning pickup. That's abandoned property, my man, on public space. Totally legitimate source for DNA evidence. The Founding Fathers would say, 'Go 'head, pick it up and get the recycling while you're at it.'"

He shot a sideways glance at Rashid, not having realized he was sharing such close quarters with a future member of the defense bar.

"Yo, there's something else I want to talk to you about." Rashid's fingers wrapped around the steering wheel.

"Okay."

"So don't bug out on me, a-ight?"

"All right." Francis braced himself, realizing everything else had been a preamble.

Under the dome light, the smooth brown skin of Rashid's shaved head seemed to expand and shrink down as he tried to figure out how to begin.

"The kid," he said. "Julian."

"Yeah." Francis gave him a sullen look. "What about him?"

"If you're right about what we're doing here tonight, he didn't have nothing to do with either of these murders."

Francis made a show of running his tongue under his lip, to convey his displeasure.

"So, what's up with that?" Rashid asked. "You sent a motherfucker to jail for twenty years for something he didn't do? And then you hound him for another homicide soon as he gets out? You made that boy's life a living hell on earth."

"You talking to me as another cop or as a guy who's going to be a fucking defense lawyer in a couple of years?" Francis asked, making no effort to hide his impatience.

"I'm talking to you *as a man*. All right?"

"All right."

He went quiet, contemplating the flaws in the windshield and the places in the mid-distance where his vision began to drop away.

"What is it you want me to say exactly? Give me a hint."

"I'm just curious. How are you going to live that down?"

"Hey, I was just part of the process," Francis said, automatically going into the same rap he'd given Patti. "The jury decided on the evidence and the judge determined the sentence —"

"Bullshit, man. What kind of fucking idiot you think you're talking to? I know what time it is. I've put niggers away for dealing weight *and* I've got cousins locked up. So don't be talking shit to me about 'the process.' I know about *the process*."

"What are you, my wife? I would've never partnered with you if I knew you were going to be such a self-righteous pain in the ass."

"Well, you didn't have any choice and now you've got me in the car with you. And we are going to *discuss* this shit. If you're my partner, I want to know where you're coming from on this."

The streetlamp before the Wallis house blinked off, plunging that part of the block into sepulchral darkness for a few seconds.

"If I made a mistake, all I can do is go back and try to make it right," Francis said slowly. "I wouldn't be here otherwise."

"'Make it *right?*'" Rashid's voice cracked. "Man, how the hell you gonna make it *right?* You put that kid away when he was seventeen and he came out when he was thirty-seven."

"And so what the fuck do you want me to do about it now? Shoot myself in the head? *I'm here, aren't I?*" He paused to collect himself. "Look, I'm working the case hard as I can. All I can do is try to get it right this time. If anyone wants to come take my badge and gun after I've done that, *fine.* I'll take whatever I've got coming. I'll fall on the sword if I have to. I'm not afraid. Bring it on. All's I'm asking is, just let me be the one who does this. If you're going to make me responsible, let me fucking *be* responsible."

He realized he was starting to perspire.

"You ever thought about what it must've been like?" Rashid asked, smooth as a drawer sliding open.

"What?"

"For the guy. Julian. You ever thought what it must have been like, getting put away for something he didn't do?"

Francis rolled the window down, wondering how it got so stuffy all of a sudden.

"You ever thought about that long-ass bus ride he must have taken with all these hardened criminal motherfuckers? This little kid not even out of parochial school, walking through the cellblocks. Can you imagine how scared he must have been? They threw him in the shark tank, man, before he even knew how to swim."

"All right, I got the point." Francis hung his arm out the window, taking deep breaths.

"I wonder if you do. I wonder if you ever really thought about what it would be like to miss the last twenty years of your life. . . ."

"Knock it off, already. I heard you."

He stuck his head out the window, trying to get some air. Not wanting to be looked at. He watched the silhouettes of more men putting their garbage out. Twenty years. He found his mind going backward, like a film rewinding, reversing every moment of joy he'd experienced from the age of thirty-seven to seventeen. He found himself giving back promotions, leaving the hospital without his babies, retreating from the church where he got married alone.

"Hey, those lights just went off." Rashid nudged him.

"Where?"

"Downstairs and upstairs. They're both going to sleep."

"All right." Francis sat up and slipped his latex gloves on, glad to be moving. "Ease up on the brake and go about halfway down the block. I'll hop out."

The car rolled about forty feet, crunching leaves and twigs under its tires, and then stopped.

"I went a little bit past the house so they wouldn't see you getting out, case one of them looks out the window," Rashid said.

Francis hesitated, seeing the streetlamp was still out.

"What're you waiting for?" Rashid fixed the rearview. "I thought you weren't afraid to get your hands dirty."

"Dirt*ier*." Francis opened the door and got out of the car like he was leaving an airplane mid-flight.

He instantly realized he'd made a mistake, not bringing

a small flashlight, after getting lost in Red Hook. Rashid had cut the headlights, so he didn't even have those to guide him. He heard a gust of wind riffling garbage bags, a flutter of pigeon wings, and a window sliding open. Every sound sharpened and accentuated by the enveloping darkness.

He heard his pulse thumping in his ears. *Don't panic. It's just a temporary thing.* He felt his way between parked cars and tried to judge his distance from the sidewalk by the sound of his footsteps. *Come on, ya bastard, tell me where I am already.* He stumbled over the curb and heard a group of passing teenagers, skunky from smoking weed in Riverside Park, laugh raucously at his expense, thinking he was nothing more than an old drunk trying to find his way home.

Shut up. His fear shaded into anger and humiliation. He bumped into a barrel full of empty cans and the sound of jostled aluminum echoed loud enough to wake half the Upper West Side.

Get a grip. He took a deep breath and smelled the odors of rotting vegetables, sour milk, and coffee grounds in one of the nearby barrels. The blackness around him relented a little, giving him a slim diagonal of light from a window across the street. It fell on two garbage cans with the numbers 655 spray-painted on their sides. Somehow he'd found himself directly in front of the Wallis house. Rashid, double-parked close by, revved the Buick's motor impatiently.

He started rummaging through the barrels, pulling out a small bag and knowing from its weight that it was the one just left by the German shepherd's walker. He tossed it aside and started to reach in for a larger bag just as he realized someone was standing right beside him.

"What're you doing, Francis?"

He lurched back as Tom's milky white face swam out of the darkness.

"*Aaay*, Tom . . ." Francis stuck his gloved hands in his pockets.

"What's going on?" Tom asked. "Why are you out here?"

"Tommy, Tommy. The years. The fuckin' years. Sometimes you just have to come remind yourself what it's all about."

"Are you drunk, Francis?"

"I might've had a couple of smarteners." Francis played along as he tried to ease the gloves off without taking his hands out of his pockets.

"Keep your voice down. My mom's sleeping on the first floor."

"Yeah, I just wanted to talk to her, Tom. Tell her how bad I feel about the way things are turning out. . . ."

It had been so long since he'd actually tied one on that he had to be careful not to exaggerate his performance.

"Go home, Francis. It's the middle of the night."

"Is it?"

He heard the engine still idling down the block and worried that Rashid was about to come over and blow the act here. "I just wanted to let you guys know, I'm still on it."

"Still on what?" Tom asked, getting aggravated.

"Still on, you know, what happened to your sister. I haven't forgotten. That's the problem in the world. Too many people fuckin' forget things. . . ."

"Francis, I never even wanted you to open this case again, if you recall." Tom cinched the belt on his bathrobe.

"I don't know who this benefited, but it certainly wasn't us. All we wanted was to be left alone."

"Yeah, yeah, *closure*. I remember." Francis nodded. "I've been thinking about that a lot since you said it."

"What about it?"

"It's one of those new words, isn't it?"

"I think you'd find it in most dictionaries."

"No, but people use it differently now. They say, 'closure,' like it's the end of some crappy TV show. Like you can just wrap everything up in a half hour and never have to think about it again. But we know it doesn't work that way. Right, Tommy? You're always thinking about it. Even when you don't think you're thinking about it, it's still dinging around in the back of your mind. That's why I wanted to talk to your mom. Let her know I'm still thinking about it too."

"Why don't you just dry out instead?" Tom made a small scratching sound at the back of his throat. "Christ, Francis. No wonder you're having trouble with this case. You can barely stand up straight. You call that honoring our family?"

"Well . . . we all do what we can."

They stared at each other wordlessly. For a few seconds, Francis had the odd sensation that the blanket of the night had lifted and rippled over him, straightening itself out and making a little breeze.

"Go home, Francis." Tom sighed. "You're embarrassing yourself."

"Sorry you feel that way, Tom. I'm just trying to do my job."

"Jesus Christ. Enough already. I'm going to bed."

He turned and walked back into the house, shaking his head and locking the gate after himself. Francis grabbed

two bulging bags out of the barrels and stumbled his way
back to the Buick.

"How'd you do?" asked Rashid.

"Okay, I guess." Francis threw the bags in the back.
"At least he didn't call the cops on me."

54

THIS TIME, SHE was waiting for him. She heard him closing the door and slowly coming up the stairs, each tread giving a long deep mahogany groan from the pressure of his step.

She burrowed deeper under the covers, the girls huddling close next to her in the single bed, their little frames shivering by her rib cage. *A thing doesn't stop just because you pretend it isn't happening. It just goes on and on. You have to make it stop. You have to take control.* She held her breath, hearing him hesitate on the landing, an animal presence just outside the door. *Please don't come in. I'm not strong enough yet.*

Michelle, the little one, wheezed and coughed, as Eileen pulled up the blanket. *You have to wrap them in layers.*

The door swung open and Tom walked in, silhouetted, the limp ends of his bathrobe belt dangling down at his sides in a way that seemed both menacing and somehow obscene. He had brought something dark and confused into the room with him.

She hugged the girls tight, feeling herself start to shiver as well.

"Mom?" He stopped at the foot of the bed. "What the hell are you doing in here?"

55

On THE LONG walk down to Red Hook, Hoolian started having a whole *Officer and a Gentleman* fantasy about sweeping Zana off her feet, then triumphantly carrying her past the wharves while Eddie skipped alongside of them, trying to keep up. Old longshoremen would wave them on, tugboats would sound their horns, and Wall Streeters across the river would throw confetti from their windows while "Lift Us Up Where We Belong" blared in the background.

Instead, he ended up leaning on her buzzer in vain and then hiding in the doorway of a building across the street, with a new toolbox, a MetroCard for the kid, and an F train T-shirt he'd bought near City Hall with money he'd borrowed from Ms. A.

A little after three, Zana's friend Ysabel came walking up the block, holding Eddie by one hand and her own little girl by the other, taking her turn picking the kids up from day care.

"Heyy, how's my big man?" Hoolian crossed Coffey Street, intercepting them. "You ready to take a ride with me out to Coney Island?"

The boy slipped from Ysabel's grip and went running over, throwing his skinny arms around Hoolian's knees.

"Look what else I got here, man. We can finish fixing the bathroom now."

He started to show off the new toolbox, but Ysabel was teetering up, shouting at the top of her lungs in Spanish. *"¡Larga de aqui! ¡Vete a bañar!"*

She was a big woman who put on makeup and high heels just to go to the bodega.

"Whatcho doing around here?" She pulled Eddie back and got between the two of them. "I thought they locked your ass up again."

"They figured out they made a mistake. What time's Zana getting back? I need to talk to her."

Ms. A. had warned him not to tell anybody about what had just happened at the DA's office, seeing how badly he'd screwed everything up before by literally shooting his mouth off.

"Didn't she tell you she don't wanna see you no more, *culo?*"

"Yeah, but that was before. . . ."

Eddie tried to hug him again, but Ysabel held him back by the hood of his sweatshirt and in her distress swatted absently at her own daughter, who'd been standing there, innocently sucking her thumb.

"Yo, don't be like that, *mami,*" Hoolian protested. "You don't know what happened to me."

"I know the police woke up half the damn neighborhood, looking for you last week."

Hoolian watched the boy start to edge away from him, hiding behind Ysabel's thigh, knowing something was wrong. It wasn't supposed to go like this. This was supposed to be a good day. He'd been vindicated — almost.

He wasn't the bad guy anymore. That was someone else now. On the way down here, he'd even dared to allow himself a moment of relief, thinking maybe everything would be all right after this. But the rest of the world hadn't got the news. He was still the monster on the block, frightening people away.

"Can I at least give the kid his presents?" he asked, holding up the toolbox, MetroCard, and T-shirt. "I walked all the way, from Smith Street."

"Keep them." Ysabel grabbed both kids by the hand. "Nobody needs nothing from you, nohow."

56

THANKS FOR COMING in on a Sunday, Tom." Francis walked in the room and dropped a thick manila file folder on the table. "I know how hard it is leaving the kids on a weekend when you're away most of the week."

"Well, you may need to do some explaining to my wife, but I'm okay with it." Tom Wallis settled into one of the metal chairs.

"And sorry about the other night again."

Instead of assuring him that it was okay, Tom hunched forward. "So, what's doing?"

"I think I mentioned to you on the phone this morning, some new evidence has developed and we could use a hand figuring out what it means."

"Whatever it takes to bring this all to a conclusion." Tom put his hands flat on the table. "Like I said before, we just want it to end."

"Right. We're on the same page there." Francis half smiled. "Anyway . . ."

"Anyway . . ."

"I wonder if I could take you back a couple of steps. The night your sister was murdered."

"Okay." Tom nodded, his brow folding into two distinct lines.

"I know it's a pain in the ass, having to rehash these old details again, but we just have to nail them down one more time. S*oo* . . . She called you twice around midnight. Any idea what that was about?"

"I think that's probably in your notes." Tom glanced at the unopened file. "We talked about where we were going to have my mother's birthday dinner. I was thinking Tavern on the Green. My sister thought we could find some place more intimate, so she called back a couple of times with suggestions."

"Remember what they were?"

"No, but what does that matter? We never went."

"Of course. You're right. It doesn't matter." Francis sat down, trying to get into a rhythm. "I just needed to check. You didn't go by her apartment after that, did you?"

"What, *that* night?"

"Just checking to make sure we have the chronology right. Julian Vega's lawyer is challenging us on all these piddly little details. Real ballbuster, this lady."

"Sure. I understand."

"So you definitely didn't stop by after you spoke to her, right?"

"Francis, it's in the court record. I testified about it in 1984. *No*." Tom looked him straight in the eye. "Why is this coming up again?"

"See, what's happened is" — Francis hitched up his belt, making sure his gun was visible — "a new witness has come forward."

"Really?" Tom shook his head, as if to say, *How*

do you like that? Isn't life full of odd memorable little characters?

"You know, it might just be bullshit," Francis said. "People coming out of the woodwork because they smell money in a civil case. Hey, it happens. But we still gotta run down every lead. At this point."

"Sure, I understand."

Tom let his attention wander for a fraction a second, just long enough to confirm the presence of the one-way glass and the handcuff bar on the wall.

"So who is this, by the way?"

"Someone who worked in the building. I wouldn't think you'd know the name."

"No, probably not." Tom crossed his legs.

"Thing is, he says he saw you leaving the building after midnight."

"Me?" Tom touched a button halfway down his shirt. "What're you, kidding?"

Francis let that sit for a while. Giving him a chance to feel how things had changed. That even though the walls were still about twelve feet apart and the ceiling was still about ten feet from the floor, the dimensions of the room had somehow shrunk just a little.

"There's been a mistake," Tom said, bouncing in his seat and noticing that the legs of his chair were a little short. "I don't know who it is you're talking to that has such a photographic memory after twenty years. How exactly does he know who I am in the first place?"

"He says he'd seen you before. Red-haired man about your height and build, with almost the same complexion as his sister upstairs. That's a pretty specific description, don't you think?"

"Then he's wrong about when he saw me. I'm not sure

how old this person is, but I think they're getting a little confused."

Sharp, thought Francis. *He's thinking ahead like a lawyer. Figuring the witness might be an old man, whose ID a good lawyer could pick apart on cross-examination.*

"Yeah, but see, like, there's this other thing that keeps fucking us up."

"What's that?"

Tom sat up, still playing the earnest grad student trying to help the absentminded professor.

"This thing with the DNA analysis," Francis said. "What was in the newspapers."

"Uh-huh."

"See, you're in the field of medical supplies. You probably know about all this stuff already."

"Not me," Tom deferred. "I just pass along the information I get from the sales conferences and trade journals. I'm no Ph.D."

"I'm sure you're being way too modest, but let me come back to that. The point is, we were looking at this all wrong."

"And why's that?"

Francis shifted his chair, putting his back to the door. "See, the analysis came back XX, female, with half its genes from your mother. Like she had another daughter she wasn't telling us about."

"So you've been saying."

"But, you know, everybody's got a few kinks, here and there. Am I right?"

"I'm not sure what you're getting at, Francis."

"I mean, every human being has mutations, but not all of them necessarily show up in the course of a lifetime," said Francis. "And one of the things that can happen is you can have somebody who looks and acts like a man in every single way. But when you send their DNA out for analysis, the profile comes back female."

Tom took a long deep breath that sounded like a broom's stiff bristles moving across a stretch of pavement.

"It's not the first thing the people at the ME's office think of. In fact, it's pretty unusual. One of the research citations came back from Charles Sturt University in Wagga Wagga, Australia."

Tom was not amused.

"But what happens is there can be a mutation or a deletion that keeps the Y chromosome from showing up when they test the gene that normally tells you what somebody's sex is. They call it the amelogenin locus."

Tom took a slightly longer look at the one-way glass, correctly intuiting there might be a crowd gathering on the other side.

"Pretty interesting once you get into it," Francis continued, as if it were all just a matter of academic interest. "Little things can throw the test off. Like if you have certain kinds of cancer. But probably you knew all that already."

He watched the subtle constriction of Tom's throat muscles.

"So once we figured that out, it was a whole other ballgame." Francis moved his chair closer. "It opened up the possibility that we might be looking for a man. Just like we thought in the first place."

Tom lifted a finger to his forehead and leaned away, starting to understand exactly where this was going.

"Sounds like there've been a lot of mistakes in this case," he said.

"True," Francis admitted. "But things are starting to come together."

Tom started rubbing the space between his eyebrows. Probably trying to calculate the downside of asking for a lawyer at this point. Go slow, Francis reminded himself. Ease back on the throttle a little. Give him a way out. Nothing good comes from a man knowing he's cornered too soon.

"I need you to help me out here." Francis scraped his chair legs across the floor, deliberately disrupting his train of thought. "It appears we have blood under your sister's nails that comes from a male relative."

"I thought you also had stains in her apartment from Julian Vega."

"Absolutely. But right now, I'm trying to understand how this relative's blood got on her."

"Well, you know I broke a glass that day," Tom said agreeably, not missing a beat.

"When was this?"

"In her kitchen, just after dinner. I stopped by with some papers I needed her to sign, to do with our grandmother's estate. I broke a wineglass and she bandaged me up."

Nice. Francis almost smiled in admiration. You'd normally have to go to a Washington press conference or a corporate shareholders' meeting to hear this accomplished a liar.

"I told you about it at the time," Tom said, anticipating the next line of attack.

"That's strange, I don't remember seeing it in my notes." In fact, he now had a clear recollection of Tom wearing his collar buttoned and his sleeves rolled all the way down back then, long before it was fashionable; no conspicuous defensive scratches would've been visible on his forearm.

"Well, I have no idea what you did or didn't write down," Tom said, looking injured. "But I distinctly recall showing it to you. I'm amazed you don't remember that."

He's good. Francis had to give it to the man. In the confines of this small room, the story could be taken apart and revealed for what it was: a frail little lie barely on life support. But in a courtroom, it would have a chance to breathe and grow stronger. It would rise to the occasion and fight. Tom would get on the stand, with his open farm-boy face and his voice shaking with just enough emotion, and he would sound far more credible to a jury than a ruddy old cop with devilish eyebrows and failing eyes.

"I see." Francis nodded. "So that's why we would've found your blood under your sister's nails?"

"If that's what you found," said Tom, making sure to give nothing away for free.

"Well, that's great. Clears everything up. It leaves me with only one problem."

"What's that?"

"Why we found an exact match for that DNA under Christine Rogers's nails."

Tom's face seemed to slowly dissolve into static, like an image on an old TV with a broken antenna.

His lips moved without making noise, his features became blurry, his eyes lost focus. He took a few seconds to readjust and sharpen his attention again on Francis sitting just a couple of inches away, leaving no way to the door except straight through him.

"Wait a second," Tom said. "How do you know that's *my* DNA? I don't remember giving anybody a specimen."

"Yeah, there is that." Francis scratched the back of his ear. "You know, your family's been through so much already, there was an argument against getting a subpoena invading anybody's privacy and forcing them to give a sample against their will. So we just used what's available to the general public."

"What are you talking about?"

"Thursday night's garbage night in your neighborhood, right? Sidewalk is public property."

The little pools of skin under Tom's eyes turned just the faintest shade of blue, as if a pair of thumbs were pressing into them.

"You went through *my garbage?*"

"Hey, I was against it," Francis fibbed, playing good cop for the moment. "I said, 'You guys are crazy. You're gonna make asses out of yourselves and see Tom had nothing to do with it.' But the department lawyers said go ahead. It's been done before. Garbage bags are like Disneyland for DNA. The Magic Kingdom, where dreams come true. And it just so happens this time a condom turned up."

Tom listened impassively. His light-colored brows no longer looked childlike, they made him look like something slightly inhuman, without expression or moral compunction. This was the scary part. He could lawyer up at any moment. Francis tapped a pen on the table. They were close here, but not that close. He couldn't let Tom leave without making a statement of some kind. There was no room for doubt this time. He needed to get a confession.

"I'm not sure if what you did here is legal," Tom said. "Maybe I should call my lawyer."

Francis gently put the pen aside. "Well, I have no

problem with you bringing a lawyer in, Tom. Only then we're not going to be able to tell you what else we have."

He saw that register, bringing Tom's chin up and making his eyes jitter for a half-second; just long enough for him to figure out that it probably was in his interest to hear all the evidence they had.

"Listen, we've known each other a long time," Francis said. "I'm sure you can explain why things look this way."

"Yeah, you screwed up."

Francis nodded. Yeah, that's right. You're smarter than me. You don't need a lawyer. I'm just a dumb half-blind donkey who put some poor kid in prison for twenty years for something he didn't do. But that's all right. I'm not mad. It's not weighing on me. It's not eating me up inside. It's not making me physically sick. It's not killing me. Go on. I can take the stain on my soul. It was dirty anyway. It's okay. Do it. You can get over on me again.

"Well, it's possible the samples got mixed up at the lab. There's always room for human error."

"I'll say."

"So you never met this other woman, Christine. Right?"

"Who?"

"Christine Rogers. Lady doctor who was killed a couple of weeks ago. You know."

"I meet a lot of people," Tom said in a flat voice. "I'm in and out of hospitals all the time, making sales calls and telling staff about our products. That's my job."

"But you don't remember this woman specifically, do you?"

The lightness of his eyebrows made him seem eerily unmoved by the question. "Sometimes I'll come in to give a demonstration on how a piece of equipment works and there'll be a lot of doctors in the room. I'm not always good with names."

"I'd think that'd be a handicap in sales."

Tom looked at the clock, trying to figure out how long he'd been here.

"See, I'll tell you something that wasn't in the papers." Francis leaned over, slipping the hook in deftly before the subject of a lawyer could come up again. "This girl— *woman* — when we searched her apartment, turned out she had a bunch of news clippings about your sister's case hidden away."

Tom began to fiddle with the button on his shirt again even as his expression remained unchanged.

"Seems she had kind of an obsession about it," Francis continued. "Even told a few of her friends she thought Julian Vega got a raw deal."

He saw Tom turning the button this way and that, as if he were about to twist it off. But his face remained the same: remote, innocent-looking, perhaps mildly curious. It was as if he had no idea what his hands were up to.

"It's odd, but I don't see what it has to do with me," he said. "Probably she knew Julian from around the neighborhood, and he sold her that whole sorry line about how he went to jail when he was innocent. Then he turned around and did the same thing to her that he did to my sister. That's what he does. He gets close to these girls, and then when they don't give him what he wants, he murders them."

"Yeah, that's what I thought too. People have a way of repeating certain patterns in their lives, over and over, until they get things to come out right."

Francis allowed himself a brief knowing smile.

"So anyway after we got this witness coming forward and the DNA hit, we began looking in other places and seeing these details we didn't know about before. Like that your mother came into the ER at St. Luke's one night when this Christine was on duty."

"Meaning what?" The lines in Tom's throat deepened ever so slightly. "What's the connection?"

"We compared signatures and figured out you were the one who signed in for her that night at Admissions. We're thinking maybe that's when you met Christine."

"Come on, that's ridiculous, Francis." Tom waved his hand. "That's a huge emergency room with a lot of doctors and nurses. I've been in and out of there a hundred times, making calls. I certainly don't remember meeting that woman."

"Right, we kind of thought you'd say that," Francis said, nodding agreeably. "But then yesterday we turned up a security guard at the hospital who recognized your picture and said he'd seen you two having coffee in the cafeteria a few months ago."

"He's wrong."

"He's *wrong?*" Francis gave him a smashed-mouth smile.

"Yes, I read about witnesses making false identifications all the time."

"So the guy who worked in your sister's building is wrong about seeing you the night she was killed *and* the hospital security guard is wrong about seeing you with Christine. Is that what you're telling me?"

"I don't know who these people are or what their agenda is. It could be that they just saw my picture in the newspaper and got confused. It happens."

"Then what about the cell phone?"

"What cell phone?"

"She was making two, three calls a week to a phone registered to your outfit."

"How should I know?" Tom asked. "Maybe she was friends with somebody else at the company."

"Tom, *come on*." Francis touched his knee lightly. "You were seeing her. The longer you deny it, the worse it's going to look."

"Okay," Tom said abruptly. "I don't think I want to say anything else."

Francis exerted just the slightest bit of extra pressure on Tom's knee before he took his hand away. *No, you're not going anywhere this time.* Jerry Cronin and the rest of them were on the other side of the glass, silently begging for him to wrap it up, thinking they probably had enough to make an arrest here. But he needed *more*. He needed actual words, he needed to have the bones and viscera of this crime spilled out across the table so that everyone would see, so there'd be no doubt or second-guessing, no sending the wrong man away this time.

"Help me understand this." He turned his chair around and straddled it, going nose to nose with Tom. "I'm sure it wasn't your fault. You and your mother met this girl at this hospital. And then I guess your mother got to be friends with her there, because we can see they called each other a couple of times afterward. Mother looking for her daughter, daughter looking for her mother. That kind of thing . . ."

He could see from the way Tom turned his head that he was on the right track here.

"So I'm thinking maybe the three of you socialized a bit, had dinner, you sort of saying thanks for looking after my mom. And you maybe got a little involved with her.

Okay. It happens. Nobody's making any judgments here. I mean, cops and marriage . . . *whew* . . . You're not going to get *me* to cast the first stone. . . ."

Tom was tapping his forehead, no doubt trying to remember his lawyer's number. *I can do this,* Francis told himself. *I can get anybody to give it up. Natural talent. Like Mantle hitting a baseball or Pavarotti singing opera.*

"But this girl . . ." He shook his head, pressing his case. "She was one of those types, can never let anything go. She's seeing this guy, nice guy, treats her really well. Takes her out to dinner. Buys her nice jewelry. . . ." He lowered his chin and looked up at Tom, not needing to spell out that they'd pulled his Amex records and had the charges. "But she keeps bugging him, asking him questions about his family. Shit that happened a long time ago, that's none of anybody's business . . ."

Come on, man. Give it to me. I'm your friend. You can trust me. All his life, he'd found ways to bond with people who'd committed savage, brutal, and sometimes unforgivable crimes. He'd treated them as equals, compared unhappy childhoods with them, minimized the seriousness of their crimes. *You robbed a bank? So what? It's not like you killed somebody. Oh, you did kill somebody? Hey, it was an accident. It's not like you went and deliberately robbed a bank.*

"I mean, she starts sneaking around behind his back, talking to people, collecting newspaper articles after this other guy gets out. It's sick, really. She's trying to stir shit up just when his family's most vulnerable."

Tom turned his head almost ninety degrees, keeping one eye trained on Francis, as if he were afraid to look away.

"So then she starts drawing conclusions," Francis said. "Talking about things she doesn't know about."

A certain restiveness was growing between them, a sense he'd been making his circles too wide. It was time to get in close and risk getting gored.

"So then she starts throwing accusations around, about him and his sister."

The room filled with the deepest silence Francis had ever heard in his life. He could hear filaments buzzing in the fluorescent lights, the hydraulics of Tom's digestive system, glue loosening its grip on the floor tiles, as if the whole room were coming apart, molecule by molecule.

"What are you saying to me, Francis?" he asked in a tense staccato voice.

"I'm saying things happen in a family that no one outside it can understand. And this girl, Christine, might've intimated certain things that she shouldn't have."

Bad smells were beginning to emanate from Tom, even as he sat here expressionless, in his oxford shirt and khaki pants.

"I think I'm going to be sick."

Francis pulled a little garbage can from under the table and parked it beside Tom's chair. "Do what you need to do."

"I can't believe you're saying this to me. I used to have some respect for you."

"You used to have some respect *for me?*" Francis's lip curled.

Tom started to rise, but Francis pushed him back down, with the flat of his palm to the chest.

"Sit the fuck down," he said. "We're not through here."

He wiped his hand on his pant leg in disgust. He saw the

one-way glass quiver and knew Jerry Cronin and the rest on the other side were probably all having coronaries.

"I know what you did to her." Francis pressed in on him, closing the distance. "I know you had her put henna streaks in her hair so she'd look a little more like your sister. I know you gave her some of your old science fiction books. I know you were trying to get back to that thing you had with Allison. . . ."

It was no good. He'd lost him. He knew it the second he wiped his hand on his pant leg, like he'd just touched something less human. He'd broken the bond and his own rule with that gesture, letting the suspect know exactly what he thought of him. Tom was just staring at him now, unblinking. Not feeling the heat at all anymore.

"My lawyer," he said. "I've heard enough."

Words weren't going to do it this time, Francis realized. He needed another kind of leverage.

"Okay, we don't have to talk anymore," he said. "I just want to show you something."

He opened the file folder that had been sitting in the middle of the table, undisturbed until this moment.

"Here, this is Christine." He took out a Polaroid that Rashid had taken at the crime scene: the girl with her trachea severed and her blood seeping into the bathroom grout. "I can see why you went for her. She's kind of the same type as your sister. Maybe a little older-looking. Not so much of that little-girl thing happening. But you can't always get so hung up on age, can you?"

Tom kept staring, his expression unchanging even as the smells from him started becoming more pungent and unhealthy.

"And this is Allison." Francis took out a second photo before Tom could object. "But I guess you knew that."

Tom looked down at his sister's one intact eye staring up at him from the bloody lava pit he'd made of her face.

"Come on, look at it." Francis leaned over, almost putting his hand on the scruff of Tom's neck. "What're you afraid of? She's dead. She's not gonna tell anybody how you used to do her."

Tom tried to turn away, but his pupils jerked back twice as if drawn by magnets. "Come on, Tom. Is this helping you? Is this giving you *closure?*"

Without warning, Tom bent over and threw up next to the garbage can, spattering Francis's shoes.

"Okay." He rested his forehead on the table after he was done. "I think I'd like you to let me either call a lawyer or go home and see my girls."

"Tom, I got news for you." Francis reached for a box of Kleenex. "You're not seeing your girls tonight."

57

IN A WAY, he'd always been a stranger to her, sealed off, distant, and unreachable. Eileen stood by the pass-through window, watching him from behind at the kitchen table. Whose child was this, reading the papers the day after he'd been arrested and eating his way through two pints of ice cream, one after the other, without gaining any weight? Where did he get that habit of constantly rubbing the middle of his forehead with one finger? Certainly not from her or his father, that potbellied satyr. She realized now that from the very moment the nurse at Lenox Hill had put him on her chest, damp and blue, staring at her in eerie silence, there'd been something in him that she didn't quite recognize.

It was as if he were only disguised as a member of their family; alien and frightening things were going on behind the nearly invisible eyebrows. At first, she told herself she was just imagining it. He wasn't that different from other boys. A little sneaky sometimes, a little furtive. But then she began to notice that he was a devastatingly good liar, as if one side of him were wholly unaware of what the other side was doing. Who broke that vase, Tom?

Jesus, I dunno, Mom. I was out all day. What happened to that money I left on top of the dresser? *I never saw it.* The bigger the lies got, the more she realized he was deliberately keeping parts of himself hidden from her. *Why is your sister crying? What did you say to her? What were you doing in her room last night?*

It must have started when he was about eleven and she was six. No, she still couldn't think about it. It was like staring at the sun. You could know a thing was there but not be able to look at it. It would burn the eyes right out of your skull. She listened to the rhythmic clank of his spoon on porcelain in the empty kitchen.

She'd tried. She took him to the cream of the Upper West Side therapists and psychiatrists. But they could never figure out who or what had damaged him. Tom always insisted no one had ever touched him, and as far as she knew it was true. There was just a terrible hunger inside him. Some things you couldn't explain. So she sent him away, first to boarding school and then to live with his father, when she knew she couldn't control him anymore. But he kept coming back with a greater appetite. How could you keep a brother and sister apart? Each time they saw each other the attraction was stronger, as if they were continually rediscovering long-lost parts of themselves.

She'd thought growing up and getting married would change him, cure him of whatever it was that had made him that way. But the girl he chose was ill-equipped and overmatched, in no way up to the task. She was like Thumbelina: a small person who would never get any bigger. Hardly more than a child herself, barely able to handle the demands of city living, let alone raising two small girls in a wolf's den.

When Eileen tried to talk to her about the future this

morning, saying they couldn't pretend anymore, they had to make themselves strong and think of the girls, she'd just shut down and had one of her sinking spells. Sat on the quilt with the lights low and the E! channel playing, surrounded by magazine articles about chronic fatigue and Epstein-Barr virus, saying all she wanted to do was sleep. Tom had told her it was all lies, false witnesses, murderers and crooked investigators trying to divert the blame from themselves. Everything was going to be all right because *he said it was going to be all right.* And how could Eileen blame her? For most of her life, she'd been the same. Only slowly waking up now that the sun was beginning to scorch the earth.

She heard Stacy, six years old and the spitting image of her aunt at the same age, coming down the stairs, looking for dessert.

"Daddy, is there any mocha almond fudge left?" She appeared at the far kitchen doorway, crossing her ankles and chewing the end of her braids the way Allison used to.

"I'm sorry, sweetie." From the pass-through, Eileen saw him deliberately take the Häagen-Dazs carton off the table and place it on the chair beside him, where the child wouldn't see it. "We don't buy that anymore. Mommy thinks you guys are getting a little heavy."

Stacy stuck out her lip in disappointment.

"Come here, baby," Tom said. "Daddy's had a hard couple of days. He needs a hug."

Reluctantly, she went to him, dragging her ballet slippers over the tiles, the soles making a sound like match heads sliding across charcoal.

"Can I run a bath for you instead?" He put an arm around her.

"Oh-okay." She leaned against him and sighed dramatically.

"'At's my girl."

Eileen felt herself go impossibly stiff, watching his hand drift down and squeeze the little pink heart patched onto the back pocket of her jeans. A voice in her head screamed as his hand stayed there and kept squeezing, as if it were her very own heart in his grip. Not wanting to see it, but not daring to look away. Finally he let go, but the voice kept screaming. *A thing doesn't stop. A thing doesn't stop until you make it stop.*

She climbed the stairs and crossed the landing into the bathroom so she'd be there waiting to take over from him when they came up.

58

O N MONDAY MORNING Hoolian found himself back in Part 50 of the New York State Supreme Court in Manhattan, like a time-traveler in a *Twilight Zone* episode returned to the very instant his life fell apart.

"The *People of New York* versus *Julian Vega*," the clerk called out.

He stood up and instinctively assumed the classic guilty-looking defendant's pose, hands behind his back, head bowed, glancing once over his shoulder, checking to see if Zana or any of the other people he'd left messages for had shown up.

"Ms. Aaron." Judge Bronstein raised her voice, making sure the press in the back rows could hear her. *"Approach."*

Ms. A. stepped up beside him, straightening her lapels.

"Your Honor, we're filing a motion to dismiss the indictment against Mr. Vega."

"Mr. Raedo?" The judge looked left to the prosecution's table. "Any last-minute issues you want to raise?"

"No, Your Honor. We're not going to oppose it."

The ADA didn't even bother to look up. Just pretended to fuss with his papers, like he had more important matters on his mind. It made Hoolian feel small, disrespected, as if the value of his life wasn't even worth acknowledging. He had half a mind to go over, grab that *hijo de gran puta* by the back of the neck, and bounce his face off the table two or three times, to remind him of his manners.

"Okay." The judge slammed the gavel. "The indictment is dismissed. Mr. Vega, you are free to go. On behalf of the court, I'd like to say what happened to you is very unfortunate. No one goes into this business to send innocent people to prison. . . ."

Her voice seemed to fade as she kept talking and gesturing. He found himself getting light-headed and disoriented, missing some of what was being said.

". . . And so I personally want to wish you good luck with the rest of your life and if you're ever in my courtroom again, I hope it's only as a visitor."

He heard hollow fake-sounding laughter from the press section as the judge reached down to offer a withered bony hand that somehow made him think of thorny rose stems wrapped in thin tissue. As he stood on tiptoe, shaking it, he felt Ms. A. tugging on the back of his jacket, prompting him to another task.

He turned and saw Paul Raedo waiting, his hand offered limply like a beggar's cup.

For a moment, everything seemed to freeze. The court officers, the assembled reporters, the other attorneys waiting for their cases to be called, all leaned forward to see what he would do. Coppery-tasting saliva gathered at the back of his mouth, bringing up the urge to hock in the man's face. It was the least Raedo deserved. But then his eye fell on the row right behind the defendant's table, where his father had sat day after day at the original trial in his best lobby suit, trying to show the world what kind of people they really were.

He pressed his lips together and offered his hand, silently cursing himself for his good manners.

"All right, man." He squeezed until he had the minor satisfaction of seeing the prosecutor wince. "There you go."

"I'll call you about the settlement." Ms. A. leaned over Hoolian's shoulder. "Think in the low sevens."

"I'll be in the office." Raedo wrung his hand out. "But don't get your hopes up."

Out in the lobby a few minutes later, Hoolian hesitated before the metal detector, instinctively putting his arms out.

"It's all right." Ms. A. came up behind him and touched his elbow. "You don't have to let them search you anymore. We're *leaving*."

He edged past the Phantom Tollbooth–like frame, still bracing for a guard to call, *"Halt."* Instead, the court officers just went on searching bags and waving their wands over the people heading *in*to the courthouse, as if he'd suddenly become invisible to them.

He followed Ms. A. through the revolving doors and out to the sidewalk, with the uncanny sensation that he was moving backward through time.

Two dozen news cameramen and reporters had set up under blue scaffolding over the pavement, not far from where they'd been standing the day the jury found him guilty nineteen years, eight months, and twelve days ago.

"Julian, how you doing?"

"Julian, do you feel vindicated?"

"Julian, are you bitter?"

He looked up, recognizing this last voice as the one that had been calling, *"Hooleeyaaan,"* over and over in falsetto outside the 19th Precinct. He saw that it was a short bearded guy with a press pass from the *Post* who had pages falling out of his notebook; his midsection was soft and inviting, as if you'd never get your fist out once you buried it there.

"We're not going to have any further comment, for the moment." Ms. A. stepped up to the microphones as the bright lights went on and the camera shutters started clicking. "We believe the cause of justice was finally served today. Mr. Vega wishes to thank all his supporters. He's looking forward to spending time with his friends and family. . . ."

Hoolian nodded along pleasantly, becoming an actor for the occasion, his facial expressions and modest gestures having nothing to do with the storm of emotions raging in his head.

"Julian, what are your plans for the future?" a girl reporter with bobbed hair and tiny teeth called out.

"I dunno," he said. "Maybe I'll go for my law degree. I already know the system pretty good. . . ."

He saw a few of them already starting to peel off as Ms. A. stepped up to say they had no further comment at the moment. The spotlight was moving on. They had what they needed. There was no reason to linger. He realized his exoneration was probably only a page-three story. All the juice had been in the original accusation. He saw some of the correspondents take their microphones and start to run down the block, where another story had obviously caught their attention. Through the crush of bodies, he caught a glimpse of Tom Wallis looking white-faced and terrified. Ms. A. had said he'd be coming to court this afternoon to be arraigned for his sister's murder. A pruny old lawyer in a natty bow tie stood at his side, batting away questions. Hoolian didn't give a damn what they did to Tom in prison. But as the crowd moved by, in a traveling swarm, Hoolian saw that the mother was with them as well, a spectral presence in red hair and tinted glasses. He thought she must be the loneliest woman on the planet right now. How could you go on, knowing that your only son had killed your only daughter? You'd either have to go crazy or do yourself in.

He watched them all go up the steps and through the revolving doors, entering the immense gray machine he'd just gotten out of.

So that was it. The circus was leaving. Tom would be the headline tomorrow. The Julian Vega story was over. Shouldn't the sky be splitting open? Shouldn't a heavy rain be coming down and washing the streets clean? Shouldn't the sun be rising in the west and setting in the east? Shouldn't God be making his own presence known and explaining himself? Shouldn't there just be . . . *more* somehow?

But the day had no special character. A lawyer in a Burberry coat stepped in front of him to hail a taxi. A couple of reporters straggled behind, talking to Ms. A. about her other cases. A police car hurtled past with its siren on, paying him no mind at all.

He should have been overjoyed. It was finally done. He could do anything now. But instead, he felt lost and a little afraid. He watched a fleet of yellow taxis go by and it dawned on him that every single driver, even the newest immigrant off the plane who barely spoke English, had something he lacked — a license. He wasn't even sure which was the gas pedal. All at once, he was awash in all the unfamiliar details of daily life. Insurance deductibles, health-care premiums, tax-deferred savings. He'd heard of them but had been afraid to ask anyone what they were. How would he ever catch up?

He realized he was at sea out here. He'd work on his civil suit for a while, but once that was settled, he wouldn't know what to do. Without this case, without this cause, his life would have no direction, no structure, no organizing principle. And once he opened the clenched fist inside him that had been holding him together for so long, everything he had would blow away.

All of Foley Square seemed to spin around him. Everyone moving by him with a sense of purpose that made him feel more shiftless, lonely, and vulnerable. A blue-and-white Department of Correction bus pulled around the side entrance of the courthouse, to take prisoners from the holding pens off to jail. He had a premonition that if he wasn't careful, he'd be taking that ride again soon himself.

But then he felt the tremor of the Lexington Avenue subway right beneath his feet and in the gust of wind coming up through the grating he sensed, for just an instant, the presence of his father again.

He'd find his way, he told himself. Something would tell him where to go. And as the last of the reporters finally walked away, he saw that Zana had been standing with Eddie at the rear of the pack all along, waiting for him. And as he staggered over to them in gratitude, he saw that the boy was holding, like a fallen banner he'd picked up in the street, a half-unfolded, crayon-annotated map of the New York City subway system.

"Can we go to Coney Island now?" the kid asked, like he was sick of waiting.

59

JUST AS FRANCIS turned from the Starbucks counter holding two scalding-hot cups of coffee, an ungainly girl with a shaved head came zooming out of his blind spot on Rollerblades, flailing her arms and heading right at him. It was too late to get out of the way and there was no room to move. But somehow he managed to catch her in his arms, spin her around gracefully like a waltz partner, and let her go without spilling a drop or burning either of them.

"Surprised you made it," said Hoolian, once Francis had navigated back to the table and sat down, slightly red-faced and worse for wear.

"Yeah, they ought to make people take their skates off when they come in."

"I meant I was surprised you showed at all."

Francis handed him his coffee, a little surprised to find himself here as well. When he first got the word from Deb Aaron a few weeks back that Hoolian wanted a sit-down, just the two of them, he'd simply crumpled up the pink message slip and dropped it in the wastebasket, the way any sensible person would. But over the next couple of days, he noticed that it somehow didn't go out with the rest of the trash but stayed there lodged in a corner of the basket, like a discarded organ still pulsing.

"Case is over." He shrugged, glad he'd insisted they do it in a public place. "We might as well be strangers."

They stared at each other in awkward silence for a while, and then both turned to look out the window at the same time. A fine pre-Christmas dusting was falling over the construction site near Cooper Union, the kind of precipitation that could turn into rain or snow at a moment's notice.

"You know, I hate this weather." He watched the orange netting on the upper floors start to disappear in the mist. "First dead victim I saw was right before Christmas. Old lady got killed up in Harlem and lay there a week. Body all bloated. Maggots crawling out of the eye sockets. The smell was so ripe that guys with twenty years were throwing up. I washed my uniform three times afterward. But you know, you can't just throw your hat in the Maytag with the rest of your clothes. I had to leave it. So the next time I was on foot patrol, it rained. And that awful smell just came washing down all over me again, running straight down my face. It brought it all back, like I was still in that apartment."

"There you go, motherfucker. You can't get away from some things. Sorry you didn't catch pneumonia."

Francis gave him the once-over, noticing Hoolian had on the same tweed jacket and maroon shirt he wore to court every time. He was wearing the same black tie as well, knotted a little too tightly around the throat. So much for letting things go. This probably did not mark the beginning of National Brotherhood Week.

"So, what'd the city give you for a settlement anyway?"

Francis reached for a napkin and blew his nose, still not able to get rid of the cold that had been nagging him since Thanksgiving. "Fifty, sixty thou?"

"I'm getting my life together." Hoolian pointedly ignored the question and pushed his face across the table. "But whatever it was, it wasn't enough to make up for what you did to me."

Eighty, ninety grand, Francis figured. With a third going to Deb Aaron as her contingency. Otherwise, Hoolian would've shown up wearing a brand-new flashy designer suit, just to rub his old adversary's face in it.

"You're probably lucky you got anything." Francis looked past him. "I don't know how your lawyer ever thought she could prove malicious intent."

"You know what you did," Hoolian said in a cutting voice.

"I worked the case as hard as I could. Never anything personal."

"You flaked me and we both know it."

"Believe what you like, son. It's nothing to do with me —"

"Why the fuck did you do that anyway?"

Francis forced a smile. "You seriously expect me to answer?"

"I had my whole life ahead of me, man. Look at this. . . ."

Hoolian made a sudden move for his inside pocket and Francis lurched back.

"Easy now." Hoolian's eyes glimmered with amusement as he took out an old yellowing business envelope and laid it on the table between them.

"What's this?" Francis leaned over it, his blood pressure rising.

"Just open it."

Francis hesitated and then smoothed back the flap, his veins starting to pump like fire hoses at a three-alarm.

"If this is a sample of Allison Wallis's DNA you been carrying around for twenty years to use at a crime scene, I'm telling you right now that I'll shoot you in the head, right before I shoot myself."

"Just open the fuckin' envelope, man. Don't be a pussy."

He took out and unfolded a brown-stained crinkled letter, set it down on the table, and then studied it awhile, trying to make sense of the words.

"*. . . we are pleased to inform you that you have been accepted into the class of 1988 . . . Additional materials will be sent to . . .*"

His jaw slowly retracted into the lower part of his face. "Is this your college admissions letter or something?"

"I've been carrying it around for twenty years." Hoolian nodded. "It came the second week I was in Attica. I just sat on my bunk, reading it over and over. They were going to give me a full scholarship."

Francis wiped the table beneath the letter to make sure it wasn't damp. "And what do you want me to do with it?"

"I want you to keep it, man. I want you to put it right next to your family pictures. So you look at it every day the rest of your life."

Francis grunted, as if he'd just had a medicine ball heaved at him. *Why the hell did I come today?* I should be home, spreading salt on the sidewalk and making sure all the storm windows are closed. I should be trying to get my kids on the phone. I should be helping my wife paint the bathroom while I still can. I'm not even getting paid for this.

"I just want you to tell me one thing." Hoolian pushed the letter more toward Francis's side of the table, trying to get him to take it. "How do you live with yourself, knowing what you did?"

"Nature of the beast," Francis said casually, even as he found he couldn't quite meet Hoolian's eye.

"And what the hell's that supposed to mean?"

"I had a dead girl on my hands. I did what I thought I needed to do."

"And so you needed to set me up?"

Francis found himself shifting and fidgeting, like some common criminal just brought into the precinct.

"I'm sorry you got caught up when we should've been looking at somebody else," he said carefully. "It's every cop's worst nightmare. In twenty years, I never had another case like that. . . ."

"Sorry I got *caught up?*"

Hoolian pushed back from the table and several of the women sitting near them looked over.

"That's all you have to say to me? You're sorry I got 'caught up'? Like I'm Charlie the fuckin' tuna in a net?"

"Well, what else do you want?" Francis dropped his voice, embarrassed.

"I want you to admit it."

"Admit what?"

"What you did to me. I want you to say the words."

"Why's that so important to you?" Francis turned sideways, his legs getting cramped.

"Because it *is*. You took the best damn years of my life. I got so much hate for you, man, that it's poisoning me."

"Still?"

"Yes, *still*. How am I supposed to get past it? Tell me that. I thought everything was going to be okay now, but

I'm still all fucked up about it. I can't relax. I can't smile most of the time. I can't eat in a restaurant without trying to bring the silverware back to the front. I can't even enjoy being in the first fucking adult relationship of my whole life."

Francis shook his head, silently insisting it all had nothing to do with him.

"It got so bad the other day, I went back to my old school and I saw the priest who wrote my college recommendation. Ninety-seven years old and still remembers my last report card. And you know what he said to me? He said I had to *forgive* you."

"Might be something to that."

"But how can I forgive you when you won't even say what you did?"

Francis's eyes drifted down to the letter on the table again and he felt a subtle increase of pressure inside his chest.

"I'm sorry, son. I can't give you what you're asking for. That's just never going to happen."

Get up. His head was sending messages to the rest of his body. You don't have to stay here. You're under no obligation to take this. Just because everybody else needs to confess doesn't mean you have to.

"I figured you'd say that." Hoolian clasped his hands, nodding furiously and trying to keep himself under control. "I really did. But you know what kills me anyway?"

"No. What?"

"It's knowing you're going to do the same thing to somebody else that you did to me."

"No, I'm not." The throb of blood was so loud in his ears, it sounded like footsteps across the ceiling.

"Of course you are. Why wouldn't you? You're not

fucking *sorry*. You're not having to pay for what you did."

Francis felt the pressure in his chest move, becoming more spread out and harder to sit with comfortably. "You always end up paying."

"What do you mean, 'you always end up paying'? That's just some weak shit people say to get you out of their office. You're not paying. Look at you. You're fat and sassy. You're probably about to retire with all your benefits and half your salary. You're not suffering —"

"I'm going blind," Francis said before he could stop himself.

"Yeah, right."

"I'm serious. My eyes are going."

"Get the fuck out of here, man. Is that supposed to be funny?"

"Not to me, it isn't."

Hoolian fell silent and studied him for a few seconds, still trying to tell if it was a put-on. He stuck a finger in front of Francis's face and slowly began to move it rightward. Francis tracked it for a few inches until it disappeared. Then he heard Hoolian snapping his fingers somewhere beside his ear.

"No fucking way."

"It's the truth." Francis leveled his gaze. "I'm seeing less and less all the time."

He must have lost his senses. He still hadn't even broken it to the kids.

"And . . . so . . . *what?*" Hoolian fell back, flustered. "You want me to feel *sorry* for you or something?"

"Not at all," Francis said. "But you're sitting here, telling me that I'm off the hook for how I did you so bad. And I'm just telling you, it ain't so. Everybody gets something."

What had he just done? He felt like he'd jumped out of a plane without a parachute. He was in free fall. Hoolian could tell the whole world now. They could reopen dozens of his old cases and question his testimony about things he'd claimed to have seen. They could go after his pension for allegedly lying on the stand and not telling anyone about his condition. They could strip him bare and leave him in the street.

Why don't you just reach over and hand him your gun while you're at it, Loughlin?

But there was something heady and exhilarating about it as well. He felt his lungs open up and his heart beating faster. Noticed the coolness of air on his skin and the renewed vividness of colors around him. All his senses were keener and more alive than they'd been in weeks. So this was what it was like to be on the other side of the interrogation table. Until this moment, he'd never really understood why people ever confessed and told him the things they should have never told anybody else. Now he got it. It was almost like being high, but better. For just a second, at least, he'd let someone see him as he truly was, and there was not just relief but a kind of knife-edge grace in that.

"Everybody gets something."

Hoolian didn't want this. Didn't want to see things the way this man did. He was better than that. It served that bastard right, what was happening to him.

Just the same, when he closed his eyes for a half-second, he found himself wondering how he'd handle going blind. How would you not go crazy, knowing you'd never read another comic book, look into your lover's eyes, or see the spokes of the Wonder Wheel go off one by one? How would you find your way home? How would you *not* think it was some sort of punishment?

"So you're not going to ask me for forgiveness or any of that shit?" Hoolian said, opening them up again.

"Screw that." Loughlin pushed back from the table. "I don't need to cop a plea. You can either stand up to what you did or you can't."

They both slowly got to their feet. For twenty years, Hoolian had fantasized about what he'd do if he ever came upon Loughlin in a vulnerable spot. He'd plotted things he was going to do with lead pipes, thick ropes, and car trunks. He'd even gone so far as to think of alibis he'd use if he got arrested. But now for the second time he reached down into that vast reservoir of rage he'd been maintaining for years and found nothing. Just half-dry muck at the bottom. Where did it all go?

He looked down and saw his own hand rise and hang in midair, waiting for Loughlin to grasp it.

The cop didn't see it, though, because it was just outside his line of sight and Hoolian quickly let it drop back down to his side.

"All right, man. Don't put any more people in prison who don't belong there."

"Sure. You make it sound easy."

The cop smiled dourly and put the letter in his wallet, as if he were manacling a briefcase bomb to his wrist.

"Oh, look, it's snowing out there." Hoolian peered out the window.

"Jesus, I didn't even notice the changeover." Loughlin

sneezed, the end of his nose already turning red. "I hope I'll be able to find my car."

"Yeah, you're probably going to need to do some digging out."

"Tell me about it."

He walked out the door, leaving his cup half full on the table, then paused before the window. The wind was lifting the snow into wide grainy arcs under the streetlamps, as if some magnetic force was trying to draw it back up to the clouds. Hoolian saw him turn around twice, trying to get his bearings as the night fell over him and cars skittered around the sugar-dusted cube in the middle of the plaza.

Then he hunched his shoulders, thrust his hands into his pockets, and started trudging south toward the Bowery, past the cranes and cement trucks, a hulking figure heading into the whiteout, getting smaller and smaller until he finally disappeared.

CODA

STARING AT THE SUN

60

 ⊺OM WAS IN the kitchen, looking up at the ceiling, with his hair still damp from the shower, his blue work shirt unbuttoned at the collar, and a pair of scissors buried in his chest just below the sternum.

Francis checked his Swatch against the clock on the stove and noted his time of arrival at 10:42. Then he carefully navigated his way out of the kitchen and found Eileen on the living-room sofa, with an iodine-red blood smear on the front of her white turtleneck.

"You want to tell me what's going on?"

She looked at the Christmas tree in a daze, its colored lights blinking on and off erratically while her granddaughters and their mother sobbed hysterically upstairs.

"It was happening again," she said.

"What?"

"I told you before. Children have secrets."

He sat down beside her, making sure not to touch anything on the floor or the coffee table. "If you want me to help you, you're gonna have to do better than that."

"I know he couldn't stop himself," she said in an

unnaturally calm voice, as if she were just waking from anesthesia. "My own child. What do you do if your own child turns out to be a monster?"

Francis tried to keep his mind clear as he started to take notes.

"You know but you don't know. You want to pretend that it's not happening. But what can you do? You can't keep them apart forever, a brother and a sister."

Francis put down his notepad, unable to make himself write any more.

"You know, she wanted it to stop." Eileen picked at Scotch tape wrapped around her finger. "She tried to tell me, but I couldn't stand to hear it. It was too much for me."

Francis nodded, the last part of the picture finally coming together. No wonder she'd been going around saying Allison was still alive, haunting him with hang-ups on the answering machine, trying to keep him from forgetting about the case. *They buried the wrong child.*

"It was starting to happen again, with his own children." She put her hands on her knees, steadying them. "I caught him this morning with the older one in the bathroom. His own daughter. And I couldn't let it happen again. Could you, Francis?"

"I don't know. I don't know what I'd do."

"Yes, you do." She raised her chin defiantly. "I think you'd know *just* what to do."

For a moment, all the grief-stricken madness and medicated excuses were gone. She was the mother beast with blood on her claws from trying to keep the young from eating each other.

"If someone gave you a chance not to make the worst

mistake of your life twice, you'd move heaven and earth. And don't tell me you wouldn't."

Rashid, now in the task force, and Jimmy Ryan arrived five minutes later and found Francis in the kitchen, standing over the body and taking notes.

"What do you say, X Man?" Jimmy snapped his gum. "What comes around goes around, eh?"

"I'm thinking he bled out right away." Francis barely glanced up. "Mom was home and he was dead by the time she called nine-one-one."

"Yeah?" Jimmy hunched down beside the body, studying the way the blood soaked through the shirt. "That's some fuckin' entry wound. Looks like it got one of the main arteries."

"Yeah, he must've been pretty determined."

"What?" Rashid did a double take, almost losing his toothpick. "You're calling this a suicide?"

"I'm not calling it anything." Francis's pen kept moving across the page. "It's up to Crime Scene to lift the prints off the handle and the ME to decide the cause."

"Excuse me, I'm going to go call JC and let him know what's doing." Jimmy stalked out of the room, wanting no part in the deal.

Rashid crouched down beside the body. "That's a helluva tough angle for somebody stabbing himself, G.," he said. "Most people would aim the blade down."

"Why don't you ask him why he did it that way?" Francis kept writing. "Fucking scumbag. He probably knew he had cancer from the DNA tests we gave him and he knew his trial was starting in a couple of weeks.

Probably figured killing himself was the best option. Would've been the only decent thing he ever did."

Rashid stood up very slowly. "Uh-uh, chief, I don't like it."

"Who asked you anyway?"

"I'm saying, I got a lot of respect for you, because I've seen the way you handle yourself. But if it turns out somebody's been fucking with evidence at a crime scene, I don't want any part of it."

Francis lowered his pad and slapped it against the outside of his leg. "You *implying* something, Detective?"

Rashid thrust his chin out. "You heard me. The leopard don't change its spots. Don't jam me up because you got some history that don't sit right."

"Fuck you, I'm doing this by the book. Anybody says otherwise is a liar."

Rashid bowed his head and looked up at Francis from a low angle, trying to get a word in with the man behind the mask. "Don't do this, G.," he said. "It's not your job to make things work out the way you want —"

"Excuse me." Francis cut him off. "You wanna throw stones, throw stones. You wanna be my partner, be my partner. That means we don't have to talk about it. We just do what needs to be done and we don't send anyone to the can, doesn't belong there. This lady's trying to raise her grandchildren. She needs some understanding. If you can't get your head around that, step off right now."

Rashid stared at him a long time before he knelt down next to the body again, chewing his toothpick and shifting it from one side of his mouth to the other.

"Still looks kind of funny to me," he said. "Guy

stabbing himself with a pair of scissors. There's easier ways to do it. He didn't leave a note, did he?"

"Not that I noticed." Francis started to walk away. "But look around for yourself. You don't always see everything the first time."

ACKNOWLEDGMENTS

I WOULD LIKE TO give thanks to the following people for their generosity in making this book possible:

Chauncey Parker, Lisa Palumbo, Mark Desire, Joseph Calabrese, Laurey G. Mogil, M.D., Joyce Slevin, Bob Slevin, Luke Rettler, John Cutter, Jennifer Wynn, Stephen Hammerman, Arthur Levitt, Mark Graham, Anthony Papa, Mitchell Benson, Peter Neufeld, Jim Dwyer, Peter Garuccio, John Hamill, Steve Kukaj, Peter Walsh, Charlie Breslin, Ron Feemster, Svetlana Landa, Daniel Perez, Charles Shepherd, Leon Maslennikov, Katya Zhdanova, John Nelson, Ron Kuby, Nelson Hernandez, Joel Potter, Vicky Sadock, Sam Bender, Daniel Bibb, Mark Stamey, Bilial Thompson, Shqipe Biba, June Ginty, Bob Stewart, Kevin Walla, John McAndrews, Kim Imbornoni, Chris Smith, Tom Grant, Ed Rendelstein, James Watson, Molly Messick, David Segal, James McDarby, Steve Lamont, Steve DiSchiavi, Darryl King (the real one), Sophie Cottrell, Richard Pine, Michael Pietsch, and Judy Clain.

I would also like to give a special tip of the fedora to my old neighbor and friend Jim Knipfel for his graciousness and his excellent books, including *Slackjaw* and *Ruining It for Everybody*.

All of the above are hereby absolved of all responsibility for any factual mistakes made between these two covers, as well as for the character defects and crimes of moral turpitude described therein. All of those truly belong to the author.

ABOUT THE AUTHOR

PETER BLAUNER is the author of five other novels, including *Slow Motion Riot,* which won an Edgar Allan Poe Award for best first novel of the year, and *The Intruder,* a *New York Times* and international bestseller. His work has been translated into sixteen languages. He lives in Brooklyn, NY, with his wife, Peg Tyre, and their two children.

For more information, visit www.peterblauner.com.

Enjoy another
scintillating thriller
from master storyteller

PETER BLAUNER!

Please turn this page
for a preview of

SLOW MOTION RIOT

Winner of the Edgar Award
for Best First Novel.
Available in April 2007.

1

NOW THAT THE baby was two months old, she seemed to be waking up at least twice a night. But since he was doing a four-to-midnight tour in the city today, Franklin "The Ambler" Sheffield could afford to sleep in a little. He woke up around noon with a mouth full of cotton, the silky threads of a sex dream coming apart in his head and the child screaming in her crib. His wife had already gone to work, though, so there was nothing to do except gulp down the NutriSystem breakfast, warm up the milk Felicia had expressed and stored in the refrigerator, and hope the baby would take the bottle from him this once.

It was just after three in the afternoon when the man with the dreadlocks came into the boy's bedroom. All the lights were out, and the floor was strewn with model airplanes and fierce-looking toys called GoBots and Transformers. The boy, whose name was Darrell King, was lying on the Star Wars sheets with one arm thrown over his face.

The man with the dreadlocks knelt over him and put

the Smith & Wesson right over the words "The World's Greatest Daddy" on Darrell's T-shirt.

"It's time," he said.

The Ambler adjusted his seat belt, making room for the twelve pounds he'd strapped on in sympathy with his wife's pregnancy, and started to fiddle with the car radio until he got "Love on a Two-Way Street." He liked a lot of things about driving in to work on these cold winter afternoons. The stillness of the air and the silence of the other houses as he pulled out of the driveway. The snow and the neighbors' plaster saints on the front lawns. The cars going the opposite direction on the Long Island Expressway. The Christmas decorations outside the Manhattan stores as he drove north from the Midtown Tunnel. The Salvation Army Santa ringing a bell near the 125th Street subway entrance and the wreath over the entrance to the Twenty-Fifth Precinct.

The scene brought back an oldtime feeling he still had about the neighborhood. Mom shopping for presents after the holidays at Blumstein's. Listening to the brothers up on their ladders preaching revolution in front of Mr. Michaux's African Unity bookstore. Hearing the choir sing at the Fountain of Living Waters Ministries. Seeing Herman "Helicopter" Knowings stuff a ball down on Connie Hawkins at the Rucker basketball tournament. Accompanying Dad to Rolys Barbershop. The neighbors yelling, "There's colored on TV!" from across the hall when Sammy Davis Jr. showed up on a Bob Hope Christmas Special.

His parents would've hated it that he wound up working around here again. They'd both busted their backs trying to get him through Cardinal Hayes High School and Mercy College. Once, when he was eleven, he got a five-dollar tip for running across the street to buy a pack of cigarettes for one of Nicky Barnes's crew outside Big Wilt's Small's Paradise, and his mother almost beat the black off him, like he'd been dealing smack himself. *Hell, no!* No child of hers was getting into that mess. He was getting up and out of the city. The day they closed on the house in Roosevelt was the day she knew she could die with a satisfied mind. But when he'd been assigned back to patrol in Harlem, he didn't fight it. A part of him had never really left the neighborhood, never believed it was right to forget where he came from. In his mind's eye, he was still that little kid keeping an eye on the block.

Darrell King, the boy with the gun, didn't go straight to work. It was too early anyway. Instead, he went downtown and found some friends at the Playland video game arcade in Times Square. A couple of them wanted to catch a "Live Love Acts" show at one of the nearby theaters, but Darrell was too distracted thinking about what he had to do tonight. He was seventeen, with hard, bony features and a high, handsome forehead slowly emerging from the soft round pie of a face he'd had as a child. To conquer his nerves, he beamed up to see Scotty in the alley behind the arcade, and when the others came out to get high with him, he lifted his coat flap and showed them what he had tucked in his belt.

"Thirty-eight-caliber revolver," said Darrell. "Just like he police carry."

*　　　*　　　*

A *damn* shame, a wife needing an order of protection against her own husband a week before Christmas. Franklin Sheffield sat in the patrol car parked outside a short brown tenement on 128th Street, missing his wife and his daughter. To need someone guarding your front door against the man you'd married. Snowflakes fell slowly, changing shades as they flitted in and out of the streetlight. They landed on the windshield and melted before his eyes. A family should be together for the holidays, he thought. He hoped he wouldn't be on call on Christmas Day. Though the overtime would help pay for the gold earrings he'd picked out for Felicia at Fortunoff and the real estate taxes were going up five percent next year. And they'd already sunk half his overtime for the year into the baby's room. And now Felicia was starting to talk about doing the kitchen over. He was going to need that promotion to sergeant next year and the raise that went with it.

Darrell King and his two friends were coming up on the opposite side of the street. It was after eleven o'clock and below fifteen degrees. The only other people who were out now were the Dumpster divers, the truly hardy ten-dollar-a-pop skeezers and five-dollar-a-bottle crack slingers, and they were mostly gathered around a trash can fire around the corner, trying to stay warm.

Darrell walked briskly, a couple of steps ahead of his friends. Smoke streamed out of his mouth, and the gun rode high in the waistband under his coat. The police car was only half a block away now, just out of range of the streetlight.

"You're not gonna do it," the bigger of Darrell's two

friends, Bobby "House" Kirk taunted him. "You ain't got the heart."

"Watch me," Darrell King said.

The car's heater was starting to make Franklin feel sick to his stomach and sweaty, so he turned it down a little and put his hat on. There was a light rap on the window and he looked up. A skinny young kid with a flattop hairdo and a harelip was staring at him and saying something. Franklin rolled down the window to hear him.

"Yo," the kid said.

"What's up?" Franklin gave him his hard-ass face, the one that in his mind made him look like Fred "The Hammer" Williamson in *Black Caesar*.

Meanwhile, Darrell and Bobby Kirk were sneaking around to the other side of the car.

Bones throbbing deep inside his skull, Darrell steadied himself against the door frame. Then he lifted his shirt to pull the gun out of his waistband. Just as he started to get a grip on the handle, though, the cop turned and looked straight at him. And for a second, he could've sworn the brother didn't look angry or surprised, but almost disappointed.

Darrell yanked hard on the gun, but it stayed stuck in his waistband, pulling the crotch seam of his jeans up into the nether region between his balls and ass. Everything seemed to slow down, like a frame-by-frame video crawl. The cop fumbling for his own gun. Aaron's eyes widewalling as he mouthed, "*OH, SHIT!*" in an underwater voice. Bobby flailing wildly at his shoulder and trying to take the gat from him, so he could do the job right.

The thirty-eight finally jerked free, and Darrell extended

his arm. He saw the cop's eye focus on the hole, ready for the muzzle flash. And each time he pulled the trigger, the police car lit up like a furnace in the snow.

Later on that night, Darrell told his family what happened while they sat around chilling out on weed and the Yule log on TV.

"His hat flew off, like 'bing,' the first time I sparked him up," Darrell said. "And I seen Aaron jump back. You know what I'm saying? I pushed that nigger's wig back. Aaron was like, 'Oh, shit, man, I seen his brains. I seen that nigger's brains come flying outta his head—'"

"What you mean 'nigger'?" Darrell's older sister, Joanna, turned slowly to look at him. "You mean, like a brother?"

Darrell sat up. "Yeah, I just said, 'I pushed that nigger's wig back—'"

"But Darrell, that cop who was ripping off our crack house was a white boy. Didn't Winston done tell you he was a blondie?"

Darrell's face went dim. It was like the moment when a TV set went off and all the light shrank down to a hard little point in the middle of the screen.

"*Damn*," his sister said. "That's a fucked-up way to start the holiday."

2

$\mathbf{S}$OME MORNINGS AT Probation, I like to play a little game called "What's My Crime?" The idea is to try to guess the crime my client has committed just by looking at the Polaroid clipped to the outside of his file folder. It's one of my ways of relieving the tension and telling myself that I don't give a shit anymore.

Delilah, the heavyset secretary behind the reception desk, puts down *The Watchtower*, the Jehovah's Witness magazine, and holds up the first picture.

It's of a Hispanic guy in his early twenties, with a friendly smile and a dreamy warmth in his eyes. His hair is long on the sides and he keeps his chin low, like he was trying to sweet-talk a girl when the photo was taken.

"Looks like a nice guy," I say.

Delilah slips the Polaroid across the desk so I can give it a better look. "I dunno," I say finally. "Small-timer. Nickel-and-dime pot dealer, something like that?"

Delilah is already frowning at the file opened on her lap.

"This boy's a crack-smoking schizophrenic," she says. "He blew his landlord's head off with a shotgun."

"*Ho, shit.*" I push the photo back at her.

Now I have to make space in my life to see this guy. I could have him come by after Maria Sanchez on Friday. But Maria always leaves me feeling wrung out, so I put him off until Monday.

My union rep walks by. "Mr. Jack Pirone," I say.

"Mr. Steven Baum."

Fat Jack. Two hundred and fifty pounds of institutional memory and petty grievances, dressed like a Miami bookmaker in a black fedora and a white polo shirt. Before he was my union rep, Jack Pirone was my training instructor. His line then was *"Every time you reach for a new assignment at Probation, you're reaching for your passport to adventure."*

I can always count on the Fat Man to watch my back when he isn't busy kicking my butt.

"How you doing this morning, Mr. Baum?"

"Laughing on the outside, crying on the inside."

"Try the other way around," he says, slapping me on the shoulder and ambling on down the hall. "You'll live longer."

It's almost nine o'clock and behind me I hear the waiting room full of probation clients grumbling at each other. I take a quick look over my shoulder and see a bunch of them sprawled out on the wooden benches, like a wayward congregation spilling out of the church pews. The air conditioner is broken, so there's no relief from the June heat. The air is dank and it smells of stale smoke. The walls are painted a deep, intense orange. You'd think they would've chosen something a little more calming, like pale blue or ocean green. Instead, this orange is disturbing, maybe even inciting. It's like a "GO" sign for the mentally ill.

One woman is standing up and throwing pieces of a

Styrofoam coffee cup around the room. She's probably getting in the mood to see her probation officer. I hope she's not one of mine.

Delilah hands me the last file. "This one don't have a photo," she says.

Instead, it has a sticky yellow note from my supervisor, Emma Lang, on the front. "Special!" it says. "Attention must be paid." The new client is named Darrell King.

I check the sign-in sheet to make sure he isn't here yet and then look once more across the smoky civil-service purgatory where people are waiting. That woman has finally stopped throwing Styrofoam around. The bleary fluorescent light gives everyone a slightly greenish tint, and there are piles of cigarette butts and suspicious-looking puddles on the linoleum floor. I check out one guy lying face-up with his eyes closed and his legs in stone-washed jeans extended stiffly off the end of the bench. Making sure he's not dead. With my hangover I'm not feeling so hot myself.

The one thing that picks me up is the hairstyles on the younger guys here. An excellent summer for hair so far. I see one guy has his shaped like an upside-down bottle cap—a new one on me. I know all about the Fade: that's the flattop with lightly shaved sides. Then there's the Wave, a lopsided ski jump of hair sloping up on one side. And of course, my favorite is the Cameo, a high ebony tower of hair that looks like an Egyptian headdress. I wonder if the bottle cap has a name yet. The Ripple, maybe. One thing certain is that, in a year or less white kids will be wearing it, and picturing that, I smile to myself.

Six expressionless eyes turn to stare at me. Three teenage boys with big white sneakers and eerily dulled-out eyes. The term Fat Jack would use is "lacking in affect."

Not that they'd be real intimidated anyway. They look at me and see a tall, skinny Jew with curly hair in his late twenties. The free weights are starting to give me broader shoulders and my hands are big, but you wouldn't automatically give up your seat for me on the subway or anything. Far as they're concerned, I'm just another clueless white guy trying to tell them how to run their lives.

Just then, somebody catches my eye over near reception. An emaciated black teenage girl, with a purple scarf and a gold front tooth. She's squinting at Ronald Reagan on the guard's tiny black-and-white TV. I can't quite tell if she's one of mine. I've got 250 people on my caseload, and I know about half by sight. Two small boys are next to her on the bench. One is about five. The other is about a year old. The older one wears thick brown glasses and has big gaps between his teeth. When he thinks no one is looking, he pulls his little brother close and kisses him on the forehead.

I reach into the pockets of my windbreaker to see if I have a piece of candy to give him. Usually I carry my whole life around—keys, change, pens, scraps of paper, peppermint patties, and Reese's Pieces—I can't deal with those fanny packs. No candy today, though, so I just give him a little wink.

The two boys look remarkably similar, except for some ugly scabs and bruises on the older one's face. He clings his baby brother like he's trying to protect a smaller, unspoiled version of himself. Their mother suddenly turns, sees the older boy with his arm around the sleeping baby, and slaps him hard with an open hand across his cheek.

"Travis, don't you touch him," she barks.

Travis looks scared and takes his hand off his little brother. The baby wakes up and starts crying.

"You know, he wasn't doing anything," I tell her.

"Mind your own fucking business," she says, looking down and picking at her thumbnail.

She goes back to watching the television. The baby keeps crying. And Travis, the five-year-old, tightens his body and stares down at his folded hands in his lap.

Thanks a lot, lady, I think. I'll probably have your son as a client in ten years.